Anonymus

Daniels Brothers - Amateur Gardeners

Anonymus

Daniels Brothers - Amateur Gardeners

ISBN/EAN: 9783741196713

Manufactured in Europe, USA, Canada, Australia, Japa

Cover: Foto ©Andreas Hilbeck / pixelio.de

Manufactured and distributed by brebook publishing software
(www.brebook.com)

Anonymus

Daniels Brothers - Amateur Gardeners

THE ✢ ROYAL ✢ NORFOLK ✢ SEED ✢ ESTABLISHMENT,

NORWICH,

ENGLAND.

Seed Warehouses.
EXCHANGE STREET
AND BEDFORD STREET

Chief Offices..
BEDFORD STREET.

Seed Grounds.
IPSWICH ROAD AND EATON.

Nurseries.

THE TOWN CLOSE NURSERIES,
NEWMARKET ROAD.

BANKERS—MESSRS. GURNEY AND CO., NORWICH.

TERMS OF BUSINESS, &c.

☞ All orders from unknown Correspondents must be accompanied by a sufficient Remittance or satisfactory References; and to save cost and trouble of Booking, a Remittance should in all cases be sent with Orders under 10s. in value.

DISCOUNTS.—All accounts are due net in three months, we however allow a discount of 1s. in the pound on all orders of 20s. and upwards when accompanied by a remittance, or when paid within fourteen days of date of invoice.

CHEQUES, MONEY ORDERS, AND POSTAL ORDERS.—Please make payable to DANIELS BROS., and cross "GURNEY & Co.," Norwich.

POSTAGE-STAMPS AND COIN.—All letters containing postage-stamps should be registered before being posted. The registration fee is now only 2d., and this ensures a safe delivery. Letters containing coin *must* be registered.

VEGETABLE SEEDS, CARRIAGE FREE TO ANY PART.—We send all Vegetable Seeds Post or Carriage Free to any part of the United Kingdom.

SEED POTATOES CARRIAGE FREE.—All general orders for Garden Seeds (including Seed Potatoes), to the value of 10s. and upwards Free to any Railway Station on the Great Eastern System; and of the value of 20s. and upwards, Carriage Paid to any Railway Station or Steam Port in the United Kingdom.

FLOWER SEEDS.—All orders for Flower Seeds we send Post or Carriage Free to any part of the United Kingdom; and all orders of 10s. value and upwards we send free to any part of the world.

CARRIAGE OF ROSES, FRUIT TREES, MUSHROOM SPAWN, &c.—We do not undertake to pay carriage on general orders for Roses, Fruit Trees, Ornamental Shrubs and Plants, but continue to enclose extra plants free of charge to compensate for carriage; nor can we undertake to pay carriage of such horticultural requisites as Mushroom Spawn, Silver Sand, &c. All plants, trees, shrubs, &c., will be so packed as to stand a journey of a week or ten days without injury. Should the packages arrive at their destination during a severe frost, it will be advisable not to unpack them, but keep them cool and moist out of the reach of the frost, until a change of weather takes place.

CO-OPERATION IN SENDING ORDERS.—Allotment holders, Cottagers, and others requiring but small quantities of Seeds and Seed Potatoes, by joining together in sending their orders, can have the advantage of our terms of Free Carriage, and will be allowed a special discount of ten per cent., taken in seeds, besides the usual discount of five per cent. for cash, thus:—for every 20s. remitted 23s. worth of seeds may be ordered. No order can be recognised under these terms unless accompanied by at least one pound in cash. Every care will be taken to pack each lot of goods separately, according to order, and they can all be despatched in one parcel. Full name and address of each customer ordering under this arrangement should be sent, so that copies of future editions of our *Illustrated Guide* may be posted as published.

EMPTY PACKAGES.—All packages are charged at the lowest cost price, and are not returnable unless sent back in good condition, and Carriage Paid, within fourteen days after receipt of goods. Customers are particularly requested to have their name and address on each package, and to advise us by post when returned, or they cannot be credited.

CHANGE OF RESIDENCE.—We shall esteem it a favour if our customers, on changing their residence, will kindly favour us with their new address, that we may be able to send them our Catalogues as usual.

RECOMMENDATIONS.—The many kind recommendations to new customers with which we have been honoured during the past season have been very gratifying. Should any of our customers have friends requiring Seeds, Bulbs, &c., and to whom a copy of our *Illustrated Guide* would be acceptable, we shall feel much obliged for intimation of the fact.

IMPORTANT NOTICE.—We are extensive growers of several years' experience, and take the greatest possible care to supply only reliable seeds of the finest stocks and quality; we however wish it to be distinctly understood that we give no warranty express or implied as to description, quality, or productiveness, or any other matter relating to the seeds or plants we supply, and will not in any way be held responsible for any failure of crop.

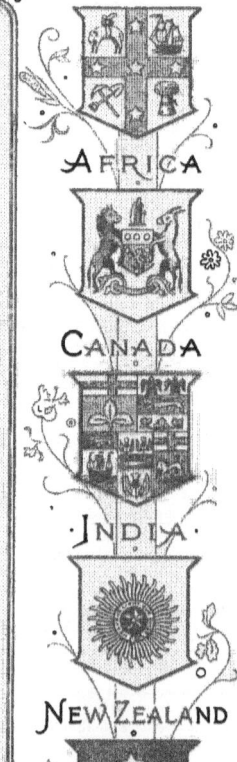

DANIELS' NEW PEA
MATCHLESS MARROW

ARTICHOKE

NEW WHITE MAMMOTH

New & Select Garden Seeds for 1892.

RUNNER BEAN—DANIELS' GIANT WHITE.

RUNNER BEAN—DANIELS' GIANT WHITE.

This is without doubt the finest type of Runner Bean extant, bearing in profusion long, green, thick, fleshy pods, upwards of twelve inches in length, and nearly two inches in breadth. This variety, besides the best for culinary purposes, will also be found a grand exhibition kind.

Per pint 1s. 6d.; per quart 2s. 6d.

RUNNER BEAN—TITAN (new).

The following is the raiser's description: No other Scarlet Runner approaches this in appearance, size, and productiveness, and asserts that the pods are twice the size of those of any Scarlet Runner; the pods, which are broad, straight, and handsome, are produced in clusters, and are very fleshy and almost stringless. This variety is very hardy, and most useful to grow, either for table or market, while for exhibition purposes it is unequalled.

In Sealed packets 1s. 6d.

NEW BEAN—BLUE-PODDED DWARF.

A great novelty in the way of French Beans. The foliage is tinted with metallic purple, and the pods, produced in abundance, are of a dark bluish purple, giving the plant a very distinct appearance. When cooked they have the same delicate flavour of other dwarf beans, and form quite a novelty on the table.

Per quarter-pint packet 1s.

NEW BEET—DANIELS' BLACK QUEEN.

This is the darkest foliage Beet in cultivation. Its dwarf habit and dark foliage will highly commend it for bedding purposes; whilst for culinary use it is all that can be desired; the roots of a deep blood colour, are intermediate between the turnip-rooted and the long red.
Per packet 6d; per oz. 1s. 6d.

NEW ONION—DANIELS' NEW RED GLOBE.

The finest red Onion in cultivation. The bulbs are large, of a fine globular shape, and of a beautiful dark crimson. Besides being very attractive in appearance, it has the mild flavour and good keeping qualities of the very best of the White Spanish type.
Per packet 9d.; per oz. 2s.

NEW ONION—DANIELS' NEW GOLDEN GLOBE.

A grand Onion, same shape as the White Globe; colour, yellow; very handsome, and an excellent keeper. Per pkt. 1s.

NEW ONION—WHITE PORTUGAL.

A silver-skinned variety from America; one of the best of the white flat Onions; a most excellent keeper and good yielder.
Per packet 1s.

RADISH—DANIELS' "PERFECTION."

This is a new long Radish; colour, beautiful bright scarlet, very tender; makes a fine appearance on the table, and is excellent for market purposes. Per packet 4d.; per oz. 1s.

RADISH—IMPROVED SCARLET, OLIVE-WHITE TIP.

This is a great improvement on the French Breakfast; colour, bright crimson, very tender, and quick growing; fine for market purposes. Per packet 6d.; per oz. 1s. 6d.

TURNIP—NEW EARLY SCARLET.

This is quite distinct; in shape, round and flat; the colour is a rich glowing scarlet; top small and neat; flesh white and of excellent flavour. Per packet 6d.; per oz. 1s. 6d.

NEW TOMATO—GOLDEN SUNRISE.

First Class Certificate, Royal Horticultural Society. This fine variety was sent by us for trial to the Royal Horticultural Society, and obtained a First Class Certificate, as being the best of the Golden-fleshed varieties. Per packet 1s.

NEW MELON—QUEEN OF SHEBA (see coloured illustration, outside cover).

This is a remarkably fine-flavoured and aromatic Melon, the fruit are long ribbed and netted, weighing 7 to 8 lb. each, skin brownish yellow when ripe, flesh thick, green, melting, juicy, and of rich aromatic flavour. Per packet 1s. 6d.

DANIELS BROTHERS, NORWICH, SPRING, 1892.

New & Select Garden Seeds for 1892.

NEW PEA—THE DANIELS.

This grand new Pea is the result of a cross between Best of All and Alpha, and is quite distinct. The haulm is robust, and grows about 4 feet in height, is of light green colour, up to the present it has exhibited no trace of mildew. The pods are long and handsome, averaging 5 to 6 inches in length, and filled with 10 to 12 delicious marrow Peas of exquisite flavour; it is a maincrop variety, and will take a high place for exhibition purposes, while its heavy cropping qualities will recommend it to the market grower.   **In sealed quarter-pint packets 1s. 6d.**

PEA BLUE BEAUTY.

The distinctive feature is its unusually regular habit of growth, of a uniform height 1½ feet, the growth is very smooth and level, and resembles a well kept hedge. It is a blue round Pea, nearly as early as American Wonder; pods medium size, and well filled; it is very prolific, and of excellent flavour.   **In sealed packets 1s. 6d.**

DANIELS' MATCHLESS MARROW (*see coloured plate*).

This grand Pea having given such universal satisfaction we have determined to give it greater prominence by the introduction of a coloured plate, representing specimens grown at our seed grounds of an improved stock of this variety.
Price, per pint 1s. 9d.; per quart 3s; stock limited.

NEW VEGETABLE— CROSNES (Stachys tuberifera).

CROSNES (Stachys tuberifera) OR CHINESE ARTICHOKE

First Class Certificate, Royal Horticultural Society. This is a new tuberous vegetable introduced from Japan. It is a hardy plant, producing a large quantity of tubers in the same way as the Potato. Its culture is very easy, as it grows well in any good garden soil, and is readily propagated by means of its numerous tubers. They may be left in the ground until required for use, as the severest frost does not injure them in any way. The best and simplest way of cooking this vegetable is to boil in water with a pinch of salt, then fry them. They are of delicate flavour, somewhat resembling boiled Chestnuts.
Fine English grown tubers, per lb. 9d.; 3 lb. 2/-; 7 lb. 4/-.

NEW MELON— DANIELS' WESTLEY HALL.

First Class Certificate, Royal Horticultural Society.

THE DANIELS.

DANIELS' WESTLEY HALL.

A First Class Certificate from the Royal Horticultural Society may be considered equivalent to the hall mark on a piece of plate denoting its sterling value.

This grand new Melon was raised by Mr. Bishop, of Westley Hall Gardens, Bury St. Edmund's, and is a cross between Read's Scarlet Flesh and High Cross Hybrid. It has the high quality of the former for flavour, with the free setting qualities of the latter. The skin is beautifully netted, sometimes slightly flushed with yellow towards the ripening period. The flesh is thick, scarlet, and intermixed with streaks of green; with a most sweet and delicious flavour. The fruit slightly oval in shape, weighing 7 lb., are pronounced by those who tasted them to be the best flavoured and most delicious Melon that has been sent out for years.
Per packet 1s. 6d. and 2s. 6d.

NEW MELON –ELY'S SEEDLING.

Certificate of merit, Royal Horticultural Society. It is a green fleshed variety, rather large and oval, skin deep green and finely netted, flesh bright green, firm, and of most delicious flavour; it is a free setter and strong constitution, one of the best for frame culture, average weight about 4 lb.
Per packet 1s. 6d.

New & Select Garden Seeds for 1892.

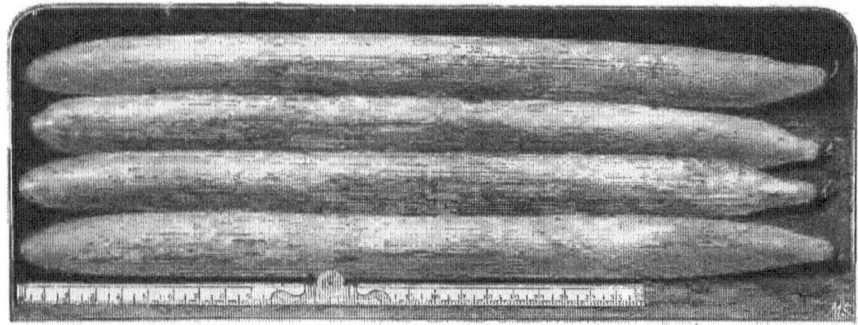

DANIELS' RELIABLE.

NEW HYBRID CUCUMBER—DANIELS' RELIABLE.

This magnificent variety, raised by Mr. J. Catton, of Saxlingham Hall Gardens, is a cross between Daniels' Duke of Edinburgh, and Tender and True, combining the extra fine qualities of each. The plants are strong and robust growers, and extraordinarily prolific bearers, two and three fruit 20 to 30 inches long at a joint, and are of a dark green colour, and very symmetrical and handsome. For exhibition and market work it is unsurpassable (*see coloured frontispiece*). **Price in sealed packets 2s. 6d. each.**

TEN POUNDS IN PRIZES

Will be offered by us for this Cucumber at the Norfolk and Norwich Rose Show, to be held in Norwich, about 7th July, 1892. **First Prize, best brace, £4; 2nd, £3; 3rd, £2; 4th, £1.** To be grown from seeds supplied from us direct in 1892.

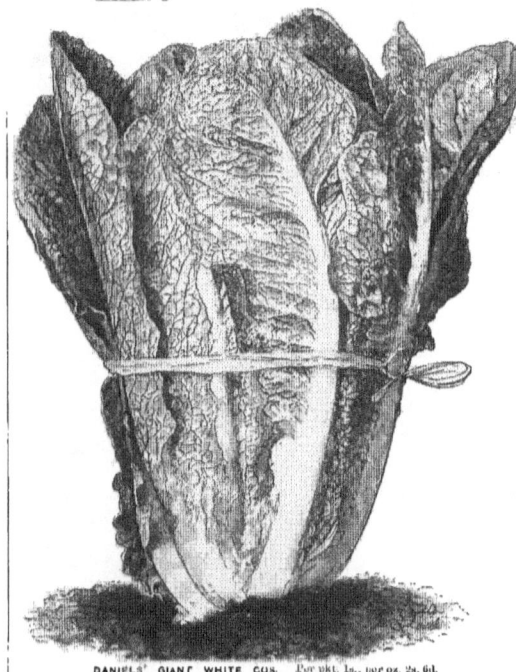

DANIELS' GIANT WHITE COS. Per pkt. 1s., per oz. 2s. 6d.

DANIELS' GIANT WHITE COS LETTUCE.

The finest and largest Cos Lettuce in cultivation, very tender and crisp, with fine solid hearts, require no tying, and will stand a long time without running to seed; should be grown in all gardens; unrivalled for exhibition purposes. **Per packet 1s.; per oz. 2s. 6d**

NEW LETTUCE— DANIELS' SOLID BROWN COS.

This fine Lettuce has been grown and selected by a Norfolk gardener for many years past. It is most excellent both for Summer and Winter use. The plants are medium size, solid, crisp, and juicy. Will be found a valuable addition to the gentleman's garden, and also for market growers. **Per packet 1s.**

NEW RED CELERY—HATCH'S CONQUEROR.

An exceedingly fine variety, and has obtained many First Prizes during the past year, and will be found the best red for market purposes. **Per packet 1s. 6d.**

EVIDENCE OF QUALITY.

"I am well pleased with the Lettuces. They are the best I ever had; the **Brown** and **White Cos** being of immense size, and cut so tender."—Mr. **UPTON**, Maidstone.

"I have grown your **Giant White Cos Lettuce** for years, and have always been much pleased with it. This year they have grown to a wonderful size, and are the talk of the town and neighbourhood."—Mr. F. **ROWE**, Huntingdon.

"I beg to say that I have had your Seeds for six years, and have not had one failure, and your **Giant White Cos Lettuce** is the finest I ever saw. I gave a market gardener some plants, and he told me he made eightpence each of them."—Mr. H **DEAN**, gardener to R. Jones, Esq., West Hill, Putney.

"I am pleased to add my testimony to the general excellence of the Seeds you supplied me with. I cut three of your **Giant White Cos Lettuces**, weighing together over 14 lbs."—Mr. J. **ELLIOTT**, Paignton.

DANIELS BROTHERS, NORWICH, SPRING, 1892.

New & Select Potatoes, &c., for 1892.

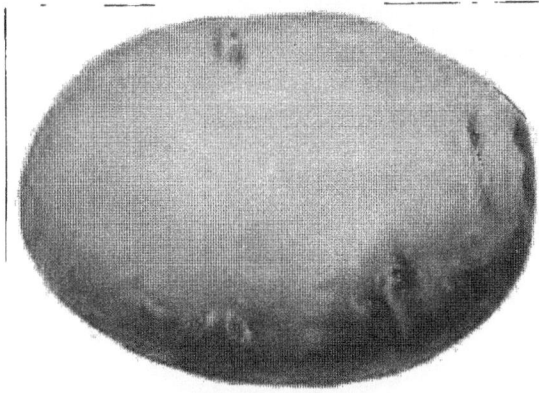

DANIELS' SPECIAL.

DANIELS' NORFOLK BLACKBIRD.

NEW DISEASE-PROOF POTATO DANIELS' "SPECIAL" (see engraving).

This new seedling has been selected for extraordinary cropping, combined with its superb cooking qualities. It is a handsome White Round main crop variety with eyes even with the surface, consequently there will be no waste in the peeling, and, when cooked, like balls of flour. We have grown this year at the rate of twelve tons per acre on medium soil, and free from disease, thus proving its great productiveness. As an exhibition variety it is one of the handsomest of the White Rounds. Stock limited. 7 lb. 3s.; 14 lb. 5s.; 56 lb. 18s.

NEW POTATO—DANIELS' NORFOLK BLACKBIRD.

A great novelty in the way of Potatoes, raised at our trial grounds. The tubers are long, handsome, kidney-shaped; the eyes few and quite even with the surface; the skin is smooth and glossy, and almost jet black. The flesh, which partakes largely of the colour of the skin, is dry and mealy when cooked, and of very fine flavour, making a very novel dish for the table. It is the handsomest and best black Potato ever raised, and will be found invaluable to give variety to an exhibition collection.
1 lb. 1s.; 3 lb. 2s. 6d; 7 lb. 4s. 6d.; 14 lb. 8s.

NEW POTATO—RED ROBIN KIDNEY.

A very handsome exhibition Potato. The tubers are medium size, and of a rich crimson colour. The flesh is of a bright golden yellow; dry, mealy, and of excellent flavour when cooked. It is also a most abundant cropper, and a good disease resister.
1 lb. 1s.; 3 lb. 2s. 6d.; 7 lb. 5s.

EVIDENCE OF QUALITY.

"Your Red Robin Potatoes have turned out splendidly as croppers; and for resisting disease I have not seen anything to equal them."—Mr.—WYMER, Scotton.

DANIELS' EARLY CRIMSON FLOURBALL.

This is the earliest Red Round Potato yet introduced, and will be found most valuable for early exhibitions; but the most valuable feature is the fact that the young tubers, even when the size of walnuts, are fit for use, and can be dug a fortnight earlier than the Beauty of Hebron or other early kinds furnish any potatoes fit to eat. The tubers are round in form, clustering compactly about the stems, which never grow more than a foot in height. The skin is of a beautiful rosy crimson colour, the eyes shallow; the flesh is beautifully white, dry, mealy, and fine flavoured. 1 lb. 1s.; 3 lb. 2s. 6d.; 7 lb. 5s.

ARTICHOKE—NEW MAMMOTH WHITE (see coloured plate).

Any improvement in the way of Vegetables is always welcome. This is a new departure and a great acquisition, the tubers having a clear white skin instead of the purplish red tint of the old variety. Being more regularly formed, tending to the globular shape, and of excellent quality; it must soon displace the present type, especially for market work. This is said to be the first step gained in the advancement of this useful nutritious and easily cultivated Winter Vegetable, and should tend to increase its popularity; being perfectly hardy, and not affected by disease or severe frost. In districts where the population depends largely on the Potato crop, this should be supplemented by a good batch of Artichokes, which would stand in good stead in case of a disastrous season, bringing in its wake a Potato famine. They yield from 150 to 1000 bushels per acre, and are excellent food for any kind of stock, especially hogs and cows. Price, per lb. 6d.; 7 lb. 3s.; 14 lb. 6s.; 56 lb. 20s.

The Artichoke, like the Potato, can be cut to single eyes when planted.

DANIELS BROTHERS, NORWICH, SPRING, 1892.

We shall feel much obliged if you will kindly recommend our Firm to the notice of any of your friends who are likely to require Seeds, Bulbs, or Plants, and shall, when requested, have great pleasure in sending Catalogues, free of charge, to their addresses.

CORRESPONDENCE:—Our Customers having occasion to write to us respecting any order previously sent by them, would much facilitate attention to their letters if they would kindly state the date on which the order was sent, and name amount remitted with it; this would enable us the more readily to identify their orders on reference to our Registers.

ADDRESSES:—Full Name and Address should be sent with every communication, and both Postal and Rail Address should accompany all orders, as much time is thereby saved to us, especially in our busiest Season, when we are receiving from 1000 to 1500 letters daily.

BLICKLING HALL, FROM A PHOTOGRAPH BY BOND, NORWICH.

HINTS TO AMATEURS
IN MAKING A NEW LAWN OR TENNIS GROUND.

In constructing a new Lawn or Tennis Court, the ground should be carefully prepared. An open level piece of ground, naturally well-drained, should, if possible, be selected; but where a good natural position is not to be obtained, the soil must be removed from the higher to the lower parts until the surface is perfectly level; and if the ground be too moist or retentive, it should be thoroughly well drained. Let the ground selected be well dug to the depth of eighteen inches or two feet, and an equal depth of soil obtained. If poor, a good coating of well-decayed manure should be incorporated with the soil. After digging, rake down level, and roll or beat the surface to an equal firmness all over. A frequent mistake is made in carting the soil on to the plot to be laid down, instead of having it wheeled on planks laid down for the purpose. The cart-rut so made is much harder than the surrounding ground, and when the natural subsidence takes place a very uneven surface is left. The surface soil to the depth of three inches should also be as nearly as possible of equal richness, in order that the grass should grow evenly and of the same colour. April and September are the best months for sowing, and the quantity of seed from half a pound to one pound to the rod, or from three to six bushels to the acre. All weeds should be removed as soon as they make their appearance, and when the grass has grown to the height of three or four inches it should be cut and rolled. Frequent cutting and rolling are of great importance where a fine, close, and soft turf is required, and an occasional dressing of **Daniels' Eureka Manure** will also be found of great service in promoting a healthy growth of the young sward. The renovating and improving of old lawns is also a work of importance at the proper season—say, in April. Daisies and other weeds should be eradicated. The holes that those weeds are taken from should be filled up with soil, which should be beaten hard into them; and the surface of the lawn ought then to be sown over moderately thick with **Finest Lawn Mixture**, and covered with another heavier sowing of sifted soil, the whole being rolled down. This rolling should be done when no fear exists of the soil adhering to the roll. It is surprising what good can be effected (to say nothing of the pleasure derived from the improved appearance) from a small outlay annually, by employing cheap labour for a short time each year, and by giving an annual surface-dressing. Grass seeds can never be fairly sown too thickly for making a new or improving an old lawn, as it is found that the thicker the seed is sown, the finer will be the turf. As many varieties of small birds are very fond of grass seeds, it will be well, when sown, to give some protection for a short time till the plants are up.

Daniels' Mixtures of Lawn Grass Seeds
FOR TENNIS LAWNS, CROQUET AND CRICKET GROUNDS, &c.
Carriage Free in quantities of not less than 2 lbs.

Mixture of Dwarf Grasses, for producing a fine close turf ... ... per lb. 1s. 0d. per bush. 20s.
Fine Mixture of Dwarf Grasses, for producing a dark green velvety turf ... ... ,, 1s. 6d. ,, 25s.
Finest Mixture of Dwarf Evergreen Grasses, extra choice ... ... ,, 2s. 0d. ,, 30s.

Our Lawn Grass Mixtures can be supplied with or without Clover as required.

"The Lawn I sowed with your **Grass Seeds** this Spring, has given great satisfaction."—Mr. W. COLLINS, Byculla Park, N.

"The **Lawn Grass Seed** you sent is wonderful, we shall be able to play tennis upon the grass this Summer to the astonishment of our neighbours."—Mrs. BURKE, Rathfarnham.

Garden Economy. Seeds Carriage Free.

KITCHEN GARDEN SEEDS.

DANIELS BROS.' Complete Collections are carefully made up with seeds of finest quality in best varieties from each class, with a view of furnishing an ample supply of Choice Vegetables throughout the year. These collections will be found extremely valuable for those who have not sufficient time nor experience for making their own selection.

N.B.—Our Collections will be made up in the same liberal manner as heretofore. Intending purchasers will kindly bear in mind that it is only by preparing them in large numbers that we can be so liberal in the quantity of the Seeds supplied for the amount charged, and that by ordering our selections, instead of making their own, they will reap an advantage of at least 25 per cent. below the general Catalogue prices. Therefore no reduction, alteration, or substitution can be allowed in any of the collections. When ordering please quote Number and Price.

Daniels' Complete Collections.

ALL PACKAGE AND CARRIAGE FREE.

No. 1.	Contains 28 quarts of Choice Peas	And		£5 5 0
No. 2.	Contains 20 quarts of Choice Peas	all		£4 4 0
No. 3.	Contains 16 quarts of Choice Peas	other	...	£3 3 0
No. 4.	Contains 10 quarts of Choice Peas	Seeds in		£2 2 0
No. 5.	Contains 8 quarts of Choice Peas	proportion		£1 11 6

EVIDENCE OF QUALITY.

"I beg to inform you that the **Seeds** I had from you last year were a great success. I took Twenty-two Prizes in our two Local Shows, one of the Prizes being a **SILVER CUP** for Collection of Vegetables."—Mr. J. **WOODS**, Surbiton.

"I have sent to tell you that your **Collection of Vegetable Seeds** turned out well, taking the First Prize with **Parsnip** and **Onions**. Six Parsnips weighing 2½ lbs.; Onions measuring 14 inches round."—Mr. C. **WESTALL**, Mildenhall.

No. 6. Daniels' Complete Collection, £1 1 0

Package and Carriage Free.   All the best kinds for succession for a Villa Garden.

14 pints	PEAS	2 pkts.	CAULIFLOWER	4 ozs.	ONION
3 pints	BROAD BEANS	2 pkts.	CELERY	1 pkt.	PARSLEY
1½ pint	FRENCH BEANS	1 pkt.	COUVE TRONCHUDA	2 ozs.	PARSNIP
1½ pint	RUNNER BEANS	8 ozs.	CRESS	4 ozs.	RADISH
1 pkt.	BEET	2 pkts.	CUCUMBER	4 ozs.	SPINACH
1 pkt.	BORECOLE	1 pkt.	ENDIVE	3 ozs.	TURNIP
1 pkt.	BRUSSELS SPROUTS	2 pkts.	GOURD or PUMPKIN	1 pkt.	VEGETABLE MARROW
3 pkts.	BROCCOLI	1 pkt.	LEEK	4 pkts.	HERBS, Sweet and Pot
3 pkts.	CABBAGE	3 pkts.	LETTUCE	2 pkts.	TOMATO
¼ oz.	SAVOY	6 ozs.	MUSTARD	1 pkt.	CAPSICUM
3 ozs.	CARROT	1 pkt.	MELON		

No. 7. Daniels' Complete Collection, 12s. 6d.

Package and Carriage Free.   All the best kinds for succession for a Small Garden.

7 pints	PEAS	1½ oz.	CARROT	1 pkt.	MELON
1 pint	BROAD BEANS	1 oz.	CAULIFLOWER	2 ozs.	ONION
1 pint	FRENCH BEANS	1 pkt.	CELERY	1 pkt.	PARSLEY
1 pint	RUNNER BEANS	4 ozs.	CRESS	1 oz.	PARSNIP
1 pkt.	BEET	2 pkts.	CUCUMBER	2 ozs.	RADISH
1 pkt.	BORECOLE	1 pkt.	ENDIVE	2 ozs.	SPINACH
1 pkt.	BRUSSELS SPROUTS	1 pkt.	GOURD or PUMPKIN	2 ozs.	TURNIP
2 pkts.	BROCCOLI	1 pkt.	LEEK	1 pkt.	VEGETABLE MARROW
2 pkts.	CABBAGE	2 pkts.	LETTUCE	3 pkts.	HERBS, Sweet and Pot
1 pkt.	SAVOY	3 ozs.	MUSTARD	2 pkts.	TOMATO

No. 8. Daniels' Complete Collection, 7s. 6d.

Package and Carriage Free.   All the best kinds for succession for a Cottage Garden.

4 pints	PEAS	1 oz.	CARROT	1 oz.	ONION
1 pint	BROAD BEANS	1 pkt.	CAULIFLOWER	1 pkt.	PARSLEY
½ pint	FRENCH BEANS	1 pkt.	CELERY	1 oz.	PARSNIP
½ pint	RUNNER BEANS	2 ozs.	CRESS	2 ozs.	RADISH
1 pkt.	BEET	1 pkt.	CUCUMBER	1 oz.	SPINACH
1 pkt.	BORECOLE	1 pkt.	GOURD	1 oz.	TURNIP
1 pkt.	BRUSSELS SPROUTS	2 pkts.	LETTUCE	1 pkt.	VEGETABLE MARROW
1 pkt.	BROCCOLI	1 pkt.	LEEK	2 pkts.	HERBS
1 pkt.	SAVOY	1 oz.	MUSTARD	1 pkt.	TOMATO
1 pkt.	CABBAGE				

No. 9. Daniels' Cottager's Collection, 5s. 0d.

Package and Carriage Free.   Thirty varieties for succession, including Peas and Beans.

No. 10. The Cottager's Packet, 2s. 9d.

Post Free.   Containing sixteen varieties of Vegetables, including Peas.

EVIDENCE OF QUALITY.

"I am pleased to say your Seeds gave me satisfaction. I took Fifteen Prizes at the High Wycombe Show, First for Collection of Vegetables."—Mr. T. SLANDAGE, High Wycombe.

"I won Twenty-eight Prizes at Shelton Flower Show, Nineteen Firsts and Nine Seconds, with Vegetables and Flowers grown from your Seeds."—Mr. W. CHILTON, Barwell.

"I cannot speak too highly of Seed purchased from you. I took Fifteen Prizes out of sixteen exhibits at our Show."—Mr. W. BOWER, Stanton.

"Last year your Seeds turned out very well. I obtained Forty-six Prizes at our Shows."—Mr. W. MORRIS, Aberdulais.

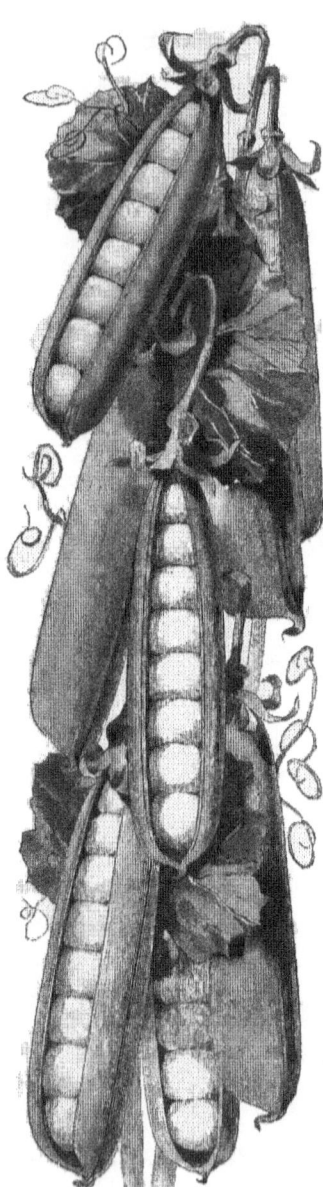

DANIELS' NEW PEA—GEM OF THE SEASON.

Peas.

Cultivation.—The Pea is one of our most important crops, and to be successfully grown, must be liberally treated. A deep rich soil, well pulverized and incorporated with a fair allowance of well-decayed manure, should be chosen for the principal crop in summer. For early Peas the ground does not require to be so rich. Sowings of **William the First, Gem of the Season,** and other first early varieties should be made in November, December, and January. The second early sorts, including **Lye's Favorite, Supreme,** and **Gladiator,** three splendid varieties, may be sown in February, and others including **Daniels' Matchless Marrow, Yorkshire Hero, Veitch's Perfection, Ne Plus Ultra,** and **Maincrop Marrow** for main crops, from March to the end of May. For last crop sow a few of the first early varieties in June or July.

In sowing Peas those of ordinary height should be in drills three or four feet apart; the taller varieties five or six feet. They can also be grown to advantage in rows twelve feet apart, and some other crop between them, as by this means both sides of the row get the full benefit of light and air, and yield a greater abundance of pods. When a crop is grown between the rows, the rows should run, if possible, from north to south, to give both the Peas and the intervening crop free access to the sunlight.

Staking up should be commenced when they are three inches high. The dwarf varieties may be grown without sticks, but all are benefited by being kept from the ground. Peas, when making their appearance above ground, are very subject to the depredations of sparrows, &c.; this may be easily prevented by placing a short stout stick at each end of the row, and then leading from one to the other a single black thread or cotton at a distance above the ground of two or three inches. We have found this by experience to be at once the most simple and efficacious remedy that will apply with equal benefit to *any kind of seed* subject to the depredations of birds, whether sown in drills or seed beds; if the latter, the threads should be stretched from end to end at intervals of about nine inches.

Section I.—Earliest Varieties.

ht. pr quart.
in ft. s. d.

DANIELS' NEW PEA.—Gem of the Season.
The earliest Pea in cultivation. Height three feet, and very prolific. This magnificent early Pea is the most valuable for general use ever sent out. Is always the earliest, whether sown in Autumn, Winter, or Spring. Is also the hardiest, resisting frost better than any other kind, and is not affected by mildew. Being very prolific and of a most delicious flavour, will be found most desirable for marketing, and invaluable for the private garden ...   .   — 2 0

"I have much pleasure in stating that considering the late heavy frosts and the dry weather we have had, the **Gem of the Season Peas** have done extraordinarily well. I gathered over three pecks of splendid Peas last week, and there are none in this neighbourhood to equal them."—**Mr. E. HENDERSON,** Cosham.

"I planted your **Gem of the Season Peas** at the same time with several other sorts, and gathered the **Gems** seven days before any of the others, and I led them very heavy croppers, and of delicious flavour. I shall always grow them as a first early."—**Mr. J. BAKER,** Chilham.

American Wonder. A first early Pea, some days in advance of William the First. For small gardens it is unsurpassed, owing to its earliness, productiveness, and the small space it occupies 1 2 0
Lightning (Carter's). Very early variety 3 1 6
Dillistone's First Early. Very early. Known also as **Carter's First Crop** and Sutton's Ringleader   ...   3-4 1 0
Early Sunrise (Day). Very hardy and prolific 2½ 1 0
Earliest of All (Laxton). A round blue-seeded Pea of excellent and rich flavour; is dwarfer than Ringleader, more prolific 2 1 6
Early Paragon. A blue wrinkled Marrow of fine flavour. It is the earliest of the large wrinkled marrows   ...   4-5 2 0
Kentish Invicta. A fine early blue Pea 2½ 1 3
Little Gem (McLean's) 1 1 6
Sangster's No. 1 ...   .   — 0 9
Sangster's No. 1 Improved. Extra select stock ...   2½ 1 6
William Hurst. An early blue wrinkled variety, similar to American Wonder. An abundant bearer, of first-rate quality; as an early Pea it should be grown in every garden ...   1 2 6
William the First. One of the finest early green Marrows, combining flavour, earliness, and productiveness   ...   3 1 6
William the First. Selected stock 3 2 0

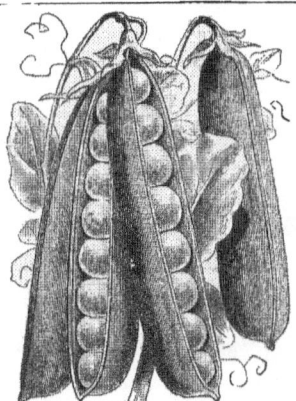

BISHOP'S LONG-PODDED DWARF.

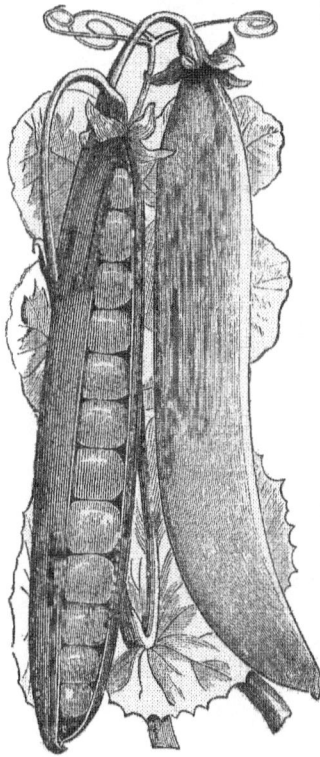

LYE'S FAVOURITE.

Peas *(continued).*

Section II.—Second Early & Main Crop.

ht.   pr quart.
in ft.   s.   d.

NEW PEA.—DANIELS' MATCHLESS MARROW. Height four feet, bearing a profusion of handsome well-filled pods, each containing ten to twelve large Marrow Peas of the most delicious flavour. For use late in the season this Pea is unequalled, and cannot fail to become a leading kind for market purposes, possessing as it does all the good qualities of Ne Plus Ultra and Veitch's Perfection combined *(see coloured plate)* ... ... per pint 1s. 9d.   4   3   0

" I was highly pleased with the Matchless Marrow Peas I had from you."—Mr. T. THOMAS, Gwaeiodynnev.

" I took two First and two Second Prizes with your Matchless Marrow Peas."—Mr. J. GIBSON, Yafforth.

" Daniels' Matchless Marrow Peas are the finest in the neighbourhood. People keep inquiring where I got them and the name. They are a splendid flavoured Pea and very fine."—Mr. H. LANGLEY, Sandridge.

" Matchless Marrow has produced one of the heaviest crops of Peas I have ever seen. The pods have nine or ten well developed peas, which can only be fully appreciated when on the table."—The Rev. A. GARLECH, M.A., Donington.

" I am very pleased with your Matchless Marrow Peas, the pods are very large, and well filled, and the flavor delicious, and I think they are unsurpassed."—Mr. W. BAGGLEY, Fredingham.

" Your Matchless Marrow Pea continues to hold its own. At Ongar Show yesterday I was awarded First Prize."—Mr. H. BALLS, Moreton.

" Prolific Peas.—On Friday a monster peapod, Daniels' Matchless Marrow was picked by Mr. J. S. Geary, Brentwood, from his garden. It was six inches long and nearly three inches in circumference. It was well filled with peas, and weighed nearly 1¼ oz."—THE CHELMSFORD CHRONICLE.

LYE'S FAVOURITE. This magnificent Pea was raised by Mr. James Lye, Clyffo Hall, Market Lavington, Wilts. First Class Certificate, Royal Horticultural Society. It is a second early variety, bearing a profusion of handsomely curved pods, well filled with delicious Marrow Peas. Ten to eleven peas in a pod 3½   2   0

" I have much pleasure in sending you a specimen of the Pea I got from you this year, Lye's Favourite. It is the best Pea I ever had, and has done splendidly in my garden. It is a perfect picture; my friends are all delighted with it."—Mr. MANSFIELD, Clifden.

" Your Lye's Favourite Pea for a second crop are the finest I have ever seen or grown. Large pods, ten to eleven peas in a pod, and the wonder of hundreds who have visited our gardens."—Mr. YALLOP, The Gardens, Framlingham Hall.

Daniels' Early Long-pod. The want of a good Early Long-pod Pea for market purposes has long been felt by every one. It grows to the height of four feet, and comes into use closely following the first-early kinds, and bearing a heavy crop of fine long pods, having ten to twelve peas in each 4   2   0

Duke of Albany. A fine long-podded variety. One of the best for exhibition, and of very fine flavour 4-5   2   6

Bishop's Long-podded Dwarf. An excellent dwarf variety, requiring no sticks, very productive 1½   1   0

Leicester Defiance. A most profitable variety for picking green. It is of the same class as Prize-taker, being very hardy can be sown with success in the Autumn 4   1   0

Gladiator. The plant is very robust and vigorous, stem branched, growing about three feet in height, exceedingly productive, bearing in pairs an abundance of long, curved, handsome pods, which are very closely filled with medium-sized peas of excellent quality. First Class Certificate R.H.S. 3   1   6

Nelson's Vanguard. A fine second early wrinkled Marrow; haulm densely covered from the bottom with fine handsome pods, well filled with peas of excellent flavour 2½   1   6

Stratagem. This is a splendid variety, with pods five to six inches in length, containing eight to ten large fine-flavoured peas. First Class Certificate, Royal Horticultural Society 2   2   6

TELEGRAPH. A valuable market variety of first-class quality ... 4   1   0

Champion of England or Fortyfold. Large blue variety ... 5   1   3

Harrison's Glory. Large blue variety 3   0   9

Fillbasket (Laxton) 3   1   6

Supreme (Laxton). This is a first-class blue round Pea, and an enormous bearer 4   1   0

PRIZE-TAKER 4   1   0

" THE DANIELS " *(see Novelties.)*
In sealed quarter-pint pkt. 1s. 6d.   —   —

Peas (continued).

Section III.—For Late and Main Crops.

bt. pr quart.
in fl,   s.   d.

DANIELS' MAIN CROP MARROW. We have great pleasure in stating that this splendid Marrow Pea has stood the test of several years and has become a favourite. It is of the same flavour as the old Ne Plus Ultra; but the pods are longer. It is very prolific, and should be largely grown as a Main Crop Pea for all purposes ... per pint 1s, 6d. 4   2   6

"Your **Main Crop Marrow Pea** has done wonderfully. It is a splendid bearer and eater." **Mr. A. K. EVANS**, Clonbela.

"I may say the **Main Crop Marrow Peas** I had from you in the Spring are the finest flavoured I have ever tasted."—**G. K. CAREY**, Esq., Bexhill-on-Sea.

"I do not think any one could wish for better Seeds than you sent us; your **Main Crop Marrow** is a splendid Pea, and of good flavour."—**Mr. CHARLES KING**, The Gardens, Holme Hale Hall.

"I wish to acknowledge my appreciation of the valuable results from your Seeds, both Flower and Vegetable, and especially your **Main Crop Marrow Peas** have been all that could be desired."—**Mrs. G. STACEY**, Beccles.

"We have not had such a crop of **Peas** for ten years."—**Miss LYTLE**, Portglenone.

"I may state your **Main Crop Marrow Pea** was something really delicious." **Mr. W. L. CLISSORD**, Fisherton.

Evolution. A main crop variety of fine flavour, pods and foliage rich dark green; very hardy and prolific 4   2   0
Dr. Maclean. A blue wrinkled Marrow, of vigorous growth, wonderfully productive, flavour of the first quality 3½   1   6
Maclean's Wonderful, or Prince of Wales 3   1   9
Queen (Sharpe). A blue wrinkled Marrow Pea of sturdy branching habit. It requires to be sown thinly. The pods are large, dark green, slightly curved, and well filled; the peas are of delicious flavour when cooked 2-2½   2   6
Superiority (Eckford). The seed is very large, wrinkled, and pale-blue in colour; haulm very robust, bearing an abundance of well-filled pods over its entire length 5   2   0
Yorkshire Hero. A fine dwarf Marrow Pea of the Veitch's Perfection type, very prolific, bearing a profusion of well-filled pods, containing six to eight large peas each; flavour first-class 2½   1   6
Triumph (Sharpe). A blue wrinkled Marrow, of exquisite flavour; the pods are long and well filled, each containing nine to eleven large peas. In constitution it is robust and hardy ... 2-3   1   6
Telephone. First Class Certificate, Royal Horticultural Society. This fine variety is good either for exhibition or market purposes 4½   2   0
NE PLUS ULTRA. Delicious Marrow Pea, very prolific, quality first-class, fine for general crop 6   1   3
NE PLUS ULTRA. Extra select stock 6   2   0
British Queen. Very long pods, productive, quality first-class, a great bearer 6   2   0
Oxford Tom (the true variety). We have succeeded in obtaining a true stock of this grand old kind, the best-flavoured of all the tall Marrow Peas 6-8   2   0
Veitch's Perfection Marrow 3   1   3
Veitch's Perfection Marrow. Extra select stock 3   2   0
Walton Hero (Laxton). Raised from a cross between Telephone and British Queen. Walton Hero is a very fine podded, white wrinkled, main crop variety 5   2   6
Charmer. A blue wrinkled Marrow, very prolific; pods handsome and well-filled with fine peas of good marrow flavour ... 4   1   6

EVIDENCE OF QUALITY.

"Your Seeds have all come up very nicely; I have a splendid show of **Peas**." **Mr. M. CALDER**, West Blanerne.

"Everything I had from you turned out remarkably well. The **Peas** were simply wonderful."—**The Rev. J. A. JENNINGS**, Donaghpatrick.

"Your Seeds gave me great satisfaction, especially the **Peas**, which were the best croppers in the neighbourhood."—**Mr. J. PETERS**, Dunyaut.

"I have much pleasure in stating that the **Peas** I had from you this Spring have all turned out well."—**Mr. E. H. BATEMAN**, Selsey.

"Last year's Seeds turned out remarkably well, especially the **Peas**, which were beautiful."—**Mr. W. D. L. LE RODGERS**, Ystrad.

DANIELS' MAINCROP MARROW.

Peas *(continued)*.

NEW AND SELECT VARIETIES.

PARROTT'S PROLIFIC.

	bt. in it.	pr quart. s. d.

PARROTT'S PROLIFIC. This fine blue wrinkled Marrow is of the Veitch's Perfection type, but more sturdy in its habit, and shorter in the haulm (about 2½ feet), bearing a profusion of well-filled pods, six to eight large peas in each, of a most delicate marrow flavour. During the past season it has proved itself to be one of the most prolific we have grown 2½   2   0

Echo. A prolific dwarf wrinkled Marrow, and a good main crop variety   2   2   6

Autocrat. First Class Certificate, Royal Horticultural Society. Is of exceedingly robust habit, much branched, foliage of a dark lustrous green. Owing to its strong constitution, it is perfectly free from mildew   4   2   6

Essential. A late wrinkled Marrow, very prolific; pods of a dark green colour, well filled with large fine-flavoured peas, which retain their beautiful colour when cooked   5   2   6

Dignity. A fine main crop Pea of robust growth; the pods averaging from four to five inches in length, well filled with fine flavoured peas. A good sort for exhibition   4-5   2   6

Empress. A main crop wrinkled Marrow, of robust habit and vigorous constitution. The pods are of large size, and well filled with six or seven very large peas of rich sugary flavour ...   5   2   6

The Don. This Pea obtained a First Class Certificate under the name of "Quality." Its flavour resembles Ne Plus Ultra, whilst it is a very heavy cropper; pods large and well filled   4   2   6

Exonian. This is claimed by the raiser to be an entirely new sort. It is a First Early Wrinkled Marrow; very productive. The haulm, which is thickly covered with pods containing six to eight peas of fine flavour, is rather light and pale green in colour. Awarded a First Class Certificate, Royal Horticultural Society.
In sealed three-quarter-pint packet 2s. 6d.   3   —

Ambassador (Eckford). Awarded a Certificate of Merit by the Royal Horticultural Society. A main-crop Wrinkled Pea, producing profusely long deep green well-filled pods, the peas are of the finest flavour, and retain their beautiful colour when cooked.
In sealed half-pint packet 2s.   5   —

Consummate (Eckford). Awarded a First Class Certificate by the Royal Horticultural Society. A main-crop green Wrinkled Marrow, producing a great abundance of long well-filled pods; a pea of exquisite flavour. Being dwarf, and a very heavy cropper, it is well adapted for field culture. In sealed half-pint packet 2s.   2½   —

English Wonder (new). A great improvement on the well-known American Wonder, in earliness, productiveness, length of pod and flavour, and being somewhat dwarfer than that variety cannot fail to become a general favourite. In sealed half-pint packet 1s.   1   3   0

Oracle (Laxton). Mr. Laxton describes this as follows:—"A splendid main-crop variety, with large handsome pods containing ten to twelve fine peas of excellent flavour. The variety is somewhat branched, very hardy and productive, and is not liable to mildew.
In sealed half-pint packet, 2s. 6d.   3   —

EVIDENCE OF QUALITY.

"The **Peas** had in your Collection of Vegetable Seeds last year all did well."—**Mrs. OWEN,** Ellesmere.

"Your **Peas** last year surpassed all I have had."—**Miss TROTTER,** Staines.

"The **Peas** I had of you last year were exceptionally fine."—**Mr. T. LERY,** Andover.

"I have grown **Gem of the Season Peas** in the open for two years, and have gathered Peas at least fourteen days before any one in the neighbourhood. They are good croppers and fine flavoured."—**Mr. J. T. HOLMES,** Reading.

"I have grown your **Seeds** for the Rev.—Isham for four years, and am pleased to say they have given me every satisfaction."—**Mr. J. KEMPSALL,** The Gardens, Carwood House.

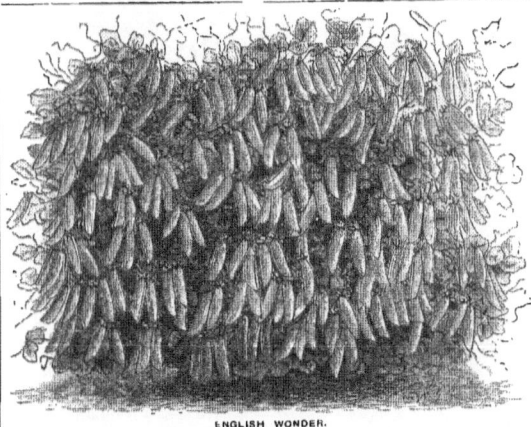

ENGLISH WONDER.

Dwarf French or Kidney Beans.

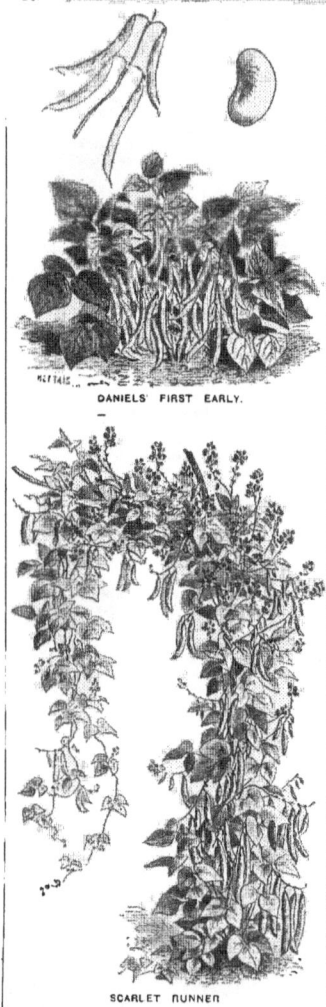

DANIELS' FIRST EARLY.

SCARLET RUNNER.

Cultivation.—These deserve far more extended culture, few esculents being more prolific or nutritious. They require a warm sunny aspect, and a rich, free, or open soil, and deep. A first sowing of **Daniels' First Early**, a very superior variety, may be made in boxes or pots indoors about the 20th April; the seedlings so formed to be transplanted on to a sheltered aspect immediately settled fine weather ensues. Sow upon a similar site in the open ground during the first week in May, and about once a fortnight subsequently for purposes of succession up to the end of July. Sow moderately thick where a good crop is required apart from show produce. They should be sown in drill rows two-and-a-half feet apart. Should many gross leaves form and young shoots push through the same, let both be neatly pinched off or removed; the former in part, so as to admit more light to the base, and assure more Bean pods and less foliage. Always keep all Beans picked off immediately they become sufficiently large for use; to permit them to remain beyond is to unnecessarily tax and impoverish the plants.

	per quart—s.	d.
DANIELS' FIRST EARLY. The finest first early Kidney Bean in cultivation; an extraordinary cropper. Pods medium length, unstained, of excellent quality and particularly tender ...	2	6
Blue Podded (*see Novelties*) ... ... per pkt. 1s.	—	
Buff. Very early	0	10
Canadian Wonder. Abundant bearer, very fleshy and tender ...	1	3
EARLY BLACK WONDER. The hardiness and productiveness of the plant, the size and appearance of the pods (rich light green in colour), show that both quality and quantity are together combined in this excellent variety	1	6
Early Golden Butter (dwarf). Pods thick and fleshy, nearly transparent, and of a bright yellow colour, which is retained when boiled ...	2	0
Early Prince Albert (true). One of the earliest and most prolific varieties grown	1	6
Fulmer's Early Forcing	1	3
Negro. Long-pod	1	3
NE PLUS ULTRA. Quite distinct in seed to any other variety; habit dwarf and compact; very delicate in flavour and very early. It is enormously productive both in doors and out. Ninety-three pods were at one time gathered from a pot containing three plants. First Class Certificate R.H.S.	1	6
Newington Wonder (or **Nonsuch**). Early	1	0
Osborn's Early Forcing	1	3
Robin's Egg (or **Chinese**)	1	0
Sir Joseph Paxton	1	6
The " Monster" Negro. First Class Certificate, R.H.S. ...	1	0
Williams' Early Prolific	1	0
All kinds mixed	1	0

Runner Beans.

Cultivation.—Scarlet Runners, as these are more commonly called, are an indispensable late Summer and Autumn vegetable. We think it desirable to point out the fact as to how well they will succeed when precisely as Dwarf Beans are, by the additional aid of constantly pinching back only; let all growers try this process therefore. For early crops many sow in boxes or in the open ground, placing a frame over the seedlings. These are transplanted on to permanent sites about the 20th of May. Sow for the main crop about April 20th, and reserve half the seed for another sowing on or about the 5th of May. We advise the seeds to be sown somewhat more thickly than is customary, by which means the crop will be forwarded and increased. Sowings made for staking should be four-and-a-half feet apart in the rows, and for pinching back three feet apart in the rows. Should a very arid period exist about Midsummer, it will be very advantageous to syringe the blooms occasionally towards the evening. Keep the produce well and constantly picked off as it becomes large enough for use. They require a deep rich soil, and the more it is worked up the better.

	per quart—s.	d.
DANIELS' GIANT WHITE (*see Novelties*) per pint 1s. 6d.	2	6
TITAN (*see Novelties*) ... ... sealed pkt. 1s. 6d.	—	
CHAMPION or **GIANT.** Gigantic variety, pods nearly double the size of the old Scarlet Runner; an abundant cropper and highly recommended	2	0
GIRTFORD GIANT. This is an immense variety of the Scarlet Runner; pods exceedingly thick, fleshy, and of extraordinary size	2	6
Mont d'Or or **Golden Wax Runner.** Very early and productive, tender and fleshy. First Class Certificate, Royal Horticultural Society	2	0
Painted Lady. Scarlet and white blossom, very ornamental	1	6

FILLBASKET (new). Amongst the recent introductions this is well worthy of notice, on account of its enormous productiveness, and good eating qualities. Pods from twelve to fourteen inches in length, of a bright green colour. It was awarded a silver medal at the Hamburg Exhibition, September, 1887 ... ... per pint 1s. 6d. 2 6

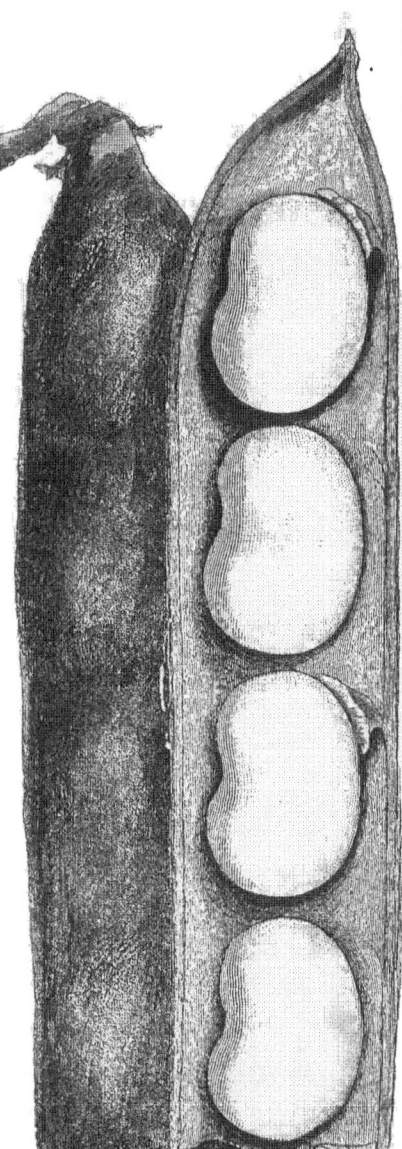

DANIELS' NORFOLK GIANT LONG-POD.

19¼ inches long, grown by W. Pound, jun. (see Testimonial).

Runner Beans *(continued)*.

per quart—s. d.

NE PLUS ULTRA (Neal's). A fine variety for Exhibition and main crop, producing an enormous quantity of extraordinary pods of splendid form, from ten to fourteen inches long, and quite straight. To grow it to perfection each bean should be planted one foot apart in the row 2 0

Giant White. Remarkably fine and distinct variety 1 9

Ruby. So named from colour of pods ... per pkt. 1s. —

Scarlet. Best for general crop 1 0

White Dutch or Caseknife. Very prolific and of good quality 1 3

Mixed. All sorts 1 3

Broad Beans.

Cultivation.—These succeed best in a deep, stiff, loamy soil, moderately enriched, and once the seed is sown require little attention, beyond earthing the plants up well by drawing the soil freely against them on either side, when the young plants are a few inches high. Immediately the plants have ceased blooming pinch off the points beyond the blooms, and should the weather prove very dry it will conduce to more quick cropping to damp the blooms over with water from a syringe, or otherwise. Early Mazagan and Long-pod varieties should be sown in November and again in February and March for early crops. Sow also at the same time during the latter months Daniels' Norfolk Giant, the best of all Broad Beans, Windsor, and Seville Long-pod, or other main crop varieties. Draw drill rows deeply, or about three inches deep, with a wide hoe, and plant the seeds in two rows, at about half-a-foot distance in each row apart, and each at right angles with the associate row. Sow the dwarfs in rows eighteen inches apart, and the tall varieties thirty inches apart.

per quart—s. d.

DANIELS' NORFOLK GIANT LONG-POD. The longest-podded Bean known, growing from twelve to eighteen inches in length, of a handsome uniform shape. First-class for exhibition, obtains first prize wherever exhibited ... 2 0

DANIELS' MAMMOTH WINDSOR. An exceedingly large-podded, very prolific variety; a great improvement, strongly recommended ... 1 6

DANIELS' SCARLET WINDSOR (*see Novelties*) 1 6

Bock's Green Gem. Excellent for small gardens ... 1 3

Broad Windsor (Taylor's). Fine selected stock ... 0 8

Giant Seville Long-pod. A very fine long-podded variety. First Class Certificate, R.H.S. 1 6

Taber's Perfection Long-pod (new). A very prolific white-eyed variety; pods long and well filled ... 1 6

Green Long-pod. Fine flavour and delicately green 0 10

Green Windsor (or **Nonpareil**). Abundant bearer 1 0

Harlington Windsor. Larger and finer pods than the old Windsor 1 0

Johnson's Wonderful (Mackie's Monarch) ... 0 6

Mazagan. Small, early, and hardy 0 6

Minster Giant Long-pod. Large and prolific ... 0 9

EVIDENCE OF QUALITY.

"I have gathered one of your **Norfolk Giant Beans**, which is 18¼ inches long and 4½ inches in circumference. About fifty persons have seen it measured."—**Mr. W. POUND, Jun.,** New Road, Chippenham.

"I had some of your **Norfolk Giant Long-pod Beans**, the pods measuring 16½ inches."—**Mr. G. DAVIES,** Hereford.

"I have taken First Prize two years following with your **Norfolk Giant Long-pod Beans.**"—**Mr. J. COLES,** Towton.

"From your **Norfolk Giant Long-pod Beans** I grew some 18 inches long. They were some of the finest Beans I ever saw."—**Mr. H. CHADD,** Godbury.

"I took First Prize at our Show here with your **Norfolk Giant Long-pod Beans.** I showed a fine dish, not one under eighteen inches long."—**Mr. G. OSBORN,** Barnet.

"I received First Prize at our Show last year with your **Norfolk Giant Bean,** against a host of competitors."—**Mr. J. WETHERELL,** Skelton.

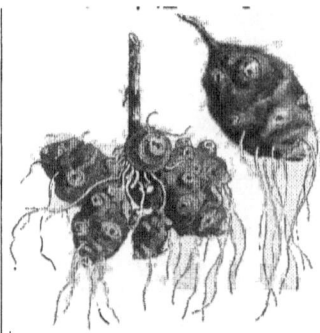

JERUSALEM ARTICHOKES.

EARLY GIANT PURPLE.

Artichokes.

		s.	d.
Globe. Plants ...	... per doz.	9	0
Jerusalem. Fine large tubers ... ... per peck 1s. 6d.; per bush.	6	0
Green Globe. Seed ... ... per oz.	1	0
Purple ... ... ,,	1	0
NEW WHITE MAMMOTH. White skinned Jerusalem Artichoke (see Coloured Plate and Novelties) per lb. 6d.; per peck	6	0

Asparagus.

Cultivation.—This, one of the finest vegetables in creation, is a general favourite, and were its medicinal qualities fully known would, considering its easy culture, be more extensively grown, and the wonder is, why all who possess any form of garden, short of an allotment, do not grow it plentifully. Nor does the preparation, and subsequent support required by the bed exceed that of other crops, if, indeed, it is nearly so much, whilst the bulk of the produce, if taken account of, perhaps exceeds that of most kinds, and that of a quality we need not accord words of praise to here. We would most impressively urge our customers to make Asparagus the first and most important consideration in planting a kitchen garden.

Asparagus likes a moderately consistent soil, and one both moisture absorbing and transmitting, or such as does not retain an excess of latent moisture. In view of this a good drained quarter is best for it, and that on a site both open and sunny. To work the bed properly, it should be deeply trenched, adding manure of any green or coarse kind plentifully to the bottom of the trenches, and such as is more decomposed and shorter, near to the upper soil. If the bed becomes somewhat elevated in the operation, so much the better. Where a good subsoil exists, and the necessary labour referred to above cannot be afforded, even then, rather than have no Asparagus bed, we advise all to thoroughly manure and dig the site most approved, and make a plantation at once. Even so treated, it will afford much and fairly good useful produce.

Asparagus plants are easily grown from seed. A rich nursery bed should be made for them, and if it can be made upon a firm bottom, and where it can be kept well manure-watered, so much the better. Sow the seeds in thin drill rows at from one to three feet apart, according to the desire that exists to grow very strong young plants. Thin the seedlings out well when they are up, and keep them free from weeds. Seeds may be sown to form plants permanently upon the beds whereon they are to stand and grow. It is best, however, to plant one year old seedlings.

The young plants may be planted during March and the first week in April, either upon beds which have been formed some four feet wide, having alleys of two feet in width between, or in rows from three to five feet apart across the whole piece, but not less than the former. Plant them in trenches or deep drill rows shovelled out, and somewhat thickly in the rows, covering them over with about three inches of soil. Always so manipulate the soil as to be able to spread the roots out straight all around.

In the Autumn, as soon as the stems turn quite yellow, cut them off below and remove them, well hoeing the ground and raking all litter off neatly. In January of the following year give a thorough good dressing of decayed manure, and a sprinkling of salt. With good cultivation till the plants are three years old, they are fit to cut from. Cut all the "blades" both large and small as they form. Cease cutting each year as soon as a fair supply has been obtained, as to do so proves a material guarantee for subsequent fine produce.

Seed.

	per oz.—s.	d.
Asparagus (True Giant) ... per lb. 4s.	0	4
,, **Connover's Colossal.** A very large variety ... per lb. 6s.	0	6
EARLY GIANT PURPLE. As grown by the celebrated French growers for Paris Market; robust variety of the most delicious flavour per lb. 7s.	0	8

Plants.

We do not advocate the Autumn or Winter planting of this seedling, as we consider March the best time for planting in the open ground. The strong roots we offer will be found very fine for forcing.

Connover's Colossal. Two and three years old

True Giant. Two and three years old, per 100, 3s. 6d. & 5s. Extra strong roots for forcing ... per 100, 12s. 6d. and 15s.

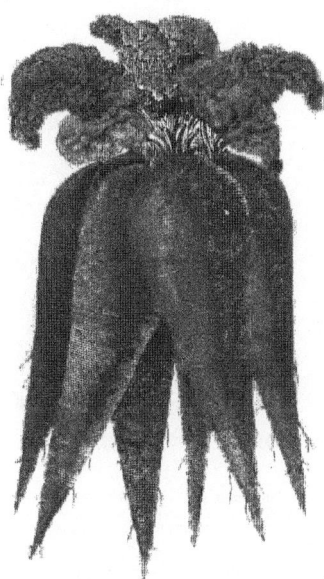

DANIELS' CRIMSON PERFECTION.

"At the Fruit and Root Show I was awarded a First Class Certificate for your **Crimson Perfection Beet.**"—Mr. **W. BAILEY,** Lamberhurst.

"Of the **Crimson Perfection Beet** every Seed seems to have germinated, and the crop was splendid."—The Rev. J. W. ANDREWS, Batcombe.

"After five years' experience of your **Seeds** of different kinds, I cannot help bearing testimony to the genuineness of same. I have not had a single crop fail, and it is with great pleasure I forward you enclosed order together with remittance."—Mr. A. BUCKINGHAM, Burford.

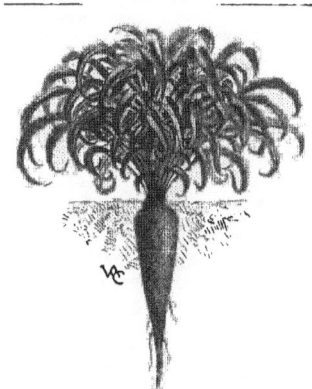

DALY BEET—DRACÆNA-LEAVED (for Flower Garden).

Beet.

Cultivation.—This is one of our most valuable vegetables, and destined to take a high place amongst them. The culture is extremely simple. A free open soil suits it best; and to grow it well a shallow bastard trench should be worked sixteen to twenty inches deep, at the very bottom of which a layer of good unctuous manure should be laid. Do not manure the layer of soil above, but fork it over just before sowing the seeds. Make an early sowing about the 10th of April, and a main sowing about the 5th of May. Sow in shallow drill rows twenty inches apart, or even less if a short-top kind is chosen, as by this means the ground is better protected from the too scorching rays of the sun. The seedlings should be thinned out to about six or eight inches 'atween" plants, or even more if large kinds are grown, which is not advisable. Hoe them occasionally during the whole Summer to ensure both the destruction of weeds and that a free soil exists around them. The earlier sown might be drawn for use as soon as they have become large enough. Take the main crop up within a week of October 1st, and during a dry day. Every root must be taken up carefully and with a fork, so as not to break off a single fibre, which is essential to their future merits both as regards colour and flavour when cooked. Never cut the leaves off; but twist them off with the hands. We would direct special attention to Daniels' Crimson Perfection Salad, which will be found a most useful and splendid variety. Also **Dracæna-leaved**; this latter, a highly desirable variety for the Flower Garden.

EGYPTIAN, TURNIP-ROOTED.

per oz.—s. d.

DANIELS' CRIMSON PERFECTION SALAD. A new dark-leaved variety with crimson flesh, of excellent quality. An acquisition in the way of ornamental Beet, having deep blood red foliage with metallic hue; fine for flower-garden decoration and for salads   ...   .   per pkt. 6d. 1 6

DANIELS' BLACK QUEEN. Fine new dark-leaved variety (*see Novelties*) ...   .   per pkt. 6d. 1 6

Dark Red Salad 0 6

Dell's Black. A fine dark-foliaged variety   ...   per pkt. 4d. 1 0

Egyptian Dark Red Turnip-rooted. One of the best for Summer Salads, as it comes into maturity very early   ...   per pkt. 3d. 0 10

Eclipse (new). A fine early Turnip-rooted variety   ...   "   4d. 1 0

Henderson's Pine Apple. Dark-leaved   ...   "   3d. 0 9

Nutting's Dwarf Red. Fine dark foliage   ...   "   3d. 0 10

OMEGA. Small top, remarkably handsome root   ...   "   4d. 1 0

DRACÆNA-LEAVED. A highly ornamental variety for the Flower Garden. The leaves are fine, long, and of a deep rich crimson; in shape they somewhat resemble the Dracæna, from which it takes its name. The root is of fine quality and excellent color. Altogether we consider it a most desirable variety, both for ornamental and culinary purposes   ...   .   per pkt. 6d. 1 6

Ornamental Chilian. Non-edible; a strikingly handsome variety, beautifully and brilliantly marked with scarlet, crimson, orange, yellow, pink, and white; invaluable for subtropical and ornamental gardening   ...   .   per pkt. 6d. 1 6

Silver Sea Kale or **Spinach Beet.** The leaves make an excellent substitute for Spinach ...   .   per pkt. 4d. 1 0

EVIDENCE OF QUALITY.

"I am pleased to tell you that the Seeds I had from you last year did remarkably well. I took First Prize with **Dark Red Salad Beet.**"--Mr. **K. LANE,** Staunton.

"I had my Seed from you last year and found it very good. I exhibited twelve varieties at our Show and received Ten Prizes." Mr. **G. MILES,** Melton.

"Mr. Oldroyd is pleased to say he took Thirteen Prizes at Thornes Flower and Vegetable Show, being the first time showing from your Seed." Mr. **W. OLDROYD,** Wakefield.

"I am very pleased with the **Seeds** which are all giving the greatest satisfaction, I think every seed growing."—Mr. **M. LOASBY,** The Gardens, Salcey Lawn.

"Please find P.O. enclosed. I am very pleased indeed with the **Seeds.** They all turned out wonderfully well."—Mr. **V. Russel,** Star Cross.

"The **Seeds** I have had these last three years have turned out well."—Mr. **NICHOLAS,** Hythe.

"I obtained the following prizes from the produce of your **Seeds,** viz.:—First, Broad Beans; First, Golden Rocca Onions; First, Giant Red Cabbage; First, Vegetable Marrow; First for the best cultivated garden."—Mr. **RHODES,** Pilsley.

Broccoli.

DANIELS' NORFOLK GIANT.

Cultivation.—As the aim of every cultivator should be to grow as constant a succession of this very valuable vegetable as possible, hence it will be necessary not only to make occasional sowings, but also to choose several distinct varieties so to treat. The first sowing should be made early in March in a gentle heat, and this should consist of Snow's Winter White, and also, if possible, Osborn's Winter White. Make other and successional sowings about once a fortnight, commencing about April 10th. In regard to culture those require a peculiar kind of soil, viz., one that is at once consistent and somewhat stiff, yet such as does not hold moisture in any great degree. The site these are to be planted upon cannot be worked too deeply, or manured too heavily, and it should always, where practicable, be trenched a month or two before the time for planting arrives. Take advantage of damp weather upon which to forward all transplanting work. The seedlings should be transplanted thickly on to what is termed nursery beds, at distances of about five inches apart. Thin out the strongest plants to treat thus, permitting the smaller ones to remain in the seed bed until they become large enough for final transplanting. So soon as the early sown plants become large enough for the latter purpose, transplant them into drill rows previously drawn for them at distances of three feet apart, and allowing a similar distance between each plant in the row. The later Winter crops should be planted a foot less apart all ways. No opportunity should be missed to give them good waterings during all subsequent dry periods, and manure water will aid them greatly. Always take care to cut the heads for use immediately the "flower" is seen through or between the apices of the leaves. It is a commendable practice to cut the top or chief head off all "sprouting" kinds so soon as it is seen to have produced the necessary bulk. The late Autumn kinds should always be protected by means of bracken fern, straw, or any similar material at the approach of frost, or if the "heads" are fit for use the plants may be drawn bodily and hung up in any cool shed until required for use. Our own specialities in this class, viz., **Daniels' Norfolk Giant**, a splendid kind, which has been grown to the enormous weight of 28 lbs., should be sown in March and April for cutting the following Spring; whilst **Daniels' King of the Broccolis**, the best late variety in cultivation, should be sown in April and May for cutting in May and June the following season.

First Division.

Sow in April, May, and June for cutting in September, October, and November the same year.

	per pkt. s. d.	per oz. s. d.		per pkt. s. d.	per oz. s. d.
Early Purple Cape	0 4	1 0	**VEITCH'S SELF-PROTECT-**		
Walcheren (true). Sow in succession every			**ING AUTUMN.** Extremely valu-		
three weeks from February till October ..	0 6	1 6	able to grow as a succession to "Autumn		
White Cape. A valuable variety	0 9	2 0	Giant" Cauliflower	0 9	1 0
White Sprouting	0 6	1 6			

Second Division.

Sow in April, May, and June, for cutting in January and February the following Spring.

	per pkt. s. d.	per oz. s. d.		per pkt. s. d.	per oz. s. d.
DANIELS' NEW YEAR. A			Penzance Early White	0 6	1 6
vigorous, compact, dwarf-growing variety,			Snow's Winter White. May be cut from		
with self-protecting foliage over-lapping			Christmas to end of January	1 0	2 6
snow-white heads, which are fit to cut from			**St. Hilary.** A splendid Broccoli of hardy,		
Christmas to end of January	1 0	2 6	vigorous constitution, dwarf, compact growth,		
Adams' Early White. A fine white variety	0 6	1 6	and large white heads, coming into use the		
Osborn's Winter White	0 6	1 9	second week in January	0 9	2 0

EVIDENCE OF QUALITY.

"Herewith I enclose one of your Norfolk Giant Broccoli, which I think is a grand acquisition, as I have this year grown eight kinds. I find yours has come through this trying winter with very few losses, whilst some of the other kinds were all killed by frost. It is a pleasure to sow the seeds you send out, as one feels they can be depended upon; and it is only fair to say that out of the eight kinds of Broccoli I have grown this year your **Norfolk Giant** is the best."—Mr. H. RIDGEWELL, Cambridge.

Broccoli *(continued)*.

Third Division.

Sow end of March and beginning of April for cutting in March and April the following Spring.

	per pkt. s. d.	per oz. s. d.
DANIELS' NORFOLK GIANT. A magnificent variety of robust and compact habit, stem short, the flower-heads exceedingly large and beautifully white, being well protected with luxuriant overlapping foliage. Have been grown to the enormous weight of twenty-eight pounds each	1 0	2 6
Dilcock's Bride. Heads pure white	0 4	1 0
Easter Day or **Springtide.** A fine variety of dwarf, compact habit and vigorous growth, one of the best kinds for the main crop in the Spring	0 6	1 6
Knights' Protecting	0 6	1 6
Leamington. Heads large and solid	0 6	1 6
Purple Sprouting. A very hardy Winter variety ...	0 4	1 0

Fourth Division.

Sow in May and June for cutting in May and June the following season.

	per pkt. s. d.	per oz. s. d.
DANIELS' KING of the BROCCOLI. This splendid variety comes in for cutting from the beginning of May to the first week in June, and as a late kind cannot be surpassed. It is of a fine dwarf habit, and being well protected is exceedingly hardy. Its heads are remarkably fine, close, and white, and of large size ...	1 0	2 6
Chappell's Large Cream	0 4	1 0
Gilbert's Victoria Late White. Very late white. First Class Certificate, Royal Horticultural Society	0 0	2 0
Gilbert's Burghley Champion	0 0	2 0
Daniels' Latest White or **Summer.** One of the best kinds for filling up the gap or period that occurs between Broccoli and Cauliflower	0 6	1 6
Queen (Sutton's). Very fine	0 6	1 6

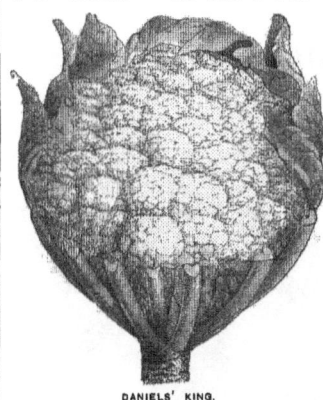

DANIELS' KING.

EVIDENCE OF QUALITY.

"The **King of the Broccolis** grown from your Seed this season have been superb."— Dr. **HARRISON**, Killough.

"Your **Norfolk Giant Broccoli** turned out the best I have seen this season, and gave great satisfaction."—Mr. R. **CLARKE**, Hampstead.

Borecole or Kale.

Cultivation.—These in their several varieties are the most hardy amongst the Brassicas. They form a link as 'twere between the many Winter and very early Spring supplies and the earliest Summer-bearing Cabbages, and as such should be considered indispensable in all gardens where a constant supply has to be maintained. Few subjects exhibit so pleasantly the result of good culture as do these; as the best strain a seedsman can send out is capable of being destroyed by bad and overcrowded culture. The seeds must be sown broadcast and thinly, in richly prepared soil, in about three successional sowings commencing March 25th, and twice subsequently between then and the 12th May. These will also repay being transplanted into nursery beds four or five inches apart, from thence they may be finally transplanted into rows three feet apart and two feet between plants in the rows, as soon as they are large enough and a showery period intervenes. They delight in thoroughly worked and enriched soils of moderate consistency, the lighter the soils, so much the more will they be benefited by copious manure waterings, and it aids them powerfully in all soils. There are some very showy and effective variegated-leaved varieties, examples of which tend to break up the monotony of and to enliven the kitchen garden, and, indeed, shrubbery borders during early Spring. They are equally adapted for culinary purposes, the flavour being much improved after frost.

DANIELS' MOSS CURLED.

	per pkt. s. d.	per oz. s. d.
DANIELS' DWARF EXQUISITE. A dwarf compact-growing variety, leaves exquisitely curled and fringed, most valuable for garnishing, it is also well adapted for culinary purposes, presenting a pleasing appearance when cooked	0 6	1 6
DANIELS' MOSS CURLED. Of medium height, very hardy, with foliage beautifully curled ...	0 6	1 6
Cottagers'. Exceedingly hardy	0 3	0 8
Dwarf Green Curled. Very hardy, dwarf-stemmed, flavour very mild, colour dark green when cooked, the best for general crop	0 3	0 8
Tall Green Curled. The Tall Scotch Kale ...	0 3	0 8
Variegated or **Garnishing.** A fine curled-leaved variety, beautifully variegated, very useful and ornamental for garnishing, also valuable for Winter gardening. Extra-fine selected stock	0 4	1 0

EVIDENCE OF QUALITY.

"Your **Broccoli, Cabbage,** &c., served splendidly last year, and your **Lettuce** was excellent."—Rev. J. C. **EDWARDS**, Aylesbury.

Brussels Sprouts.

DANIELS' COLOSSAL SPROUTS.
(*From a Photograph.*)

DANIELS' DEFIANCE.
(*From a Photograph.*)

Cultivation.—Few comestibles have a finer flavour than that of the better kinds of Brussels Sprouts; and we have much pleasure in stating that we possess the finest stock in cultivation of this delicious vegetable. **Daniels' Colossal**, a truly magnificent variety, a most abundant cropper, of mild flavour, and the best for general use, should be grown by everyone who has a garden. To ensure really good sprouts it is necessary to grow medium-sized by contrast with the very large ones, which are invariably somewhat strong-flavoured. They delight in a deep, rich, and somewhat light or moderately stony soil. Sow seeds during the early part of March, and by way of succession early in April also. The plants should be planted in drill rows, drawn two feet apart, and about twenty inches from plant to plant in the rows. Earth the plants up well when active growth has commenced. In the Autumn when the lower leaves turn yellow, and commence to ripen off, remove all such as show these symptoms, and hoe and rake neatly between the plants. Do not, as is too frequently done, cut the crowns off the plants until February, as they serve as a necessary protection to the young sprouts, and, indeed, the plants generally. They delight in Summer waterings, manure water in particular.

per oz.—s. d.

DANIELS' COLOSSAL. One of the finest and best in cultivation, of very vigorous growth, bearing sprouts of a large compact globular shape all the way up the stem; these will be found of a more delicate and fine flavour than any of the Cabbage tribe ... ... per pkt. 9d. 2 0

DANIELS' DEFIANCE. An extra select variety, half dwarf, and exceedingly productive, the stem being covered with fine compact sprouts of excellent quality ... ... per pkt. 9d. 2 0

											s.	d.
Aigburth. Extra fine	...	...	...	...	...	...	...	...	...	„	4d.	1	0
Dalkeith. Extra fine, select stock ...	...	...	...	...	...	...	...	„	6d.	1	4
Imported	...	...	...	...	...	...	...	...	...	...	...	0	6
President Carnot	...	...	...	...	...	...	...	...	...	per pkt. 9d.	2	0
Scrymger's Giant	...	...	...	...	...	...	...	...	...	„	3d.	0	9

EVIDENCE OF QUALITY.

"The **Brussels Sprouts** I had from you last year were splendid, and so much liked."—Mrs. **WIFFEN**, Northlew Manor.

"I beg to say that the **Brussels Sprouts** I had from you last year proved excellent. They were a very fine crop, and stood all Winter, while all others were cut off."—Mr. E. **WICKS**, Puttenham.

Cabbage.

DANIELS' DEFIANCE GIANT EARLY MARROW.

DEFIANCE CABBAGE (cut open). (From a Photograph).

Cultivation.—In this class of the Brassica tribe, **Daniels' Defiance Early Marrow** stands pre-eminent. This fact is testified by the thousands of packets sold during the past Spring and Autumn, and further, by the numerous flattering testimonials we continue to receive on all hands with respect to its superior qualities.

Although Cabbages would appear to occupy quite a second-rate position among the list of comestibles of the vegetable garden, Spring Cabbages are nevertheless universally appreciated for their tenderness and unquestionably delicious flavour. In the culture of them, a constant succession of quickly grown and hence tender heads should always be aimed at in preference to an undue quantity, existing as sometimes happens at any period of the year. Cabbages, as do all the tribe, delight in a deeply-worked, well enriched soil; one however that has been brought into good order by constant manuring and manipulation in the past, rather than such as has been recently so treated. This particular species of this extensive family will succeed most thoroughly in well-worked and fertilized open or stony soil. This in comparison to such other kindred subjects as have been previously referred to. It is only necessary in these regards to study one particular in regard to such, viz., if any soil is very light, it should have been well enriched, and be allowed a month or two to settle down subsequently before the crop is planted out upon it. By such means we have carried the finest possible crops upon very light stony soils, by transplanting the Autumn sown plants intended for the Spring crop upon the previously used Onion bed. This be it understood without digging it over following the Onion crop; but in fact only hoeing it over deeply, drawing the drill rows, and planting the young plants thereon. All heavy, stiff, retentive, and damp soils, it were needless to remark, must be well worked up for the crops, or they will not succeed thereon. The first sowing in the year should be made about the middle of March. These, if transplanted on in patches as they become large enough, will afford the late Autumn and Winter supply. For the main or Spring crop sow about August 11th. These must be transplanted on to an open sunny aspect, so soon as large enough for the purpose. Sow the seeds upon prepared and finely raked soil, and where practicable transplant into nursery beds, there to grow the plants on to become large enough for final planting out. Good Cabbages should be thirty inches apart in the rows. A sowing of Rosette Colewort, made about the middle of July and during showery weather, will often form very excellent and useful stuff for the early Autumn months, and prove useful away into the Winter.

EVIDENCE OF QUALITY.

"Please send me a packet of **Defiance Cabbage**. I have had it these four years and cannot find any way to equal it."—**Mr. S. PALMER**, Exeter.

"Your Defiance Cabbage stood the Winter when other sorts failed."—**Mr. T. THOMPSON**, Leicester.

"I have grown the best Cabbages I ever had from the Defiance and Little Queen I had of you last year."—Mr. J. BLIGHT, Torrington.

"I have had some splendid Cabbage this Summer from the Seed I had from you. They stood the severe weather remarkably well."—Mr. **W. A. FERMOR**, Harrietsham.

DANIELS' DEFIANCE GIANT EARLY MARROW. A magnificent variety, growing to the weight of from ten to twenty pounds. Remarkably early, short-legged, and compact, and of the most delicious marrow flavour. Invaluable for the market gardener or the private grower. **Per packet 6d., per oz. 1s. 6d.**

Cabbage (*continued*).

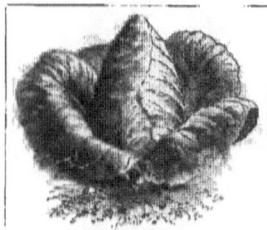

LITTLE QUEEN.

"The **Little Queen Cabbage** I had from you in July last are splendid. I cut some nice hard ones this day. I may say it is the best plot of Cabbage round here."— **Mr. C. WALKER**, Marlow.

	per oz.—s. d.
DANIELS' LITTLE QUEEN. A superior fine early dwarf variety per pkt. 6d.	1 6
ALLAN'S INCOMPARABLE. A distinct Early Cabbage, raised by Mr. Allan, head gardener to the Right Hon. Lord Suffield, Gunton Park per pkt. 4d.	1 0
Cocoa-nut. Early and distinct variety	0 6
Ellam's Early Dwarf. A first-class Early Cabbage in all respects. Being very compact, they can be planted close together, thus growing double the quantity of plants on the same space than most kinds. A fine early market kind	1 0
DANIELS' IMPROVED ENFIELD MARKET per pkt. 4d.	1 0
Early Dwarf York	0 6
Early Large York	0 6
Enfield Market. Excellent main crop variety	0 6
Ewing's No. 1 (true) A very fine early Dwarf Cabbage per pkt. 3d.	0 9
Early Rainham. Excellent	0 6
Heartwell Early Marrow per pkt. 6d.	1 0
Nonpareil Improved Dwarf. Early variety	0 10
Nonpareil. Large	0 6
Rosette Colewort	0 8
St. John's Day. A fine dwarf, very early variety	0 6
Wheeler's Imperial	0 8

EVIDENCE OF QUALITY.

"**Little Queen Cabbage** did remarkably well this year. I noticed in several gardens that early Cabbages invariably bolted, but not Little Queen."—**Mr. W. SNELL**, Chesterfield.

"I planted out three hundred of your **Little Queen Cabbage** last Autumn, they are the best I have ever grown. I only lost three, and I have cut some 7 lbs. in weight."—**Mr. H. HUMPHREY**, Stevenage.

Savoy Cabbage.

DANIELS' VICTORIA SAVOY.

Cultivation.—This, like all of its class, delights in deep, rich, moderately consistent soil, and it must be the chief object of the grower to grow good plants that may become well-established, large, and leafy by the Autumn. Sow early in March, and again about April 10th, and thinly, into a well-enriched and finely-worked soil. We are very partial to the Dwarf Ulm, Tom Thumb, or Daniels' Extra Early, as they produce such neat firm heads, and may be planted more thickly together than is ordinarily requisite. Transplant the larger kinds out permanently in drill rows two feet apart, and from eighteen to twenty inches apart in the rows. The dwarfer kinds may be planted eighteen inches apart in the rows, and fifteen inches asunder in the run. To prevent clubbing, deep and good culture, and frequent changing of crops is beneficial, often besides it proves a powerful preventive to dip the roots of all young plants into a lye formed of cow-dung, wood ashes, &c., just before planting them out into the permanent Winter quarters. If a sprinkling of lime or soot be thrown amongst the seedling plants upon the seed beds when very young, this often deters the pest from attacking them, as it sometimes does at this early date. For late use, and northern and cold climates, "**Norwegian**" cannot be surpassed.

TOM THUMB.

	per oz.—s. d.
DANIELS' NONPAREIL. Splendid variety for early use, quite distinct; the most delicately flavoured Savoy grown per pkt. 4d.	1 0
Drumhead (Selected Stock). The largest variety	0 4
Dwarf Green Curled. Very compact	0 8
Dwarf Ulm. Early, very dwarf	0 6
Golden Autumn. A distinct and beautiful variety per pkt. 3d.	0 9
Green Globe. A good hardy variety	0 6
VICTORIA. Extra large and fine quality per pkt. 4d.	1 0
Norwegian. Excellent variety for late use, extremely hardy, and well suited for northern and cold climates	1 0
Tom Thumb. The most compact variety in cultivation per pkt. 3d.	0 9
Daniels' Extra Early. Fortnight earlier than Dwarf Ulm " 4d.	1 0

We can supply all the above kinds much cheaper by the pound. Prices on application.

Red or Pickling Cabbage.

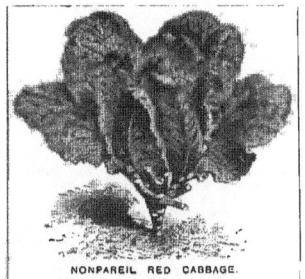

NONPAREIL RED CABBAGE.

	per oz.—s.	d.
DANIELS' GIANT RED DRUMHEAD. Very fine, grows to a large size, the finest Red Cabbage known ... ... per pkt. 4d.	1	0
Erfurt Blood Red. Dwarf, compact, small heads ... ... „ 3d.	0	9
Manchester Large Red. Fine, large, firm heads	0	8
New Early Red Nonpareil. It has a pointed head; its main feature, however, is its dark red colour throughout, besides being the earliest of all the Red Cabbages ... ... per pkt. 4d.	1	0
Red Dutch	0	6

EVIDENCE OF QUALITY.

"The **Cabbage** I had last year I believe was the best and earliest in Sussex, notwithstanding the hard Winter. They stood it well."— Mr. **W. SMITH**, Easthourne.

"Your **Red Cabbage** has taken First Prize wherever exhibited." Mr. **W. F. SMITH**, Apsley.

Cabbages for Field Culture.

Drill 4 lbs. per acre, or sow at rate of 2 lbs. per acre for Transplanting.

DWARF DRUMHEAD.

	per lb.—s.	d.
DANIELS' DWARF DRUMHEAD. Distinct from Robinson's Champion, being dwarf and much earlier, coming into use some weeks before the large Drumhead varieties ... per oz. 4d.	4	0
Thousand-headed Kale. Tall, branching, valuable for early sheep feed, extra stock, improved ... ... per oz. 4d.	2	6
DANIELS' IMPROVED CHAMPION DRUMHEAD. A very fine selected variety, producing extraordinarily large heads ... ... per oz. 4d.	4	0
Robinson's Drumhead ... ... „ 4d.	3	6

" Enclosed please find P. O. for 1 oz. of **Defiance Cabbage.** They are by far the best I ever grow."—Mr. **S. LEE**, Bridgewater.

EVIDENCE OF QUALITY.

" I am much pleased with the Cabbage Seed I had from you last year. I have had very good Cabbages from your **Defiance** and **Little Queen.** My friends have asked me to get some Seed for them, and I have sent for a few packets."—Mr. **J. WEBBER**, Molland.

" I took thirty Prizes at Millom Floral and Horticultural Show last year from your Seed. Cabbage **Defiance**, excellent, about 30 lbs., Red Cabbage over 30 lbs., Savoy Victoria 12 lbs. weight, and Drumhead (Winter) over 30 lbs."—Mr. **H. NORTHCOTE**, Millom.

" We had some splendid **Cabbages** from the Seed we had last year." Mr. **G. TURNER**, Chatham.

"The **Defiance Cabbage** turned out well with us last year."— Mr. **J. WARNE**, Wadebridge.

"The **Cabbage** Seed that we had last time gave great satisfaction, both to ourselves and others for whom we got it. We have had some very fine ones."—Mr. **M. ELLIOTT**, Cuckfield.

Corn Salad (Lamb's Lettuce)

	per oz.—s.	d.
Green Cabbaging. A fine variety, rosette-shaped per pkt. 4d.	0	9
Lettuce-leaved ... ... „ 4d.	0	9
Large Round-leaved Dutch ... „ 4d.	0	9

Chicory.

	per pkt.—s.	d.
Improved Large-leaved. Excellent for blanching	0	9
Large-rooted or Coffee	0	6
Whitloef. Equally good as a salad or boiled. Sow in June	0	6

Couve Tronchuda,

or Portugal Cabbage.

Per packet 4d., per ounce 1s.

Dandelion.

	per pkt.—s.	d.
Improved Large-leaved. Very valuable for Winter Salads when blanched	0	6
Thick-leaved Cabbaging	0	6

Egg Plant.

	per pkt.—s.	d.
Crimson	0	4
Purple { Exceedingly effective for conservatory } ...	0	4
White { decoration; also for garnishing. } ...	0	4
Mixed	0	4

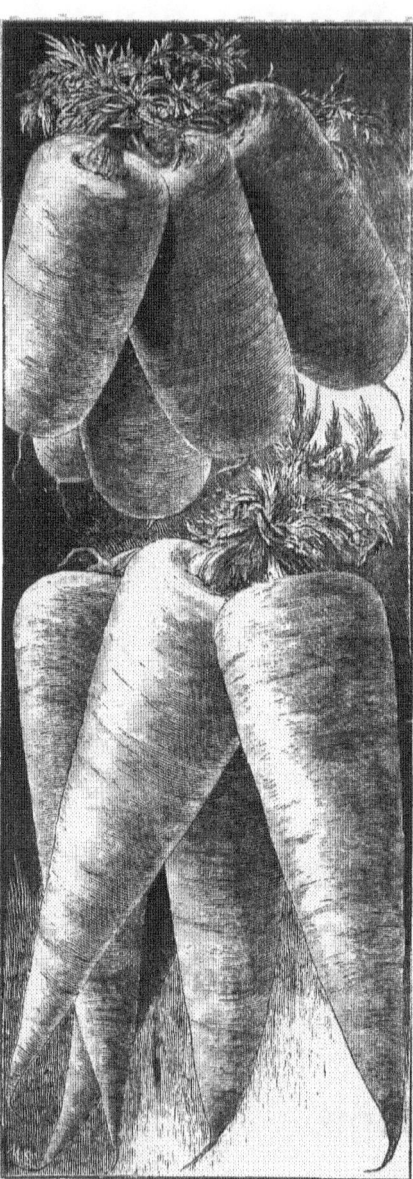

DANIELS' SCARLET PERFECTION.

DANIELS' TELEGRAPH CARROTS.

Carrot.

Cultivation.—Few subjects delight more in a free, open, sandy loam, of good depth. In preparing the ground for them it will be well to bastard trench it over, if possible, a few months before the seeds are sown. Place good decomposed manure ten inches deep for all long and intermediate kinds, and four inches deep for Short Horns of whatever variety. Whilst the soil cannot well be too open, free, and rich, wherein the roots form and swell, it will be important to make it so by working it up, and manuring it the season previously, as if it be too rich, caused by the presence of actual manure, it will have a tendency to cause the produce to become forked, and as regards symmetry and real usefulness, of inferior merit. Sow always in drill rows and but moderately deep. To promote a vigorous youthful growth, and enable the young plants to grow freely, the drills may be drawn deep enough to enable a small quantity of well-rotted manure to be placed at their bottom and covered over with a little fine soil, into which the seeds are to be sown. They must be kept scrupulously clean by frequent hoeings. Sow Horn Carrot early in August and about the 4th of September for Winter and early Spring use, in rows about eight inches apart, drawing for thinning, so soon as large enough. Make the early Spring sowings of Short Horn upon a sunny aspect in March, and the main sowings about April 10th. Mix sand with the seeds to aid in separating them before sowing.

Daniels' Telegraph Carrot is the best to grow for general crop for market or exhibition, and is becoming a general favourite with market gardeners. It has gained First Prizes this season wherever exhibited. **Daniels' Scarlet Perfection** or **Main Crop** is a most useful kind for general use, as it attains a large size in a short space of time.

per oz.—s. d.

NEW MAIN CROP CARROT, DANIELS' SCARLET PERFECTION. This is well adapted to shallow soils, being intermediate and stump-rooted (*see accompanying illustration*); is easily raised. Its symmetrical shape and its colour of bright orange-scarlet, make it a most desirable variety for the exhibition table, and also for market purposes ...   ...   per pkt. 4d.   1 0

"I took First Prize with your Scarlet Perfection Carrot."— Mr. J. J. GARNER, Sutton Bridge.

"I am pleased to tell you that I won fourteen prizes at our Show last week; I took a prize for everything I exhibited. Your **Scarlet Perfection Carrots** are splendid."—**Mr. G. GRENDON**, Oxenham.

DANIELS' TELEGRAPH. The best form of intermediate we know of. Carefully grown from selected roots; it is early, of good colour and shape (*see accompanying illustration*). A fine exhibition variety, and invaluable for market use 1 0

"I took two First Prizes with your Telegraph Carrot."—**Mr.** W. REYNOLDS, Dannel.

"I had the finest crop of **Carrots** from your Seed last year that has ever been grown about here."—**Mr. W. WILSON**, Boragh.

DANIELS' LONG RED WITHOUT HEART. Flesh bright red, without the core usually found in the Carrot 0 9

DANIELS' NEW EARLY FORCING. One of the earliest Carrots yet introduced. In shape it is nearly round; top small and neat. They can be left thickly in the row, and drawn for use as required

per pkt. 4d.   1 0

	s.	d.
Altringham Improved ...	0	6
Early Forcing Horn. Best forcing variety ...	0	9
Early French Nantes. Dwarf, stump-rooted ...	0	8
Early Scarlet Horn. For first early crop	0	6
Giant White. Much larger and of finer quality than Belgian White. Highly recommended ...	0	6
JAMES' SCARLET (Intermediate) ...	0	6
Long Red St. Valery. A very choice stock	0	8
Long Red Surrey or **Long Orange**	0	8
Studley. A superior variety	0	6

Cauliflower.

DANIELS' KING OF THE CAULIFLOWERS. Per packet 1s. 6d. and 2s. 6d.

Cultivation.—In the Cauliflower we possess at once the tenderest and sweetest delicacy that we can boast of amongst vegetables, and one universally appreciated. To grow it well it requires the richest of soils, with no stint of root moisture throughout its whole growth. Hence to insure this, deeply worked, heavily manured ground is of the first importance. To keep up a successional supply during as much of each year as possible, considerable care and attention is requisite. Advantage must be taken of many kinds of frames, handlights, &c., to grow young seedling plants under throughout the Winter months. A sowing should be made in a moderate warmth about February 12th, and as soon as the plants are large enough they should be pricked off in boxes, trays, &c., and placed in a cool frame. When the plants are somewhat stronger transplant into frames or under handlights, give air during mild weather, and about the middle of May remove the covering entirely. Sowings in the open air, to produce a crop to succeed the above, should be made about the 10th of April, May, June, and July successively. Transplant on good soil and water constantly, draw the soil up to and around them freely. As it is necessary not only to maintain moisture over the roots, but also to ward off the somewhat too direct rays of the sun during hot dry weather, when practicable, mulch with some rich moisture-retaining materials. The Autumn crop, which consists of Walcheren and Veitch's Autumn Giant, must be looked through daily, to see if any need gathering, and all that are ready should be pulled up and laid in, in a cool situation till wanted. For Spring work the Early Snowball and Daniels' **Dwarf Mammoth** are good, and to sow in Spring for Summer culture **Daniels' King of the Cauliflowers** is the best. Spring sowings are particularly liable to the depredations of White Fly, which cluster on them or destroy their centres, and so cause what is termed "blindness." To prevent this, sprinkle the leaves over when damp with soot, or the hearts with tobacco powder. Finally take care to use the heads when young, white, and solid; and to insure the production of such, the fewer sudden changes the plants are subject to the better. Irregularities in culture cause them to button or "bolt," as they sometimes do at the earliest stage of growth.

	per oz. s. d.
DANIELS' KING OF CAULI-FLOWERS. New and distinct variety; heads large, firm, and first-class to sow for a succession throughout the Autumn and Winter per pkt. 1s. 6d. and 2s. 6d.	—
DANIELS' SNOWBALL. Invaluable, *ready to cut in four months from the time of sowing* per pkt. 2s.	—
DANIELS' DWARF MAMMOTH. A very superior early dwarf variety, the best for early forcing; heads white and compact per pkt. 1s.	2 6
Eclipse. This is an excellent large Autumn Cauliflower, and very useful for Market purposes. By successional sowings it can be had from August to Christmas per pkt 1s.	2 6

	per oz. s. d.
Early London White per pkt. 6d.	1 6
Self-protecting Autumn Giant. A fine variety, coming into use directly after Veitch's Autumn Giant, the large white flowers being well protected from the Autumn frosts by overlapping leaves; may be had in good condition up to Christmas per pkt. 9d.	2 0
Veitch's Autumn Giant. An extremely valuable late variety, perfectly distinct from any other sort, heads magnificent, beautifully white, large, firm, and compact per pkt. 9d.	2 0
Walcheren (the true kind). Sow under glass in February, to succeed the Spring Broccoli, and in beds from May to July for succession per pkt. 6d.	1 6

EVIDENCE OF QUALITY.

"Your **King of the Cauliflowers** last Summer and Autumn turned out splendid. I took First Prize in July for a collection of vegetables, open to all England; the exquisite colour and fine texture of six of your **King of the Cauliflowers** were quite a feature in the collection, and were very much praised by the judges."—**Mr. H. RIDGEWELL,** Cambridge.

Celery.

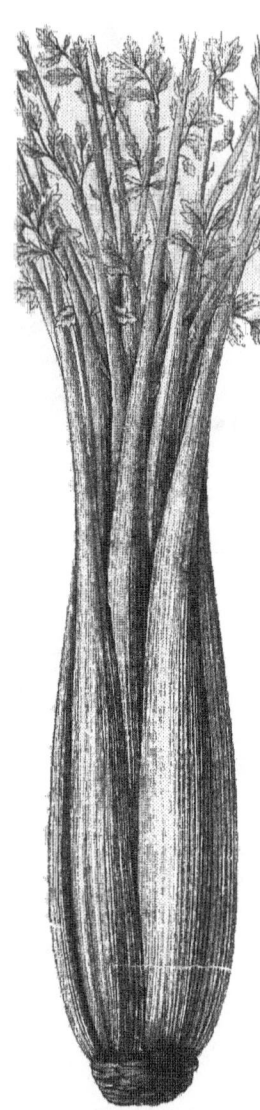

Cultivation.—Few vegetables exhibit more prominently the features which result from good culture than does Celery. If it receives any check during its entire growth, the invariable result is that the produce becomes either stringy, or bolts, and indeed, not infrequently both; and the latter sometimes happens at a very early date in the Autumn. Too early sowing also causes the latter to happen sometimes, following very arid Summers; hence it is not advisable to sow but sufficient for a few first rows when the earlier sowing has to be made. As regards the date of sowing, the grower must determine this according to the date when the earlier supply is in demand. In some establishments it is required by the beginning of September, or before; though generally consumers like it to remain until cold nights and a little frost have given to it less of that strong natural taste which it invariably has, at such times as the leaves are young, active, and in full growth. For the first crop sow in February, in pans, boxes, or upon a slight hotbed, if time and the opportunity exist to do the latter. So soon as the young plants, the produce of this sowing, become large enough for handling, prick them out thickly on to nursery beds formed upon a slight hotbed. Make another successional sowing in March, and in a like manner, and as soon as the plants, the produce of such, are large enough, prick them out in turn, either upon a warm aspect, under handlights, or any kind of protection that may exist. Make yet another sowing, out of doors, on a warm sheltered site, and in a very rich mellow soil, about the last week in April. The produce of this sowing will form excellent late sticks, and may come in useful besides for soups, &c. When the plants assume fair proportions, trenches must be prepared to finally plant them into. The trenches should be from nine to twelve inches deep, and from fourteen to eighteen inches wide, according to the earliness of planting, &c. Throw out the soil to this required size and depth, packing it up neatly on either side. Then procure, and dig in four or five inches of thoroughly decomposed rich manure; turn this over, and knock it about, so as to mix it freely together, and proceed to plant the plants therein directly. The principal attention they will require for the next month or two will consist of watering, &c., and both clear water and rich liquid manure should be given to them as frequently as it may be possible to do so. The earthing-up process should commence very early in July, or previously, when a very early supply is in demand. When it is in contemplation to proceed with this process, first go over all the plants, remove all the small leaves from around their base, and any young side or sucker shoots which are seen to form; then upon a fine dry day, chop down some of the soil from the sides of the trenches, breaking it up fine, and with the hands, aided by a trowel, place the soil in around the base of each plant neatly with the right hand, whilst each plant or stick is held firmly in position with the other. It is better to mould up at three successional times. Take care not to press the soil too firmly around the hearts, and avoid letting crumbs of soil fall into the hearts of the plants beside, as if carelessness be permitted in either case, there will be great danger that the "sticks" will grow crooked, or become "seated" as it is commonly called. All successional crops must be earthed up in rotation, and at studied intervals apart, but each should, at the advent of Winter, have sufficient soil placed around to protect all from severe frosts. **Daniels' Golden Heart, Daniels' Giant White,** and **Daniels' Giant Red** are the best, being extra selected stocks of superior merit.

						per pkt.—s. d.
DANIELS' GIANT RED. The largest grown, splendid colour, very solid, and of fine flavour	...	...	...	...	...	1 0
DANIELS' GIANT WHITE. The largest white in cultivation, very solid, crisp, and of excellent flavour	...	...	...	...	...	1 0
DANIELS' GOLDEN HEART. An excellent, sturdy, dwarf variety, very quick-growing, solid, and of fine nutty flavour, and when blanched the heart is of a pure yellow	...	...	...	...	...	1 0
Major Clark's Red	...	...	...	...	6d. and	1 0
Manchester Fine Red	...	...	...	...	3d. and	0 6
Sandringham Dwarf White	...	...	...	...	3d. and	0 6
Seymour's Superb White	...	...	...	...	3d. and	0 6
Silver Plume. A fine white-leaved variety. It blanches well by simply tying up the plants with matting	...	...	...	...	6d. and	1 0
Sulham Prize Pink	...	...	...	...	3d. and	0 6
Williams' Matchless Red	...	...	...	...	3d. and	0 6
Standard Bearer, an extra fine dwarf Red	...	...	...	...		1 0
Wright's Grove Red	...	...	...	...	6d. and	1 0
Wright's Grove White	...	...	...	...	6d. and	1 0
New Apple-shaped Celeriac, or Turnip-rooted Celery. For soups					6d. and	1 0
Curled-leaved. Extra fine	...	...	...	...	6d. and	1 0
Mixed Red and White. Useful for Cottagers				...	3d. and	0 6
Soup Celery	...	...	...	...	per lb. 2s.	—

EVIDENCE OF QUALITY.

"The **Giant White Celery** I had from you last year was excellent."—**The Rev. Canon DROWN,** The Rectory, Seaford.

"I took First Prize with your **Giant White Celery.**"—**Mr. H. GWYNN,** Bishopstone.

"Your **Giant White Celery** is the best we ever grew, and people came from all parts of the district to see it. They said it was the tenderest Celery they had ever eaten."—**Mr. E. ODDY,** Bradford.

"I have received over fifty Prizes for **Celery, Parsnip, Potatoes,** &c., at Castleford and several other shows."—**Mr. G. ROSE,** Pontefract.

DANIELS' GIANT WHITE.

"I took four First Prizes with your **Celery.** It measured four feet two inches long and sixteen inches round."—**Mr. W. SLATER,** Rochester.

Capsicum or Chili.

Cultivation.—Seeds should be sown between the beginning of March and April 20th; but the sooner the better within the above dates. Their culture is very simple, as seeds may be sown in pots or pans, and placed in moderate heat. Sow more nearly in the latter date under some kind of frame protection, or in the open border, where the above convenience does not exist. Seedlings must be transferred to single small pots, or two plants in each, as soon as they are fit to handle, and be thus grown on until the first week in June. At this date plant them out at the foot of a full South aspect wall, keeping them well watered. It is safest during all the changes of seasons to grow the crops in pots under glass, where convenience exists so to do. Even half-a-dozen pots so grown often prove very serviceable, besides coming in earlier than the general crops out of doors. The smaller kinds or Chili variety is more dwarf in its habits than the other varieties, though it is always more profitable to grow the larger ones.

		per pkt.—s.	d.
CELESTIAL (new). Very ornamental and useful			
	Gd. and	1	0
Chili or Bird Pepper. Small	...	0	4
Long Red. Large, the best for general use ...	...	0	4
Long Yellow. A very useful variety	...	0	4
Procopp's Giant (new). Superior variety with very large, glossy-scarlet, fleshy fruits, surpassing in size all other sorts of Giant Pepper. The flesh is sweet and mild, half an inch thick; fine exhibition variety Gd. &		1	0

		per pkt.—s.	d.
MONSTREUSE. Pods of enormous size ...	...	0	6
RUBY KING (new). Valuable as a decorative plant for the conservatory, besides being exceedingly useful for stews, pickles, &c.	... Gd. and	1	0
SWEET GOLDEN DAWN. Very useful as a decorative plant, also for stews and pickles, having the flavour of the Capsicum, without the hot piquancy of the Chili or Cayenne Pepper ...	...	0	6
Mixed. All kinds	...	0	6

Cress.

Cultivation.—The several varieties of Cress, consisting of the Australian, American, and commoner, not to omit that known as Watercress, all delight in a damp or moist situation; and as such is known and acted upon in practice, so is their simple growth enhanced, and the size of their leaves, &c., and more delicate piquancy increased. It is only necessary to sow the common kinds about five or seven days before they are required for use, and to keep them moderately moist, to insure a crop. The Australian, on the contrary, should be sown from early in the month of April to July, and for the Winter crop about August 20th and September 4th. The American variety sown at similar dates also comes in most usefully, and is a moderate substitute for our own popular Watercress. This latter may be produced from seeds sown upon a shady north aspect border. It is better to make a shallow basin-like bed for the seeds, and after these are sown to keep the same as constantly and copiously watered, artificially during dry weather, as possible.

		per oz.—s.	d.
DANIELS' GARNISHING or PARSLEY-LEAVED. Useful alike for salads and garnishing		0	6
American or Land. Eaten as Water-cress in Winter		0	4
Australian or Golden. This valuable Cress is a most desirable addition to all salads	... ...	0	4
Curled. For salads in the second leaf			
	per quart 1s. 9d., per pint 1s.	0	2

		per oz.—s.	d.
Plain. For curly salads, best for garden use			
	per quart 1s. 9d., per pint 1s.	0	2
Sorrel-leaved. The largest-leaved of all, dark green colour, and good flavour. A most useful salad ...	... ...	0	6
Water. Sow in a moist, shady place per pkt. 6d. and 1s.			—

Gourd or Pumpkin.

DANIELS' YELLOW MAMMOTH.

Cultivation.—Though these often succeed sown upon very rich soils in the open ground, and especially if a handlight or cloche be placed over; yet it is a far better way to sow seeds about April 25th, and so soon as the seedlings—having grown somewhat—assume the third or rough leaf, pot them off into about four-inch pots: one plant only of the large kinds should be placed in each pot. The best place to plant them is in a good thickness of soil placed upon a mound of manure. If a slight warmth exist in the latter so much the better. Plant them out about May 26th or soon after, and place some kind of protection over or around them. Do not plant them less than six or eight feet apart. The smaller-fruited kinds are best trained to upright rods or trellis-work, and are very ornamental. An abundance of liquid manure should be given to them constantly, and especially to the young plants when they commence growing freely. The fruit of the large sorts when ripe is useful for mixing with apples for pies, tarts, &c., and they keep well throughout the Winter months when stored in dry places, &c.

		per pkt.—s.	d.
DANIELS' YELLOW MAMMOTH. Seed from large handsomely netted fruit, weighing one hundredweight and upwards ...	... ... Gd. and	1	0
Bottle-shaped. Green, very ornamental		0	4
Common Pumpkin. Very useful for pies and preserves in Winter ...	... ...	0	3
Pear-shaped. Green and yellow, pretty	...	0	4
Potiron Jaune or Mammoth. A giant variety, frequently attains one hundredweight ...	... ... Gd. and	1	0
Small Orange. Strongly resembling an orange		0	4
Variegated Turk's Cap. An exceedingly handsome variety, striped orange, green, and white	... ... Gd. and	1	0

Cucumber.

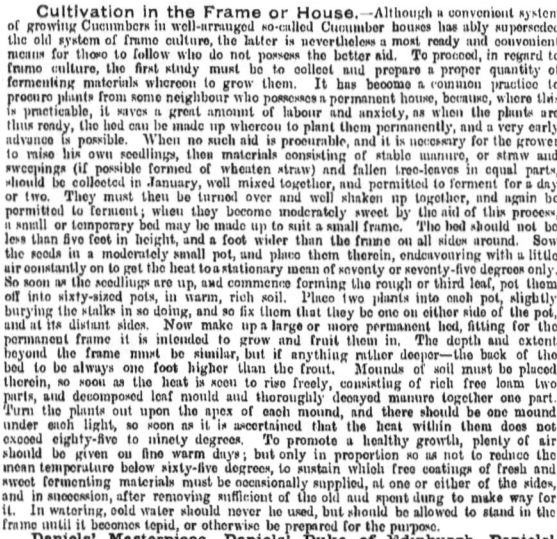

Cultivation in the Frame or House.—Although a convenient system of growing Cucumbers in well-arranged so-called Cucumber houses has ably superseded the old system of frame culture, the latter is nevertheless a most ready and convenient means for those to follow who do not possess the better aid. To proceed, in regard to frame culture, the first study must be to collect and prepare a proper quantity of fermenting materials whereon to grow them. It has become a common practice to procure plants from some neighbour who possesses a permanent house, because, where this is practicable, it saves a great amount of labour and anxiety, as when the plants are thus ready, the bed can be made up whereon to plant them permanently, and a very early advance is possible. When no such aid is procurable, and it is necessary for the grower to raise his own seedlings, then materials consisting of stable manure, or straw and sweepings (if possible formed of wheaten straw) and fallen tree-leaves in equal parts, should be collected in January, well mixed together, and permitted to ferment for a day or two. They must then be turned over and well shaken up together, and again be permitted to ferment; when they become moderately sweet by the aid of this process, a small or temporary bed may be made up to suit a small frame. The bed should not be less than five feet in height, and a foot wider than the frame on all sides around. Sow the seeds in a moderately small pot, and place them therein, endeavouring with a little air constantly on to get the heat to a stationary mean of seventy or seventy-five degrees only. So soon as the seedlings are up, and commence forming the rough or third leaf, pot them off into sixty-sized pots, in warm, rich soil. Place two plants into each pot, slightly burying the stalks in so doing, and so fix them that they be one on either side of the pot, and at its distant sides. Now make up a large or more permanent bed, fitting for the permanent frame it is intended to grow and fruit them in. The depth and extent beyond the frame must be similar, but if anything rather deeper—the back of the bed to be always one foot higher than the front. Mounds of soil must be placed therein, so soon as the heat is seen to rise freely, consisting of rich free loam two parts, and decomposed leaf mould and thoroughly decayed manure together one part. Turn the plants out upon the apex of each mound, and there should be one mound under each light, so soon as it is ascertained that the heat within them does not exceed eighty-five to ninety degrees. To promote a healthy growth, plenty of air should be given on fine warm days; but only in proportion so as not to reduce the mean temperature below sixty-five degrees, to sustain which free coatings of fresh and sweet fermenting materials must be occasionally supplied, at one or either of the sides, and in succession, after removing sufficient of the old and spent dung to make way for it. In watering, cold water should never be used, but should be allowed to stand in the frame until it becomes tepid, or otherwise be prepared for the purpose.

Daniels' Masterpiece, Daniels' Duke of Edinburgh, Daniels' Duke of Albany, Daniels' Defiance, and **Daniels' Improved Telegraph,** all superb varieties, are the very best kinds that can be grown for exhibition, market and general use.

Cultivation in the Open Air.—"Ridge" varieties alone should be grown out of doors. These consist of a shorter-fruited, hardier form of the same. The seeds should be sown early in the month of April, and in moderate warmth, and so soon as they show the rough leaf, they also must be potted off into four inch pots, three in a pot, in a free, rich, loamy soil. Shade them for a day or two subsequently, and keep them up close to the glass to ensure their being stiff and sturdy. Towards the end of April, or during the first week in May, select a warm sunny situation, a south-west aspect is best, and dig out a trench about eighteen inches deep and three feet wide, and fill it with warm, fermenting materials, to about one foot above the ordinary ground level, then cover with about nine inches of rich new soil. In a few days the plants previously prepared may be turned out thereinto, and covered over with handglasses, &c., when they should have a gentle watering with tepid water, and be shaded for a few days, and until the plants are established. Plant out three plants under each handlight, and do not plant any wider than five feet apart. As the plants grow, and are seen to fill the handlights, more and more air must be given, until the plants become moderately inured to the full outer air, at which time elevate the handlights, so that the young, growing shoots find their way from under them, and commence to ramble away freely, when the

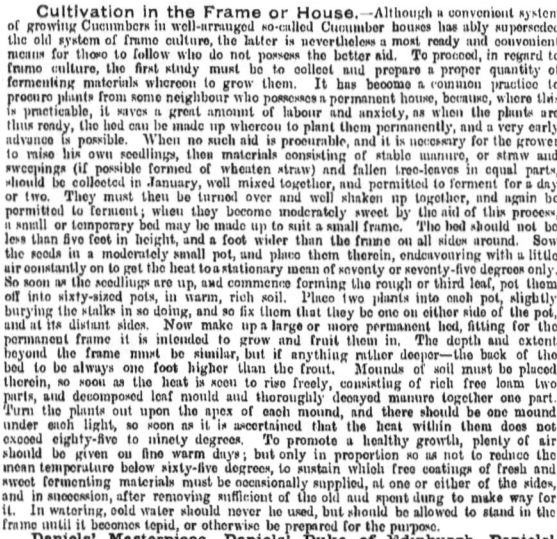
DANIELS' DEFIANCE.

handlights may, towards the latter part of June, be removed altogether. Where these simple facilities do not exist, they may be easily raised on a warm sheltered border, under a handlight alone, towards the end of April, or the first week in May. The ground should be liberally manured, and well dug up and "worked" for their reception, and the plants may be planted out under handlights about May 30th. Shade or protect them for a few days, and until the plants are established; during dry weather give plenty of liquid manure. Cucumbers sometimes succeed well so grown, and we have occasionally seen moderately good produce of the kind grown from seeds placed under the handlights, following such simple preparation of the soil as we have suggested.

Daniels' Perfection Ridge is a great improvement on the old Stockwood, and the best for ridge cultivation, being most prolific, and of extra fine quality.

Sowing in the Open Air.—A good crop of Cucumbers can sometimes be obtained by sowing the seed in well prepared ground in the open air. Sow in the first or second week in June in drill rows, six feet apart, and thin out the plants to eighteen inches apart in the row; give a liberal supply of water in dry weather. In a favourable season good crops can be produced in this way; they will grow rapidly, and produce abundance of fruit.

EVIDENCE OF QUALITY.

Cucumber *(continued).*

per pkt.—s. d.

DANIELS' MASTERPIECE. The fruit are slightly spined, and of a rich dark emerald green, twenty to thirty inches long. For colour, quality, constitution, and prolificness, it cannot be surpassed, while at the same time it is A 1 for exhibition, and will be found invaluable for market purposes ... ...   1s. 6d, and   2 6

CUCUMBER—MASTERPIECE.

"I had immense success with Cucumbers last year. My house is only 16 feet by 10 feet, and I had as many as 150 fruit hanging at one time. I cut 81, each over 22 inches in length, in six weeks. One fruit of **Masterpiece** measured 25½ inches long."—Mr. W. J. DUNRIDGE, Lewisham.

DUKE OF NORFOLK. We have much pleasure in bringing into notice this handsome and prolific Cucumber. The plant is of robust habit, short-jointed, a prolific and continuous bearer, remaining in full fruit after many other kinds are exhausted. The fruit are solid in flesh, with scarcely any seeds, and growing from eighteen to twenty-four inches in length. It is a white-spined variety. Its dark green, straight, symmetrical, and handsome fruit renders it a most valuable kind for market gardeners or the exhibition table ... ...   1s. 6d. and   2 6

"I beg to inform you that the Seeds I purchased of you last year were everything that could be desired. The **Duke of Norfolk Cucumber** I began cutting from in April, and it fruited splendidly till the middle of September."—Mr. J. DURBRIDGE, Garsington.

"Your **Duke of Norfolk** is a splendid Cucumber, growing to 2 feet 6 inches in length, and very firm."—Mr. WALFORD, Sevenoaks.

"I have much pleasure in renewing my order for Seeds, that which I obtained from you last year gave great satisfaction. I obtained First Prize for, and had a good crop of your Cucumbers **Duke of Norfolk** and **Telegraph.**"—Mr. W. PACKHAM, Sittingbourne.

DANIELS' DUKE OF EDINBURGH. A beautiful white-spined variety sent out by us, and pronounced by all competent judges to be the finest Cucumber in cultivation. It is of a fine robust constitution and habit, its fruit growing rapidly to the length of thirty to thirty-six inches, being at the same time of the most beautiful proportions, and of a fine rich green colour, which it retains to the last. A first-class variety for general use, and unrivalled for exhibition. This splendid variety has been now before the public several years, and from the many testimonials we are constantly receiving, we find it is still in favour with our customers.

Our own fine selected stock in sealed packets 1s. 6d. and   2 6

"I have much pleasure in saying that your **Duke of Edinburgh Cucumber** did exceedingly well last year. I had more and finer Cucumbers than I have had or seen her during twelve years as under and head gardener."—Mr. D. P. ROBINSON, The Rectory Gardens, Bulwick.

"I consider your Seeds the best I ever grew. I grew your **Duke of Edinburgh Cucumber** 3 lbs. in weight, without anything else but sun heat. Any one ordering from you has the satisfaction of getting Seed true to name and of best quality."—Mr. H. HANDLEY, Fence Houses.

"The **Duke of Edinburgh Cucumber** I got from you last year, were the finest that were ever grown here, one of them was over twenty-six inches long."—Mr. E. ODDY, Buttershaw.

"Last year I grew your **Duke of Edinburgh Cucumber**, and they did wonderfully well. I had some splendid fruit."—Mr. W. F. PARKER, Helion Bumpstead.

DANIELS' DEFIANCE (early prolific). A white-spined variety of hardy, robust constitution, producing in great abundance very short-necked and elegant fruit of a rich dark green colour, from eighteen to twenty-four inches in length, straight and uniform, and of the same thickness throughout; a magnificent variety for early Spring and Summer work, and first-class for market purposes and general use; is also a grand exhibition kind. Seed carefully selected from the handsomest and most prolific fruit ... ... sealed packets 1s. 6d. and   2 6

DANIELS' IMPROVED TELEGRAPH. A great improvement on the old Telegraph, bearing clean straight fruit twenty to twenty-four inches long, an abundant bearer ... B.S. 1s. 6d. and   2 6

DANIELS' EMERALD GEM. A choice variety of the Telegraph type, a most prolific kind; the fruit eighteen to twenty-four inches long, growing in clusters of three and four at a joint. Handsome, smooth, and symmetrical, and of a bright glossy emerald green 1s. 6d. and   2 6

DANIELS' RELIABLE *(see Novelties)* ... 1s. 6d. and   2 6

Cucumber (*continued*).

per pkt.—s. d.

DANIELS' DUKE OF ALBANY.

Since its introduction a few years ago, this remarkable Cucumber has obtained First Prize wherever exhibited. The increased demand and numerous testimonials we receive every season, prove it to be one of the handsomest and most prolific Cucumbers ever raised. It is a long, straight, dark green fruit, averaging from twenty to twenty-six inches in length, bearing sometimes as many as three or four at a joint, whilst its hardy and vigorous constitution, together with its remaining a long time in bearing, recommends it especially for market purposes. Few can equal this Cucumber for exhibition purposes   W.S. 1s. 6d. and   2   6

"I am glad to inform you that your **Duke of Albany Cucumber** took First and Second Prizes, and Commended at our Show last week. The judge said it was the best colour and shape he ever saw."—**Mr. T. ROWLANDS**, St. David's.

"I had a splendid crop of your **Duke of Albany Cucumber** last year. I had 240 fruit growing in my house at one time, and they averaged from twenty to twenty-four inches in length. The size of my house is 13 ft. by 11 ft."—**Mr. G. DIRALL**, Leatherhead.

"I am pleased to inform you that your **Duke of Albany Cucumber** gave me every satisfaction; they are very prolific. I took two First Prizes with them last Summer."—**Mr. COOKE**, Ashford.

LOCKIE'S PERFECTION.

This fine variety was raised by Mr. Lockie, of Oakley Court Gardens, Windsor, and is a most valuable acquisition. The fruit are produced in great abundance; medium in length, quite straight, short necked, with no ribs, and only a few black spines; are very uniform in size, and covered with a dense bloom. The flesh is solid and crisp, with few seeds. It has received seven First Class Certificates, besides numerous First Prizes

         1s. and   2   0

Abbott's Early Prolific. One of the finest and most useful varieties ...   . B.S. 1s. 6d. and   2   6

Cardiff Castle. First-class frame variety   1   0

Extra Early Frame   ...   . 6d. and   1   0

Manchester Prize. Good market variety

         W.S. 6d. and   1   0

DUKE OF ALBANY. (*From a Photograph*).

EMPRESS OF INDIA.

This splendid Cucumber is especially adapted for Summer cultivation, and will become as popular for this purpose as Rollisson's Telegraph is for Winter work. The fruit is remarkable for its handsome shape and excellence of flavour. Twenty to twenty-four inches is its average length, but it has been grown to thirty inches   B.S. 1s. 6d. and   2   6

Monro's Duke of Edinburgh. First Class Certificate R.H.S. ...   W.S.   1   0

Rollisson's Telegraph (true) ...   . B.S.   1   0

Tender and True. Superior quality and flavour   ...   ... W.S.   1   6

B.S. Black Spine.   W.S. White Spine.

Cucumbers for Ridge Cultivation.

per pkt.—s. d.

DANIELS' PERFECTION RIDGE.

A very hardy and prolific variety of extra fine quality, length fifteen to twenty inches, very straight and few seeds   ...   . 6d. and   1   0

Cluster Gherkin. For pickling, an immense bearer   0   4

Short Prickly. Very hardy, fine for pickling   0   3

Bismarck.

An American introduction which has proved to be of first-rate quality. The fruit is long, white-spined, and of a dark green colour. It is of superior flavour and of uniform and slender growth   ... 6d. and   1   0

Stockwood. Fine selected stock   ...   ... 3d., 6d. and   1   0

Prolific Pickling. One of the most prolific out-door varieties we know of; very hardy ...   . 6d. and   1   0

EVIDENCE OF QUALITY.

"I have pleasure in informing you that I took five First Prizes from the produce of your Seeds—with **Cabbage, Cauliflower**, and **Stockwood Ridge Cucumber**."—**Mr. E. WHITE**, Chapmanslade.

"The Seeds sent me last Spring have turned out well. I have taken several First Prizes at our two Shows. The **Perfection Ridge Cucumber** is, I think, the best I have ever grown, and gained First Prize at Hatfield Show."—**Mr. J. PAGE**, Hatfield.

PERFECTION RIDGE.

"I received the Seeds all right, and they gave great satisfaction. I took First Prize with your **Perfection Ridge Cucumber** last August."—**Mr. G. SARJENT**, Horley.

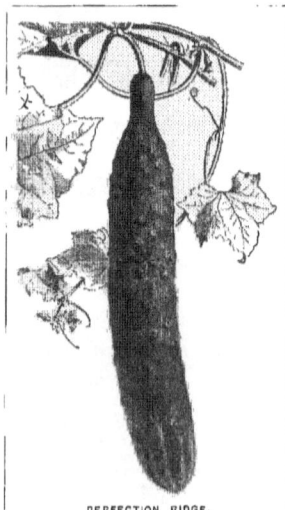

Endive.

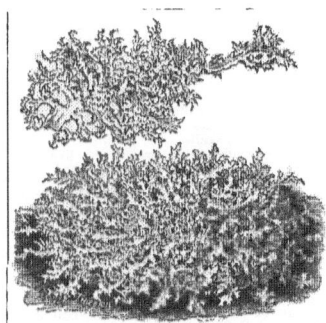

DANIELS' SUPERB CURLED.

Cultivation.—This crop is not so greatly appreciated as it should be; we think, nevertheless, that it is "growing in favour." When well grown, the curled varieties are greatly appreciated by some, when cooked as other green crops are. . To grow it well, thorough good deep soils are essential, and water in abundance during all dry periods. For an early Spring or Summer crop, sow during the first week in April on a warm sunny situation, and again towards the middle of May. The plants produced from the latter sowing should be thinned out, and stand where sown to produce thin crops. The best crops are the Autumn, Winter, and very early Spring, which are produced from successional sowings made between the last week in July and the end of August. The seedlings resulting therefrom should be transplanted successionally on to every conceivable space of good, rich soil. Some will be forward enough to blanch by means of tying them up, or placing a slate upon them, for August and subsequent uses. Others must, if at all large, be removed into a shed or frame, or be otherwise protected from sharp frosts. The lesser and later seedlings will stand out during the Winter on a warm aspect, seed or nursery beds, for use following an early Spring growth, so to maintain a supply as long as possible.

per oz.—s. d.

DANIELS' SUPERB CURLED. The best of all the Curled Endives, it blanches well, and is of first-class quality ... per pkt. 1s. —
Batavian Green. Broad-leaved, very hardy, and desirable for Winter cultivation, tie up for blanching 0 8
Green Curled. Extra 0 8

per oz.—s. d.

EXTRA BROAD-LEAVED. An excellent variety, highly recommended ... ... per pkt. 4d. 1 0
Moss Curled. Very fine ... ... „ 4d. 1 0

White Curled. Excellent variety per pkt. 3d. 0 9
Digswell Prize. A fine variety, beautifully curled, hearts well ... ... per pkt. 4d. 1 0

Herbs (Sweet and Pot).

Per packet 3d. Per dozen packets, 2s. 6d.

Angelica. The mid-rib may be eaten as Celery, or when candied makes an excellent confection.
Anise. The seeds are much used for medicinal purposes; the leaves for garnishing or seasoning.
Balm. For making balm tea, which is invaluable in cases of fever; makes also a fine-flavoured wine.
Basil, Bush. The leaves and tops impart the flavour of Clove leaves to soups, and are much used for seasoning.
  " **Sweet.** For flavouring salads and soups.
Borage. The young leaves used as salad or pot herb.
Burnet. The young leaves have the flavour of Cucumbers.
Caraway. For flavouring soups.
Chervil, Green Curled } Very fine for salads.
  Tuberous-rooted }
Coriander. The tender leaves are used for soups or salads.
Dill. The leaves are used in soups, sauces, and pickles.
Fennel. Used in sauces for fish and for garnishing.
Horehound. Makes an esteemed well-known beverage.
Hyssop. Young shoots used as pot herbs.
Marigold, Pot. The flowers impart a beautiful colour to broths and soups.
Marjoram, Pot } Aromatic and sweet flavour, used in soups and stuffings.
  " **Sweet, or Knotted** }

Lavender. Cultivated for its flowers, which are very aromatic.
Purslane, Green } The shoots and succulent leaves are cooling
  Golden } when used in Spring as salads.
Rampion. The leaves used as salads; the roots, which have a pleasant nutty flavour, used as Radish.
Rosemary. The leaves make a drink esteemed for relieving headache.
Rue, Broad-leaved. Leaves used medicinally; also used as a remedy for croup in fowls.
Sage. Used in stuffing and sauces.
Savory, Summer } The tops being very aromatic are used
  " **Winter** } in salads and soups; they improve the flavour if boiled with Peas or Beans.
Scurvy Grass. Eaten as Water-cress.
Skirret. The tubers when boiled and served up with butter are most delicious.
Sorrel, Broad-leaved } The leaves are used in salads, soups,
  Lettuce-leaved } and sauces.
Tansy.
Tarragon.
Thyme. Broad-leaved. Used in stuffings, soups, and sauces.
Wormwood. Fine tonic when taken as tea; and imparts bitterness to drinks.

Plants.

Balm, Sweet Basil, Chamomile, Horehound, Hyssop, Lavender, Pot Marjoram, Mint (of sorts), Pennyroyal, Rosemary, Rue, Sage, Winter Savory, Sorrel, Tarragon, Thyme (of sorts), Wormwood each 6d., per doz. 4s. 6d.

Mustard.

Cultivation.—Both the White and Chinese are valuable in salads as they assist digestion. Cut close to the ground the young leaves and stalks, before the second or rough leaves appear; in this state they have a delicate and piquant flavour. When a daily supply is required sow every two or three days throughout the year, in the Winter sow under glass in a temperature of 50° to 60° to hasten the growth. Mustard, as with all kinds of salad, the quicker the growth the more tender the produce.

per oz.—s. d.

Chinese. Fine salad variety ... ... per quart 3s., per pint 1s. 9d. 0 4
White. For early salads or medicinal purposes ... ... per quart 1s. 9d., per pint 1s. 0 2

Price of Mustard for Agricultural Purposes may be had upon application.

Kohl Rabi or Turnip-rooted Cabbage.

		per oz.—s.	d.
Early White Vienna	Grown as substitutes	per pkt. 4d. 1	0
Large Green	for Turnips, being	„ 4d. 1	0
Large Purple	much hardier	„ 4d. 1	0
Neapolitan Curled.	Very ornamental, leaf curled like		
Kale	.. ..	per pkt. 4d. 1	0

Leek.

Cultivation.—The Leek luxuriates in the richest of soils, and the most unctuous of manures only, and such being the case, a thorough preparation must be made for them wherever it is hoped to grow them moderately well. The finest examples are produced in shallow trenches dug out and deeply and thickly manured as for Celery. Here the seedling Leeks are planted either in single, or in double rows, or at right angles with each other. By these means the roots are kept cool during the most arid and hot weather, whilst water can be applied more directly. They like the strongest of manure waters. Sowings may be made very early in the Spring, either in boxes under shelter or on warm borders out of doors, commencing in February; for ordinary main crops sow early in March, in a rich soil and on an open sunny site, and proceed to transplant them as soon as they become large enough so to do. When the plants in either case have made a good growth, some open rich material is often applied to keep additional moisture around them, and to blanch their stems somewhat. Where shallow trenches can be prepared for them during the Winter, seeds may be sown therein early in March, and if the seedlings are subsequently thinned out, a strong and uninterrupted growth is the result.

Our supplies of these being procured from the most noted **Musselburgh and other growers,** the stocks can be guaranteed of the finest possible quality.

	per oz.—s.	d.
DANIELS' CHAMPION. A fine broad-leaved variety, highly recommended for exhibition purposes per pkt. 1s. 6d.		—
Ayton Castle Giant. Remarkably large and good, may be grown seven inches in circumference, and with one foot of blanched stem ... ... per pkt. 4d.	1	0
Carentan. Large French	1	0
CONQUEROR. First-class; very superior either for competition or culinary purposes ... ... per pkt. 1s.		—
Henry's Prize. Exceedingly large, blanches well, flavour mild, fine for exhibition ... ... per pkt. 6d.	1	6
Large Rouen. A well-known French kind per pkt. 4d.	1	3
London Flag. Large, broad-leaved	0	6
LYON (new). The largest kind grown ... per pkt. 1s.		—
Musselburgh. Extra broad-leaved, blanches to a large size, flavour mild, highly esteemed for soups; grand stock, direct from the Musselburgh growers	1	0

EVIDENCE OF QUALITY.

" I am pleased to tell you that your **Seeds** have turned out grand. The cottagers for whom I got the seeds have won all the First Prizes for the best allotments. Also the champion special."—**Mr. J. HUXTABLE,** Molton.

" Enclosed I send you an order for **Seeds** required by myself and friends, a proof of the satisfaction your seeds gave us last year."—**Mr. J. H. WORTHINGTON,** Lowick.

" Your **Champion Leek** did very well with me last year. I took several prizes with them. The six Leeks shown weighed 12½ lbs."—**Mr. A. TWIDDLE,** Longton.

" I have always received good **Seeds** from you in previous years, and trust they will be the same this year again."—**Mr. THOMAS POWELL,** Clydach.

" I cannot speak too highly of **Seed** purchased from you. I took fifteen Prizes out of sixteen exhibits at our Show. The **Daniels' Potatoes** took four Special Prizes, one dish of eight weighing 11 lbs. 12 ozs."—**Mr. W. BOWER,** Stanton-by-Dale.

" Your **Seeds** speak for themselves, they always turn out well. I have grown your **White Elephant Potato** for years, and nothing can come up to it."—**Mr. GEORGE ANDERSON** Walsingham.

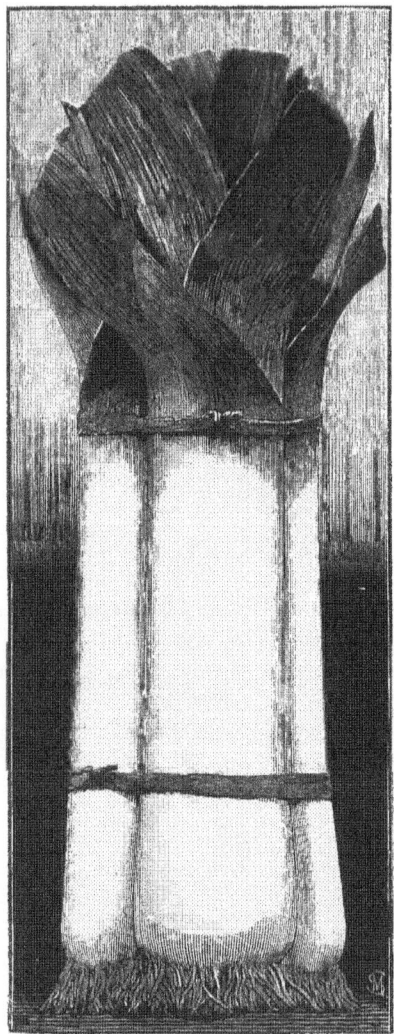

DANIELS' CHAMPION.

EVIDENCE OF QUALITY.

" I have much pleasure in informing you that I took First Prize with your **Champion Leek.** I grew them 7½ inches in circumference. I took twelve First Prizes last year from your Seeds."—**Mr. W. COOMS,** Lostwithiel.

" I have at present some tremendous Leeks grown from your **Champion Leek Seed,** several weighing 2½ lbs. each."—**Mr. W. DAVID,** Laugharne.

" I am pleased to tell you that I took seven Prizes at our show with the produce of your Seeds."—**Mr. W. FARMELO,** Bexley.

Lettuce.

Cultivation.—Of Lettuces, we give particular attention to the growth and selection of two varieties, viz., **Daniels' Giant Cos** and a capital stock of **Daniels' Continuity**. The former is the largest Lettuce grown, and very fine for exhibition, being at the same time tender and crisp, and requires no tying. The best Cabbage Lettuce is **Daniels' Continuity**, which will be found invaluable for Summer use, as it will withstand dry seasons, and continue fit for use after all other kinds have run to seed.

Lettuces are especially partial to an open, deeply worked, and enriched soil, and to an abundant supply of moisture throughout their whole growth. Not only is this necessary to insure a free growth apart from all tendencies to "bolt" or run to seed; but so also is it to ensure such an amount of crispness and natural succulency as alone constitute the higher merits of this important salad plant. Sowings should be made upon a slight bottom-heat, or in boxes, &c., early in February. Make other sowings to follow these during the month of March and again early in April. Sow this time upon warm sunny sites, and transplant a portion of the produce of each sowing only, leaving a sufficient number in the seed beds, and properly thinned, to ensure a supply thereon. For permanent Summer crops sow again during May and June, and this time upon cool open airy quarters. Sow the seed in drill rows, and so soon as the seedlings are large enough don't transplant them at this date, but thin out and throw away all but the strongest plants. Too much or too frequent waterings cannot be given them during the hot and arid Summer months. Make a somewhat large sowing or two during the month of July; this for permanent Autumn and Winter uses. The seedlings may be transplanted when the produce of these sowings are thinned out, as by so doing they succeed those which have been permitted to stand. Other sowings should again be made on or about August 11th and 25th, September 5th and 20th, which are likewise to be thinned out and transplanted as necessary for Winter and early Spring supply. Cabbage Lettuces sow in May and August.

Cabbage Varieties.

	per pkt. s. d.	per oz. s. d.		per pkt. s. d.	per oz. s. d.
DANIELS' GOLDEN SUMMER (new). This is quite distinct from Butter-cup, being more of a bronzy yellow on the outside. The large, firm, solid heads when cut open, are nearly white inside, and exceedingly tender and juicy. This is one of the best Summer Lettuces ever introduced, as it will stand a long time without running to seed	1 0	2 6	**Neapolitan.** Leaves beautifully curled and tender, one of the finest Summer sorts, grows very hard and solid	0 3	0 9
QUEEN OF SUMMER (new). This is one of the finest Summer Lettuces yet introduced. It is remarkable for its large size, splendid appearance, and for withstanding the drought. It produces fine, crisp, and tender Lettuces in the driest season	0 6	1 6	**New American Gathering or Curled.** Distinct and interesting, intermediate between the Cabbage and Cos kinds	0 4	1 0
DANIELS' BLACK-SEEDED TEXTER. Large, compact, and solid, one of the most splendid varieties in cultivation, first-class for market gardeners or family use	0 4	1 0	**Daniels' Giant White.** An exceedingly large and fine variety, crisp and juicy, and of fine flavour, stands a long time without running to seed	0 6	1 6
"All the Year Round"	0 4	1 0	**Brown Dutch.** Very large and hardy	0 3	0 9
DANIELS' ENDIVE-LEAVED (new). We have much pleasure in introducing this remarkable Lettuce to our customers. The leaves are of a bright rich green colour, and prettily fringed, whilst unlike most of its class, it has a firm crisp head of fine flavour, and it is, we should think, one of the most useful Lettuces for adding variety to the salad bowl, on account of its Endive-like foliage	1 0	2 6	**Drumhead or Malta**	—	0 6
			Buttercup. This large handsome variety is remarkable for its tenderness and delicacy of flavour, while its bright citron-coloured foliage renders it perfectly distinct from all existing Cabbage Lettuces	0 6	1 6
			Hammersmith Hardy Green	0 3	0 9
			Goldenhead (new Winter). This is said by the raiser to exceed all other Winter kinds, for hardiness, earliness, large size, firmness of head, crispness, and flavour	0 6	1 6
			Golden Spotted. A distinct and gay-coloured variety of delicate flavour	0 6	1 6
			Large White Winter	0 4	1 0
			Tennis-ball. A fine dwarf variety	0 4	1 0
			Wheeler's Tom Thumb	0 4	1 0
			Mixed Cabbage vars. All the best kinds for succession	0 3	0 9
			Mixed. All kinds, Cos and Cabbage	0 3	0 9

Cos or Upright-growing Varieties.

	per pkt. s. d.	per oz. s. d.		per pkt. s. d.	per oz. s. d.
DANIELS' SOLID BROWN (see Novelties)	1 0	—	**DANIELS' SELECTED PARIS WHITE.** Self-blanching, tender, and mild flavour	0 6	1 6
DANIELS' GIANT WHITE. The finest and largest Cos Lettuce in cultivation, very tender and crisp, with fine solid hearts, requires no tying, and will stand a long time without running to seed; should be grown in all gardens; unrivalled for exhibition purposes	1 0	2 6	**Daniels' Black-seeded Bath**	0 6	1 6
			Daniels' Green Winter. An excellent and hardy kind, valuable for Winter and early Spring work	0 6	1 6
DANIELS' MONSTROUS BROWN. Tender and crisp, requires no tying, the largest grown, fine variety for exhibition	1 0	2 6	**Daniels' Blood Red Winter.** A very handsome and hardy variety; very useful for early Spring use	0 6	1 6
			Paris Green. Blanches well without tying	0 4	1 0
			Paris White	0 4	1 0
			Mixed Cos vars. All the best for succession	0 3	0 9

EVIDENCE OF QUALITY.

"I consider your 'Continuity' one of the finest Cabbage Lettuces I have ever seen. The solid heads are perfection of what a Lettuce should be. They are now solid balls, when others sown at the same time are long since gone to seed. I shall certainly grow no other Cabbage Lettuce in future."—Mr. W. M. GEDDES, Thrumpton.

"Your Seeds did well at our Show last September. Your Giant White Cos Lettuce took all the Prizes there were to be taken, two Firsts, two Seconds, and two Thirds."—Mr. WILLIAM ROGERS, Whissendine.

Daniels' Continuity (or Perpetual).

THE BEST CABBAGE LETTUCE IN THE WORLD.

A bed sown or planted in Spring will keep up a supply of Salad throughout the Summer. No matter how hot and dry the season they will continue to maintain firm heads long after every other kind has run to seed or gone to decay. One sowing is equal to three or four of any other variety.

Whatever we have claimed in regard to its most excellent qualities has been more fully borne out in all these respects by the many testimonials we are continually receiving from our customers.

From THE GARDENER'S CHRONICLE, September 5th, 1891.

"Daniels' 'Continuity' Cabbage Lettuce.—I sowed a row of this Lettuce in the Spring, at the same time as Paris Cos, and am very pleased with it. It fully merits the name it bears, as it was at first, the Paris Cos and the ordinary Cabbage variety have both bolted long ago, but this does not, seem to get any more advanced in that direction at present. It is a brown Lettuce of good flavour, and it grows to a fair size. Ours is a heavy soil, and any those that were transplanted at that time have turned out as well as the ones that were left.—W. J. S."

"Another long-standing variety, 'Continuity,' I permit me to bring to your readers' notice another Cabbage Lettuce of sterling merit, by name Continuity. It is very appropriately named, my plants were raised from a trial packet of seed, sent me by the well-known Norwich seed firm, Messrs. Daniels. Its leaves fold over very closely, forming a compact heart, a completely blanched in the whole bowl. Our Perpetual thickly highly of this variety, white so much appreciated in the salad bowl. Our Perpetual thickly highly of this variety, and so do I. I can confidently recommend it to your readers, and say get it, you won't be disappointed.—J. KIPLING, Knebworth Park, Herts."

From THE GARDENING WORLD, August 15th, 1891.

Price, 6d. per packet; 1s. 6d. per oz.

"Your **Continuity Lettuce**, I am glad to say, has done well here during the Summer months. I would like you to send me a packet for Winter use."—**Mr. J. SMITH,** Gardener to The Earl of Hopetoun.

"I have grown your **Continuity Lettuce** for several years past in preference to all others, because it far exceeds them all in giving a continual supply. It is well named (Continuity as it remains fit for use longer than any other variety without running to seed; in hot dry weather is tender and crisp, which is so highly valued in salads."—**Mr. C. E. MARTIN,** The Hoo Gardens, Welwyn.

"I wish to say I have found your **Continuity Lettuce** the best I have known. I should think about two sowings a year you would have *Lettuces all the year round.*"—**Mr. W. CLARKE,** Gardener to The Earl of Bessborough.

"I think your **Continuity Lettuce** is the finest in cultivation for those who have to supply the salad bowl every day. I sowed it February 25th, and cut May 20th. It has kept me supplied up to August 24th. I planted it on a bank, the worst piece of ground I have."—**Mr. G. SUIN,** Gardener to General Norman, C.B.

"The packet of **Continuity Lettuce** has given entire satisfaction; in future I shall grow no other but Continuity. My employer says it is by far the best ever he tasted."—**Mr. J. L. McKELLAN,** Gardener to Lord Ashbrook.

"I gave your **Continuity Lettuce** a fair trial amongst other standard varieties, it stood the test, and came to the front as being the finest Lettuce we have had this season, and is very highly recommended for flavour by her ladyship."—**Mr. J. F. SMITH,** The Gardens, Cullen House.

"I have to-day (September 5th) cut the last Lettuce of your variety 'Continuity' from seed sown in April. I have drawn plants from the same seed-bed for various plantings, and not one bolted. It is well worthy of its name, Continuity."—**Mr. R. C. WILLIAMS,** Gardener to The Earl of Lisburne.

"Kindly send me another supply of your **Continuity Lettuce**. Major Hall says it is by far the best Lettuce he ever tasted, and I am instructed to grow nothing else. It stands a long time without running to seed."—**Mr. J. MORRISON,** Gardener to Major Hall, D.L.

"Your **Continuity Lettuce** is all that can be desired, it has a splendid firm heart, is crisp, and well flavoured. While other sorts, sown on the same day, and having the same treatment, have all gone to seed, it certainly has no tendency to seed at present (July 30th)."—**Mr. J. ANDERSON,** The Gardens, Milner Field.

"Your **Continuity Lettuce** is an acquisition. From a packet of seed sown in March I am still (August 6th) cutting large supplies of beautiful, firm, close heads, not a single plant having gone to seed."—**Mr. W. GUY,** Gardener to F. Townsend, Esq., M.P.

"I have given your **Continuity Lettuce** a fair trial, and consider it the best I have ever grown its chief feature being its lasting so long without running to seed."—**Mr. E. WHEELER,** Gardener to Lord Hylton.

CONTINUITY CUT OPEN.

(From a Photograph.)

On the left of the image:

"I sowed a packet of your **Continuity Lettuce** on May 16th, part of them were cut when ready, the remainder were left until now (September 21st), and not one of them have ran to seed. It is the most useful Cabbage Lettuce I have ever grown."—**Mr. F. JONES**, Gardener to His Grace The Duke of Buccleuch.

On the right of the image:

"Your **Continuity Lettuce** I unhesitatingly pronounce to be the best Cabbage Lettuce extant. The seed sown March 7th commenced cutting in May, and from one sowing have had splendid Lettuce up to this time (September 15th), and have some grand specimens yet remaining—six months after sowing the seed. Not one plant bolted. It is deliciously crisp and blanches well."—**Mr. R. WELLER, F.R.H.S.**, The Gardens, Clonstal Castle.

Price, 6d. per packet; 1s. 6d. per oz.

"I sowed your **Continuity Lettuce** about the middle of April, and was able to cut good heads the first week in June, and from the same sowing was still able to cut good firm heads on the 1st of October, not one bolting. It is certainly the longest keeping variety I have ever grown, and I favour first-class."—**Mr. J. BAYLISS**, The Gardens, Belvedere House, Mullingar.

"Your **Continuity Lettuce** has been grown here in company with four other varieties of Cabbage Lettuce, and has been the only one which has not given as any trouble as regards bolting; it hearts and blanches well, is of excellent quality."—**Mr. J. SUNNINGTON**, Gardener to Sir H. D. Ingleby, Ripley Castle.

"I planted **Continuity Lettuce** by the side of several well-known varieties, it came into use quite a fortnight before the others, and remained good all the summer; it is solid and of excellent flavour."—**Mr. G. FORSTER**, Glendarragh Gardens, Teignmouth.

"I find there is no exaggeration whatever in the various reports presented in favour of your Lettuce **Continuity**. It certainly is a valuable and quite correctly named sort, the hearts remaining sound and fresh longer than any other variety I am acquainted with. Its flavour too, my employer voluntarily asserts, is the best he can ever remember tasting among Cabbage Lettuces."—**Mr. R. STRUGNELL**, The Gardens, Willow Vale, Frome.

"I made two sowings of your Lettuce **Continuity** in May and June, it proved itself to be a very fine Cabbage Lettuce, standing a long time fit for use, not any running to seed. The last was used September 9th, and cut crisp and firm."—**Mr. T. SHINGLES**, Gardener to the Right Hon. Earl Ducie.

"I have given your '**Continuity**' what I consider a fair trial by frequent sowings, I have not seen one single plant offer to go to seed, others by the side of it have bolted every one of them."—**Mr. J. MATHISON**, Gardener to Lord Addington, Addington Manor.

"Early in February I sowed the seed of your **Continuity Lettuce** in a box under glass, and planted them out in the open about the 1st of April, the last one being cut only about a fortnight ago (September 23rd), and not one of them ran to seed. I have great pleasure in stating that the family was much pleased with them. It grows to a large size, is quite firm, and of excellent quality. I will give you an order for more early in the coming spring."—**Mr. G. PHILIP**, The Gardens, Blackhall Castle.

"I can speak in the highest praise of the long-standing qualities of the **Continuity Lettuce**. I have now good firm heads, without any sign of bolting, from seed sown on May 5th, and consider it a great boon where a continual supply of Lettuce is required."—**Mr. GEO. SPENCER**, The Gardens, Langford Park.

"The Cabbage Lettuce **Continuity** sent me turned out very fine indeed, a better Lettuce could not be desired."—**Mr. E. CROCKER**, The Gardens, Ham Green.

"I consider the **Continuity Lettuce** first-class all round for size, crispness, and good flavour, and consider it far and away the best variety I have ever grown, and I shall go in for it larger in future."—**Mr. A. HORSELL**, Wonersh Park Gardens.

"I have grown several sowings of your Lettuce **Continuity**, and find it a most excellent and useful variety. I intend to grow it again next year."—**Mr. J. McDONALD**, Gardener to The Right Hon. Earl of Gainsborough, Exton Park.

"It affords me great pleasure in testifying to the excellence of your **Continuity Cabbage Lettuce**. I have grown this variety through the present season, and up to the present time have found none inclined for bolting, neither do they show any signs of decay. It is a great acquisition to the class of cabbage varieties."—**Mr. S. WARD**, Gardener to Lord Windsor, Hewell Gardens.

"The "**Continuity**" were solid three weeks after all the others had bolted, therefore for summer use I consider it a most useful variety."—**Mr. W. MARTIN**, Gardener to Lord Poltimore, Exeter.

"The **Continuity Lettuce** has proved to be the best out of half dozen sorts. It well deserves its name, lasting long after all others had bolted."—**Mr. J. PROWSE**, The Gardens, Hall Barn Park, Beaconsfield.

"Having given your '**Continuity**' a good trial, I can speak very highly of it. I sowed it 25th of March, and had it good far up in August, not one running to seed."—**Mr. D. HOBBY**, Gardener to Sir S. P. Vane K.C.B.

Melon.

THE COUNTESS.

Cultivation.—What is generally designated a Cucumber house will prove also an excellent place wherein to grow Melons, and to this fact as opposed to general culturists, is to be attributed much of the success of certain growers. The cultivation of the Melon is very similar to that of the Cucumber up to and a little beyond the full swelling of the fruits. If there exists one thing more than another conducive of or to success, it consists in the maintaining of as equal a temperature as possible throughout their growth; this is not as readily insured in frames as in houses having all convenient hot-water apparatus, &c., hence some allowance must be made for frame growers. The propagation of the Melon is usually by sowing seed, although some do so by cuttings; and certainly, when several sorts are grown in the same structure, and there is a desire to continue the variety pure and unchanged, the latter mode is the best. The seed should be sown in shallow pans instead of in ordinary pots, as the roots coming in contact with the bottom of the pan extend horizontally, instead of perpendicularly, and hence become better furnished with fibres. Sow the seeds during either of the first four months of the year, according as there is a possibility of growing them early or otherwise. Pot them off, &c., in detail similarly with the above, excepting that only one plant must be placed into each pot, and it must be potted more firmly. They delight in deep rich loam, and trodden firmly. The temperature by day should average, with daily ventilation, from seventy-five to eighty-five degrees, according to the warmth of the sun, &c. By night it should not be permitted to exceed seventy-two degrees; an average of seventy degrees being a desirable warmth. Give at all times the frost possible exposure to the full sunlight, as to shade them in any degree is derogatory to their doing well, after once a crop of fruit is "set," and the plants must be kept moderately thin by judicious pruning to insure this. Weak liquid manure may be given to them up to the time of the fruit attaining the size of a hen's egg; after which water more sparingly until the fruit are seen to have commenced netting or to change colour, when it should be withheld by degrees altogether. The water given to Melons, whether superficially or as root-watering, should always be of the same temperature as the air in any kind of structure in which they may be grown.

Daniels' Green Perfection is a new and improved green-fleshed variety of great merit, beautifully netted and slightly ribbed, and of the most delicious flavour.

Abbreviations.—Those marked with an asterisk (*) have received a First Class Certificate from the Royal Horticultural Society. S.F. scarlet flesh, G.F. green flesh, W.F. white flesh.

	per pkt.—s. d.
*DANIELS' WESTLEY HALL (S.F.) *(see Novelties)*. First Class Certificate, R.H.S. ...	1s. 6d. and 2 6
DANIELS' IMPROVED GOLDEN PERFECTION. A splendid green-fleshed variety, regularly and beautifully netted; thin skin, flesh very thick, firm, of the most exquisite flavour; the plant is of fine robust constitution and a free setter; we confidently recommend this ...	1s. 6d. and 2 6
DANIELS' GREEN PERFECTION. This choice new variety is of vigorous habit, and a most profile bearer. The fruit, which are of large size, 6 to 7 lb., are slightly ribbed and beautifully netted, green at first, but assuming a yellow tinge when ripe. The flesh is very thick and of a pale green, with a rich luscious and melting flavour, and of delicate aroma ...	1s. 6d. and 2 6
*Benham Beauty (S.F.). Fruit large, globular, with yellow skin, finely netted ...	1 6
Gunton Scarlet. A fine scarlet-fleshed Melon. Raised by Mr. W. Allan of Gunton Park ...	1 6
Hero of Lockinge (W.F.). Fine exhibition variety; very prolific ...	1 6
High Cross Hybrid (G.F.). A fine variety; of excellent flavour ...	1 6
*La Favorite (G.F.). Fruit somewhat oblong in shape; skin beautiful golden yellow, thickly netted ...	1 6
*Longleat Perfection (W.F.). A smooth-skinned variety, very handsome, and of fine flavour ...	1 6
MELTON HYBRID (S.F.). This choice variety will be found a valuable addition to our list of good Melons. The fruit are large and handsome, slightly ribbed, and nicely netted. The flesh is thick, of rich salmon colour, juicy and melting, and of fine flavour ...	1 6
*Monarch (Sutton's) (G.F.). A fine netted variety of good flavour ...	1 6
Royal Ascot. A fine scarlet-fleshed Melon, beautifully netted; fine exhibition variety ...	1 6
St. Blaise (new). A splendid green-fleshed Melon. The flesh is solid, thick, rich, melting, of exquisite flavour and delicate aroma ...	1 6
*The Countess (W.F.). A cross between American Musk and Cashmere; of strong constitution, and enormously prolific; clear yellow skin, beautifully netted; flesh thick, tender, juicy, and melting ...	1 6
The Shah. This is a new green-fleshed variety, of a delicate flavour, and delicious aroma, the flesh thick, melting and juicy, and is the finest-flavoured Melon we ever tasted ...	1s. 6d. and 2 6

The following Varieties can all be supplied at 1s. per packet:—

Blenheim Orange (S.F.)	*Gilbert's Green Flesh (G.F.)	*Read's Scarlet Flesh (S.F.)
Best of All (W.F.)	*Masterpiece (S.F.)	Scarlet Perfection (S.F.)
Colston Bassett Seedling (G.F.)	*Munro's Little Heath (S.F.)	„ Premier (S.F.)
*Dell's Hybrid (G.F.)	Prince of Wales (S.F.)	„ Gem (S.F.)
Earl of Beaconsfield (G.F.)	Queen Anne's Pocket or Tom	*The Netted Victory (W.F.)
Eastnor Castle (G.F.)	Thumb	*William Tillery (G.F.)

Onion.

Cultivation.—PREPARATION OF GROUND.—The Onion is what may be termed a gross feeder; it cannot be grown to perfection without a good depth of rich and well pulverised soil and an open situation. Superficially, it would appear the reverse of this, though the roots are known to run perpendicularly downwards many feet in depth where agreeable soil exists, and for which reason very deep and good cultivation is of the first importance. In preparing a bed for Onions, therefore, always endeavour to trench it deeply, adding abundance of manure at the bottom of each trench, and throughout its various strata as the work progresses. The object to be obtained being to thoroughly break up and manure the soil to the depth of twenty to twenty-four inches, we should recommend its accomplishment in the following manner:—In October or November, or as early as possible afterwards, dig out a trench two feet wide and one spade deep, removing the soil where you intend to finish; break up the bottom or subsoil of the trench another spade deep, mixing in a liberal quantity of manure, throw on this the soil from the next space of two feet, again mixing in plenty of manure, treat the second and succeeding trenches in the same manner, until the whole plot is completed. It is found that by this means the ground will resist drought much better than when dug in the ordinary way, that heavy soils are rendered less retentive, and light soils greatly improved, and that all soils are much benefited, and will yield much finer crops in successive seasons. By timely sowing, good cultivation, and careful harvesting, Onions can be produced in this country, in size, quality, and mildness of flavour, and for culinary purposes, equal to the finest importations from Portugal or Spain. And the great wonder is that much larger quantities are not grown, as thousands of tons are imported at a cost of something like £80,000 to £100,000 annually, which could be as well produced at home to meet the great demand for this much esteemed article of food, possessing as it does such valuable medicinal and nutritious properties. An occasional dressing of soot during the Winter and Spring will be of great benefit. DANIELS' EUREKA MANURE worked into the soil, or applied in liquid form, is a powerful stimulant to growing crops.

DANIELS' IMPROVED WHITE SPANISH.

SPRING SOWING.—The early sowing, consisting of such sorts as **Golden Rocca, Daniels' Improved White Spanish, Red Wethersfield,** and **Zitteau Giant Yellow, &c.,** should be made early in February, and the main one of all kinds early in March. Always where convenient, sow in drill-rows, drawn very shallow, and about nine inches apart. Before sowing the seeds the ground should be well trodden down and raked level. Immediately the seeds are sown, level in the drill-rows neatly, then well tread over the whole surface of the bed, again raking it over to remove all stones, &c. The young seedling plants must be kept quite free from weeds by frequent use of the hoe, and immediately they are large enough, thinning should be performed, carefully drawing all weaklings out without disturbing such as are to remain, and which should be at a distance of from eight to nine inches apart, if any fine produce is aimed at. Where, however, much moderate-sized produce is in demand (and it has become the fashion to garnish with such) it is not desirable to thin nearly so much. In regard to growing "picklers," these should be sown more thickly, and receive no thinning out at all; and it may be necessary, in the case of very good ground, to sow them on to a poor site chosen for its poverty, and stony, or similar characteristics. Irrigation or any kind of artificial waterings, especially if more or less manurial, will prove of great benefit in growing large and fine produce. The maggot, which often attacks the crops, may be "kept off" by sprinkling the young seedlings thinly with fresh slaked lime immediately after thinning, and during showery weather. Watering them with the lime water has also the same effect.

AUTUMN SOWING is growing more in favour every year with most cultivators, and the many advantages to be derived from having a plentiful supply of Autumn-sown Onions cannot be well over estimated, as by transplanting they can be grown to double the size and are much milder in flavour, besides a more abundant and heavier crop can be relied on. In these Autumn sowings, the attack by the fly and consequent destruction by maggots is unknown, and if the seed is sown in fairly good time, so as to be well up before the Autumn frosts begin, they will withstand our severest Winter. By thinning the crops, an abundant supply of fresh green Onions can be had for use all through the Spring and early Summer months. **Daniels' Golden Rocca, Daniels' Giant Rocca,** and **Daniels' Crimson Rocca** are the best kinds for Autumn sowing.

TIME OF SOWING FOR STANDING THE WINTER.—Sow any time from the middle of July to the second week in September in moderately rich and well-pulverised soil, in an open situation, in beds four feet wide, (and, where convenient, make two or three sowings at intervals of ten or fourteen days). Before sowing, the ground should be thoroughly consolidated, by treading down with the feet, raked level, and drills carefully made, &c., as recommended above for Spring Cultivation. Water and clean from time to time as required. Very fine crops can be obtained in the ordinary way of cultivation by thinning the young plants out to about six inches apart, but where extra fine bulbs are required for exhibition and other purposes, we strongly recommend TRANSPLANTING.

EVIDENCE OF QUALITY.

"Last Spring I purchased from you half an ounce of **Improved White Spanish Onion Seed,** from which I grew 112 lbs. of good-sized and splendid Onions."—**Mr. H. HUTCHINGS,** Wellington.

"We had a very good Onion from you last year. **Improved White Spanish,** some 1-lb. weight."—**Mr. E. NURSE,** Penclandd.

Onion (*continued*).

Daniels' Select List of Onions for 1892.

DANIELS' GOLDEN ROCCA. One of the largest and finest Onions ever introduced. Fine globular shape, golden yellow skin, mild flavour, and with careful cultivation comes equal to the imported Portugal Onions, and keeps sound until June. This variety is the best exhibition kind known. If sown in Autumn, and kept under first-class cultivation, will grow Onions three to four pounds each ... per pkt. 6d.   1 6

DANIELS' GIANT ROCCA (true). A splendid variety, of delicate flavour, large globular shape, and light brown skin, weight two to three pounds; plant out one foot apart. If sown in Spring this variety will produce larger Onions than any Spring sort 1 0

DANIELS' CRIMSON ROCCA. Extra fine variety 1 3

SILVER-SKIN PEAR-SHAPED (new) A very fine, hardy Onion, of the same form as the yellow pear-shaped variety ... per pkt. 1s.   2 6

GIANT ZITTEAU, BLOOD RED (new). Large size, handsome, globe-shaped, a late keeper, of mild flavour; skin pure blood red per pkt. 6d.   1 6

"LONGLASTER." This is by far the longest keeping Onion yet introduced. We have had specimens in sound condition eighteen months after being harvested. This variety should be sown early in the season ... ... per pkt. 6d.   1 6

NEW RED GLOBE (*see Novelties*)   „ 9d.   2 0

DANIELS' WHITE ELEPHANT TRIPOLI. This new Italian introduction is the largest of the Tripoli sorts, the average diameter of the bulbs being six and a half to seven inches. They are flat in form, with a silvery white skin, and of fine mild flavour. This Onion is unsurpassed as an exhibition variety ... ... per pkt. 6d.   1 6

DANIELS' IMPROVED WHITE SPANISH. The most perfect type of White Spanish Onion in cultivation, specially selected by ourselves. Grows to a large size, very even, and of good flavour. This variety has been exhibited with much success during the past season, and will prove a great acquisition ... ... per pkt. 1s.   2 6

DANIELS' BLOOD RED. Fine rich colour, very hardy 0 9

ST. LAURENT (new). In shape this variety resembles James' Keeping, but of a much larger size, and is strongly recommended for its long keeping, and mild flavour; it is flat on the top, becoming narrow towards the base of the bulb, and is a very heavy cropper ... ... per pkt. 9d.   2 0

"EARLY WHITE GEM." One of the earliest in cultivation, three weeks earlier than the Queen, and comes to maturity from eight to ten weeks from time of sowing. The bulbs are medium-sized and handsome shape, it is of exceedingly mild flavour, and will be found a valuable addition to the Kitchen Garden for early use ... ... per pkt. 6d.   1 6

EVIDENCE OF QUALITY.

"It may interest you to know that my gardener sent for a supply of **Onion Seed** for the labourers in this village, and it was the best grown in this district."—**Captain W. A. CRAGG,** Folkingham.

"The **Onion Seed** I had from you last year gave every satisfaction."—**Mr. T. GILBERT,** Tenterden.

Onion *(continued)*.

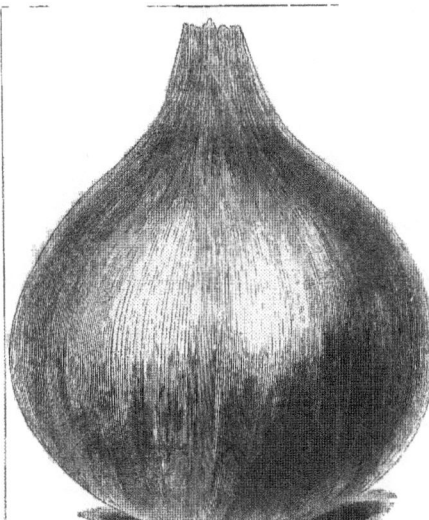

DANIELS' GOLDEN ROCCA.

	per oz.—s. d.			per oz.—s. d.
ROUSHAM PARK HERO. A magnificent variety of the White Spanish type (very scarce) per pkt. 1s.	2 6	**Neapolitan Marzajole.** A white variety, quick grower		0 9
Bedfordshire Champion	1 0	**Nuneham Park.** Much recommended, a fine variety		0 9
Brown Globe. Very useful, heavy cropper	0 9	**Silver Skin.** Of very quick growth, best for pickling		0 9
Danver's Yellow (true stock). Fine early variety	0 9	**Strasburgh or Deptford.** Well known		0 4
DANIELS' NEW GOLDEN GLOBE *(See Novelties)* per pkt. 1s.	—	**Tripoli Italian Red.** Fine dark red skin		0 9
EARLY QUEEN. Remarkably quick-growing, may be sown in July and will ripen same year, an excellent keeper	1 0	**Tripoli Italian White.** Similar to the above, but milder		0 9
		Tripoli Large Globe. Handsome large variety		0 8
Giant Madeira. Flavour excellent, grows an immense size	1 0	**Wethersfield New Red.** A capital type of Red Onion for Spring sowing, flesh pure white		0 8
Giant Red Tripoli. An exceedingly fine variety	1 0	**White Globe** (straw-coloured). A fine useful variety		1 0
JAMES' KEEPING. Excellent keeper	0 9	**WHITE SPANISH.** Ordinary stock per lb. 5s.		0 6
Lisbon White. Fine hardy variety, first-rate for drawing early in Spring	0 6	**WHITE SPANISH, Portugal, or Reading.** Fine selected stock, best for general use per lb. 6s. 6d.		0 8
NEW WHITE GLOBE. First Class Certificate, Royal Horticultural Society. Bulbs of medium size, true globular shape, remarkably firm and solid, with a very white silvery skin; very handsome and distinct	1 0	**WHITE PORTUGAL** *(See Novelties)* per pkt. 1s.		
		ZITTEAU GIANT YELLOW. A magnificent variety, of fine yellow skin, attains a large size, remains sound till June per lb. 6s. 6d.		0 8
		Mixed, for Autumn sowing „ 4s. 6d.		0 6
		„ for Spring sowing „ 4s. 6d.		0 6

PLANTS.—Strong Autumn sown, to plant out for show purposes, can be supplied in Spring of the following kinds only: **White** Elephant Tripoli, White Spanish, Golden Rocca, and Giant Rocca.
Each sort 1s. 6d. per 100; 10s. per 1000. Carriage Paid.

POTATO ONIONS. Fine select stock ... ... bulbs, per lb. 6d. ; 12 lb. 5s.

Parsnip.

DANIELS' QUEEN OF PARSLEYS.

HOLLOW-CROWNED PARSNIP.

PARSLEY—COVENT GARDEN.

Cultivation.—Rarely, if ever, is the Parsnip valued at its proper worth, or are its usefulness and high nutritive properties properly acknowledged. Perhaps there is no crop so remunerative both from the above point of view, and besides from a consideration of the heavy crops that on a system of fairly good culture, very limited space is capable of producing. As this esculent is known as being "dibble-rooted," it may not be necessary to dwell upon the great necessity of deep culture. They delight in fairly stiff soil, moderately moist, and always succeed best upon such soil either trenched, or bastard trenched, and with manure placed not less than eight or ten inches deep and in a goodly layer, and well decomposed. Sow the seeds about March 20th in drill rows fourteen inches apart, thinning out the young seedlings to distances of from eight to ten inches apart in the rows. In cases where it is not possible to insure a regular crop, owing to irregular sowing, germination of seeds, or insect pests, we have seen a fairly good produce, and a better finish given to a bed, by transplanting some of the thickest seedlings during showery weather on to vacant spaces. Hoe frequently during the Summer months, and if a good tender Parsnip is appreciated, never dig up the roots until they are actually required for use.

	per oz.—s.	d.		per oz.—s.	d.
DANIELS' IMPROVED. A fine selection of the Hollow-crowned. First-class exhibition and market variety	0	8	**Guernsey** or **Jersey Marrow.** A fine, large, and heavy cropping variety	0	6
Elcombe's Improved. Very choice stock, of fine flavour, much esteemed for exhibition	0	6	**Hollow-crowned.** Largest and best for general use; a fine selected stock	0	3
Turnip-rooted. Excellent for shallow soils	0	6	**The Student.** A first-class variety, but requires a good depth of soil	0	6

Parsley.

Cultivation.—It is only by thorough and efficient culture that good Parsley can be grown. Hence good, deep, rich soil, should always be prepared for it by trenching, manuring, &c., where practicable. Sowings should be made from about the middle of February until the end of March, according to the demand. For a limited supply only one sowing, made about March 10th, will suffice. Make another sowing about the first week in July, transplant a few seedlings from each sowing, if possible, as finer plants are formed thereby. It is a desirable plan to sow in rows ten inches apart, and to thin the plants out to like distances apart in the rows. By placing frames over some portions of the crop during Winter, or potting up bundles of the roots, and placing them into a gentle warmth, a better supply will be assured at a most acceptable season.

Daniels' Queen of the Parsleys, an improvement upon the Fern-leaved variety, is the most useful for garnishing, and is extremely valuable as an ornamental-foliaged plant for the flower border, &c.

	per oz.—s.	d.		per oz.—s.	
DANIELS' QUEEN OF THE PARSLEYS. An extra selected stock of the Fern-leaved variety, carefully grown on our own Seed Farm. The most useful for garnishing, and extremely valuable as an ornamental plant for the flower-border ... per pkt. 6d.	1	6	**Covent-Garden Garnishing.** A splendid variety, beautifully curled	0	6
			Extra-fine Curled. Fine for garnishing	0	4
			Fern-leaved. Distinct foliage, useful for garnishing per pkt. 3d.	0	9
			Tuberous-rooted (new). " 6d.	—	

EVIDENCE OF QUALITY.

"At the Fruit and Root Show I was awarded a First Class Certificate for your **Improved Hollow-crowned Parsnip.** The six weighed 26 lbs., one of the largest weighed 5 lbs."—Mr. W. BAILEY, Lamberhurst.

"All the Seeds that came from you last year were a great success, some of the **Parsnips** measuring 20 inches round."—Mr. J. FLAYER, Watlington.

"Your **Parsnips** turned out well. I took five First Prizes in five consecutive Shows with them."—Mr. T. BOOTH, Whitby.

"I have sent to tell you that your Collection of Vegetable Seeds turned out well, taking First Prizes with Parsnips and Onions; six Parsnips weighing 34 lbs., Onions measuring 14 inches in circumference."—Mr. C. WESTALL, Mildenhall.

Radish.

Cultivation.—A free open soil, enriched by real unctuous manures, best suits the Radish, and if a little bottom-heat can be insured in the Spring, so much the better the produce. To this end it is well to place soil upon any manure heap undergoing fermentation, and sow thereon. Successive sowings should be made constantly onward, commencing about the middle of February until the last week in September. The best Spring crops, it were scarcely necessary to remark, are produced under glass. If grown out of doors, however, both those for early Spring supply and the last sowings should have a warm sunny site chosen for them, and a light protection of straw; this will ward off excessive cold and aid them materially, if placed over them during cold, frosty nights, removing it during the day, &c. The China Rose and Black Spanish varieties should only be sown during July and August, and for Winter salads, for which purpose they are esteemed. *Raphanus caudatus* is an edible-podded variety only, the pods of which are exceedingly long, and are eaten, when young and tender, in the same manner as the roots of other varieties, and for pickling are a decided improvement on ordinary radish-pods. It only succeeds well under pot culture, or treated as a tender annual.

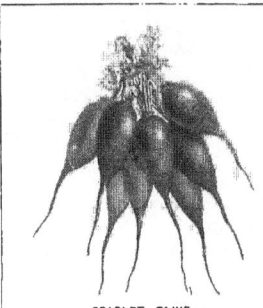

SCARLET OLIVE.

EVIDENCE OF QUALITY.

"I have taken First Prize two years in succession for six sorts of vegetables, mainly by the aid of your **Scarlet Perfection Carrot, Snowball Turnip, Norfolk Giant Broad Beans,** and **Table King Potatoes,** and have also taken First Prize for two years for garden cultivation."—

Mr. G. HYDE, Eaton.

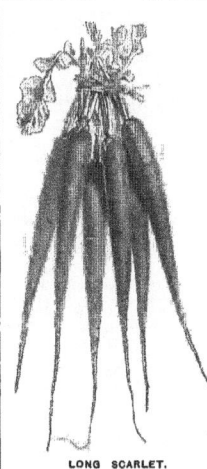

LONG SCARLET.

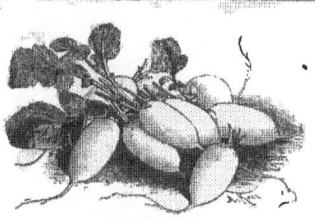

WHITE OLIVE.

EVIDENCE OF QUALITY.

"I have great pleasure in informing you of my success at the Axminster Show, 29th July last, taking twenty Prizes as follows: ten first, eight second, and two extra for **Vegetables** and **Flowers,** grown from seeds and plants, obtained from your firm."—

Mr. S. E. ENTICOTT, Axminster.

"I am much pleased with the seeds you sent me this season, I took First Prizes for **Parsnips, Carrots, Leeks, Vegetable Marrows,** and **Kidney Potatoes.** I have received twenty-four prizes in all, at the first Flower Show held in the Rhondda Valley."—**Mr. T. W. EVANS,** Ystrad.

	per oz.—s. d.
DANIELS' LONG SALMON. Similar in growth and appearance to Scarlet Short-top, but of a rich salmon colour	0 6
Long Purple. Similar in growth to Scarlet Short-top, but of a rich purple colour; forms a striking contrast with the white and scarlet kinds on the breakfast table and in the salad bowl	0 6
Long Rose, White-tipped. Excellent new sort, attaining an unusual size without becoming stringy. Its pretty rose colour passes to pure white at the end of root, a peculiarity which gives to this Radish a very pleasing appearance ...	0 8
Long White May	0 6
Long Scarlet ... per qt. 2s. 6d.; per pt. 1s. 6d.	0 3
Scarlet Short-top. Best for general crop and market purposes ... per qt. 2s. 6d.; per pt. 1s. 6d.	0 3
Wood's Early Frame. The best for early crop, forces well ... per qt. 3s.; per pt. 1s. 9d.	0 4
Raphanus Caudatus (Rat-tail or Tree Radish). Pods only eaten; useful for pickling per pkt. 6d.	—
DANIELS' PURPLE OLIVE-SHAPED, WHITE-TIPPED. This variety is equally as constant and attractive as the French Breakfast. It received the large Silver Medal at Erfurt Exhibition, the sole prize for a vegetable novelty	0 6
Olive-shaped Mixed per qt. 3s.; per pt. 1s. 9d.	0 3

	per oz.—s. d.
Olive-shaped Scarlet. Early, good forcer, very tender and mild ... per qt. 3s. 6d.; per pt. 2s.	0 4
Olive-shaped White. Of quick growth, mild and crisp, handsome shape per qt. 3s. 6d.; per pt. 2s.	0 4
Chinese Rose-coloured. Of oblong shape and mild flavour; for Winter use	0 4
French Breakfast. Scarlet, tipped white, oval shape, forces well, mild and crisp, highly esteemed in Paris ... ... per pint 2s.	0 4
Scarlet Turnip, Non plus ultra. Fine deep scarlet, very early	0 8
Turnip, Scarlet white-tipped. Delicious and handsome ... ... per pint 2s. 6d.	0 6
Turnip, Scarlet { For Summer and } per qt. 3s.;	0 4
" White { Autumn use. } per pt. 1s. 9d.	0 4
" Mixed ... per qt. 3s. 6d.; per pt. 1s. 6d.	0 3
Black Spanish. For Winter salads; sown in Autumn for Spring use	0 6
DANIELS' EARLY SCARLET TURNIP. The finest variety ever introduced, being very early, the roots are firm, solid, and of true globular shape. Colour, rich glowing crimson scarlet. This is unquestionably the earliest forcing Radish extant. It grows very rapidly, is of delicate flavour, and is fit to use in three weeks from time of sowing. The top is short, with leaves few and small ... ... per pt. 2s. 6d.	0 6

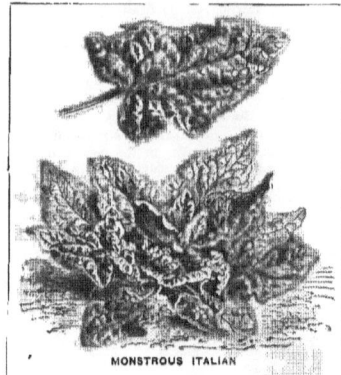

MONSTROUS ITALIAN

Spinach.

Cultivation.—Round Spinach should bo sown for Spring and Summer use at intervals from February to May; Prickly Spinach in July and August for Winter use. The New Zealand variety requires to be raised on a gentle hot-bed in April, and planted out in May on a good rich soil in a warm situation. Sow the Round and Prickly varieties in drills about an inch deep and a foot apart in good rich soil, the richer the better for the Summer crop. Abundance of moisture and an occasional dose of weak liquid manure will improve the crop.

				per oz.—s. d.
Long Standing. A most valuable variety for Summer use, as it stands the dry weather, and keeps longer fit for use than any other sort ... ... per qt. 3s. 6d., per pt. 2s.				0 6
Monstrous Italian or Viroflay. Large and superior; leaves dark green, and extremely thick and fleshy				
			per qt. 2s., per pt. 1s 3d.	0 4
New Zealand. Large and succulent	...	...	...	0 6
Perpetual or Spinach Beet ...	...	...	...	0 8
Prickly. For Winter use	...	per qt. 1s. 9d., per pt. 1s.		0 3
Round. For Summer use	...	,, 1s. 9d., ,, 1s.		0 3
Orach or Mountain. Green ...	...	...	per pkt. 6d.	—
,, ,, Red ...	...	...	,, 6d.	—
,, ,, White ...	...	...	,, 6d.	—

Salsafy and Scorzonera.

Cultivation.—To grow nice plump straight roots of Salsafy, the ground should be prepared in Autumn in a similar way to that recommended for Parsnips. Sow in April in drills fifteen inches apart, and thin out the plants to eight or ten inches apart in the row. Keep clean by hoeing, &c., during Summer, and take up for storing in November in same way as Carrots. The roots are scraped and boiled in the same way as Parsnips, and are of a mild sweetish flavour. Much esteemed on the Continent.

Scorzonera will thrive under similar treatment to that recommended for Salsafy, which it somewhat resembles, but should be allowed a little more room in the drill.

	per oz.—s. d.			per oz.—s. d.
Salsafy. Common ... ... per pkt. 3d.	0 9	**Scorzonera** ... ... per pkt. 3d.		0 9
,, **Sandwich Island Mammoth.** Splendid variety, lately introduced ... per pkt. 6d.	1 6	,, **Russian Improved**		1 0

Chives and Garlic.

	per pkt.—s. d.
Chives. Fine strong clumps ... ... each 6d.	—
Garlic, Golden Yellow (Seed). Used in same way as Common Garlic; the taste is much milder; excellent seasoning for mutton, sauces, &c.	1 0

Garlic Bulbs 1s. per lb.

Shallots.

(Sow and Cultivate as Onions.)

Far superior to Onions for pickling.

Bulbs. Fine sound bulbs ... ... per lb. 8d.; 12 lb. 6/-
Seed. New Jersey; extra large ... per pkt. 6d. and 1/-

Fruit Seeds, &c.

(various.)

	per pkt.—s. d.
Currant. Fine mixed, from a good collection 6d. and	1 0
Gooseberry. Various kinds, mixed ... 6d. and	1 0
Grape. From fine hot-house varieties ... 6d. and	1 0
Strawberry. Mixed varieties, from a fine collection 6d. and	1 0
Raspberry. Various kinds, mixed ... ... 6d. and	1 0
Apple Pips. In great variety, mixed ... 6d. and	1 0
Pear Pips. In great variety, mixed ... 6d. and	1 0

Cardoons.

	per pkt.—s. d.
Smooth Solid. Cultivated for the mid-rib of the leaf	0 6
Large Spanish	0 6

Rhubarb (seed).

Mitchell's Royal Albert ... per pkt. 6d. and 1s.
Myatt's Linnæus ... ... ,, 6d. and 1s.
Myatt's Victoria ... ... ,, 6d. and 1s.
Mixed ... ... ,, 6d. and 1s.

Plants, see page 105.

Sea Kale.

Sow early in April. Thin out the plants when strong enough. The ground should be thoroughly well hoed, and an application of weak liquid manure applied; occasional doses of manure water during the Summer months will greatly improve the size of the roots. The plants should be taken up in Spring, the roots shortened, and replanted upon deep, well-trenched, and manured ground, placing the plants in rows 3 to 4 feet apart, and about 2 feet between each plant.

New Seed ... ... per pint 2s.; per oz. 6d.
Strong planting roots ... per doz. 1s.; per 100, 7s. 6d.
Good strong roots, for forcing per doz. 1s. 6d.; per 100, 10s. 6d.
Extra strong roots, for forcing per doz. 2s.; per 100, 15s.

Tomato or Love-apple.

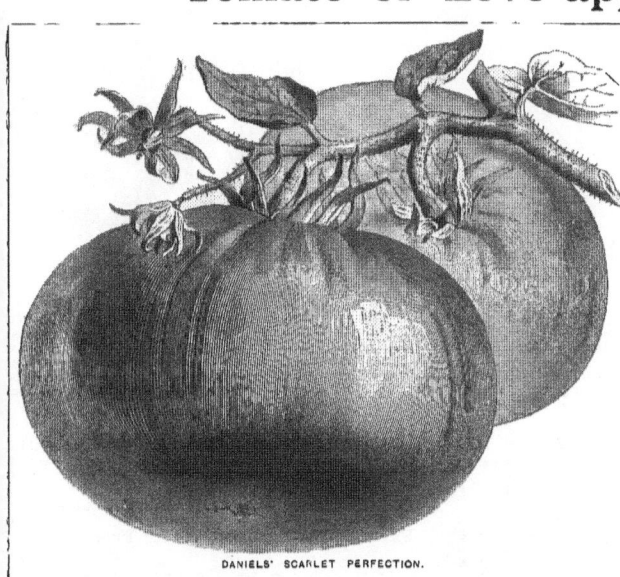

DANIELS' SCARLET PERFECTION.

Cultivation.—Sow in March on a slight hot-bed, and when two or three inches high pot off singly into three-inch pots. In middle of April place in cool frame or under handglasses to harden off. About this period great care should be taken to keep the young plants shaded from the sun, and well supplied with water. Towards the end of May plant out about four feet apart, in good rich soil, against a south wall, or close to the fence on a warm border. As the plants grow they should be trained up thinly, and nailed up or fastened. Pinch out the young branches from amongst the fruit, as it is highly important they should have the fullest benefit of sun and air to insure their full ripening. Frequent doses of weak liquid manure all through the growing season will be found of great service.

EVIDENCE OF QUALITY.

"The Scarlet Perfection Tomato I had from you was sown last February, and I commenced cutting Tomatoes 1st June, and am still cutting them regularly. Everyone who has tasted them consider them as their name perfection."— Mr. J. FLETCHER, Yate.

"I wish to inform you that the Seeds I had of your Crimson Queen Tomato have done exceedingly well, the best I have ever seen."—Mr. T. YEOMANS, The Gardens, Elsing Hall.

Red Varieties.

per pkt.—s. d.

*DANIELS' SCARLET PERFEC-TION. Very handsome, perfectly round and smooth, firm and solid, flavour first class, and of a beautiful glossy scarlet colour ... 1s. and 2 0

DANIELS' CRIMSON QUEEN. A beautiful scarlet crimson variety of extra fine form and delicate flavour, very prolific and early; a magnificent variety for exhibition purposes 1 0

Criterion. A most superior red sort, of handsome form and large size 0 6

Hathaway's Excelsior or **Stamfordian.** A fine early variety, producing in great profusion a large, smooth, round, and heavy fruit; handsome ... 0 6

*King Humbert o **Chiswick Red.** First Class Certificate R.H.S. 0 6

Lorillard. The fruit are medium large, smooth, and of a bright scarlet 1 0

*Laxton's Open-air. It is said to be the earliest and hardiest in cultivation .. ... 6d. and 1 0

*New Early Champion. Succeeds well both under glass and in the open air. It is of dwarf compact habit, fruit smooth, solid, and of a bright red ... 1 0

New Peach. Fruit is uniform in size, about as large as a medium-sized Peach, having a delicious fruity flavour not met with in any other ... 1 0

Chemin. Smooth, good shape and colour; fine market variety .. .. 6d. and 1 0

Conference. Very handsome, perfectly round and smooth, flesh firm and solid 1 0

Ham Green Favourite. Very prolific, fine handsome smooth variety; first class for market use .. 1 0

*Prelude. First Class Certificate R.H.S. Fruit solid, of good flavour, and of a rich scarlet colour .. 1 0

*Early Ruby. Very prolific, is of dwarf habit, good shape, colour bright scarlet, flesh solid, succeeds well in the open air 1 0

*DANIELS' DWARF EARLY OPEN-AIR. The earliest of all Tomatoes for the open air. Its earliness, dwarf habit and productiveness will make it a general favourite 6d. and 1 0

*DANIELS' HARBINGER. This variety, being very early and a prolific bearer, will be found extremely valuable for growing in the open air. The fruit are round, smooth, solid, and of a bright red. We have every reason to believe that this kind will soon become a favourite 1 0

Longkeeper. A new variety, selected for its long keeping qualities 1 0

Red Currant. A fine prolific variety, bearing small fruit, in racemes, of excellent quality ... 0 6

Mixed. All sorts 0 6

Yellow or Golden Varieties.

per pkt.—s. d.

*Golden Eagle. This is the most prolific variety that we know, and there is none to equal it in flavour 6d. and 1 0

Golden Queen. Smooth round golden yellow, of excellent flavour, and very productive ... 1 0

Golden Drop. Very prolific, bearing clusters of bright golden yellow fruit; round, smooth, and almost as transparent as amber, and of a most delicate flavour 1 0

*Golden Sunrise. First Class Certificate R.H.S. The fruit are large, round, smooth, and of a bright golden colour, sometimes slightly flushed with crimson; flavour excellent 1 0

Greengage. Fruit of a bright golden yellow ... 0 6

*Large Yellow Improved. A fine variety ... 0 6

Those marked thus * are the best for open air cultivation.

Turnip.

EARLY MILAN.   DANIELS' IMPROVED SNOWBALL.   EARLY STRAP-LEAVED.

Cultivation.—A rich, deep, mellow soil, with a fair amount of moisture, is the most favourable for growing nice, sweet, crisp, and juicy Turnips, but any good soil, well dug and manured, will grow them well. For the first crop sow **Daniels' Improved Snowball**, and other sorts, on a warm border towards the end of March; sow again in April, and for succession of Summer and Autumn crops, make occasional sowings up to the end of July. For Winter use sow in August or early in September. The "Orange Jelly" and "Early Munich" are best for this purpose. Turnips, to be of fine quality in Summer, should be grown quick. Sow broadcast, or in drills one foot or eighteen inches apart, and thin out the plants to one foot apart. Keep free from weeds while the plants are small, and give an occasional hoeing, which will greatly facilitate their growth.

White-fleshed Varieties.

	per oz.—s.	d.
Daniels' Improved Snowball. A distinct and beautiful Turnip. Small, solid, sweet, crisp, and of remarkably quick growth; flesh snow-white and juicy; a variety that cannot be surpassed per pint 2s.	0	6
Chirk Castle (Black Stone). Splendid Winter variety	0	8
New Early Scarlet (*see Novelties*) per pkt. 6d.	1	6
Early Milan Red-top. First Class Certificate, Royal Horticultural Society ... per pint 2s. 6d.	0	6
Early Munich. First Class Certificate R.H.S. per pint 2s.	0	6
Early White Strap-leaved. One of the earliest grown per pint 2s.	0	6
Early White Stone, or Dutch Six Weeks per pint 1s.	0	3
Veitch's Red Globe ... „ 2s.	0	6
Early Green-top Stone „ 2s.	0	4

Long or Tankard Vars. (White-fleshed).

	per oz.—s.	d.
Crimson Tankard ... per pint 2s.	0	6
Emerald Tankard „ 2s.	0	6
Jersey Navet. Fine variety from the Channel Islands	0	6
Paris Market or Long White French per pint 2s.	0	6

Yellow or Golden-fleshed Varieties.

	per oz.—s.	d.
Early Orange Jelly. Very early, fine for late sowing per pint 1s. 6d.	0	4
Golden Ball (selected) ...	0	8
Golden Tankard ... per pint 2s.	0	6
Orange Red-top. A most handsome garden Turnip, with red top and golden yellow flesh, quality first-class ... per pint 2s.	0	6
New Golden Rose ...	0	6

Vegetable Marrow.

GOLDEN CREAM.

Cultivation.—This esteemed vegetable is so nearly related to the Gourd that we may say but little in regard to it. Its treatment as regards sowing and the early transplanting, &c., should be identical therewith. Few plants delight more in copious manurial waterings than do these. Too generally the produce is permitted to become much too large before it is cut for use. This is excusable in the case of growers for market. Where, however, persons are enabled to grow their own, it seems strange that the same method should be followed. Every Marrow should be cooked whole, and this fact should alone suggest the most desirable size to grow them to. By cutting young a more abundant supply will be constantly forming than is possible when all are permitted to become more or less "seedy."

per pkt.—s. d.

Pen-y-byd (*The best in the World*). Awarded two First Class Certificates. This distinct variety is enormously prolific and a continuous bearer. The vine is extremely short-jointed, setting a fruit at every joint. The fruit is of handsome appearance, almost globular in form, sometimes very slightly ribbed, averaging about six inches in diameter, and is of a delicate creamy white colour, with thick firm flesh, which when cooked is of finest quality and delicate flavour ... ... 6d. and 1 0

per pkt.—s. d.

DANIELS' GOLDEN CREAM. Very fine and prolific 0 6

DANIELS' LARGE CREAM. Best for general use, fine-flavoured 0 6

Custard-shaped. Prolific, ornamental-shaped variety 0 6

Long Green. Good variety, forms a striking contrast with other kinds 0 4

Long White-ribbed, or Bush. Good; a prolific kind 0 4

Moore's Vegetable Cream. Very prolific, delicious flavour 0 4

Pine-apple Squash (new). From America. A useful and prolific variety ... 6d. and 1 0

Vegetable Marrow and **Squash.** Various sorts mixed 0 3

Reliable Mushroom Spawn.

⌐ This illustration (from a photograph) represents a group of Mushrooms in all stages of growth (half natural size), placed upon a brick of the Spawn.

MUSHROOMS ALL THE YEAR ROUND
MAY BE HAD BY USING
DANIELS' RELIABLE SPAWN.

COMPLETE INSTRUCTIONS FOR CULTIVATION WILL BE SENT WITH EVERY ORDER.

EVIDENCE OF SUPERIOR QUALITY AND RELIABILITY.

"The produce of your **Mushroom Spawn** is truly marvellous. My two beds are literally covered with full-sized ones, and hundreds are showing up."—**Mr. F. DRAKE**, Gardener, Catton.

"I have used your **Mushroom Spawn** for **five years**, and always found it of the best quality, and at the present time have a bed excelling all previous ones. I would recommend it to any one requiring thoroughly reliable Spawn."—**Mr. BRACEY**, Gardener to Geoffrey Buxton, Esq., Thorpe.

"I may observe that having tried your Spawn last season, I found, after strictly carrying out your instructions, the success far beyond my most sanguine expectations. I planted three bricks in a bed seven feet by three feet, and gathered over 200 lb. of fine **Mushrooms**."—**Mr. W. WRIGHT**, Derby.

"I cannot speak too highly of the crop of **Mushrooms** I had last year from the Spawn supplied by you. They exceeded any I ever had before, both in size and quantity."—**Mr. R. T. COWING**, Plumstead.

"The **Mushroom Spawn** I had of you gives me great satisfaction, the way in which the Mushrooms cover the bed greatly surprises me."—**Mr. T. I. HANCOCK**, High Wycombe.

"Your **Mushroom Spawn** has given every satisfaction."—**Mr. B. LAST**, Golborne.

"The last **Spawn** I had was A.1. I have grown and cut several 8½, 9, and 10 ounces, one was 24 inches in circumference."—**Mr. C. TWIST**, Doncaster.

"The **Spawn** has done remarkably well, and with no heat whatever the bed is a perfect picture, I have cut hundreds from a dozen cakes."—**Mr. F. BUCKINGHAM**, Ipswich.

"I may say that the **Mushroom Spawn** I had from you last year really surpasses my expectations. Grown in a cellar, I had an abundant crop beating your coloured plate into a cocked hat."—**Mr M. A. MASON**, Richmond Row, Liverpool.

DANIELS' BEST MILLTRACK.

In Bricks, each 6d., 4 bricks 1s. 6d., 16 bricks or one bushel 5s.

FRENCH MUSHROOM SPAWN.

In Boxes, 2 lbs. 2s. 9d., 3 lbs. 4s., 4 lbs. 5s. 4d., 6 lbs. 8s. (if ordered to be sent per parcel post 3d. per lb. extra).

These Boxes are the sizes generally required by Mushroom growers, and can be sent out just as received, thus preserving the Spawn from breaking.

This Spawn is of very fine quality, and is in a more concentrated form than the English make.

EFFICIENT, ODOURLESS, ECONOMICAL.

This preparation is purely and simply a Manure in a highly concentrated form, without any admixture of other ingredients to make up bulk, and will be found more CLEANLY, because it is entirely without smell, more EFFICACIOUS, because it is easily assimilated by all kinds of vegetable growths, and more ECONOMICAL, because it is cheaper in comparison with other Manures, where quantity is preferred to quality.

EVIDENCE OF QUALITY.

REPORT OF MR. FRANCIS SUTTON, F.C.S., F.I.C.
(*Analyst to the Norfolk Chamber of Agriculture*).
"NORFOLK COUNTY LABORATORY.
"I have acquainted myself by experiment and analysis with the entire nature of your **Eureka Manure**, and may say at once you have carried out practically the ideas which I myself would advocate, viz., a manure safe, odourless, and adapted for the healthy growth and development of every variety of plants."

"Your **Eureka Manure** proved upon trial an excellent aid to pot-grown plants."—**WM. EARLEY, Esq**., Ilford.

"The effect of your **Eureka Manure** is very noticeable on soft-wooded plants in about three weeks from first application, more especially on **Coleus**, the colours of which it improves amazingly."—**Mr. M. C. WILSON**, The Gardens, Hevingham Hall.

"Excellent alike for Vegetables and Flowers."—**Mr. WM. BARNES**, Ormesby.

"I have used your **Eureka Manure** side by side with other manures, on Stove and Greenhouse Plants, and all kinds of **Vegetables**, with most satisfactory results. The quantity and quality of the vegetables was surprising. I shall most certainly endeavour to promote the sale of your **Essence of Plant Life**, as I consider it to be one of the few good things of modern introduction."—**Mr. H. STEVENS**, The Gardens, Northrepps Hall.

"I gave your **Eureka Manure** a fair trial while I was in the gardens of Colonel Couchman. I also gave two other gentlemen's gardeners an equal quantity for trial, and they agree with me in testifying as to its nutritious and invigorating quality, excelling any other Manure we have yet tried.—**Mr. GEO. DEVERILL**, Brentwood.

"I got my Potatoes from you, they all gave great satisfaction and won many prizes for me, which were open to all England. I used **Daniels' Eureka Manure**, which I consider very valuable for all kinds of **Roots** and **Flowers**."—**Mr. W. VALES**, The Gardens, Needham Hall.

"I have made a trial of your **Eureka Manure** with some seedling **Coleus** in four-inch pots, and have grown some very fine specimens, which have kept the colour splendidly; all my neighbours were surprised at the small quantity of soil I used. I have also tried it with **Cucumbers** and find it highly satisfactory, and believe it to be one of the best Artificial Manures, and intend to make further trials with it this coming season."—**Mr. S. GUNN**, The Gardens, Wethersfield Place.

"I find the **Eureka** a very good manure."—**Mr. H. HORN**, Fence Houses, Durham.

"Your **Manure** is excellent."—**Mr. W. S. BOULDERSON**, Bath.

Sold in Packages, with complete Directions for Use, Postal Boxes, ½-lb. 1s., 2½-lb. 2s. 3d., 6-lb. 4s. 6d., Post or Carriage Free, at prices quoted. In Boxes, not Carriage Free, but can be enclosed in general order, without extra expense of carriage, 1-lb. 1s., 2-lb. 1s. 8d., 4-lb. 3s, 7-lb. 4s. 6d., 14-lb. 7s., 28-lb. 12s. 6d. Much cheaper by the cwt. Prices on application.

Miscellaneous Garden Requisites.

Shading & Tying Materials.

APHICIDES, or Spray Diffusers. A most useful and ingenious invention for distributing insecticides. Fitted with mouthpiece, and cork attached for mouth of bottle. Useful also as a means of sprinkling flowers when cut. 1s. 6d. each.

APPLEBY'S PATENT FUMIGATOR. There are many of these in commerce, but most of them not strong enough to stand the test of wear and tear; these are, however, exceptionally strong. 5s. and 7s. each.

EWING'S MILDEW COMPOSITION. 1s. 6d. per bottle.

FIR-TREE OIL INSECTICIDE. A preparation that has outlived many newer ones, and very effectual. In bottles 1s. 6d., 2s. 6d., and 4s. 6d. each.

FLORAL CEMENT. For fixing the petals of flowers, thereby preventing their dropping. 1s. per bottle.

FOWLER'S INSECTICIDE. In jars 1s. 6d. and 3s. each.

   „   **TOBACCO POWDER.** In tins 6d., 1s., 2s. 6d., and 5s. 6d.

GARDENERS' APRONS. In Shalloon, best make, 4s. 6d., 4s. 9d., and 5s. each. These are exceptionally strong, and should be the property of every gardener.

GENTLEMEN'S GARDENING GLOVES. Strong leather, for hedging. 1s. 6d. per pair.
   1st quality Leather. A very neat glove, and soft to the hand. 2s. 6d. per pair.
   Inseam Tan. Good cheap glove, soft and pliable. 1s. 3d. per pair.
   Oxford Tan. In several qualities; one of the strongest and most serviceable gloves made. 1s. 6d., 1s. 9d., 2s., and 2s. 3d. per pair.
   Drummond's. A one button glove by one of the best makers, and in great demand. 1s. 6d., 1s. 9d., 2s., and 2s. 3d. per pair.
   Harvest Tan. Good strong make. 1s. 4d. per pair.
   Wash Leather. Suitable for light work generally, or for housemaids. 1s. and 1s. 6d. per pair.

LADIES' GARDENING GLOVES.
   Short Tan. Of neat and strong manufacture. 1s. 2d. per pair.
   Long Tan. Composed of more material than the foregoing. 1s. 4d. per pair.
   Leather Gauntlet. A really stylish and at the same time useful glove for more than one purpose. 2s. 6d. per pair.

GISHURST COMPOUND. A very effectual insect destroyer. 1s. and 3s. per box.

GISHURSTINE. Is a perfect dubbing, invaluable to gardeners as a means of rendering boots absolutely waterproof. 6d. and 1s. per tin.

LEMON OIL INSECTICIDE. Per pint 1s. 6d., per quart 2s. 9d.

LETHORION (vapour cone). New Fumigator. Supplied in sizes for 50, 100, 500, and 1000 cubic feet, at 6d., 9d., 1s. 3d., and 2s. each, with full directions for use.

McDOUGALL'S TOBACCO SHEETS (a new form of distributing Tobacco Fumes in greenhouses). Highly approved of by many gardeners as being very destructive to all insect pests. 1s. each; 9s. per dozen.

MATS, Large Archangel. 2s. each; 18s. per doz.

   „   St. Petersburg. 1s. to 1s. 6d. each; 10s. 6d. and 15s. per doz.

   MAW'S TERRA COTTA LABELS. The cleanest looking and best for showing up the names written thereon that we know of. It is simply necessary to apply a little white lead paint on the surface before writing. In all shapes and sizes. 1s. 6d. to 8s. 6d. per 100.

METALLIC GARDEN WIRE. For tying roses and suspending labels, from No. 12 (thick) to No. 20 (thin). 1s. 6d. to 2s. per lb.

   „   **INK.** Produces indelible black writing. 6d. and 1s. per bottle.

   „   **LABELS.** Suitable for Gardens, Conservatories, Greenhouses, Ferneries, Flower Pots, &c. From 2s. to 5s. per 100.

ROFFEA GRASS. For tying. 6d. and 1s. per bundle; 1s. 6d. per lb.

SILVER SAND. Best Reigate. 4s. per bushel.

STYPTIC. For preventing bleeding in Vines. 3s. per bottle.

TAM O'SHANTER HONE. A first-class implement for sharpening knives and small tools. 6d. to 2s. 6d. each.

TANNED NETTING. For Fruit Trees, &c. Six feet wide, 3d. per yard; twelve feet wide, 6d. per yard.

TAR TWINE. In balls, thick or thin. ½-lb. 9d., per lb. 1s. 3d.

   THERMOMETERS. Boxwood (Spirit or Mercury), 9d., 1s., 1s. 6d., and 2s. 6d. each.
     Boxwood, with storm glass, 2s. 6d. and 3s. 6d. each.
     Cast metal scales; for the garden, 3s. 6d. each.
     Maximum and minimum registering; boxwood scales, tin japanned case. 5s. 6d. each.
     The same as the preceding, but of better finish, and with bright steel scales; in handsome case japanned white. 7s. 6d. each.
     Porcelain (Mercury), bevelled edge, first quality. 5s. 6d. and 6s. 6d. each.
     For hotbeds; box scales. 12 in., 5s. 6d.; 18 in., 10s.; 24 in., 12s. 6d. each.

TIFFANY. For shading purposes. In pieces twenty yards long, thirty-eight inches wide, 6s.

VERBENA PINS (Galvanized Wire). For pegging down Verbenas, &c., in order to strike. Per box of one gross (three inches long) 1s.

VIRGIN CORK. Quarter-cwt. 6s.; half-cwt. 11s.; per cwt. 20s.

WATERING POTS, New High Level (patented), (*see illustration*). A long felt want for watering top shelves in greenhouses, no steps or ladder required. Made in the following sizes, and so simple that any one can manage them with facility. Complete with shaft, 1 quart 3s. 6d., 2 quarts 4s., 3 quarts 4s. 6d.

WEED KILLER, The Perfect. 2s. per gallon (to make 25 gallons), cheaper in quantities.

Saynor's Celebrated Pruning and Budding Knives, &c.

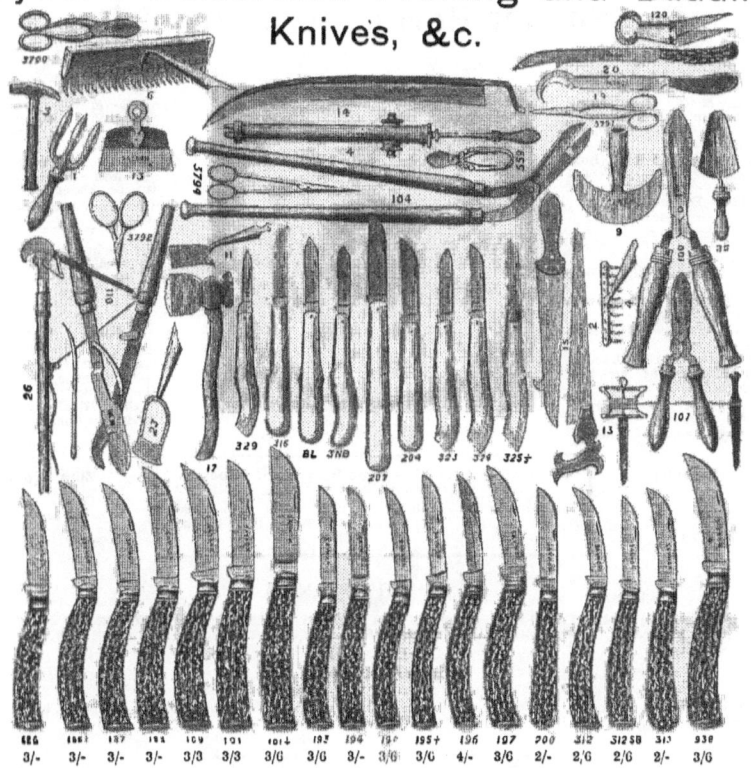

BUDDING KNIVES. No. 329, 3/6; 316, 3/-; BL, 3/-; 3NB, 3/-; 207, 3/6; 204, 3/-; 323, 2/6; 324, 3/-; 325½ 3/6.
,,   ,,   No. 204n, "The Gardener's Favourite," brass bound, 3/6 each.

SCISSORS. Flower-gathering—No. 3791, 6-in., 3/-;
                8-in., 4/-;
,,   Pruning—No. 3790, 6-in., 2/6; 7-in., 3/6;
                8-in., 4/-.
,,   ,,   With slide, 5/6, 6/6, and 7/6 per pair.

SCISSORS. Vine—No. 3794, 6-in., 2/6; 7-in., 3/6 per pair.
SECATEURS. New, all bright, with improved spring,
                7-in., 4/6; 8-in., 5/- per pair.
,,   ,,   With spring, 6-in., 4/-; 7-in., 5/- per pair.
,,   ,,   Patent spring, 2/- per pair.

SYRINGES. Benton & Stone's best quality, fitted with Cooper's Patent Protector, and Stone's Patent Adjustable Plunger.
     No. 8106, 14 by 1, 5 -; No. 5, 14 by 1, 7/6; No. 5, 18 by 1½, 10.6; No. 4, 16 by 1½, 12.6; No. 3, 18 by 1½
     (Ball Valve), 18/6; No. 3, 20 by 1½ (Ball Valve), 21/-

No. 26.	**Averruncators.** 6-ft. long, 20/- per pair.	
,, 1.	**Ladies' Digging Forks.** 2/6 each.	
,, 3.	**Garden Hammers.** No. 1, 2/-; No. 2, 2/6.	
,, 23.	**Dutch Hoes.** 5-in., 1/3; 6-in., 1/6.	
,, 13.	**Draw Hoes.** 5-in., 10d.; 6-in., 1/-; 7-in. 1/2.	
,, 17.	**Gentlemen's Hatchets.** Claw head, 4/6 each.	
,, 4.	**Iron Rakes.** 8 teeth, 1/4; 10 teeth, 1/8, 12 teeth, 2/-	
,, 6.	**Daisy Rakes.** 7/6 each.	
,, 18.	**Garden Reels.** 2/6 each; Lines for ditto, 1/6 and 2/6.	
,, 110.	**Sliding Pruning Shears.** 8/6, 9/6, and 12/6 each.	
,, 107.	**Grass Shears.** 4/-. No. 100, 4/6 each.	
,, 104.	**Edging Shears.** 7/6, 8/6, and 9/6 each.	

No. 120.	**Sheep Shears.** 3/6 each.
,, 15.	**Pruning Saws, with Bill Hook.** 9/- each.
,, 2.	**Pruning Saws, cast Steel.** 3/6 each.
,, 9.	**Edging Irons, cast Steel.** 3/6 each.
,, 25.	**Bright Steel Trowels.** 6-in., 2/3; 7-in., 2/6.
,, 19.	**Gooseberry Pruners, with hook.** 3/- each.
,, 20.	**Gooseberry Pruners, straight.** 3/- each.
,, 14.	**Scythe Blades.** 36-in., 4/6.
,, 11.	**Cast Steel Spuds.** 1/6 each.

Duns Switching and half-cut over Bills, best make, 4/6 each.

Wreaths, Crosses, Bouquets, Grasses, Gnaphaliums, and Sundry Horticultural Requisites.

Wreaths in White Cape Flowers. 2s., 2s. 6d., 3s. 6d., 4s. 6d., 5s. 6d., to 10s. 6d. each.

Wreaths—Metal Leaves and Porcelain Flowers. 2s., 2s. 6d., 3s. 6d., 4s. 6d., 5s. 6d., 10s. 6d., to 42s.

Wreaths—Artificial (best French flowers). 7s. 6d., 10s. 6d., 12s. 6d., 15s., 21s., to 42s.

Wreaths—Porcelain. Very choice. 12s. 6d. to 63s.

Cape Flowers, white. Wired, 2s. per 100.

Cape Flowers, in colours. Wired, 2s. per 100.

*Pampas Plumes. Natural, white, 1s. to 1s. 6d. each.

*Pampas Plumes. Coloured, 1s. to 1s. 6d. each.

*Uva Plumes, 1s. to 1s. 6d. each.

*Uniola Plumes, 8d. per doz.; 4s. 6d. per 100.

* These are very stately growing Grasses, the plumes of which form valuable objects for house decoration.

Crosses in White Cape Flowers. 6s., 7s. 6d., 10s. 6d., 12s. 6d., and 15s. each.

Crosses—Metal Leaves and Porcelain Flowers. 6s., 7s. 6d., 10s. 6d, 12s. 6d., and 15s. each.

Crosses—Artificial (best French flowers). 7s. 6d., 10s. 6d., 12s. 6d., 15s., 21s., to 42s.

Crosses—Porcelain. 10s. 6d. to 42s.

Grasses—In bouquets. Natural or coloured, from 6d. to 5s. each.

Bouquets of Dried Flowers, in great variety. 9d., 1s., 1s. 6d., 1s. 9d., 2s., 2s. 6d., and 3s. 6d. each.

Moss—French. Natural and dyed green. 4d. and 6d. per bunch.

Dried Flowers—Gnaphaliums—Blue, Crimson, Green, Magenta, Pink, Purple, Violet, White, Yellow, Mixed. From 1s. 6d. to 2s. 6d. per bunch.

Zinc Troughs.

For Wreaths of fresh cut flowers.

All sizes, 1s. 3d. to 3s. each.

WREATH CASES.—Dome Shaped, of superior pattern and best quality.

8-in. diameter 3s. 3d., 9-in. 3s. 9d., 10-in. 4s. 3d., 11-in. 4s. 9d., 12-in. 5s. 6d., 13-in. 6s. 6d., 14-in. 7s. 6d., 15-in. 10s., and upwards.

Zinc Troughs.

For Crosses of fresh cut flowers.

All sizes, 1s. 6d. to 3s. 6d. each.

FLOWER STAKES.

Unpainted Deal. In bundles of 100, 1-ft., 1/-; 1½-ft., 1/6; 2-ft., 2/-; 2½-ft., 2/6; 3-ft., 3/-; 3½-ft., 3/6; 4-ft., 4/-.

Stout, Green Painted. Per doz., 1-ft., 6d.; 1½-ft., 9d.; 2-ft., 1/9; 2½-ft., 2/3; 3-ft., 3/-; 3½-ft., 3/6; 4-ft., 4/-; 4½-ft., 4/6; 5-ft., 5/-; 6 ft., 6/-.

WOOD LABELS.

Best English Make, Painted. In bundles of 100, 4-in., 8d.; 5-in., 10d.; 6-in. 1/-; 7-in., 1/3; 8-in., 1/6; 9-in., 1/9.

Plain. 4-in., 6d.; 5-in., 8d.; 6-in., 10d.; 7-in., 1/-; 8-in., 1/4; 9-in., 1/6; 12-in., 2/6.

SUSSEX TRUCK BASKETS.

Indispensable to every garden.

No 2, 11½-in. by 6-in., 1/-; No. 3, 13½-in. by 7½-in., 1/3; No. 4, 15-in. by 8½-in., 1/6; No. 5, 17½-in. by 9½-in., 1·9; No. 6, 20½-in. by 10½-in., 2/3; No. 7, 23-in. by 12-in., 2/6; No. 8, 26-in. by 14-in., 3/-; No. 9, 28-in. by 15-in., 3/6.

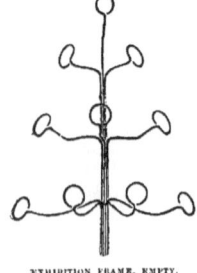

EXHIBITION FRAME, EMPTY.
No. 1

PATENT FLOWER SUPPORTS.

FOR THE WALL.   FOR THE TABLE.   FOR THE MANTELPIECE.

For the arrangement of Cut Flowers these are unequalled.

Various Shapes in Stock.

Artistic arrangement is greatly obviated by the invention of these Patent Frames. All the frames are enamelled green.

		each—s.	d.
No. 1.	Exhibition Bunches (without cups) for 10 Flowers ...	0	9
„ 2.	Exhibition Bunches (without cups) for 6 Flowers ...	0	6
„ 3.	Wall Suspenders with cup for 10 Flowers ...	1	0
„ 4.	Wall Suspenders with cup for 6 Flowers ...	0	9
„ 5.	Table Decoration, with raised centre ...	1	6
„ 6.	Table Decoration, with raised centre, with Dish ...	2	0
„ 7.	Table Decoration, without raised centre ...	1	3
„ 8.	Table Decoration, without raised centre, with Dish ...	1	6
„ 9.	Circular for Vase or Bouquet ...	1	0

Price per dozen on application.

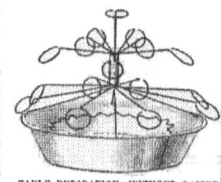

TABLE DECORATION, WITHOUT RAISED CENTRE, WITH DISH.
NO. 8.

Daniels' Seeds for Song Birds.

We have much pleasure in introducing to the notice of our customers the following choice bird-seeds. Norwich has long had a world-wide reputation for song birds, more especially the beautiful Norwich Canary, many thousands of which are annually bred and sent to various parts. Having been in the habit of supplying some of the best breeders with our choice seeds, we feel confident the seeds now offered will give every satisfaction, and prove a boon to many of our customers residing in distant parts, who are desirous of obtaining, at a small cost, the choicest seeds for their favorite songsters and cage-birds. The samples have been thoroughly cleaned, and are free from all impurities.

		per quart. s. d.		per peck. s. d.		per bush. s. d.
CANARY, Superfine Spanish		0 5	2s. 6d. to 3 0	9s. 6d. to 10 6
Rape		2 6	…	9 0
" German		0 6	3 0	10 6
Turnip		0 4	2 3	9 0
Hemp		0 3	.1 9	6s. 6d. to 7 6
Linseed. Small		0 4	2 3	9 0
" Large		0 5	2 6	9 6
Mustard. Brown		0 8	4 6	17 0
Maw	6d. per pt., 8d. per lb.	—	—	—
Inga		0 6	3 0	—
Lettuce	1s. to 2s. per lb.	—	—	—
Millet. Best French		0 6	3 0	10 6
" Ears	8d. per doz.	—	—	—
Cress		0 5	3 0	10 0
Maize. Small for parrots		0 3	1 6	4 6
Our own Special Mixture for Canaries		0 8	3 0	10 6

These very low prices do not include carriage unless the order amounts to £1 and upwards, but they can be sent free along with a general order for other seeds. The above prices are subject to Market variations.

SPECIAL QUOTATIONS FOR LARGE QUANTITIES.

EVIDENCE OF QUALITY.

Daniels' Selected Home-grown Farm Seeds.

HAVE PRODUCED SOME OF THE HEAVIEST CROPS ON RECORD.

Our new **Farm Seed Catalogue**, published March 1st, will be forwarded gratis and post free on application. Not bound by these prices after March 1st, 1892.

Daniels Bros. have as usual given special care and attention to the selecting and improving of their choice stocks of Swedish and other Turnips, and also of Mangolds, which for size, quality, and smallness of top are considered the finest grown. Their stocks of all the well-known sorts have been grown expressly for their retail trade, and may be relied upon as being true to name, of the best quality, and saved from selected roots.

Swede Turnips.

per bush.—s. d.

DANIELS' NORFOLK GIANT PURPLE-TOP. The success this magnificent variety has met with during the past season shows it to be superior to most sorts now in commerce, and we have no hesitation in recommending it to our customers. The roots are somewhat oval, and of a deep rich purple. It is a heavy cropper and excellent keeper. All farmers should give it a trial. per pk. 7d. 30 0

DANIELS' IMPROVED PURPLE-TOP. A carefully selected and splendid variety ... ... per pint 7d. 28 0

DANIELS' DEFIANCE GREEN-TOP. A first-class variety for grazing purposes; very hardy ... ... per pint 7d. 30 0

Skirving's Purple-top. An old-esteemed variety „ 6d. 25 0

White-fleshed Turnips.

DANIELS' NORFOLK GREEN ROUND. Excellent for main crop, the hardiest of the Globe varieties ... per pint 6d. 24 0

DANIELS' PURPLE-TOP MAMMOTH. An early Turnip, very heavy cropper, large and handsome roots ... per pint 8d. 30 0

Bell or Decanter. Extra selected stock ... ... „ 6d. 24 0

Pomeranian or White Globe. Fine for early use „ 6d. 24 0

Stone or Stubble. For late sowing ... ... „ 6d. 24 0

Yellow-fleshed or Scotch Turnips.

GREEN-TOP YELLOW SCOTCH or BULLOCK. Grows a heavy crop, flesh solid and juicy, much relished by cattle per pint 8d. 32 0

Purple-top Yellow Scotch or Bullock. A very superior variety, nearly equal to the Swede in quality ... per pint 9d. 40 0

Special low quotations for large quantities.

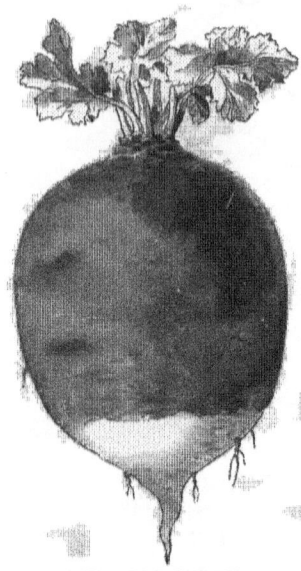

NORFOLK GIANT PURPLE-TOP.

Mangolds.

Long Varieties.

per cwt.—s. d.

DANIELS' IMPROVED MAMMOTH LONG RED. Our stock is very fine and can be highly recommended, having been selected by us for many years ... ... per lb. 9d. 75 0

DANIELS' GOLDEN TANKARD. Specially selected for its yellow or golden flesh, its richness in saccharine matter, and handsome shape ... ... per lb. 9d. 75 0

DANIELS' SELECTED LONG YELLOW. This we can highly recommend as a select stock of Long Yellow per lb. 9d. 75 0

DANIELS' GOLDEN GATE-POST. The colour and quality of the flesh are equal to the Golden Tankard, being of rich yellow and full of saccharine matter ... ... per lb. 1s. 100 0

DANIELS' INTERMEDIATE or GATE-POST. One of the finest Mangolds ever introduced. The crop is uniform, and the roots heavy, handsome, and clean, with single tap-root per lb. 10d. 84 0

Yellow Intermediate ... ... „ 9d. 75 0

Globe Varieties.

DANIELS' CHAMPION ORANGE GLOBE. Our own unequalled stock, highly recommended for its neat top, fine clear skin, and tap root, a heavy cropper of splendid quality per lb. 10d. 84 0

DANIELS' GOLDEN GLOBE. One of the finest selected stocks introduced of late years ... ... per lb. 1s. 100 0

DANIELS' SELECTED RED GLOBE. Very heavy cropper per lb. 9d. 75 0

Yellow Globe. Good stock ... ... „ 9d. 75 0

Special low quotations for large quantities.

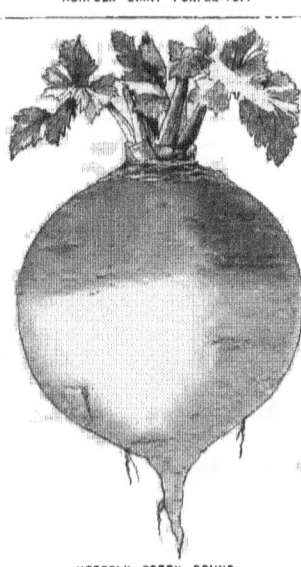

NORFOLK GREEN ROUND.

Cleaned Grass Seeds and Clovers

For all Soils & Situations, for Pasturage, Ensilage, &c.

Samples and Special Quotations on Application.

Grass Mixtures.

per acre.—s. d.

1.—MIXTURES FOR ALTERNATE HUSBANDRY OR ROTATION CROPS.

Rye Grasses and Clovers for one year's lay   12s. 6d. to   17 6

Rye Grasses and Clovers for one year's lay, and one year's pasture   ...   ...   18s. to   25 0

Rye Grasses and Clovers for one year's lay, and two or three years' pasture   ...   20s. to   27 6

2.—MIXTURE FOR PERMANENT PASTURE OR MEADOW.

This comprises a selection of the Finest Perennial Clovers, Cocksfoot, Crested Dogstail, Fescues, Golden Oat Grass, Meadow Foxtail, Parsley, Peas, Rye Grasses (Italian and Perennial), Sweet Vernal, Timothy, &c.   25s. to   35 0

3.—MIXTURE FOR PERMANENT PASTURES IN PARKS, ORNAMENTAL GROUNDS, CEMETERIES, &c.

Made up of Perennial Clovers, Crested Dogstail, Fescues, Golden Oat Grass, Meadow Foxtail, Peas, Evergreen Perennial Rye Grass, Sweet Vernal, &c.   25s. to   35 0

4.—RENOVATING GRASSES AND CLOVERS. For improving old or worn-out pastures, mending patches, &c. Sow 10 to 12 lbs. per acre   ...   per bush. 20s.; per lb. 1s.   —

All orders should be accompanied with a description of the nature of the land to be laid down, and the measurement in statute acres.

BROAD-LEAVED ENGLISH RED CLOVER.

Rye Grasses, Clovers, &c.

Finest Qualities Selected, and Cleaned by the best Machinery.

Prices subject to the variation of the Market.

Evergreen Perennial or **Devon Eaver**   per bush. 4s. to 6s.

Italian (*Lolium Italicum*) English   ...   per bush. 4s. to 5s. 6d.

     ,,   Foreign   ...   per bush. 5s. to 6s.

Perennial (*Lolium perenne*) Scotch   ...   per bush. 4s. 6d. to 6s.

     ,,   **(Pacey's)**   ...   per bush. 4s. 6d. to 6s.

Alsyke or **Hybrid** (*Trifolium hybridum*) per lb. 1s. to 1s. 3d.; per bush. 65s. to 80s.

Giant Cow Grass or **Perennial Red** (*T. perenne*) per lb. 9d. to 1s.; per bush. 56s. to 70s.

Red or **Broad-leaved** (*T. pratense*) per lb. 6d. to 10d.; per bush. 35s. to 60s.

White or **Dutch** (*T. repens*)   per lb. 10d. to 1s. 3d.; per bush. 56s. to 80s.

Yellow or **Trefoil** (*Medicago lupulina*)   per lb. 6d.; per bush. 25s. to 35s.

Yellow or **Red Suckling** (*T. minus filiforme*)   ...   per lb. 9d.

Clover Mixed for Alternate Husbandry per lb. 1s.; per bush. 45s. to 65s.

Crimson Clover (*Trifolium incarnatum*)   ...   ...   market price.

Perennial Clovers in Mixture   ...   ... per lb. 1s.; per bush. 60s.

Sainfoin, Giant. Sow four bushels per acre; specially adapted for growing on light, dry, chalky soils, producing a considerable amount of bulk for using green; it also makes very good hay   per bush. 5s. 6d. to 6s. 6d.

Sainfoin, Common ...   .   per bush. 5s. to 6s.

Spring Tares or **Vetches** ...   ... per bush. 6s. 6d. to 7s. 6d.

   ,,   ,,   **New Zealand** or **Golden** ...   ... per bush. 7s. 6d.

EVIDENCE OF QUALITY.

"Please send me sixteen acres **Grasses** and **Clovers** same as last year. My layers look better this year than they have ever done before."—Mr. G. BAGNALL, East Dereham.

"The meadow I have now growing from your **Clovers** and **Grasses** of last year is excellent, there is nothing like it for miles round."—Mr. P. DONOHOE, Killancooly.

SMOOTH-STALKED MEADOW GRASS.

This magnificent new Potato is a cross between the Magnum Bonum and the White Elephant, combining the excellent qualities of both; but it more resembles the White Elephant in shape, size, enormous productiveness, and fine cooking qualities, with the advantage of having a pure white skin. The introduction of such choice varieties as the Magnum Bonum and White Elephant has caused quite a revolution in the Potato trade, their immense productiveness and excellent table quality have had a great influence in moderating the prices on the Market. This new variety, The Daniels, combining as it does the excellent qualities of both, is likely to become a general favourite. We sent it out for the first time in 1887, and from the numerous unsolicited testimonials received of its superior merits, have no hesitation in saying it is the best second early white-skinned variety in cultivation, and is sure to give satisfaction.

In the circular issued by the Board of Agriculture, Intelligence Department, October, 1890, after an exhaustive enquiry in regard to the Potato Crops throughout the United Kingdom, the "DANIELS" is reported as one of the varieties most free from disease.

Price, per peck 2s. 6d., per bush. 8s., per cwt. 14s. Much cheaper by the Ton

---

EVIDENCE OF SUPERIOR QUALITY AND PRODUCTIVENESS.

From the *JOURNAL OF HORTICULTURE*, Nov. 5th, 1891.

A correspondent to the above Journal writes:—**The Daniels.** "This variety, the result of a cross between **Magnum Bonum** and **White Elephant** gave me an agreeable surprise, as neither of these varieties is of any use here either as disease resisters or for eating purposes. Their "Bairn," however, turned out like them in being an enormous cropper with large tubers of even size and handsome form, and not a trace of disease; of first-rate quality when cooked, being very floury, first-rate exhibition potato."

From Hundreds of Unsolicited Testimonials received we select the following:—

"I have won First Prize for **The Daniels Potato** in the Gaerwen Show in 1889, and in 1890."—**Mr. T. EVANS,** Gaerwen.

"I am pleased to say my employer is so pleased with the quality of **The Daniels Potato**, as to desire me to send no other main crop to the table."—**Mr. JAMES WYATT,** Gardener, Kit's Croft.

"**The Daniels Potatoes** which you sent me last season were truly magnificent."—**B. A. LEONARD, ESQ.,** Ballycarney.

"I beg to say that out of 14 lbs. of **The Daniels Potatoes** that I planted last year reproduced 175 lbs., and am very pleased with them."—**Mr E RABBITS,** Poole, Dorset.

"Mr. H. Smith cannot speak too highly of **The Daniels Potato**, it was excellent in all points." **Mr. H. SMITH,** Clobham.

"Your Potato, **The Daniels**' is the best flavoured potato out of 30 sorts grown by me."—**Mr. T. HAYNES,** Stapenhill.

"**The Daniels Potato** last year produced nearly double any other, and I have about thirty I tried in field and garden with equal success."—**Mr. A. CLARK,** Ballater.

"From 1½ lbs of the **Daniels Potato** I had from you, I have just raised 740 lbs., this is the second year I have grown them they are a splendid Potato."—**Mr J. T. BILLINGS,** Walthamstow.

GENERAL LIST OF SEED POTATOES FOR 1892.

EARLY WHITE HEBRON. *Half natural size.*

FIRST EARLY VARIETIES (White).

EARLY WHITE HEBRON. The finest first early white-skinned Potato in the World. For many years past the Beauty of Hebron has held a first place amongst the earliest varieties for productiveness, earliness, and first-class cooking qualities. The Early White Hebron possesses, in addition to all the well-known and appreciated qualities of above-named kind, a clear white skin, which renders it more valuable for market purposes. We can therefore give it our highest commendation to all who are desirous of securing a stock of this most valuable variety. It will be found all that can be desired for the gentleman's table, whilst its great productiveness renders it a most profitable kind for the market grower.

Price, 14 lb. 2s. 6d., 56 lb. 8s. 6d., cwt. 15s.

EVIDENCE OF QUALITY.

"The Seed Potatoes I bought from you have turned out to my entire satisfaction. From 7 lb. Early White Hebron I got 116 lb., and from 7 lb. Daniels, 180 lb."—Mr. J. CHAMBERS, Langley Mill.

"The Seed Potatoes which I received from you were very good indeed. From the Bushel we had Half-a-ton of good Potatoes, the best we ever grew."—Mr. A. HICKS, Seal.

"The White Hebron Potatoes I had from you last year beat any Potatoes we ever had in this part of the country. They are a splendid cropper, and free from disease."—Mr. W. BOND, Northwold.

		per 14 lb. s. d.	per 56 lb. s. d.	per cwt. s. d.
DANIELS' "HARBINGER." A first early Round variety of great excellence; first-class for earliest crop, in frames or out of doors. Height one foot		3 6	12 6	21 0
Defiance Ashleaf. The earliest and best kind, cooks well, and of fine flavour		4 0	14 0	21 0
Early Ashleaf		2 6	7 6	14 0
Early Primrose. A first early Kidney, coming in at same time as Early Ashleaf, but is more prolific; the tubers are of the most excellent quality and flavour, and when cooked the flesh is beautifully mealy and of a delicate primrose colour, hence its name. From its handsome shape it is a most desirable exhibition kind		3 6	12 6	21 0
Early White Beauty. Handsome Kidney, eyes few and shallow, heavy cropper, of good quality		2 6	8 6	15 0
Kentish or Mona's Pride Ashleaf. Small foliage, heavy cropper		2 6	8 6	15 0
Myatt's Ashleaf. A fine old variety		2 6	8 6	15 0
Old Ashleaf (true). The finest-flavoured first early known (scarce)		3 6	12 6	—
Rivers' Royal Ashleaf. Very productive		2 6	8 6	15 0

EARLY PURITAN.

EARLY PURITAN. An early variety of great excellence. It is claimed by the raiser to be the earliest pure white-skinned variety in cultivation. The tubers can be used when half grown, as they are wonderfully dry and of fine flavour. The plant is of vigorous constitution, and very productive. We have again grown this Potato in our trial grounds this season, and can thoroughly recommend its numerous good qualities. Price, 14 lb. 2s. 6d., 56 lb. 8s. 6d., cwt. 15s.

EVIDENCE OF QUALITY.

"The **Daniels** and the **Puritan** Potatoes are the best croppers I have ever grown, and I am recommending them to all my neighbours."— **Mr. J. DEAKIN**, Fazeley.

"From the Potatoes which I had from you last year, I gained First Prize at Coseley and Bradley Flower Show with your **Daniels** Potato, and a Special Prize for six dishes. **Early White Hebron, Early Puritan, Table King, Universal, Dreadnought, & Remarkable.** I never raised finer tubers before, and they were praised by all potato growers in the show for their fine colour and clean eyes."— **Mr. S. CLARKE**, Hallbrook.

"... I was very successful with **Potatoes** from your Seed last year, I only exhibited at two shows, and at one obtained First and Second Prizes and at the other First Prize."— **Mr. E. MACKIE**, Polmont.

"All the **Seed Potatoes** you sent in the Spring have turned out splendidly. **Table King** A 1 for quality and quantity; **Early Puritan** and **Thorburn** magnificent, rolling out of the ground like dumplings."— **Mr. J. STONE**, Exeter.

"I took 49 Prizes in all with your **Potatoes** last year. I had Second First Prize for collection of Potatoes two years consecutively."— **Mr. T. W. BEVERIDGE**, Wemyss.

"You have always supplied me with my **Seed Potatoes**, and successfully too, so I now write to give you my entire order for seeds required."— **Mr. E. A. SMITH**, Pennover.

"I am pleased to tell you the **Potatoes** you sent me last year turned out well. I took First Prize for the best collection, and First for the best twelve tubers."— **Mr. T. MORTIMER**, Upton.

SECOND EARLY VARIETIES (White).

	per 14 lb. s. d.	per 56 lb. s. d.	per cwt. s. d.
American Breadfruit or **Pride of Ontario.** An excellent variety ...	2 0	7 6	12 6
Matchless (Sutton). Round, second early variety, very free from disease, of fine quality, and a good keeper	3 6	12 6	—
Norfolk Hero (Daniels). A Kidney of superior excellence, the tubers being handsome, with clear skin; fine for exhibition, while its great productiveness and good cooking qualities should recommend it to every Potato grower ...	2 6	8 6	15 0
RURAL NEW YORKER, No. 2. The tubers are large and unusually smooth, eyes few and shallow, form oblong inclining to round, skin and flesh white, the latter being of superior quality; it is a very heavy cropper, and well deserves a trial ...	2 6	8 6	15 0
Sutton's Seedling. A white Kidney, eyes few and shallow, skin somewhat netted, very handsome, and of fine flavour, ripens at the same time as the Beauty of Hebron ...	2 6	8 6	15 0
Windsor Castle. An excellent variety, tubers oblong or pebble shaped, very heavy cropper, flesh firm, white, and of splendid quality ...	3 6	12 6	

MAIN CROP AND LATE VARIETIES (White).
DANIELS' TABLE KING.

DANIELS' TABLE KING. This remarkably handsome Potato has now been some time before the public. It is a second early and will be found a valuable market variety to follow the first earlies. The tubers are somewhat kidney-shaped, but many are nearly round. They are mealy when cooked and of a most excellent flavour. The eyes are few and quite even with the surface. Its dwarf habit (one foot) renders it a most desirable sort for all gardens, and its handsome appearance, combined with its great productiveness, will soon make it a favourite market variety. For exhibition it is first-class. Price, 14 lb. 2s. 6d., 56 lb. 8s. 6d., cwt. 15s.

EVIDENCE OF QUALITY.

From *JOURNAL OF HORTICULTURE*, November 5th, 1891.

A correspondent writes:—"**Daniels' Table King.** So far I must pronounce this variety the best of all. It is the most floury Potato I have seen in Ireland, and what is of equal importance it is of first-rate flavour, very prolific. In size and shape a gem for the exhibition table, while not a diseased tuber was found when lifting them.'

DANIELS' REMARKABLE. This variety was raised by us some few years since, and after repeated trials has proved itself a first-class cropping variety, a good keeper, and of splendid table quality. The tubers are of an oblong round shape, white, large, and handsome; a fine exhibition variety. Price, 14 lb. 3s. 6d., 56 lb. 12s. 6d., cwt. 21s.

DANIELS' GOLDEN FLOUR-BALL. A fine late yellow-fleshed Potato of handsome shape, a good keeper, and of fine quality late in the season. Price, 14 lb. 2s. 6d., 56 lb. 8s. 6d., cwt. 15s.

DANIELS' SPECIAL (*See Novelties*). Price, 7 lb. 3s., 14 lb. 5s., 56 lb. 18s.

	per 14 lb. s. d.	per 56 lb. s. d.	per cwt. s. d.
Abundance (Sutton's). A white round late variety, haulm robust, eyes few and shallow, excellent alike for exhibition and table purposes ...	2 6	8 6	15 0
Best of All (Sutton's). A fine maincrop variety, tubers flattish round, very handsome, eyes very shallow, flesh white, and of excellent table quality ...	3 6	12 6	21 0
Champion of the World, or Scotch Champion. A good kind for moist and heavy soils ...	2 0	7 0	14 0
Chiswick Favourite. First Class Certificate, Royal Horticultural Society. A splendid round, late variety; an enormous cropper ...	2 6	8 6	15 0
DANIELS' KING KIDNEY. A remarkably robust grower; and producing a very heavy crop of handsome, marketable tubers, of superior cooking quality. It is the best disease-resister that we know of, and a first-class kind for poor soils; and fine for exhibition ...	3 0	10 6	20 0
DANIELS' ROYAL NORFOLK RUSSET. This is one of the most remarkable Potatoes ever raised; the tubers are of medium size and roughly netted, eyes few and shallow, flesh white, fine grained, boils like a ball of flour, and of the finest flavour. Since sending this variety out we find it has been named by our Scotch friends "The Village Blacksmith" ...	5 6	*Very scarce.*	
Dunbar Regent. We have procured a limited quantity of this well-known variety, which is second to none for its grand cooking qualities ...	2 0	7 0	12 0
Harvester. Handsome oblong round, of fine appearance on the exhibition table, extra cropper and fine quality ...	2 6	8 6	15 0
The Celt. Tubers slightly oblong and flattish, eyes medium, flesh firm and mealy, very strong grower ...	2 6	8 6	15 0

Main Crop and Late Varieties (White) (continued).

DANIELS' UNIVERSAL.

EVIDENCE OF QUALITY.

"I like the **Universal** very much, as they are a nice size and good yielders." **Mr. FUTTER**, Tuttington.

"**Universal** is a good Potato and all that can be desired."— **Mr. A. STANNARD**, The Gardens, Coxford Abbey.

"I must say the **Universal** are all that can be desired, when cooked they are of a beautiful white floury nature."— **Mr. A. BOOTY**, Bottisham.

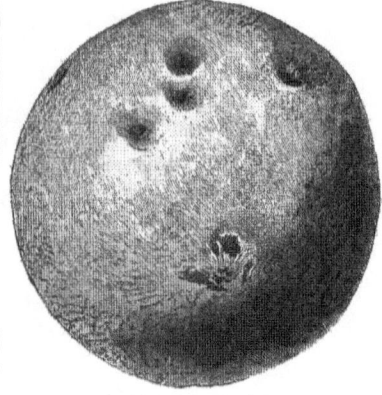

EVIDENCE OF QUALITY.

"I find **Daniels' Universal Potatoes** yield well, and have stood the disease better than any other sort I have previously grown, and I also find the **Table King** a good early Potato, and well worth cultivating."— **Mr. WM. BARNES**, Hindringham.

"The **Universal Potato** is a good cropper, and of excellent cooking quality." — **Mr. W. SELF**, Gunton Hall.

DANIELS' UNIVERSAL. New seedling Potato (1888). A round white variety, of the size and shape of a cricket ball; eyes few and shallow, skin slightly netted, flesh white and floury when cooked. A first-rate cropping variety, and an excellent keeper. We sent this variety out in 1888 for the first time, and the steadily increasing demand shows that it is giving general satisfaction to our customers.   Price, 14 lb. 2s. 6d., 56 lb. 8s. 6d., cwt. 15s.

DANIELS' DREADNOUGHT. New disease-resisting main crop variety. This magnificent Potato somewhat resembles the Magnum Bonum, but far excels that variety in vigour of constitution and enormous productiveness; grown side by side with Magnum Bonum it produced one third more tubers, of handsome shape and fine table quality.
          Price, 14 lb. 3s. 6d., 56 lb. 12s. 6d., cwt. 21s.

FUTURE FAME. A grand Seedling of the Magnum Bonum type, and, like that variety, a great disease-resister, but is at least a fortnight earlier, and a heavy cropper, and when cooked is white, dry, and mealy, and of faultless flavour. (As this variety is likely to prove one of the great food producers of the future, we recommend all growers to at once possess themselves of the stock.)   Price, 14 lb. 2s. 6d., 56 lb. 8s. 6d., cwt. 15s.

EVIDENCE OF QUALITY.

"Your **Dreadnought** is a grand cropper, free from disease. I planted it side by side with other varieties, which were all more or less diseased, but there is not a sign of it in Dreadnought."— **Mr. W. SHAW**, The Gardens, Heacham Hall.

"The **Future Fame Potatoes** are the best that grow. Cook well all the year round."— **Mr. J. TURNER**, Bourton.

"From **7 lbs.** of your **Future Fame Potatoes** I obtained a splendid sample of over 170 lbs."— **Mr. A. REBBIE**, Chipstead.

"I beg to inform you that the **Dreadnought Potatoes** I had from you yielded well; fine tubers and sound."— J. T. **KITCHING**, Esq., Bexhill.

"I have grown your **Daniels** and **Future Fame Potatoes**, both of which I consider first-class varieties."- **Mr. T. LINDLEY**, Epworth.

"The **Future Fame Potatoes** purchased from you last season have turned out well."- **Mr. S. MILLS**, Newport, Mon.

	per 14 lb.		per 56 lb.		per cwt.	
	s.	d.	s.	d.	s.	d.
Imperator. This is a most excellent variety, and is far superior to the Champion	2	0	7	6	11	0
Magnum Bonum. A well-known first-class main crop variety	2	0	7	0	14	0
Satisfaction. In shape it is almost round, or rather pebble-shaped, eyes upon the surface; a very heavy cropper, and of fine cooking quality	3	0	10	6	20	0
Schoolmaster. A well-known variety, tubers uniformly round and handsome. First Class Certificate, Royal Horticultural Society. Fine for exhibition	2	6	8	6	15	0
Snowdrop. Handsome Kidney, clear skin, eyes few and shallow; white and mealy when cooked. First Class Certificate, Royal Horticultural Society	2	6	8	6	15	0
The Bruce. A new Scotch variety; late Kidney, robust grower, of good quality, and very prolific ...	2	0	7	6	14	0
The Village Blacksmith (see **Royal Norfolk Russet**)	4	6	—		—	

FIRST EARLY VARIETIES (Coloured).

THE THORBURN. A new early American variety of the White Elephant type, and is said to be the best of all the early kinds, and will rapidly find a place in the front rank of the early market varieties.   Price, 14 lb. 2s. 6d., 56 lb. 8s. 6d., cwt. 15s.

	per 14 lb. s. d.	per 56 lb. s. d.	per cwt. s. d.
Beauty of Hebron. A well-known excellent variety	2 0	7 6	14 0
Daniels' First Early. A variety of the Early Rose type, but ripening ten days earlier than that well-known kind	2 6	8 6	15 0
DANIELS' EARLY CRIMSON FLOURBALL (*See Novelties*) 1 lb. 1s., 3 lb. 2s. 6d., 7 lb. 5s.	—	—	—
Early Gem. A fine first early of the American Rose type, but a heavier cropper; fine table quality	2 6	8 6	15 0
Early Rose. A well-known variety. Fine for early use on light soils	2 0	7 6	14 0
Early Sunrise. This is the true type of Early Rose; very early, and of excellent quality	2 0	7 6	14 0
Extra Early Vermont. A first-class early variety; fine for light soils	2 6	8 6	15 0

SECOND EARLY VARIETIES (Coloured).

Adirondack. Abundant cropper, late keeper, and of finest quality	2 6	8 6	15 0
Late Rose. A well-known variety of fine quality and productiveness	2 6	8 6	15 0
RED ELEPHANT. This is of the same robust constitution as the White Elephant, being of similar shape and habit, and an enormous cropper like that variety; will be found invaluable for light sandy soil, producing an abundant crop of fine quality tubers where many other best kinds would fail	2 6	8 6	13 0
WHITE ELEPHANT. The original and true stock	2 0	7 6	14 0

MAIN CROP AND LATE VARIETIES (Coloured).

Australian (Red Skin). A very large variety from Australia, resembling the old Red Skin Flourball, but larger and a heavier cropper	2 6	8 6	15 0
Edgcote Purple. A remarkably handsome deep purple Kidney; tubers very smooth, flattish, and straight. It is a good cropper, of splendid quality and flavour	2 6	8 6	15 0
Empress of India. A handsome oblong round coloured Kidney; skin rich purple, mottled with cream colour; flesh yellow, floury, and of fine flavour when cooked	3 0	10 6	—
Lord Tennyson (new). A very heavy cropper, tubers large, purple blotched, and of fine quality; good for exhibition. First Class Certificate, Royal Horticultural Society	3 0	10 6	—
NORFOLK BLACKBIRD (*See Novelties*) 1 lb. 1s., 3 lb. 2s. 6d., 7 lb. 4s. 6d.	8 0	—	—
Peerless Rose. A flat, smooth, very handsome Kidney-shaped Potato; eyes even with the skin; fine quality, and excellent for exhibition	4 0	14 0	—
PURPLE PRINCE (Daniels) (new). This variety was first offered in 1891; the tubers are round and of a bright purple, slightly shaded with crimson; it is a heavy cropper, and cooks well; for exhibition it cannot be surpassed	2 6	8 6	15 0
Queen of the Valley. A well-known coloured Round, sometimes flat in shape; exceedingly fine table quality	4 0	—	—
RED ROBIN (*See Novelties*) 1 lb. 1s., 3 lb. 2s. 6d., 7 lb. 5s.	—	—	—
Vicar of Laleham. Skin of a rich dark purple, good cropper, cooks well, and fine for exhibition	2 6	8 6	15 0

EVIDENCE OF QUALITY.

"The **Vegetable Seeds** and **Collection of Potatoes** I had from you gave the greatest satisfaction, better cannot be obtained anywhere else."—Mr. **R. BATTERBEE**, Crawley.

"Your Potatoes were the best at our show here last year."—Mr. **G. W. BRINDLEY**, Milford, Derby.

"In March last I bought of you one stone of your new Potatoes (The **Daniels**), they were taken up last week, and the produce was over bi stone and no disease. I consider this very good as my garden is well planted with fruit trees." **R. FITCH**, Esq., J.P., Heigham.

"I had two sacks of Potatoes from you, one the **Thorburn**, the other, **Daniels**, and they realised 20 sacks with which I was well satisfied." Mr. **C. RAYNER**, East Hoathly.

"I had an immense crop from your **Daniels** and **Thorburn** Potatoes." Mr. **J. MERRETT**, Malvern, Wells.

"The **Daniels** Potatoes are fine croppers and good quality. I took the prize at the show held on August Bank Holiday." Mr. **S. BINKS**, Haverhill.

NEW AMERICAN VARIETIES.

	per lb. s. d.
Bill Nye. A white Kidney; late, eyes very shallow; heavy cropper, and good keeper	1 0
Delaware. A valuable Potato; tubers round but inclined to oblong; grand cropper, and of excellent quality	1 0
Howes' Premium. Very early; round, skin pink, very handsome; flesh white	1 0
Livingstone's Standard. Early white Kidney; flesh white and floury when cooked; very productive	1 0
Munro County Prize. An oblong white Kidney, second early; flesh white; good cropper	1 0
New Queen. A seedling of the Beauty of Hebron, white Kidney, very early; flesh pure white; quality good	1 0
Polaris. Tubers somewhat oblong; eyes few and shallow, very early; heavy cropper, and of fine quality	1 0
Pride of the West. A flattish round red-skinned variety, medium late, unusually strong grower; heavy cropper	1 0
Brownell's Winner. The tubers large, long, oval, slightly flattened, are very smooth and handsome with few eyes. The colour is a light rose-pink; medium late; heavy cropper, and good quality	per 7 lb. 3s. 0 6
Late Puritan. This Potato is identical with Early Puritan in appearance, colour, and quality, and was originally found growing amongst this variety, but ripens much later, and is a heavier cropper	per 7 lb. 3s. 0 6

The Collection, ten varieties, 1 lb. each 7s. 6d., 3 lb. each 18s., 7 lb. each 30s.

POTATOES.

NEW AND SELECT VARIETIES FOR 1892.

DANIELS' RELIABLE.

NEW SEEDLING—DANIELS' 'RELIABLE' *(see engraving).* This is a handsome White Kidney of extra cooking qualities and most excellent cropper; its eyes are few and quite even with the surface. It is a second early, and will make a fine exhibition kind.
Price, 7 lb. 3s., 14 lb. 5s., 56 lb. 18s.

NEW SEEDLING—INDIAN PRINCE. This is a remarkably handsome Black Kidney, long, flat, and smooth. Although the colour is quite black, it is only skin deep, the tubers being beautifully white and floury when cooked; it is also a most excellent cropper, and of handsome appearance on the exhibition table.
Price, 1 lb. 1s., 7 lb. 6s., 14 lb. 10s. 6d.

NEW SEEDLING—COLONEL LONG. This handsome Kidney, raised at The Gardens, Hurts Hall, Saxmundham, the residence of Colonel Long, has proved itself to be possessed of so many excellent qualities that we have determined to offer it to the public. The tubers are of large size, smooth, long, and handsome; an exceedingly good cropper, floury, and of most excellent flavour when cooked. This variety should be in every collection.　　　　Price, 7 lb. 3s., 14 lb. 5s., 56 lb. 18s.

LYE'S SEEDLING. This variety was raised by Mr. James Lye, Market Lavington, and will be found a most excellent addition to any list of Potatoes. The tubers are very handsome, of a long White Kidney shape; it is an excellent cropper, good cooker; fine for exhibition. It took First Prize at Bath Show as a New Potato.　　　　Price, 7 lb. 2s. 6d., 14 lb. 4s., 56 lb. 14s.

EMPEROR FREDERICK. A fine exhibition Potato. The tubers are large handsome Kidney-shaped; skin a rich purple, mottled with crimson. It is a most excellent cropper; flesh white, dry, mealy, and of fine flavour when cooked *(see coloured illustration outside cover).* Price, 7 lb., 2s., 14 lb. 3s. 6d., 56 lb. 12s. 6d.

DANIELS' LONGKEEPER.

NEW SEEDLING—PRINCESS MAY. This is by far the handsomest Red Kidney ever raised, being a seedling from Edgcote Purple and Peerless Rose. The tubers are flat Kidney shape, eyes shallow, the skin being of a bright glossy red. The flesh is of excellent quality when cooked. It is a good cropper and invaluable in a collection of exhibition varieties *(see coloured illustration outside cover).*
Price, 1 lb. 1s., 3 lb. 2s. 6d., 7 lb., 5s.

DANIELS' LONGKEEPER. A fine red round variety of the Red Skin Flourball type, but a later keeper. This has been selected from many others for its good cropping and late keeping qualities. The tubers, when cooked, are white, firm, and dry, but not mealy. This kind of Potato is preferred by many to the very mealy kinds.
Price, 3 lb. 2s., 7 lb. 3s. 6d., 14 lb. 6s.

General Collection.

General Collection.

		per 7 lb. s. d.	per 14 lb. s. d.
Albert Victor	... Early white round; very prolific, good table quality	1 9	3 0
American Purple	... Purple kidney; good shape; fine for exhibition	1 9	3 0
Charter Oak ...	... Handsome white round, suffused with pink about the eyes; fine cropper, of good quality, maincrop	1 6	2 6
Clarke's Maincrop	... A well-known white kidney of great excellence	1 9	3 0
Cole's Favourite	... A handsome white kidney of fine quality; First Class Certificate R.H.S., maincrop variety	1 9	3 0
Crimson Beauty	... Handsome red kidney; fine exhibition kind; stock limited	2 6	4 6
Daniels' Advancer	... A second early white kidney; first class quality; good cropper	1 6	2 6
Epicure ...	... White round, good cropper, flesh yellow, and of fine quality	2 0	3 6
General Gordon (Daniels)	Round variety, tubers large, handsomely marked with purple; fine for exhibition	2 0	3 6
Hanworth Superior ...	Tubers pebble-shaped, skin white; an abundant cropper of excellent flavour	1 6	2 6
Maincrop Kidney	... White kidney of superior quality, good cropper	2 0	3 6
Napoleon	... Well-known red round variety, yellow flesh; fine cooking quality ...	1 6	2 6
President	... A large handsome kidney; heavy cropper; fine for exhibition	2 0	3 6
Perfect Peachblow	... Coloured round; good quality; useful for exhibition	1 6	2 6
Reading Giant	... A maincrop kidney; heavy cropper of fine quality	1 6	2 6
Reading Russet	... A red round variety; good quality; very good for exhibition	1 9	3 0
Red Fluke Seedling..	... Red round of superior merit	1 9	3 0
Superior (Burpee)	... A handsome kidney from America; heavy cropper and of fine quality ...	1 9	3 0

Many other choice varieties in stock, nearly every variety in commerce can be supplied.
POTATO SEED (from a fine collection), Early, Main Crop, and Late kinds, per packet 1s.

A CHANGE OF SEED ALWAYS PAYS.

Daniels' Superb Collections of the Choicest Seed Potatoes.

From General List, for Exhibition and Table Use.

DANIELS BROS.' long experience in the growth and selection of Seed Potatoes suitable for all purposes, and having by far the largest and best collection of any house in the Kingdom, enable them to give their customers many advantages not to be obtained elsewhere in the selection of sorts suitable to their particular soil and district, &c.

			3 lb. each. s. d.	7 lb. each. s. d.	14 lb. each. s. d.
Six choice varieties, Daniels Bros.' selection }		Early,	4 6	7 6	12 6
Twelve " " " }		Medium,	8 6	14 0	22 6
Eighteen " " " }		and Late.	12 0	20 0	33 0

50 distinct kinds, including all the newest, correctly named, one tuber
each 10s. 6d.; 1 lb. each £1 5s.

Each collection will be made up of distinct kinds correctly named. In all cases the selection must be left to DANIELS BROS., but customers will do well in ordering to give a list of the kinds they already possess, so that they may not get the same again; also state the nature of their soil, in order that we may send suitable kinds.

OUR STOCKS are true to name and free from DISEASE, all being carefully selected at time of growth, and afterwards hand-picked at least three or four times before being sent out, and all inferior or damaged tubers carefully discarded.

CARRIAGE FREE. All Orders for Potatoes to value of 10s. and upwards Free to any Station in the Eastern Counties. All Orders of 20s. value Free to any Railway Station or Steam Port in the United Kingdom. See also Terms on the front cover inside.

PARCEL POST. Six pounds of tubers can be sent by Parcel Post to any address in the Kingdom for 1s., and ten pounds for 1s. 6d. *extra for postage*, in addition to the cost of the Potatoes.

N.B.—Being large growers we can offer many kinds much cheaper by the Ton.

POTATO BAGS.—Good strong Bags can be supplied at 4d. each, to hold one bushel; 6d. each, to hold 1 cwt.; 1s. each, to hold one sack.

The amount for Bags should be added to remittance when ordering.

SEED POTATOES

Have for many years received our special attention; and we have always on hand many first-class varieties, unobtainable elsewhere, selected with great care from the hundreds of seedlings we annually raise, retaining only those of handsome shape, great productiveness, and good cooking qualities. Besides we are constantly adding to our collection all the best varieties raised by other growers. We have now the largest, most varied, and best collection in the world for market, exhibition, or family use. Being large growers, we can offer most of the leading kinds much cheaper by the ton. Customers requiring large quantities are kindly requested to get our special quotations.

NEW "MARGUERITE" DAHLIA.

DANIELS' "MARGUERITE" DAHLIA, FROM A PHOTOGRAPH.

OPINIONS OF THE PRESS.

From
*THE GARDENERS'
MAGAZINE,*
October 31st, 1891.

"The Single Dahlia named
Marguerite from Messrs.
Daniels Bros., Norwich, is
distinct, the colour white, and,
as shown in a bouquet, very
charming."

From *THE GARDEN,*
October 31st, 1891.

"Messrs. Daniels and Co.
sent a novel kind of Single
Dahlia (white) with narrow
petals, called **Marguerite.**"

From
*THE MIDDLESEX
COUNTY TIMES,*
December 12th, 1891.

"But many other curious
flowers and plants were exhibited, amongst them being
noticeable a fine stand of a
new variety of a white Single
Dahlia, the **Marguerite,**
shown by Messrs. Daniels Bros.,
the well-known Norwich
nurserymen and florists, and
so named from its star-like
petals and general similarity
to the Marguerite Daisy."

SINCE the introduction of the Dahlia into this country more than a hundred years since, it has sported into many different forms and colours, all of them more or less beautiful, so much so that it has been found necessary to divide them into distinct classes, as "singles," Pompon or Bouquet, Show, Fancy, Cactus, &c. Before the introduction of the beautiful Scarlet Cactus Juarezi with its bristling petals, nothing was tolerated but the most rotund and symmetrical forms. This is all changed, the bristling forms of the Cactus in its many beautiful colours fast gaining upon the public taste, in the same manner as the once despised ragged form of the Japanese Chrysanthemum.

In introducing this new and very distinct variety, we have decided to give it the name of "Marguerite," owing to its striking resemblance at a short distance to a large Marguerite Daisy. This will be found a most valuable addition to the white flowers now used for decorative purposes, it being admirably adapted alike to church and table decoration, and will be found exceedingly useful for all kinds of bouquets, wreaths, and crosses. This, the first of its kind, can only be looked upon as the harbinger; others of the same class in many beautiful and brilliant shades of colour have already been raised by us, and will follow in successive seasons. Bouquets made up of these and Maiden-hair Ferns have a very novel and charming appearance. We therefore have every confidence in introducing this variety, and it is sure to be highly appreciated by all lovers of flowers.

Price 2s. 6d. each; 3 for 6s. 6d.

FRUIT TREES AND ROSES.

We are large growers of choice Fruit Trees and Roses, which are a specialty of our business, and to meet the constantly increasing demand amongst our customers, we annually rear many thousands of Apples, Pears, Plums, Cherries, Peaches, Apricots, &c., besides many thousands of Hybrid Perpetual, Tea-scented, and other Roses. All are grown hardily, and our soil being especially favourable to their growth, the plants lift with abundance of fibrous root, a very essential requirement for their successful transplantation and after productiveness.

NEW APPLE VICAR OF BEIGHTON.

NEW APPLE—VICAR OF BEIGHTON.

We have much pleasure in introducing this fine Apple to the horticultural public, who, we feel sure, will highly appreciate its many good qualities. A seedling raised in the Vicarage Gardens at Beighton, Norfolk, it has proved itself one of the handsomest, most prolific, and best keeping apples in cultivation. The fruit is large and roundish, and when ripe of a deep bright crimson colour, mottled and striped with yellow and green, giving it the most beautiful appearance, which, if well kept, it retains till April or May; whilst its pale yellow flesh is of fine flavour, juicy, and all that can be desired in a first-class kitchen Apple. Will prove a most valuable sort for market growers on account of its very handsome appearance and excellent keeping qualities.

Dwarf Bushes or Maidens, each 2s. 6d.; Pyramids, each 5s.; Fine Standards, each 7s. 6d.

From **COLONEL SANDERSON**, Glenloggan.
Nov. 27th.
"The **Fruit Trees** have arrived in safety, and we are much pleased with them and with the admirable manner in which they were packed."

From **Mr. GEORGE BAKER**, Redan Hill, Aldershot.
Oct. 27th.
"The **Fruit Trees** arrived quite safe, and I am very pleased with them, they are far beyond my expectations, and I must say that, after dealing with your firm for sixteen years, I have never been disappointed with anything I have ordered from you."

From **Miss DALTON**, Bamford, Wigton.
"The **Fruit Trees** I had from you have done extremely well."

From **Mrs. WALKER**, Thornhill, N.B.
Oct. 27th.
"Mrs. Walker has had a splendid crop of very large Apples from the **Trees** sent her last by Messrs. Daniels, when those of the neighbourhood have had a very indifferent crop."

From **Mr. D. E. FANNER**, Cheam, Surrey.
Oct. 2nd.
"All the **Fruit Trees** I received from you are doing well; the Raspberries have been a picture, with very large fruit on them all."

From **Mr. LUDLOW**, Alcombe.
Nov. 25th.
"Mr. Ludlow begs to enclose cheque for account received yesterday. He is very much pleased with the **Fruit Trees** sent him."

DANIELS'
SUPERB STRAINS
of
Calceolaria hybrida,
Gloxinia hyb grandiflora
Pansies, Prize Blotched.
· 1892 ·

DANIELS BROS. NURSERYMEN & FLORISTS. NORWICH

GREAT·AND·INCREASING·SUCCESS·OF

DANIELS'

WORLD·FAMED FLOWER·SEEDS

Choice·Flower·Seeds·are·a·special feature·of·our·extensive·business·and·our reputation·for·their·superior·quality·is·World·Wide

EVIDENCE · OF · QUALITY

AUSTRALIA

AFRICA

CANADA

INDIA

NEW ZEALAND

FROM AUSTRALIA.

From Mr. W. CARTER, Hamilton, Victoria.

"The Seeds forwarded in August came duly to hand, and those sown have so far germinated splendidly, better than anything I have had previously from any Seedsman."

From Mr W. H. DODD, Kadina.

"I received the Seeds in June in good order, and plants are doing well."

From C. A. HIGGINS, Esq., Hamilton, Victoria.

"I have much pleasure in informing you that the produce from your Seeds gave great satisfaction, and gained First Prizes at three Shows."

From Mrs. C. STEWART, Sandhurst, Victoria.

"The Seeds I had from you last, gave great satisfaction, and shall be pleased if those now ordered turn out as well."

FROM SOUTH AFRICA.

From A. WEAKLEY, Esq., Queenstown, Cape of Good Hope.

"The Pansies from your Seed were very much admired, in fact, they were far better than any others here."

From Mr. J. PERRIN, Durban.

"The Balsams and Dianthus I have raised from your Seed have been magnificent and greatly admired."

FROM NORTH AMERICA.

From LAWRENCE PARKER, Esq., St. John's, Newfoundland.

"The Trees I had from you I am well pleased with; they have turned out most satisfactorily."

From Mr. HENRY BRAGG, Montreal.

"I was very much pleased with the Plants, especially the Primulas, which bloomed splendidly."

FROM SOUTH AMERICA.

From Senor J. W. A. HAMLY, Sante Fé.

"I brought out a few of your Seeds with me, two years ago, and they have done remarkably well, especially the Sweet Peas, which bear a profusion of the most gorgeous bloom."

From The GOVERNMENT BOTANIST, Trinidad.

"In reference to the Plants, the last transaction was a great success, and is, I think, a very great triumph of horticultural ingenuity. I should esteem it a favour if you would repeat the compliment."

FROM INDIA.

From Major HALEMAN, Trevandrum, Madras Presidency.

"I am much pleased with the prompt manner in which you have complied with my request, and the selection of Seeds you have sent seem remarkable for the price."

From A. P. WEBB, Esq., Meerut, N.W.P.

"I must give you credit for having enabled me to possess the best Balsams, best Petunias, and best Portulacas that I have ever seen in any garden or anywhere else."

From The DEPUTY COMMISSIONER, Mysore Commission, Bangalore.

"I must not forget to tell you that the Asters this year were splendid, better than any I have ever seen, also the Phlox, amongst which there were some new colours."

From The CHIEF INSPECTOR OF POLICE AND FORESTS, Bangalore.

"My Dianthus were of wonderful brilliancy and variety of colouring, the Mimulus also were beautiful; the Phlox Drummondi were excellent and of choice variety, and the Gloxinias and Cyclamens were very good."

FROM NEW ZEALAND.

From Mr. T. L. PRIME, Auckland.

"I beg to thank you for the choice selection of Seeds received from you: the Calceolaria produced some remarkably fine flowers."

From Mr. C. G. WARD, Dillmanstown West Coast.

"I was very pleased with your Gloxinia Seed, the flowers were very beautiful, and drew visitors from far and near to see them."

From G. MILLAR, Esq., Roslyn.

"I am very much pleased with the Begonias you sent me last year, and have taken five out of six prizes at our last show."

From Mr. J. O. JOSLING, Rangiori, Canterbury.

"The Flower Seeds sent last year came out in splendid order, every variety growing well. The Asters, Phloxes, and Dahlias were magnificent, and much admired."

From Mr G. M. SMALL, Christchurch.

"I have looked through dozens of Catalogues, but have not seen one that appears to do business so straightforward as your firm, this is saying a great deal. I know from experience that your Seeds are the best obtainable."

From Mr. FRANCIS H. RICHMOND, Awatere.

"I am pleased to say that the Seeds I have had from you previously have given me entire satisfaction."

In addition to the above, we have many customers in Canada, British Columbia, United States, Brazil, Falkland Islands, Egypt, Ceylon, Straits Settlements, China, Japan, and other parts, besides all countries in Continental Europe.

Floral Novelties for Spring 1892.

NEW COMET ASTER. PURE WHITE.

ASTERS.

COMET, PURE WHITE. We have much pleasure in offering this beautiful variety, which is undoubtedly one of the grandest novelties of the season. The flowers, which are larger and more perfectly double than those of the other varieties, are of the most exquisite pure glossy satiny white, and the petals being longer and more twisted, give them a peculiar and elegant appearance. The blooms closely resemble a large-flowered, pure white, Japanese Chrysanthemum. This is a splendid novelty that cannot be too highly recommended for exhibition or decorative purposes.
Per packet 1s. 6d.

BALL OR JEWEL, ROSE AND WHITE. A very handsome variety, with large densely double flowers, which are so symmetrically incurved as to form a perfect ball or globe. The colour of the flower is a lovely deep rose, the petals being edged with white. Per packet 1s.

MIGNONETTE.

RED MAMMOTH. A very fine red variety of the largest flowering Mignonette; the plants are distinguished by their robust habit of growth, and their exceedingly bright and large spikes of deliciously scented reddish coloured flowers.
Per packet 1s.

BEGONIAS, STRIPED-FLOWERED TUBEROUS-ROOTED.

BEGONIA TUBEROSA VITTATA (*see illustration*). An entirely distinct and novel class of Striped-flowered Begonias, combining both attractiveness and originality ; with the exception of white all the colours common to the older varieties, with the addition of a rich chrome-yellow, are comprised in this new class, and the flowers are marked or striped after the manner of a Carnation, with a great variety of pleasing shades of white, red, and yellow, which particularity is apparent even in the flower-buds. The seed offered will produce at least 45 per cent. of plants with flowers striped in the way described. Per packet 1s. 6d.

CARDINAL POPPY (*Papaversomniferum nanum fl. pl.*)

This fine novelty, in the dwarf robust and compact habit of its growth, differs entirely from all other Poppies. The plant attains a height of about 18 inches, is furnished with deeply-cut dark green foliage, and throws up ten or twelve enormous and very double flowers, colour a glowing scarlet on a white ground. This brilliant and effective annual it is predicted, will, on account of its extreme showiness, soon be in great request. Per packet 1s.

ZINNIA, NEW DOUBLE STRIPED.

SCARLET AND GOLD. A distinct and splendid strain. The very large and perfectly-formed double flowers are of a pure golden-yellow colour, elegantly striped with brilliant scarlet ; the effect produced by the mixture of these colours is very fine, and makes this novelty one of the most valuable of the year. Per packet 1s. 6d.

TULIP POPPY (*Papaver glaucum*).

A quite new and splendid annual from Armenia. The plant rises to a height of from 12 to 14 inches, and produces well above the bluish-green foliage fifty or sixty large and splendid flowers of the most vivid scarlet imaginable. The two outer petals of the flower bear a similarity to a saucer, in which are set two erect petals of the same colour, forming a pouch-like receptacle, enclosing and seemingly protecting the anthers. It commences blooming early in June, and flowers abundantly and in uninterrupted succession for a period of six or eight weeks. Sown where the plants are to bloom, the minute seeds lie several weeks before germinating, sown on a hot-bed it comes up in about eight days. Per packet 1s. 6d.

GLOXINIA HYBRIDA GRANDIFLORA.

CORONA (Benary). Splendid new hybrid, referable to the class of French spotted or dotted Gloxinia and to the very finest of which it will in respect both to size and beauty of flower form a worthy companion. Its distinguishing characteristics are enormous blooms, 3 to 4 inches across, with six, and often seven, divisions or lobes, and a large richly-veined throat of deep violet red, passing into a beautiful indigo towards the orifice, this colour gradually disappears, and the pure white outer ground is marked with innumerable dark blue dots. To these merits of size and handsome colouring may be added that the Gloxinia "Corona" comes as true from seed. Per packet 1s. 6d.

Good Things of Recent Introduction.

BEGONIAS, NEW STRIPED.

CARNATIONS.

MARGARET. A fine new strain of these popular flowers, and one that will prove of immense value alike to the grower for market and the amateur. The seed produces at least eighty per cent. of fine double flowers, and sown in February or March on a gentle heat may be had in bloom within four months of coming up, and will furnish an abundance of beautiful flowers throughout the summer. Per packet 1s. 6d.

NICOTIANA COLOSSEA (New Giant Tobacco).

A strikingly handsome ornamental plant of imposing appearance. It grows upwards of 8 feet in height, with leaves 3½ feet long, by 2½ inches wide, and planted singly or in groups is very effective and picturesque. Sow in March or April under glass, and plant out in May.
Per packet 1s. 6d.

GODETIAS.

DUKE OF FIFE. Intensely rich satiny crimson, blooms of fine form and substance, the individual blooms measuring 4 to 4½ inches across, with perfect habit of plant. A magnificent and valuable addition to our hardy annuals. Received an Award of Merit from the Royal Horticultural Society, September 9th, 1890. Per packet 6d. & 1s.

DUCHESS OF FIFE. A most superb variety of the same fine habit of growth as the preceding, and bearing equally large flowers. The colour, however, is a lovely satiny white, each petal being distinctly marked by a brilliant carmine blotch. The blooms are produced in the greatest profusion, and for a long period the plants have the most charming appearance. These superb annuals are quite hardy, and should be considered indispensable in every flower garden. Duchess of Fife has been awarded a First Class Certificate by the Royal Horticultural Society during the past season. Per packet 6d. & 1s.

ARNEBIA CORNUTA.

A new and charming Asiatic annual, discovered by Dr. Regel. The plant attains a height of about two feet, is much branched, and furnished with linear oblong leaves. Its curious and exceedingly beautiful flowers expand daily in succession, and are produced on each branch. They are slightly smaller than a shilling, of a pleasing rich yellow, and marked with five large black spots; the latter turn, the second day, to a deep maroon, the third day the colour vanishes and becomes a clear pure yellow. The *Arnebia cornuta* flowers with profusion during the whole of the Summer, and one hundred spikes of flowers may often be seen on one plant; its flowers, cut and placed in water, retain their freshness for more than a week, whilst the plant is highly effective for the garden. Sow the seed in February or March on a gentle heat, and plant out in April or May on rather poor soil. Per packet 1s. 6d.

GLOXINIA HYBRIDA GRANDIFLORA.

DEFIANCE. A grand new Gloxinia of the *hybrida erecta* type, bearing magnificent upright flowers of the most intense glowing crimson scarlet colour; the edges of the petals are delicately fringed or wavy, giving the individual blooms the most charming appearance, whilst its great beauty is much enhanced by its rich dark velvety-green foliage with pretty silvery white venation. This superb variety comes quite true from seed, and has proved a splendid acquisition. Per packet 1s. 6d.

PANSY, NEW BEDDING.

METEOR. This splendid new Pansy is of a novel and most attractive tint of colour, and will be found most useful and effective for groups and bedding. The colour is a bright terracotta red, which in the sunshine throws a most striking fiery reflex such as is quite novel in Pansies. The medium-sized flowers are of good shape and substance, and are produced very freely. Per packet 1s. 6d.

ASTER.

SNOWBALL or PRINCESS. An exquisitely beautiful variety, growing about one foot high, and producing quite a profusion of pure white handsomely imbricated flowers. This will make a capital pot plant, and be of great value where cut flowers are in demand. Per packet 1s. 6d.

CHRYSANTHEMUM ANNUUM.

NEW DOUBLE-FLOWERED HYBRIDS. A new and splendid race of the popular Annual Chrysanthemums. The flowers are very double, and remarkable for their brilliant and varied colours, which range from white and yellow to the richest crimsons and purples, with all the intermediate shades of rose, lilac, &c. Per packet 1s.

COLEUS.

NEW LARGE-LEAVED HYBRIDS. This is a grand strain of large-leaved and brilliantly coloured varieties, invaluable for the decoration of the greenhouse or conservatory. The seed offered has been carefully hybridised, and will produce a splendid variety of beautiful foliage. Per packet 2s. 6d.

POPPIES.

NEW SHIRLEY. A magnificent class, bearing large single flowers of the most charming and varied colours, and which last for a long time when cut and placed in water. The plants continue in bloom for a long period; highly recommended. Per packet 6d. & 1s.

SNOWDRIFT. A valuable and beautiful variety from the United States. The plants grow only about two feet high, and the large pure white delicately fringed flowers may be best compared to Japanese Chrysanthemums. This is a very showy plant for the garden, whilst the flowers are first-class for cutting. Per packet 6d.

New Florists' Flowers, &c., for 1892.

NEW PINK, HER MAJESTY.

NEW ZONAL PELARGONIUMS.
(PEARSON'S 1891.)

AYESHA. Salmon, suffused with warm shade of orange, lighter centre; beautifully formed flower, and very free blooming. Each 1s. 6d.

CONDE. Deep crimson scarlet, shaded plum colour; a fine variety in the style of *Falstaff*, but better colour and constitution. Each 1s. 6d.

CYCLOPS. Very dark rich crimson, smooth well formed flower, with distinct white eye; plant of dwarf habit and very free. Each 1s. 6d.

ERIC. Purple scarlet, beautifully shaded, white eye, large well formed flower, smooth, and good substance. Each 1s. 6d.

ETHEL PELTON. Beautifully shaded flower, with tints of pink, orange, and cerise; the largest and finest flower we have raised in this class. Each 1s. 6d.

ETNA. Rich crimson scarlet, suffused with plum colour, wonderfully free flowering, very effective variety. Each 1s. 6d.

HECLA. Crimson scarlet, immense truss, large bold pip, of fine shape and substance. Each 1s. 6d.

JULIET. Ground colour salmon pink, shaded rosy pink and orange, a charming mixture of colour, habit dwarf and free. Each 1s. 6d.

MIDSUMMER. Pale salmon, lighter edge, a lovely delicate shade, flowers large and finely formed; received an award of merit from the R.H.S. Each 1s. 6d.

PROSERPINA. Salmon, shaded orange, fine well formed flower, free flowering variety of good habit. Each 1s. 6d.

REV. H. JOHNSON. Very dark crimson, flower larger and better shape than any dark variety yet distributed; very fine truss, habit of plant good. Each 1s. 6d.

SHIRLEY HIBBERD. Rich scarlet, shaded plum colour, immense truss, individual pips also very large and fine; habit dwarf and spreading, will be a grand exhibition plant. Each 1s. 6d.

One each the above twelve superb varieties, 15s.
Six superb varieties, our selection from the above, 8s.

GRAND NEW HAIRY-PETALLED CHRYSANTHEMUMS.

W. A. MANDA. A most beautiful variety of the Incurved Japanese type, and with the same hirsute character as *Mrs. Alpheus Hardy* and *Louis Boehmer*, but in a mere marked degree, whilst the petals are broader and the whole flower is of better form. The colour is a beautiful deep chrome or golden-yellow throughout, and the plant, which is of a good dwarf strong habit of growth, is a profuse bloomer. This is a flower of exquisite beauty and one that will become highly popular.
Strong plants in April, each 5s., or three for 12s. 6d.

H. BALLANTINE. This is another superb variety of the "Hairy Family." The flowers are large, well formed, and of a beautiful soft terra-cotta or bronzy colour, the outer petals changing to a delicate straw-yellow. The plant is of strong habit like *Louis Boehmer*, whilst it is a free bloomer and easily managed. Will prove a most valuable addition to the Incurved Japanese section.
Strong plants in April, each 4s., or three for 10s. 6d.

NEW GARDEN PINK—HER MAJESTY

We have much pleasure in drawing attention to this charming novelty, which is far away the finest and best White Garden Pink in cultivation. The plants are of sturdy compact growth, the flowers are very large, resembling those of a Carnation, pure white, and of the most delicious fragrance. Splendid as a cut flower, and a first-class variety for forcing. Has been awarded nine First Class Certificates.
Each 1s. 6d., or three for 4s.

GRAND NEW PELARGONIUMS.

M. GUNTHER (Zonal.) Full double flower, of large size and excellent form, colour a rich and brilliant carmine-crimson; plant of dwarf sturdy growth, splendid variety. Each 3s. 6d.

THEODORE DE BANVILLE (Zonal). Fine double flowers, colour a brilliant orange-scarlet; a very distinct and telling variety. Each 3s. 6d.

G. GOESCHKE (Zonal). A very fine dwarf-growing variety, bearing fine trusses of large perfectly double flowers, of an intense deep blood scarlet colour; superb. Each 3s. 6d.

LOUIS MAYET (Ivy-leaved). Very large and splendidly formed perfectly double flowers, colour a bright rosy purple; extra fine. Each 3s. 6d.

EBLOUISANT (Ivy-leaved). Very large semi-double flowers, colour a brilliant fiery scarlet; splendid showy variety. Each 3s. 6d.

SIR RICHARD WALLACE (Ivy-leaved). Beautifully formed perfectly double flowers, colour a lovely rosy-carmine; a very free flowering and charming variety. Each 3s. 6d.

One each above six superb varieties, 17s. 6d.
One each any three varieties, 9s. 6d.

CALLA ÆTHIOPICA—LITTLE GEM.

A charming miniature variety of the well-known Arum Lily, growing only about one foot high, and bearing flowers of a purer white than those of the old variety. This will be found a pretty and easily grown plant, well suited for window or conservatory decoration, and especially useful where cut flowers are in demand. Special Certificate, Royal Horticultural Society. Each 2s. 6d. and 3s. 6d.

LILIUM WALLICHIANUM SUPERBUM.

A magnificent variety growing to the height of four to five feet, and producing very large trumpet flowers of a beautiful creamy yellow colour, and deliciously scented. Will thrive in a sheltered position in the garden, and is a splendid variety for the greenhouse or conservatory. Each 3s. 6d.

Daniels' Superb Prize Asters.

We are justly celebrated for our magnificent strains of English, French, and German Asters, which form an important branch of our Flower Seed business, and would mention that our seeds of those having been grown especially for our retail trade may be relied on as the very finest procurable.

Cultivation of French and German Asters.

When well grown nothing can exceed the chaste loveliness and exquisite colour-blendings of a nicely arranged bed of choice Asters, and certainly no plant can be more easily raised and grown to perfection. The principal types of form are represented in the Pæony-flowered, having noble blooms with long incurved petals; the Victorias, with their beautifully imbricated and perfect flowers; the tasselled, as shown in the Chrysanthemum-flowered; and the quilled, or Globe-flowered. As a rule Asters should not be sown before the first week in April, and to ensure a succession of fine bloom another sowing should be made in about a fortnight; and a final sowing about the second week in May. These latter, although they will not probably produce such fine blooms as those sown earlier, will be found exceedingly useful for planting in any out-of-the-way place for furnishing a late supply of cut-flowers. Sow the seed in boxes or pans of light rich soil, covering very lightly, and after giving a gentle watering, place under glass where the young plants, when they come up, can have full benefit of sun and air. As soon as large enough to handle, the earlier sown plants should be pricked out in boxes or pans of good rich soil, and placed in a light and airy position under glass to strengthen. In about three weeks, if fairly attended to, these will be found to have made nice sturdy plants with good tufts of fibrous roots, and which, if carefully transplanted to their blooming quarters, will grow on without a check. Asters will thrive and flower well in almost any good garden soil, but if really fine blooms be required for exhibition, &c., it is advisable to have the ground well broken up, and a good quantity of thoroughly decayed manure worked in. The healthy growth of the plants, and the development of fine blooms, are greatly assisted by occasional applications of weak liquid manure up to the time of the plants showing the flower, when it should be discontinued, and the buds of those intended for exhibition thinned out to three or four on a plant, generally removing the centre bud; and neat stakes should be placed to the taller-growing varieties requiring support.

Daniels' Improved Pæony-flowered Perfection.

These Asters are of the greatest perfection, producing noble flowers of the most perfect Pæony form, and in a great variety of beautiful and brilliant colours. A decided improvement on the old form of Pæony-flowered Aster usually sent out, and are invaluable for exhibition. Have been awarded numerous First Prizes during the past season.

			s.	d.						s.	d.
1	An assortment of 16 splendid vars.		4	6	8	Dark scarlet and white	...	... per pkt.	1	0
2	,, ,, 12 ,,		3	6	9	Dark purple violet	...	... ,,	1	0
3	,, ,, 6 ,,		2	0	10	Pure white	...	... ,,	1	0
4	Brilliant crimson	...	per pkt. 1	0	11	Dark blood red	...	... ,,	1	0
5	Sky blue ...	...	,, 1	0	12	Splendid mixed ...	...	... ,,	1	0
6	Delicate rose	...	,, 1	0	13	,,		smaller pkt.	0	6
7	Light blue and white	...	,, 1	0						

Daniels' Improved Victoria.

A truly magnificent class, growing to the height of about eighteen inches, and producing an abundance of perfectly double and beautifully imbricated flowers, which frequently measure four and a half to five inches across. The plants are of a handsome pyramidal form, and when grown for exhibition should be planted eighteen inches apart.

			s.	d.						s.	d.
14	An assortment of 16 beautiful vars.		4	6	19	Dark crimson and white	...	... per pkt.	1	0
15	,, ,, 12 ,,		3	6	20	Bright rose	...	... ,,	1	0
16	,, ,, 8 ,,		2	6	21	Rich purple	...	... ,,	1	0
17	Dark crimson	...	per pkt. 1	0	22	Finest mixed	...	... ,,	1	0
18	Pure white	...	,, 1	0	23	,,	...	smaller pkt.	0	6

Daniels' Dwarf Perfection.

A quite new and superb strain of beautiful varieties. The plants grow only about twelve or fifteen inches high, with stiff upright stems and branches, and form handsome circular bushes. The flowers are of immense size, perfectly double, imbricated, and of the most beautiful form. This will be found a grand strain for garden decoration, for bedding out, or for exhibition.

			s.	d.						s.	d.
24	An assortment of 6 superb varieties	...	3	6	27	Pure white	...	... per pkt.	1	0
25	Crimson ...	...	per pkt. 1	0	28A	Dark blue	...	... ,,	1	0
26	Rose	...	,, 1	0	28	Choicest mixed	...	... ,,	1	6

DANIELS' SUPERB   PRIZE ASTERS.

1. COMET.   2 & 3. DANIELS' IMPROVED VICTORIA.   4. IMPROVED PÆONY-FLOWERED.
5. DANIELS' PRIZE QUILLED.

Daniels' Superb Prize Asters.

ASTER—NEW COMET.

The New Japanese Chrysanthemum-flowered Aster "COMET."

(See illustration.)

NEW and extremely beautiful class of the same height and habit as the Dwarf Pæony Perfection Aster, forming fine, regular pyramids twelve to fifteen inches high, and covered profusely with large double flowers. The shape of the latter deviates from all classes of Asters in cultivation, and resembles very closely a large-flowered Japanese Chrysanthemum, the petals being long and somewhat twisted or wavy-like curled, are recurved from the centre of the flower to the outer petals in such a regular manner as to form a loose but still dense semi-globe. Well grown plants produce from twenty-five to thirty perfectly double flowers, measuring from 3½ to 4½ inches in diameter, and are very handsome in appearance.

			s.	d.
29	An assortment of six beautiful varieties	...	2	6
30	Pure white (new). Beautiful ... ... per pkt.		1	6
31	Rose and white, splendid variety ... ,,		1	0
32	Light blue and white, beautiful ... ,,		1	0
33	Choicest mixed seed ... ... ,,		1	0

Dwarf Chrysanthemum-flowered

THIS fine class is a decided acquisition. It commences blooming when other Asters are off, and is invaluable for a late display; its height is only nine inches, and in consequence of its fine dwarf habit of growth it is admirably suited for beds, edgings, pots, &c.

			s.	d.
34	An assortment of 12 fine varieties	...	3	0
35	,, ,, 8 ,,		2	0
36	Fiery scarlet ... ... per pkt.		1	0
37	Pure white ... ... ,,		1	0
38	Choicest mixed ... ... ,,		1	0
39	,, ... smaller pkt.		0	6

Daniels' Improved Prize Quilled.

A FINE strain of splendid varieties, producing beautifully formed, perfectly double flowers of the most charming colours. First-class for exhibition.

			s.	d.				s.	d.
40	An assortment of 12 choice varieties	...	2	6	42	Choicest mixed ... ... per pkt.		1	0
41	,, ,, 6 ,,	...	1	6	43	,, ... smaller pkt.		0	6

NEW DWARF QUEEN. A novel and beautiful class not more than ten inches high, with large double imbricated flowers. Splendid.

| 44 | Pure white ... ... per pkt. | 1s. | 0d. |
| 45 | Brilliant crimson ... ... ,, | 1s. | 0d. |

VICTORIA NEEDLE. Very beautiful varieties of the most brilliant colours, all the blooms being handsomely quilled.

| 46 | Six fine varieties ... ... | 2s. | 0d. |
| 47 | Choicest mixed ... ... per pkt. | 1s. | 0d. |

WASHINGTON (new). Very large splendid flowers, extra double, and exceedingly valuable for exhibition purposes.

| 48 | Six choice varieties ... ... | 2s. | 6d. |
| 49 | Choicest mixed ... ... per pkt. | 1s. | 0d. |

DWARF VICTORIA. A fine new strain, having all the symmetry and beauty of form of flower and habit of plant as Victoria Perfection, but growing only ten inches in height.

| 50 | An assortment of 6 beautiful varieties ... | 2s. | 6d. |
| 51 | Choicest mixed ... ... per pkt. | 1s. | 0d. |

GIANT EMPEROR. Remarkably fine flowers, frequently measuring six inches across, perfectly double.

| 52 | An assortment of 8 fine varieties ... | 2s. | 6d. |
| 53 | Choicest mixed ... ... per pkt. | 1s. | 0d. |

SNOWBALL or PRINCESS. An exquisitely beautiful variety, growing about one foot high, and producing quite a profusion of pure white handsomely imbricated flowers. This will make a capital pot plant, and be of great value where cut flowers are in demand.

| 54 | Per packet ... ... | 1s. | 0d. |

IMBRICATED POMPONE. Beautiful little plants about nine inches high, bearing a profusion of brilliantly coloured, perfectly double flowers, all of which have conspicuous white centres; very charming.

| 55 | An assortment of 8 beautiful varieties ... | 2s. | 6d. |
| 56 | Choicest mixed ... ... per pkt. | 1s. | 0d. |

IMPROVED PYRAMIDAL BOUQUET. Only one foot high, and branches vigorously; one plant often produces one hundred blooms, all perfectly double.

| 57 | An assortment of 8 choice varieties ... | 1s. | 6d. |
| 58 | Choicest mixed ... ... per pkt. | 0s. | 6d. |

DWARF PÆONY-FLOWERED. A beautiful new class of Pæony-flowered Aster with the same form of incurved perfect flowers as the older varieties, but with a much more compact and handsome growth, the plants reaching only twelve inches in height.

| 59 | An assortment of 8 choice varieties ... | 2s. | 6d. |
| 60 | Choicest mixed ... ... per pkt. | 1s. | 0d. |

CROWN or COCARDEAU. A brilliant and showy class of beautiful varieties growing about fifteen inches high, the flowers all having conspicuous white centres.

| 61 | An assortment of 6 choice varieties ... | 1s. | 6d. |
| 62 | Choice mixed seed ... ... per pkt. | 0s. | 6d. |

"MIGNON," PURE WHITE. A very beautiful variety somewhat resembling the Victoria. The flowers are of the most refined form, and of the purest white; splendid for cutting.

| 63 | Per packet ... ... | 1s. | 0d. |

Daniels' Superb Ten-week Stocks

From Mr. J. YOXALL,
Coppenhall.

Feb. 25th.
"I took First Prize for my Flower
Garden last year. The Stocks and
Asters were splendid, and contributed
much towards my success."

From Mr. R. TRACEY,
Orange Gardens, Pembroke.

Feb. 18th.
"I am very pleased to inform you,
that I have taken First Prize for the
past two years with Stocks grown
from your Seeds."

DANIELS' LARGE-FLOWERED TEN-WEEK STOCKS.

From Mr. C. CARTER, Hamilsdon.

Sept. 11th.
"The Ten-week Stocks, Asters, and Zinnia Seed I obtained from you
in the Spring have produced some splendid double flowers which have been admired
by all."

From Mr. J. H. NEWTON, Colwyn Bay.

Feb. 23rd.
"I beg to inform you that I am very pleased with your Giant Ten-week
Stocks, which have been greatly admired by all who saw them ; visitors calling to
know where I got the Seeds from."

From Mr. A. C. BAXTER, Plumstead.

Jan. 30th.
"I had a splendid show of Stocks last year from your Seed ; the centre spikes
were ten inches long, four and a half inches broad, and the colours exceedingly choice."

From Mr. J. J. LEE, Plumstead.

Feb. 5th.
"The Stocks I had from one of your sixpenny packets last year turned out
splendid, fully 80 per cent. of the flowers being double, of large size, and brilliant
colours."

Daniels' Superb Ten-week Stocks.

Cultivation of Stocks.

THE superb Large-flowered and other varieties of this beautiful class of annuals are all highly desirable, and we may say indispensable, for the Summer decoration of our gardens. Planted in groups or beds, such choice colours as scarlet, white, rose, purple, yellow, &c., are very telling in their effect with other plants, to say nothing of their delicious perfume; whilst large beds planted with some twelve or more distinct colours in carefully arranged lines, are very charming, and continue in their full beauty for a long period. The seed may be sown at any time from February to the end of April, but as a rule, the earlier the better. Sow in pans or boxes of light rich soil, scattering the seeds thinly and evenly (about four to the square inch is sufficiently thick), cover very lightly with fine soil, and give a gentle watering; after which place the boxes or pans under hand-lights, or in a frame close to the glass. Keep close and shaded for a few days, and when the young plants come up gradually admit air on fine warm days. Prick out to strengthen, as soon as the young plants can be handled, in pots, and place under hand-lights or in a frame close to the glass; shade from strong sun, and when established give plenty of air on fine days. Plant out about the end of April, or beginning of May, in good rich soil, nine inches or one foot apart in groups, beds, &c., as required. It is an excellent plan to pot up a score or so and grow on in small pots; these are very handy when coming into flower to replace any with single blooms which have shown on the borders and been removed. For succession sow in April and May under hand-lights, or in a sheltered place on a warm border, and plant out when ready. In planting out select, if possible, warm showery weather, and keep the plants well shaded and watered for a few days. A few sown in July and grown in pots will make nice plants for the greenhouse or conservatory in Winter. In planting

out seedlings of Ten-week and other Stocks, it is customary with many to plant only the strongest and throw away the weaker as useless. This should never be done, as the weaker and smaller plants of a batch of seedlings almost invariably produce a large percentage of double flowers, and the "fine plants," which will be found to produce but single flowers. If care be therefore taken to select in preference plants of a medium size, and having a nice tuft of fine fibrous roots, a much larger percentage of double flowers will be the result than if the plants are put out one and all indiscriminately, or the strongest only are selected.

Intermediate Stocks.—These are exceedingly useful for the greenhouse, or for window decoration in Winter and Spring. They do not require artificial heat, and are easily grown if protected from too severe frost. Sow the seeds in July or August, and prick the young plants into five inch pots, three in a pot, using a light rich soil, and place them in a cool frame or pit. Keep fairly moist and give plenty of air; liquid manure may be given with advantage at intervals, till the plants bloom.

Brompton Stocks.—The best time for sowing seeds of these is in May, and the most suitable place for planting out is where they receive some amount of shelter from severe frosts. Open spaces on shrubbery borders, or any similar position in the garden, will suit them well if they get a fair amount of warm sunshine, and the ground is tolerably rich. Sow the seeds thinly on beds of fine soil, and prick out six inches apart to strengthen, when the young plants have made three or four leaves. These will make nice sturdy plants for transferring to their blooming quarters in August or September; or the young plants may be taken from the seed bed, and planted out at once where intended to flower, if the ground is ready.

Daniels' Large-flowered Dwarf Ten-week.

This is undoubtedly the finest strain of Ten-week Stocks ever raised, and, where space is limited, should always be grown in preference to others. It is the same in height as the old Ten-week, and with the same compact habit of growth; but its flowers when well grown are nearly double the size, of great substance and brilliancy, with the most delicious fragrance.

						s.	d.						s.	d.
64	24 Superb varieties	...	...	...	...	5	6	72	Canary yellow	...	...	... per pkt.	1	0
65	18	,,	...	...	...	4	6	73	Light blue or mauve	...	...	,,	1	0
66	12	,,	...	...	...	3	0	74	Bright rose	...	...	,,	1	0
67	6	,,	...	...	...	1	6	75	Brilliant crimson rose	...	...	,,	1	0
68	Deep scarlet	...	...	per pkt.	1	0	76	New dark blood red	...	...	,,	1	0
69	Dark purple	...	...	,,	1	0	77	Improved sulphur yellow	...	...	,,	1	0
70	Pure white	...	...	,,	1	0	78	Choicest mixed	...	...	,,	1	0
71	Purple carmine	...	...	,,	1	0	79	,,	,,	...	smaller pkt.	0	6

Daniels' Giant Perfection Ten-week.

A GRAND class of tall-growing beautiful varieties. The plants attain a height of 2½ feet, are of a handsome pyramidal form, and throw up long central spikes of large, beautifully double flowers. This is an exceedingly fine strain that we can highly recommend.

					s.	d.						s.	d.
80	Fiery crimson	...	...	per pkt.	1	0	82A	Pure white	...	...	per pkt.	1	0
81	An assortment of 6 superb varieties	...	2	0	82	Choicest mixed	...	...	per pkt. 6d. and	1	0

Dwarf German Ten-week.

A FINE and compact-growing class, with handsome double flowers of the most beautiful colours and delicious fragrance.

					s.	d.						s.	d.
83	An assortment of 12 choice varieties	...	2	0	85	Choicest mixed	...	...	... per pkt.	1	0
84	,,	,,	6	,,	,,	1	6	86	,,	,,	...	...	smaller pkt.	0	6

Daniels' Superb Ten-week & other Stocks

TEN-WEEK STOCK—WHITE PERFECTION.

Large-flowered Miniature Ten-week—

		s.	d.
87	An assortment of 6 distinct varieties ...	1s.	6d.
88	Choicest mixed ... ... per pkt.	0s.	6d.

Large-flowered Globe Pyramidal Ten-week—

		s.	d.
89	An assortment of 8 choice varieties ...	2s.	0d.
90	Mixed seed ... ... per pkt.	0s.	6d.

Dwarf Bouquet Ten-week—

		s.	d.
91	An assortment of 8 distinct varieties ...	1s.	6d.
92	Finest mixed ... ... per pkt.	0s.	6d.

Large-flowered Wallflower-leaved Ten-week—

		s.	d.
93	An assortment of 8 varieties	2s.	6d.
94	Choicest mixed ... ... per pkt.	1s.	0d.

New Perpetual Ten-week.

A FINE new class, growing to the height of eighteen inches, and producing an abundance of bloom from July to November. First-class for cutting.

95   An assortment of 8 choice varieties ...   ... 2s. 6d.

"White Perfection."   This superb variety is of exquisite beauty and deserves the highest recommendation. It grows to a height of 1½ feet, is much branched, and almost a perpetual bloomer. If sown early in the Spring, it will flower with the beginning of June, continuing to bloom till destroyed by frost. In September and October, when other Stocks are off bloom, this is at its perfection, the mass of bloom is really remarkable. The individual flowers, having a fine rosette-like shape, are uncommonly large and of a snowy whiteness, and being borne on stems about three inches long, are also excellent for cutting.

		s.	d.
96	Per packet...	1s.	0d.
97	Choicest mixed ... ... per pkt.	1s.	0d.

From Mr. **E. SHERWOOD**, Blythe

Mar. 31st.
"The Ten-week Stocks which I had in a 7s. 6d. Collection last year were very fine indeed, in fact the best I have had or seen this season. The Balsams were handsome double flowers."

From Mr. **P. C. STEVEN**, Cluut.

May 8th.
"I took First Prize with three grand spikes of Stocks; also First Prize with four bunches of Annuals; all grown from your seeds."

From Mr. **JAMES BEARD**, Burton-on-Trent.

Feb. 28th.
"The Stock Seed I had from you last year was the best I ever saw. I took First Prize at our show, having beaten all competitors there last two years."

From Mr. **J. DANIELS**, Stonegate, Ticehurst.

Dec. 3rd.
"The Seeds I had from you this year turned out splendid, they were the talk of the neighbourhood; I have grown flowers for years but never had such a show of Stocks and Asters like these before."

Intermediate Stocks.

East Lothian Autumnal—
Splendid for late blooming on the open border or for Winter decoration in the greenhouse.

		s.	d.
98	An assortment of 4 distinct varieties...	1	9
99	**Scarlet** ... ... per pkt.	1	0
100	**Crimson** ... ... ,,	1	0
101	**Purple** ... ... ,,	1	0
102	**White** ... ... ,,	1	0
103	**Choicest mixed** ... ... ,,	1	0
104	,, ,, ... smaller pkt.	0	6

Large-flowered Emperor—
Remarkable for their large flowers and vigorous habit. If sown in March will produce a magnificent effect in Autumn.

		s.	d.
105	An assortment of 10 splendid varieties	2s.	6d.
106	Finest mixed ... ... per pkt.	0s.	6d.

Autumn-flowering Intermediate—
A fine class for late flowering.

		s.	d.
107	An assortment of 8 splendid varieties	2s.	6d.
108	Choicest mixed ... ... per pkt.	0s.	6d.

Brompton Stocks.

Giant or **Brompton**. Produce immense spikes of flowers and are very double. Sow in May or June, and plant out early in Autumn, for blooming the following Spring.

				s.	d.
109	An assortment of 12 choice varieties ...			3	0
110	,,	8	,,	2	0
111	,,	6	,,	1	6

			s.	d.
112	**Cottager's Scarlet.** Very fine and double per pkt.	1	0
113	**New Snow White.** Splendid double ,,	1	0
114	**Choicest mixed** ... ... per pkt. 6d. and	1	0

Daniels' Complete Collections of

Choice Flower Seeds for Amateurs.

Carefully arranged to ensure a fine display of flowers throughout the Summer and Autumn, and specially adapted to the requirements of the Cottage, Villa, or large Garden.

Collection A.—Price 5s. Post Free.

A choice assortment of twenty-four Hardy and Half-hardy Annuals, containing one full-sized packet of each of the following :—

Aster, Pæony-flowered	Convolvulus minor	Rhodanthe maculata	Calliopsis tinctoria
Clarkia integripetala	Lupinus nanus	Larkspur, dwarf Rocket	Phlox Drummondi
Collinsia bicolor	Linum grandiflorum	Candytuft, crimson	Briza maxima
Nemophila insignis	Mignonette [rubrum	Leptosiphon albus	Marigold, dwarf French
Sweet Pea, mixed	Stock, Dwarf German	Viscaria, scarlet	Zinnia, fine double
Convolvulus major	Nasturtium, Tom Thumb	Helichrysum	Nasturtium, climbing

Collection A A.—Price 7s. 6d. Post Free.

8 Choice vars. Victoria Aster	6 Half-hardy Annuals, including	1 Packet Zinnia, finest double
6 ,, Dwarf Ten-week Stock	Phlox, Marigold, Portulaca, &c., &c.	1 ,, Helichrysum, mixed
8 Choice Hardy Annuals	1 Packet Petunia, finest mixed	1 ,, Rhodanthe maculata
1 Packet Balsam, choice double		1 ,, Briza maxima
		1 Oz. Flower Seeds, dwf. mixed

Collection B.—Price 10s. 6d. Post Free.

6 Choice vars. Pæony Aster	12 Choice Hardy Annuals, the most useful and showy kinds	1 Packet Camellia-flowered Balsam
6 ,, Dwarf German Ten-week Stock	4 Choice varieties Everlasting Flowers	1 Packet Portulaca, fine double
6 Varieties New Double Zinnia elegans	2 Choice Ornamental Grasses	1 ,, Verbena, choice mixed
6 Choice Half-hardy Annuals for bedding out	1 Packet Petunia, choice mixed	1 Ounce Mignonette
		1 ,, Mixed Flower Seeds

Collection C.—Price 15s. Post Free.

6 Choice vars. Pæony Aster	12 Choice Half-hardy Annuals for bedding out	1 Packet Camellia-flowered Balsam
6 ,, Dwarf German Ten-week Stock	6 Hardy Perennials, including Pansies, Hollyhock, &c.	1 Packet Portulaca, fine double
6 Choice varieties New Double Zinnia elegans	4 Choice varieties Everlasting Flowers	1 ,, Verbena, choice mixed
12 Choice Hardy Annuals, the most useful and showy kinds	2 Choice Ornamental Grasses	1 Ounce Nemophila insignis
	1 Packet Petunia, choice mixed	1 ,, Mignonette
		2 Ounces Mixed Flower Seeds

Collection D.—Price 21s. Carriage Free.

12 Choice vars. Pæony Aster	12 Choice varieties Half-Hardy Annuals, for bedding-out, pots, &c.	1 Packet Calceolaria, choicest mixed
8 ,, Victoria Aster	6 Hrdy. Perennials & Biennials	1 Packet Cineraria, choice mxd.
12 ,, Ten-week Stock	6 Choice varieties Everlasting Flowers	1 ,, Primula, choice frngd.
6 ,, Double Zinnia	1 Packet Petunia, choice mixed	1 Ounce Nemophila insignis
8 ,, Phlox Drumm.	1 ,, Verbena, fine mixed	1 ,, Sweet Peas, mixed
12 ,, Showy Hardy Annuals		1 ,, Mignonette
4 Choice Ornamental Grasses		2 Ounces Mixed Flower Seeds

Daniels' Complete Collections of Flower Seeds for Amateurs *(continued).*

Collection D D.—Price 31s. 6d. Carriage Free.

12 Vars. Pæony Aster	12 Vars. Half-hardy Annuals for	8 Choice varieties Everlasting
8 ,, Victoria Aster	bedding out, &c.	Flowers
12 ,, Dwarf Ten-week Stock	12 Hrdy. Perennials & Biennials	6 Ornamental Grasses
6 ,, Giant Ten-week Stock	including Dianthus, Del-	1½ Ounce Mignonette
8 ,, Phlox Drummondi	phiniums, &c.	1 ,, Nemophila insignis
6 ,, Double Zinnia	6 Vars. of Seeds for the Green-	2 Ounces Sweet Peas
6 ,, Camellia-flowd. Balsam	house, including Calceolaria	2 ,, Mixed Flower Seeds
18 ,, Showy Hardy Annuals	Cineraria, Primula, &c.	

Collection E.—Price 42s. Carriage Free.

12 Vars. Victoria Aster	4 Vars. Brompton Stock	12 Hrdy. Perennials & Biennials
12 ,, Pæony Aster	6 ,, Double German Wall-	including Dianthus, Pansy,
6 ,, Prize Quilled Aster	flower	Polyanthus, Hollyhook, &c.
12 ,, Dwarf German Ten-	12 Vars. Everlasting Flowers	6 Greenhouse Perennials and
week Stock	6 Ornamental Grasses	Biennials
6 Vars. Giant or Tree Ten-week	18 Hardy Annuals, the most	6 New or very choice Annuals
Stock	useful and showy sorts	1 Ounce Nemophila insignis
8 Vars. Phlox Drummondi	8 Choice Half-hardy Annuals	2 Ounces Mignonette
6 ,, New Double Zinnia	for bedding out, &c.	4 ,, Sweet Peas, mixed
6 ,, Camellia Balsam		3 ,, Mixed Flower Seeds

Collection F.—Price 63s. Carriage Free.

12 Vars. Pæony Aster	8 Vars. Portulaca	12 Choice varieties Everlasting
12 ,, Victoria Aster	6 ,, Wallflower, Double	Flowers
12 ,, Dwrf. Chrysanthemum	6 ,, Hollyhock	6 Choice Ornamental Grasses
Aster	30 ,, Showy Hardy Annuals	6 Choice vars. Hardy Climbers
12 Vars. Prize Quilled Aster	18 Choice varieties Half-hardy	6 Vars. ornamental-foliaged
12 ,, Ten-week Stock, Dwf.	Annuals for bedding out,	plants for sub-tropical gar-
6 ,, Giant Ten-week Stock	pots, &c.	dening
6 ,, Giant Brompton Stock	12 Choice varieties Hardy Per-	1 Ounce Nemophila insignis
6 ,, Camellia Balsam	ennials and Biennials	8 Ounces Sweet Peas, mixed
12 ,, Phlox Drummondi	12 Choice varieties of Seeds of	4 ,, Mignonette
12 ,, Double Zinnia	Greenhouse Plants	4 ,, Mixed Flower Seeds

The Amateur's Packet of Choice Flower Seeds.

(Entered at Stationers' Hall.)

Price 2s. 6d. post free, 2 packets 4s. 6d.

Contains the following Choice Assortment in full-sized beautifully coloured illustrated packets.

Aster, choicest Pæony-flowered	Sweet Peas, mixed	Zinnia, finest double, mixed
Stock, Ten-week, finest double	Scarlet Linum	Godetia, splendid mixed
Phlox Drummondi grandiflora	Mignonette, Victoria Giant	Nasturtium, Empress of India
Night-scented Stock	Clarkia integripetala rosea	Leptosiphon densiflorus albus

---

OPINIONS FROM THE PRESS.

"Messrs. DANIELS BROTHERS, of Norwich, have sent one of their Amateur's Packets of Choice Flower Seeds as a specimen. It is remarkably cheap, and the varieties are well selected."—*Morning Post.*

"We have received from Messrs. DANIELS one of their half-crown packets of a dozen varieties of Flower Seeds. We caused one of these packets to be tried last year and the results were most satisfactory."—*Illustrated Sporting News.*

"We have great pleasure in acknowledging an Amateur's Packet of Flower Seeds sent us by Messrs. DANIELS, the well-known seedsmen of Norwich. Last year we were favoured in a similar manner, and from our experience of results obtained, we predict that this collection will become one of the most popular with amateur gardeners. The Asters and Stocks are from a very choice strain."—*Lady's Pictorial.*

English and Foreign Flower Seeds in Collections.

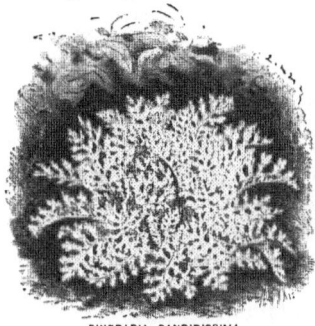

CINERARIA CANDIDISSIMA.
Per packet 1s.

PERILLA NANKINENSIS.
Per packet 3d.

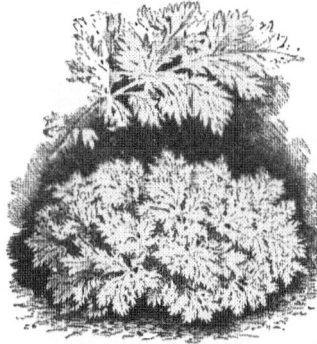

PYRETHRUM SELAGINOIDES.
Per packet 6d.

HARDY ANNUALS—
115 One hundred showy and useful varieties, including Godetia, Nemophila, Viscaria, Clarkia, Collinsia, Convolvulus, Sweet Pea, &c.   16s. 0d.
116 Fifty ditto ...   .   8s. 6d.
117 Twenty-five ditto   ...   .   5s. 0d.
118 Twelve ditto ...   .   2s. 0d.

HARDY AND HALF-HARDY ANNUALS—
119 One hundred choice varieties, including Aster, Stock, Nemophila, Marigold, Phlox, Sweet Pea, &c.   ...   ...   21s. 0d.
120 Fifty ditto   ...   .   11s. 0d.
121 Twenty-five ditto   ...   .   6s. 0d.
122 Twelve ditto ...   .   3s. 6d.

HARDY PERENNIALS AND BIENNIALS—
123 Twenty-five choice varieties, including Pansy, Carnation, Hollyhock, Polyanthus, Auricula, &c.   ...   ...   10s. 0d.
124 Twelve ditto ...   .   6s. 0d.

STOVE & GREENHOUSE PERENNIALS & BIENNIALS—
125 Twenty-five choice varieties, including Calceolaria, Cineraria, Primula, Gloxinia, Begonia, &c.   ...   ...   18s. 6d.
126 Twelve ditto ...   .   10s. 6d.

PLANTS FOR THE SUB-TROPICAL GARDEN—
127 Twelve superb varieties   ...   .   4s. 6d.
128 Six ditto   ...   .   2s. 6d.

EVERLASTING FLOWERS—
129 Twenty-four choice varieties   ...   .   5s. 0d.
130 Twelve ditto ...   .   2s. 6d.

ORNAMENTAL GRASSES—
131 Twenty-five choice varieties   ...   .   5s. 0d.
132 Twelve ditto ...   .   2s. 6d.

CLIMBING PLANTS, Hardy and Half-Hardy Annuals—
133 Twelve choice varieties   ...   .   3s. 6d.
134 Six ditto   ...   .   1s. 6d.

CONVOLVULUS MAJOR—
135 An assortment of 12 beautiful colours   ...   2s. 0d.

GODETIAS—
136 Six new and beautiful sorts   ...   ...   1s. 6d.

ORNAMENTAL GOURDS—
137 Twelve beautiful miniature varieties   ...   2s. 6d.

LARKSPUR, Giant Rocket, Hyacinth-flowered—
138 Six fine and distinct sorts   ...   ...   1s. 6d.

LARKSPUR, Double Dwarf Rocket Hyacinth-flowered—
139 Twelve extra choice varieties   ...   ...   2s. 6d.

MARIGOLDS, African—
140 An assortment of 6 choice varieties   ...   1s. 6d.

MARIGOLDS, French—
141 Six varieties   ...   .   1s. 6d.

DWARF PLANTS FOR ROCKWORK—
142 Twelve fine sorts, annual and perennial   ...   3s. 0d.

NASTURTIUM, TOM THUMB, Dwarf—
143 Eight brilliant varieties   ...   ...   1s. 6d.

NEMOPHILAS—
144 Ten beautiful sorts   ...   .   2s. 0d.

POPPIES, Double Dwarf Ranunculus-flowered—
145 Six brilliant varieties   ...   .   1s. 6d.

POPPIES, Double, Carnation-flowered—
146 Twelve fine varieties   ...   .   2s. 0d.

SCABIOUS, Large-flowered double German—
147 Eight fine varieties   ...   .   1s. 6d.

TROPÆOLUM LOBBIANUM, AND HYBRIDS—
148 Twelve splendid varieties   ...   ...   2s. 6d.

SWEET-SCENTED ANNUALS—
149 Twelve fine varieties   ...   .   2s. 6d.

SALPIGLOSSIS GRANDIFLORA—
150 Six beautiful varieties   ...   .   1s. 6d.

SWEET PEAS, Eckford's Superb New Varieties—
151 An assortment of 12 choice sorts   ...   ...   7s. 6d.
152 Six ditto   ...   .   4s. 0d.

PEAS, Sweet, ordinary class—
153 Twelve choice varieties   ...   .   2s. 0d.

MIGNONETTE—
154 Six choicest varieties   ...   .   1s. 6d.

PLANTS FOR BEES (Annuals)—
155 The Apiarian's Packet, containing 14 selected varieties, in full-sized packets   ...   ...   2s. 6d.
156 An assortment of 8 choice varieties   ...   ...   1s. 6d.

Daniels' Choice Florists' Flower Seeds.

In the rearing of Florists' Flowers from seed the first essential point is to secure carefully hybridized seed saved from the finest flowers of the finest kinds, the chances of success in raising some really good varieties being vastly greater from a few plants from seed of the choicest quality than from a large number raised from seed of an inferior description.

PRIZE AURICULA.

Auriculas.

per pkt—s. d.

			s.	d.
157	**DANIELS' PRIZE MIXED.** From a fine collection of choice named flowers, including the green-edged and grey-edged sorts; highly recommended		5	0
158	" "	smaller pkt.	2	6
159	**ALPINE.** From a superb collection, including all the most beautiful shades of colour; a very hardy and desirable class		1	0

From Mr. D. BROWN, Cathays.

April 26th.
"The packet of Auriculas I had from you two years ago has produced some splendid flowers, no two of them are alike. Altogether they make a beautiful show."

Antirrhinums.

THESE brilliant and free-flowering hardy border plants have been highly improved during the past few years, and should be found in every garden. Treated as half-hardy annuals they bloom freely the first year from seed, and afford a valuable display during the Summer and Autumn months. Many of the varieties are very beautiful. The colours vary from intense crimson to carmine, rose, primrose, yellow, pure white, &c. Some of the kinds have conspicuous white-throated flowers, which make them very attractive, whilst the flowers of some are handsomely striped. The Tom Thumb varieties are only about six inches in height when fully grown, and are very pretty for dry rockeries, &c. Sow in March in light rich soil, and place in a gentle heat; or sow in April under a hand-light, prick out to strengthen, and plant out soon as large enough. These will flower the first year from seed, and furnish a fine display of bloom during Summer and Autumn.

per pkt—s. d.

			s.	d.
160	An assortment of 12 brilliant tall vars., with names		2	6
161	" 6 "		1	6
162	Tall varieties, choice mixed		0	6
163	" "	smaller pkt.	0	3
164	**TOM THUMB,** 6 brilliant varieties with names		1	6
165	" " Choicest mixed		0	6

DANIELS' CAMELLIA-FLOWERED BALSAM.

Balsams, Daniels' Camellia-flowered.

We have much pleasure in again offering our magnificent strain of these superb Balsams, the seed of which has been carefully grown and selected under glass during the past season, and which we have no hesitation in saying, will be found of an unsurpassably fine quality, our Balsams being noted for their large size, perfect doubleness and symmetry of form, with the most brilliantly striking and exquisitely delicate and beautiful colouring. Have been awarded numerous First Prizes.

per pkt—s. d.

			s.	d.
166	An assortment of 6 splendid vars., 25 seeds each		2	6
167	Vermilion-scarlet		1	0
168	Pure white		1	0
169	Delicate rose		1	0
170	Crimson		1	0
171	Violet		1	0
172	Choicest mixed		2	6
173	" "	smaller pkt.	1	6
174	Camellia-flowered German. Mixed seed	6d. and	1	0
175	Rose-flowered. Double; fine mixed	6d. and	1	0

From Mr. M. T. ADAMS, Tring.

Jan. 27th.
"I gained First Prize for Balsams grown from your seed last year, the flowers were greatly admired, and many wanted to purchase the plants."

Daniels' Choice Florists' Flower Seeds.

Begonias—Tuberous-rooted Hybrids.

This magnificent class of handsome flowering plants has been highly improved of late years, and being so admirably suited for greenhouse or conservatory decoration, and for bedding out, should be grown by every one having accommodation for them.

DOUBLE-FLOWERED BEGONIA.

THE many noble additions made within the last few years to this magnificent class of flowering plants, have certainly placed the tuberous-rooted Begonias in the foremost rank of our choicest Florists' Flowers. The blooms of many of the newer varieties reach the large size of from three to five inches across, and are possessed of the most brilliantly varied and delicately beautiful shades of colour, including the richest crimson, scarlet, orange, rose, pale yellow, &c., to the purest white. The plants are wonderfully floriferous, and continue in their full beauty throughout the Summer, and late into the Autumn months. Their cultivation, which is very simple, places them within the reach of all having a greenhouse, or even a warm frame. Sow the seeds in February or March on the surface of well-drained pots or pans of rich sandy loam and finely-sifted leaf-mould, and place in a heat of about sixty-five degrees. When sowing make the soil tolerably firm, level and sprinkle the surface with tepid water, after which sow the seeds; no covering of soil is necessary, a piece of glass placed over the pot to retain the surface moisture being all that is required. As the seed of Begonias does not germinate very quickly or evenly, and a long interval will often occur between the first and last plants coming up, the young seedlings should be carefully lifted as soon as large enough to handle, and pricked into pots or pans to grow on, and this will make room for the succeeding young plants.

Those sown in February or March if grown on freely will commence blooming in June, and will make really fine plants for the succeeding year. Seeds may also be sown in July or August, the plants of which will form nice healthy roots before Winter. The roots may be stored during Winter in a similar way to Dahlias, and should be kept dry; but they should not be subjected to a lower temperature than forty-five or fifty degrees. The tuberous-rooted Begonias are all charmingly suited for the decoration of the greenhouse, conservatory, or window, and planted out of doors in fairly sheltered positions make fine showy beds, and are much superior to Geraniums.

		per pkt.—s.	d.
176	**DANIELS' PRIZE DOUBLE.** A superb strain, carefully hybridised, saved from finest varieties	2	6
177	smaller pkt.	1	6
178	**DANIELS' PRIZE SINGLE.** Carefully saved from a grand collection of the choicest English varieties, will produce some splendid flowers	2	6
179	„ „ „ smaller pkt.	1	6

Coleus, Choicest Mixed.

CAREFULLY saved from the newest and finest varieties. These beautiful ornamental-foliaged plants are easily raised in the way recommended for tuberous-rooted Begonias, and being of rapid growth, soon form nice plants for the greenhouse or drawing-room, their exquisite and varied markings and variegations making them highly interesting.

		s.	d.
180	**An assortment of 12 choice sorts,** 10 seeds each	3	0
181	**Choicest mixed** ... ... per pkt.	1	6

Chrysanthemums.

THESE superb Autumn-blooming hardy perennials will bloom finely the first year from seed sown in Spring on a gentle heat, and the plants grown on freely. The seed we offer has been carefully saved from a fine collection of choice named varieties, and may be expected to produce some grand flowers.

		per pkt.—s.	d.
182	**Large-flowered,** incurved, &c., choicest mixed	1	6
183	**Japanese.** Fine new	1	6
184	**Pompone.** Miniature vars.	1	6

Fibrous-rooted Begonias.

			per pkt.—s.	d.
185	**Semperflorens alba**	Very useful varieties for bedding out or edging.	1	0
186	„ **rosea**	Highly recommended	1	0
187	**Schmidti.** White shaded with rose. Very free bloomer. Sown in heat in February may be had in bloom throughout the Summer and Autumn		1	6
188	**Rex, Varieties.** Beautiful plants for the stove or greenhouse. Saved from choicest sorts	...	1	6

Fuchsias.

Sow in February or March in a gentle heat, and treat as recommended for tender annuals. These beautiful free-flowering plants will bloom well the first year from seed, and plants raised from a first-class strain will produce the most satisfactory results. The single varieties are all handsome in flower and elegant in growth of plant; and the double-flowered, with white or purple corollas, are very fine and desirable.

From a fine collection, including all the newest and best white corolla and other varieties.

		per pkt.—s.	d.
189	**Choicest mixed.** Single	2	6
190	„ Double	2	6
191	**Boliviana.** A fine species, with long racemes of splendid scarlet flowers	2	6

Daniels' Choice Florists' Flower Seeds.

Daniels' Superb Calceolarias.

(See coloured plate.)

We have much pleasure in offering our splendid strain of Calceolaria hybrida, which has been carefully saved from a magnificent collection during the past season, and which has been awarded many First Prizes. The flowers will be found of large size, beautiful form, and tigred and spotted with the most exquisite and brilliant markings.

Sow the seeds in May, June, or July, in well-drained pots or seed-pans; cover the drainage with rough fibrous loam, and fill up the surface with fine light sifted mould and silver sand; water with a fine rose water-pot, after which sow the seed, placing a piece of glass over the pot to retain the moisture, no covering of soil being required. Place the pots in a cool frame or under a hand-light, taking care to shade from the sun. Remove the piece of glass as soon as the plants are up, and when large enough to handle, prick off one inch apart into pots or pans made up as before, placing in a somewhat close situation, and when of sufficient size pot off singly, and treat in a similar manner to that recommended for tender annuals. Calceolarias should however be always kept in a cool, moist position, a dry heated atmosphere being very prejudicial to their growth, and should be kept well supplied with fresh air.

DANIELS' PRIZE CALCEOLARIAS.

				per pkt.—s.	d.
192	**DANIELS' CHOICEST MIXED**		...	5	0
193	,,	,,	,, smaller pkt.	2	6
194	,,	,,	,, smallest pkt.	1	6
105	**NEW DWARF.** A beautiful strain of handsome varieties growing only about ten inches high, and bearing a profusion of large brilliantly marked and spotted flowers			2	6
106	,,	,,	,, smaller pkt.	1	6

Carnations and Picotees.

Sow in March or April in pans of rich soil, scattering the seeds thinly, and covering to the depth of about a quarter of an inch, and after watering place under glass. Prick out on well-prepared nursery beds to strengthen when the young plants have made four or five leaves, and plant out in September where intended to bloom, or pot up for the greenhouse. Those remaining in the open ground should have the benefit of a slight protection in severe weather, and be planted in a warm and dry position. A first-class strain of seed will produce at least eighty per cent. of fine double flowers, and the choicer varieties should be set aside for propagation by layering or cuttings.

CARNATIONS AND PICOTEES.

				s.	d.
197	**CARNATIONS.** An assortment of 50 choice varieties, including the finest of the self, flake, yellow, fancy, bizarre, and perpetual-flowering varieties		...	10	6
198	,,	25 varieties ...	... ...	6	0
199	,,	12 choicest self varieties	...	4	6
200	,,	12 ,, flake varieties	...	4	6
201	,,	12 ,, bizarre varieties ...		4	6
202	,,	12 ,, yellow flake varieties		5	0
203	,,	12 ,, fancy varieties	...	4	6
204	,,	12 ,, yellow fancy varieties	...	5	0
205	,,	**DANIELS' CHOICEST MXD.** per pkt.		5	0
206	,,	,, ,, smaller pkt.		2	6
207	,,	,, ,, smallest pkt.		1	6
208	,,	choicest yellow		3	6
209	,,	pure white. Very choice ...		3	6
210	,,	**NEW DWARF.** Very fine and compact		2	6
211	,,	**GRENADIN.** A fine early-flowering variety with brilliant scarlet, double flowers		1	6
212	,,	**DANIELS' PERPETUAL or TREE.** Very choice; magnificent for pot culture		5	0
213	,,	,, ,, smaller pkt.		2	6
214	**PICOTEES.** An assortment of 50 choice varieties, including the finest white-ground, yellow-ground, and perpetual-flowering varieties		...	10	6
215	,,	25 varieties		6	0
216	,,	12 choicest white-ground varieties...		5	0
217	,,	12 ,, yellow-ground varieties...		5	0
218	,,	**DANIELS' CHOICEST MIXED** ...		5	0
219	,,	,, ,, smaller pkt.		2	6
220	,,	,, ,, smallest pkt.		1	6
221	**GARDEN PINK.** Very choice double, mixed 1s. 6d. and			2	6

Daniels' Choice Florists' Flower Seeds.

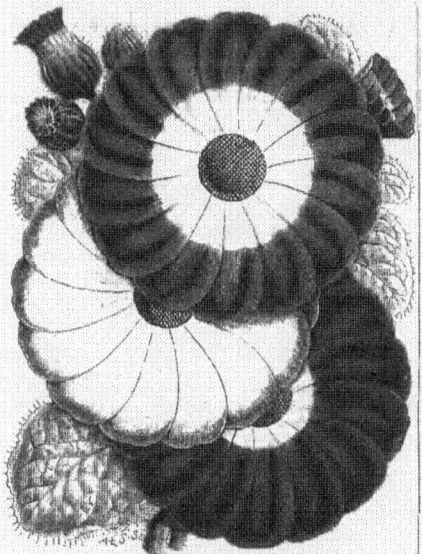

DANIELS' SUPERB CINERARIAS.

Daniels' Superb Cinerarias.

Our grand strain of Cineraria hybrida, as figured, has been carefully saved from our fine collection of named and choicest seedling flowers, and which we have every confidence in recommending as unsurpassable. The colours will be found varied and brilliant, combined with a faultless habit of plant and form of flower.

WHEN required for a general display in early Spring, the seeds should be sown in July or early in August, and when for Winter blooming, a few should be sown in March or April. Where the quantity of glass available is somewhat limited, the July sown will, however, be found the most useful. Sow in well-drained pots or pans of light rich soil, giving the seeds but a very slight covering, and place in a cool frame or under a hand-light in a shady spot, pot off singly into small pots as soon as the young plants are large enough, and shift as required. Good Cinerarias may also be easily raised by sowing in July or August in a moist shady situation in the open air, taking care to pot up in September. Cinerarias will bear a great amount of cold, but should never be exposed to frost. Green fly, damp, excessive waterings, and extreme dryness should also be carefully guarded against.

			per pkt.—s. d.
222	DANIELS' CHOICEST MIXED	...	5 0
223	„ „ smaller pkt.		2 6
224	„ „ smallest pkt.		1 6
225	„ BLUE. Fine dark		1 6
226	NEW DWARF. A fine compact-growing class with large handsome flowers, height from four to six inches, exceedingly floriferous. Choicest mixed		2 6
227	DOUBLE-FLOWERED. Very fine, will produce a large percentage of handsome double flowers		5 0
228	„ „ smaller pkt.		2 6

Cyclamen Persicum.

THE best time for sowing the seeds is in October or November, and again in January, February, or March, for a succession. When sowing, use a light rich soil, press down firmly into the seed pots or pans, placing the seeds about half an inch apart on the surface, and covering them about a quarter of an inch deep with soil; water carefully and place in a gentle heat. As the young plants become large enough to handle they should be carefully lifted and potted off singly into small pots, shifting them into larger as these fill with roots, and finishing with the forty-eight size, which will be large enough for blooming. The best soil to use for potting Cyclamens is composed of about equal parts of fibrous loam and leaf-mould, with a portion of well-decayed cow-dung and sufficient silver sand to keep the soil porous. The essential conditions of successful cultivation of Cyclamens are a moist and even temperature—sudden changes are especially to be avoided—a free circulation of air, an abundance of light and water, and the plants should be kept free of insects. After flowering, and during the Summer months, the plants should have less water than when in full growth and bloom, and should be in a position shaded from strong light, but should on no account be allowed to suffer from want of moisture.

		per pkt.—s. d.
229	DANIELS' GIANT PRIZE MIXED. A magnificent strain of a highly improved type, having large, beautifully mottled coriaceous leaves and stout flower stalks. The blooms, which are carried well above the foliage, are of splendid size, each flower frequently measuring from two and a half to three inches in length, with broad petals of great substance ...	2 6
230	„ „ smaller pkt.	1 6
231	Wiggins' Covent Garden. A fine large-flowered strain of beautiful varieties as grown for Covent Garden Market	1 6
232	Persicum, choice mixed. In a beautiful variety of colours	1 0

Cockscombs.

WHEN well grown, these singularly formed and magnificently coloured oddities have a very rich and fine appearance, and are well worth the trouble of cultivation, for although it may not always be easy to produce such grand specimens as we occasionally see exhibited at our flower shows, those of only medium size, or even smaller, are valuable for the richness of their colouring and their pleasing effect in association with other plants. Sow the seeds in February or March in pots or pans of light rich soil and plunge in a good heat. The object being to keep the plants in free growth without a check, the young plants should be carefully pricked out into small pots as soon as they can be handled, and as these fill with roots they should be shifted into larger pots. Those of eight inches diameter are large enough to finish with, but the plants must be kept in heat till the combs are formed, which will take place when the plants become pot-bound. Should some of the plants be too tall when grown but have fine combs, the defect of height may be easily remedied by cutting off the combs with a sufficient length of stem, potting them firmly into five or six inch pots, and plunging them for a few days in a good hot-bed. These will strike readily, and fine combs on dwarf handsome plants will be the result. A light rich friable soil is the best, and the plants when in full growth will be much improved by an occasional dose of weak liquid manure.

		per pkt.—s. d.
233	Daniels' Giant Prize. A magnificent strain, saved from combs measuring thirty-six inches by twelve inches, of the richest deep crimson colour; when well grown are unrivalled for exhibition ... ... 1s. 6d. and	2 6
234	Dwarf crimson. Rich crimson	0 6
235	Crimson-feathered } Long handsome plumes,	0 6
236	Golden-feathered } splendid for conservatory	0 6
237	New dwarf feathered. Splendid mixed ...	0 6
238	An assortment of 6 fine dwarf vars. ...	1 6
239	Choicest mixed. Dwarf	0 6

Daniels' Choice Florists' Flower Seeds.

SINGLE-FLOWERED DAHLIA.

Dahlias—Single and Double.

Sow in February or March in light rich soil, and place in a gentle heat; when the young plants are about two inches high, pot off simply into small pots, place in a frame or greenhouse where a gentle heat is maintained, gradually hardening them off preparatory to planting out towards the end of May. After they are transferred to the open air, give them a slight protection for a few nights if the weather be cold. A liberal application of weak liquid manure in dry weather will greatly assist in the development of fine flowers.

The single-flowered varieties are especially valuable for cultivation in this way. They commence blooming in July or August, and continue with a profusion of lovely flowers till killed by the frost; are exceedingly useful for cut flowers, and should be grown freely in every garden.

per pkt.—s. d.

240	**SINGLE-FLOWERED HYBRIDS.** Carefully saved from our grand collection of choice named flowers, and may be expected to produce some fine novelties	1 0
241	,, ,, ,, smaller pkt.	0 6
242	**LARGE-FLOWERED DOUBLE.** Carefully saved from our superb collection of upwards of 250 choicest show and fancy varieties. Will produce a large percentage of fine double flowers	1 6
243	**POMPONE or BOUQUET.** Beautiful miniature varieties with handsome double flowers	1 6

From Mr. JAMES FRANCE, Chapel, near Spalding. March 12th.

"The Seeds I have had from you this last six years have all turned out well—very may especially mention the Asters and Dahlias. From the Mixed Victoria Asters I had more than twenty splendid varieties; from the Dahlias seed I had forty two varieties. I raised the plants in an ordinary frame and found them very easy to manage, although I had not raised any from seed before. The blooms were very fine and of every conceivable colour; on some of the plants I counted more than fifty blooms, and in one case seventy-five on all out at one time."

Delphiniums.

BEAUTIFUL hardy border perennials, with noble spikes of handsome flowers, varying in colour from pure white to the richest blues and purples; exceedingly useful for cut flowers, &c.

per pkt.—s. d.

244	**Barlowi.** Dark blue, shaded red	1 0	250	**Formosum.** Rich dark blue, beautiful	0 4
245	**Cardinale.** Scarlet, fine	1 6	251	,, **coelestinum.** Beautiful light blue	0 6
246	**Cashmerianum.** Very fine dark blue	0 6	252	**Hermann Stenger.** Violet mauve, double	1 0
247	**Chinense pumila alba.** White, dwarf	0 6	253	**Nudicaule.** Orange scarlet, very distinct, fine	0 6
248	,, ,, **cœrulea.** Light blue, dwarf	0 6	254	**Choicest mixed single.** In beautiful variety	0 6
249	**Elatum "Le Mastodonte."** Bright blue with white centre	0 6	255	**Double-flowered, choicest mixed.** Fine new varieties	1 0

DIANTHUS DIADEMATUS FL. PL.

Dianthuses.

THE Chinese or Indian Pinks constitute one of the most brilliant and splendid groups of hardy biennials in cultivation. All the varieties are easily raised from seed; and sown early in Spring under glass and transplanted, they make charming beds during the Summer and Autumn. The Heddewigi section produce the largest flowers, and are perhaps the most beautiful; but all are richly deserving of extensive cultivation, and no garden should be found without some of the varieties.

per pkt.—s. d.

256	**Heddewigi, Crimson Gem.** Splendid dark crimson; single	1 0
257	,, **Snowflake.** Splendid pure white; single	1 0
258	,, **diadematus fl. pl.** *(The Diadem Pink).* Fine double flowers	0 6
259	,, **atropurpureus fl. pl.** Large dark blood red. Splendid	0 6
260	,, **laciniatus.** Beautiful fringed flowers	0 6
261	,, **Choicest mixed single**	1 0
262	,, ,, smaller pkt.	0 6
263	**Chinensis** *(Indian Pink)."* An assortment of 12 choice double-flowered varieties	2 6
264	,, **Finest double, mixed**	0 6
265	,, **alba fl. pl.** White, double	0 6

Daniels' Choice Florists' Flower Seeds.

GAILLARDIA HYBRIDA GRANDIFLORA.

DOUBLE HOLLYHOCK.

Gaillardia hybrida grandiflora.

SPLENDID hardy perennials, blooming the first year from seed sown in March or April in a cool frame. The very large and beautiful flowers are almost unique in their charming blendings of the many rich shades of brown, maroon, and golden yellow, and being of good substance are first-class to cut for indoor decoration. The seed we offer has been carefully saved at our Nurseries during the past season, from a choice collection of the finest named and seedling varieties.

		s.	d.
266	Choicest mixed seed, saved from a charming collection of named flowers ... ... per pkt.	1	0

Gloxinias.

THESE, the most exquisitely beautiful of all greenhouse plants, bloom freely the first year from seed, and should be grown largely by every one having accommodation for them. Sow in February or March on a good moist heat, in the way recommended for Calceolarias. Pot off singly into small pots as soon as the young plants can be handled, and shift into larger as required, keeping the plants going with a good liberal warmth, and finally potting off into pots of about six inches diameter, using a light and rich soil, and continuing with a moderate heat and giving air on warm days. Treated in this way, a charming display of bloom may be had during July and August, and from a good strain of seed some really grand flowers will be the result.

Gloxinia hybrida grandiflora erecta.
(*See coloured plate.*)

We have much pleasure in offering our fine strain of seed, which has been grown expressly for our retail trade. The blooms will be found of immense size, and of the most brilliant, varied, and beautiful colours and markings. The leaves, which are large, and of great substance, have a rich velvety appearance, and being finely reflexed, the plants are exceedingly handsome.

		per pkt.—s.	d.
267	"Defiance." A grand new variety, bearing large upright flowers of the most intense scarlet-crimson colour; comes quite true from seed ...	1	6
268	Striped and spotted varieties. Very choice...	2	6
269	Splendid varieties, mixed ...	5	0
270	,, ,, ,, ... smaller pkt.	2	6
271	,, ,, ,, ... ,,	1	6

Hollyhock—Daniels' Prize.

THESE magnificent flowers, with their stately spikes of handsome bloom, form grand and conspicuous objects in the flower garden during Summer and Autumn, and should always be grown where convenient. They are easily raised from seed, and sown in January or February in a good heat under glass will bloom splendidly the same year. When grown in this way a light rich soil should be used; the plants should be potted singly into small pots as soon as large enough to handle, shifting into larger as these fill with roots, gradually hardening off, and finally planting out early in May. The seed we offer has been grown especially for our retail trade, and may be relied on to produce some grand double blooms in the most beautiful variety of colours.

		s.	d.
272	Daniels' choicest double, mixed ... per pkt.	2	6
273	smaller pkt.	1	6
274	Twelve superb double-flowered varieties, separate	5	0
275	Six ,, ,, ,, ,,	2	6

Daniels' Choice Florists' Flower Seeds.

AFRICAN MARIGOLDS.

DANIELS' STRIPED FRENCH MARIGOLDS.

Daniels' Superb Marigolds.

We give special attention to the growth and selection of our choice strains of Marigolds, and can highly recommend our Orange and Lemon African and Striped French as being the finest procurable.

per pkt.—s. d.

276 **ORANGE AFRICAN.** A magnificent selection from a prize strain, bearing immense brilliant, orange-coloured, perfectly double flowers, often seven to eight inches across 1 0
277   ...   smaller pkt. 0 6
278 **LEMON AFRICAN.** The same as preceding in size and form of flower, and habit of plant, but varying in colour 1 0
279   ...   smaller pkt. 0 6
280 **DANIELS' STRIPED FRENCH (Scotch Prize).** A fine strain of beautifully striped flowers of the most perfect form and doubleness. Grown expressly for our retail trade by one of the best growers in Scotland 2 6
281   ...   smaller pkt. 1 6
282 Mixed striped. Ordinary class ... 3d. & 0 6
283 **Aurea floribunda.** Dwarf golden yellow ... 0 6
284 **Pulchra nana.** Golden yellow, dark centre, very dwarf 0 6
285 **Dwarf Brown French** 0 3
286 **Signata pumila.** Excellent for bedding ... 0 3

Pentstemons.

This beautiful class of showy hardy free-flowering herbaceous perennials has been much improved of late years. The plants are easily raised from seed sown in Spring on a gentle heat, and will afford a splendid show throughout the Autumn months. Some of the varieties with white throats are extremely handsome.

per pkt.—s. d.

287 **Gentianoides.** Very fine, various beautiful colours 1 0
288 **Lobbi.** Splendid yellow 1 0
289 **Murrayanus.** Brilliant scarlet 1 0
290 **Palmeri.** Peach-coloured, fine 1 0
291 **Wrighti.** Fine scarlet 0 6
292 **Choicest mixed hybrids.** From named flowers 1 0

Pelargoniums—Geraniums.

Sow in February or March in pots or pans of light rich soil, covering the seeds to the depth of about one-eighth of an inch, and place in a heat of about sixty-five or seventy degrees. Pot off the young plants singly into small pots, and shift into larger as these fill with roots. With liberal treatment these will bloom the first year, and, although many will not be up to the standard of first-class florists' flowers, some really beautiful varieties may be expected from a good strain of seed, and all will be found well worth the small amount of time and trouble expended. Seeds may also be sown in July and August for blooming the following Spring.

per pkt.—s. d.

293 **Large-flowered Show.** Very choice mixed ... 1 6
294 **French Blotched or Spotted.** Magnificent ... 2 6
295 **Fancy.** Choicest mixed 1 6
296 **Impregnated Tricolor and Bronze Leaved** 2 6
297   "   "   smaller pkt. 1 6
298 **Zonal and Nosegay.** From the newest varieties 2 6
299   "   "   smaller pkt. 1 6

From Mr. A. B. DRIMBAR, Donegal.

Nov., 18—.
"The Seeds I got from you this year have done very well, the **Scotch Prize French Marigolds** were splendid."

Daniels' Choice Florists' Flower Seeds.

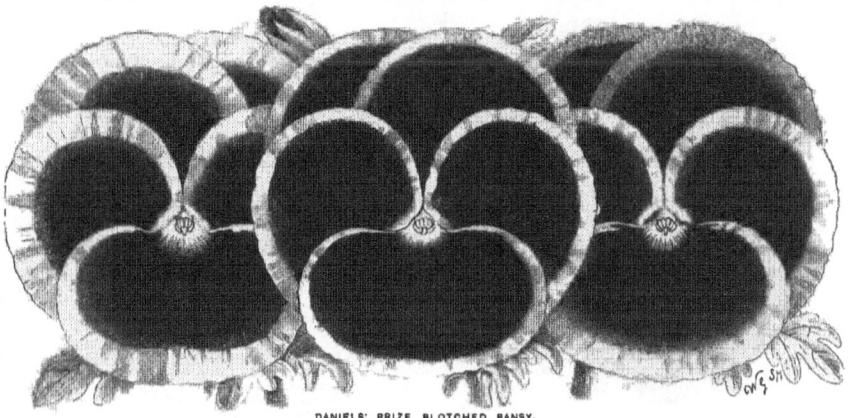

DANIELS' PRIZE BLOTCHED PANSY.

Daniels' Superb Prize Pansies.

Our Strains of Pansy are very fine.

THESE beautiful free-flowering hardy plants are easily raised from seed, and will richly repay the small cost and trouble required to grow them to perfection. For blooming in Summer and Autumn, sow in February, March, and April, in pans or boxes of light rich soil placed in a gentle heat, and as soon as the young plants are large enough, prick out about two inches apart on rich soil to strengthen, and finally plant out six or eight inches apart, in ground into which a good quantity of well-decayed manure has been worked. Pansies delight in a somewhat shady position, and plenty of moisture in dry weather. The finest blooms are produced the second year, but grand flowers may be had by sowing in July or August in the open ground, and planting out in the following Spring into good rich soil.

		per pkt.—s.	d.
300	**DANIELS' PRIZE BLOTCHED** (*see coloured plate*). A magnificent strain of fine varieties, producing large, handsome flowers of great substance and variety of colouring, the petals of which are beautifully blotched or stained. Splendid varieties mixed ...	2	6
301	smaller pkt.	1	6
302	**ENGLISH SHOW AND FANCY.** Carefully saved from a fine collection of choice English Show and Fancy varieties ...	1	6
303	**IMPROVED STRIPED.** A fine class producing large, beautifully formed flowers of the most brilliant and exquisite tints in colouring, the blooms being handsomely striped. A great improvement on the striped Belgian varieties ...	1	0
304	**New Victoria Red.** The first really brilliant red-flowered Pansy yet raised, and the brightest and most striking colour yet obtained ...	1	6
305	**Giant Emperor William.** A superb new variety, with very large deep ultramarine blue flowers ...	1	6
306	**Giant King of the Blacks.** Fine large flowers of an intense dark colour, almost as black as jet ...	1	6
307	**Giant Lord Beaconsfield.** Beautiful variety of a rich deep purple violet colour, shading off in the top petals to white; a very effective bedder ...	1	6

		per pkt.—s.	d.
308	**New Giant Striped.** The perfection of striped Pansies. The plants are of sturdy, compact habit of growth, and the very large flowers are elegantly striped with the most brilliant and charming colours ...	1	6
309	**TRIMARDEAU or GIANT.** An entirely distinct and splendid class of vigorous compact growth, producing immense flowers of good form and colour ...	1	0
310	**Candidissima** (Snow Queen.) Delicate satiny white, very pretty ...	0	6
311	**Emperor William.** An exceedingly fine variety for bedding out, &c.; colour a rich ultramarine blue; distinct and beautiful ...	0	6
312	**Quadricolor.** Very beautiful and distinct ...	0	6
313	**Blue King.** Bright deep blue; fine for bedding	1	0
314	**Cliveden Yellow.** Fine golden yellow	1	0
315	**Purple.** Purplish maroon	1	0
316	**Light blue.** Beautiful colour	1	0
317	**Pure white.** Very beautiful	1	0
318	**Pure yellow.** Bright golden yellow	1	0
319	**Rich purple.** Lovely dark colour ...	1	0
320	**King of the Blacks.** Black as jet	1	0

{Exceedingly valuable and beautiful varieties for Spring bedding; very floriferous and constant bloomers.}

One packet each last twelve sorts, 8s. 6d.

			s.	d.
321	**Mixed.** Ordinary class, good showy varieties 3d. &		0	6
322	**An assortment of 12 beautiful vars.** (German)		2	6
323	„ „ 6 „ „		1	6

Daniels' Choice Florists' Flower Seeds.

DANIELS' SUPERB MIMULUS.

From Mr. J. W. WHITROW, Newport, Mon.

Jan. 1st.
"I have a **White Primula** now in bloom, 14 inches across, grown from Seed obtained from you."

From Mr. J. LANES, Norbriggs.

May 6th.
"I have taken several First and Second Prizes with flowers grown from your **Seeds** this season."

From Mr. WILLIAM BRIDGEMAN, Shaw.

Sept. 10th.
"I can again recommend your **Prize Asters**. They took the First Prize at Purton this year."

Mimulus.

THESE beautiful flowers are easily raised from seed, and will well repay the small amount of trouble required in rearing and growing them. The individual blooms of some of the newer and choicer sorts attain an immense size, and are possessed of all the rich and varied colours and markings of the finest Calceolarias. They are quite hardy, but succeed much better when raised under glass. Sow the seeds in March or April on the surface of pots or pans of firmly pressed light rich soil, cover very slightly with fine soil and sand, sprinkle gently with a fine rose water-pot, and place in a gentle heat of about sixty degrees, not more. A piece of glass laid over the pot or pan will assist germination by ensuring an even moisture. When the young plants come up, keep near the glass and give plenty of air, and soon as they can be handled pot off singly into small pots, or prick out five or six in a five-inch pot to strengthen, give plenty of air and moisture, and plant out in May, or shift into larger pots for continuing under glass. A somewhat shady position is the most favourable for blooming, and, when planted out, a north or north-westerly aspect will be best, and the plants should have an abundance of water in dry weather.

		per pkt.—s.	d.
324	**DANIELS' LARGE-FLOWERED.** A magnificent break, remarkable for the great size and rich colouring of the flowers and the vigorous habit of the plants. First-class for pot culture in the greenhouse, conservatory, or window. Confidently recommended as one of the finest strains in cultivation. Choicest mixed	1	0
325	,, smaller pkt.	0	6
326	**Giant Emperor, Duplex.** A superb large-flowered variety of the hose-in-hose type. The calyx is of large size, and of the same rich and beautiful colouring as the flower itself. A charming plant for pot culture or the garden	1	0
327	**Cupreus Brilliant.** Orange scarlet	0	4
328	**White-ground varieties.** Choice mixed ...	0	6
329	**Hose-in-Hose varieties.** Mixed ...	0	6
330	**Choice mixed.** Good varieties ...	0	3
331	**Moschatus** (*Musk plant*). Well known ...	0	4
332	,, **compactus.** A new and excellent variety of the preceding, very dwarf and compact	1	0

Lobelias.

To secure fine plants of the *erinus* or *speciosa* varieties of these for bedding out the following May, some prefer to sow the seed in Autumn, but February or March is good time for sowing if the plants have careful attention and are grown on freely. Sow the seeds thinly in pans or pots of sandy loam, cover very lightly, and place in a gentle heat of about sixty degrees, keep moist, and soon as the young plants can be handled, pot off singly into small pots of light rich soil, keep near the glass in a gentle heat, and give plenty of air on fine days. Carefully picking off all the flower buds will greatly assist their growth, and they should on no account be allowed to suffer from want of moisture. Other excellent methods are to prick the young plants five or six in a five-inch pot, or, better still, to plant them thinly in shallow trays of rich soil, keeping in gentle heat, giving air, &c., as recommended. These will generally form compactly-grown sturdy

plants, that will quickly produce a beautiful effect when planted out. Lobelias intended for pots or window boxes succeed best when planted out thinly in good soil in an open situation, and carefully lifted when they have formed nice tufty plants: these will at once commence blooming, and produce an effect that could not be otherwise obtained.

The beautiful perennial *L. fulgens Victoria*, growing about two feet high, with its rich metallic foliage and brilliant scarlet flowers, comes quite true from seed, and sown in February or March on a gentle heat will make nice plants for bedding-out in May or June for blooming the following Autumn. The roots of these should be protected in severe weather by a covering of cocoa-nut refuse, ashes, or any light similar material, or they may be lifted after flowering, and stored in a cool pit or frame for the Winter, and planted out again the following April or May.

		per pkt.—s.	d.
333	**Speciosa** (true). Fine dark blue ...	0	6
334	,, **alba.** White ...	0	6
335	,, **White Perfection.** Very fine white, compact	1	0
336	**Paxtoniana.** Blue and white, pretty ...	0	3
337	**Erinus compacta.** Bright blue ...	0	6
338	,, ,, **alba.** White ...	0	6
339	,, ,, **Blue King.** Very fine...	0	6
340	,, ,, **Distinction.** Bright rose, distinct	0	6
341	,, ,, **Emperor William.** Rich dark blue	0	6

		per pkt.—s.	d.
342	**Erinus compacta. Cobalt blue.** Very fine dark blue	1	0
343	,, **Prima Donna.** A beautiful compact-growing variety, first-class for bedding out; flowers a rich velvety maroon colour, very distinct. First Class Certificate R.H.S. ...	1	0
344	**Gracilis.** Blue	0	3
345	,, **alba.** White	0	3
346	**Pumila magnifica.** Splendid dwarf compact variety, with large dark blue flowers ...	1	0
347	**Ramosa.** Dark blue	0	3
348	,, **alba.** White	0	3
349	**Fulgens, Queen Victoria.** Brilliant scarlet	1	0

Daniels' Choice Florists' Flower Seeds.

PRIMULA—CRIMSON KING.

DANIELS' SUPERB FRINGED PRIMULAS.

DANIELS' SUPERB FRINGED PRIMULAS.

We give great attention to the growth and selection of our superb strains of choice Primulas, and we can highly recommend the seed we offer, which has been grown expressly for our retail trade. In habit of plant, size, brilliancy, and form of flowers, our Primulas are acknowledged to be unsurpassable.

THE beautiful varieties of *Primula sinensis* may be sown in March, April, May, and June. The earlier sown are, however, to be preferred for making fine strong plants with an abundance of bloom. Great care must be taken to have a well-drained pot or seed-pan filled to within half an inch of the top with sifted leaf-mould; leave the surface rather rough, and sprinkle the seeds thinly upon it. The most successful raisers do not cover with soil, but after sowing the seed press down the surface tolerably firm, and place a square of glass over the pot. Place in a good strong heat, shaded from strong light, and water very gently when the soil becomes dry. The seeds will germinate in two or three weeks, after which remove the glass and keep in a shady position. Pot off into small pots when the young plants are about half an inch above ground, and place near the glass in the frame or greenhouse. In their after culture Primulas should be kept as near as convenient to the glass, have plenty of fresh air, and never be kept for a long period in a high temperature, or in a dry heated atmosphere.

		per pkt.—s.	d.
350	DANIELS' CHOICEST RED } Our own	1	6
351	„ „ WHITE } splendid	1	6
352	„ „ MIXED } strain	2	6
353	„ „ smaller pkt.	1	6
354	CRIMSON KING. By far the most splendid of all the high-coloured varieties yet sent out. The flowers are of great size and substance, and of the most brilliant and intense deep crimson-scarlet colour, whilst the plants are of a compact sturdy habit of growth, with the most handsome foliage; highly recommended	2	6
355	ALBA MAGNIFICA. Beautifully fringed, pure white flowers, with citron-yellow eyes	2	6
356	BLUE FRINGED. Carefully saved from beautifully fringed flowers of perfect form and of the deepest shade of blue	3	6
357	CHISWICK RED. Brilliant crimson-scarlet, very robust in habit, finely-cut foliage	1	6
358	Alexandra. Beautiful white flowers, with large yellow centre	1	6
359	Coccinea magnifica. Brilliant scarlet, with clear sulphur yellow eye, exquisitely fringed, large flowers	2	6
360	Florence. Scarlet, shaded madder red	1	6
361	Marginata. Lilac, with white border, distinct	1	6
362	Punctata. Rich velvety carmine, spotted white	1	6
363	Purpurea magnifica. Rich crimson purple, splendid	1	6
364	Village Maid. White, striped with carmine, beautiful	1	6
365	The Bride. Pure white, red-stemmed, very fine	2	6
366	Fern-leaved, new crimson scarlet, splendid	1	6
367	„ choicest red } Beautifully fringed	1	6
368	„ „ white } and remarkably	1	6
369	„ „ mixed } handsome varieties	1	6
370	Double-flowered. Brilliant magenta red	2	6
371	„ „ Choicest white	2	6
372	„ „ Prince Arthur. Glowing scarlet	2	6
373	„ „ Choicest mixed. Beautiful vars.	2	6

Hardy Primulas.

		per pkt. s.	d.
374	Primula japonica. Choice mixed	0	6
375	„ rosea. Beautiful hardy species	1	6
376	„ cortusoides. Fine showy spring-flowering variety	0	6
377	„ denticulata. A fine summer-flowering species	1	0

Daniels' Choice Florists' Flower Seeds.

PETUNIA, DOUBLE FRINGED—"LADY OF THE LAKE."

Daniels' Superb Petunias.

PETUNIAS in their many beautiful varieties form a highly interesting and desirable class of free-flowering plants for pot or garden culture; those of the *grandiflora* section, both single and double-flowered, being especially valuable. The blooms of these are of immense size, beautifully formed, and of the most charming and delicate colours; some of the flowers are exquisitely veined or pencilled, others blotched or striped. The new "Fringed" varieties, both double and single, produce some charming flowers, the edges of the petals being elegantly cut or fringed, whilst the colours are most varied and beautiful. The seed we offer has been carefully saved from fecundated flowers of the finest varieties; but, as Petunias raised from seed have a tendency to "sport," we cannot guarantee more than sixty or seventy per cent. of flowers true to description. All will, however, be found well worth growing, and occasionally some fine novelties may be secured. Petunias for indoor cultivation may be sown in January or early in February, but those intended for bedding out do not require to be sown before March. A soil composed of two parts leaf-mould and one part loam, with the addition of a little sharp sand, forms an excellent compost for these, but the seeds being very small require special care in sowing. Fill your pots or seed pans to near the rim and press the soil down firmly and evenly, sow thinly, and cover the seeds very slightly with fine soil, sprinkle gently with a fine rose water-pot, and place in a gentle heat of sixty or sixty-five degrees, not higher, and keep nicely moist. As soon as the young plants can be handled, prick them out about one inch apart in pots to strengthen, and when sufficiently advanced in growth pot off singly into small pots, gradually harden off when established, and plant out about the middle of May, or shift into large pots as required. In planting Petunias out of doors, ground should be selected that has not been freshly manured, otherwise a superabundant foliage will retard the flowering.

Petunias—Daniels' Superb Fringed.

A NEW and splendid class, producing large and strikingly beautiful flowers, the edges of the petals being elegantly laciniated or fringed.

		s.	d.
378	Single, very choice, mixed ... per pkt.	2	6
379	" " " smaller pkt.	1	6
380	Double, an assortment of 6 superb vars.	3	6
381	" Choicest mixed	2	6
382	" " " smaller pkt.	1	6
383	Lady of the Lake. (*See Illustration.*) Beautiful large fringed, pure white, double flowers, superb	2	6

Petunia—Double-flowered.

SAVED from carefully hybridized flowers, will produce a good percentage of large handsome double flowers.

		s.	d.
384	Very choice, mixed ... ... per pkt.	2	6
385	" " smaller pkt.	1	6
386	An assortment of 6 choice sorts ...	2	6
387	Green-edged double varieties. Very choice, mixed	2	6
388	Large-flowered Striped. Very choice ...	1	0
389	New Dwarf Striped. A fine new compact and distinct variety, growing about eight inches high; bearing a profusion of pretty striped flowers	1	0

Petunia hybrida grandiflora.

A FINE and distinct class of beautiful, large-flowering varieties, producing blooms of immense size, and of the most charming colours; much superior to the old varieties of *Petunia hybrida*. The plants are robust in habit of growth, and admirably suited as pot-plants for the greenhouse or conservatory.

		per pkt.—s.	d.
390	An assortment of 12 choice varieties ...	3	6
391	" 6 "	2	0
392	Alba. White, beautiful " ...	1	0
393	Kermesina. Fine, bright crimson	1	0
394	Maculata. Blotched, very handsome ...	1	0
395	Marginata. Fine large-flowered, bordered and veined with green	1	0
396	Prince of Wurtemberg. Beautiful rose, very large, extra fine	1	0
397	Purpurea. Fine dark, splendid	1	0
398	Rosea. White-throated, rose and white, very lovely	1	0
399	Superbissima. Magnificent variety, enormous flowers, fine robust plants	1	6
400	Venosa. Veined varieties	1	0
401	Violacea. Splendid bright deep violet ...	1	0
402	Choicest mixed	2	6
403	" " smaller pkt.	1	6

Petunia—Ordinary Class.

		s.	d.
404	Choicest mixed. Beautiful showy varieties for beds or borders	1	0
405	" " ... smaller pkts. 3d. &	0	6

Daniels' Choice Florists' Flower Seeds.

Phlox Drummondi.

ALL the varieties of this beautiful class of annuals are worthy of extensive cultivation, especially those of the *grandiflora* class, which produce such a charming profusion and diversity of their large beautifully formed and brilliantly coloured flowers. Those of the *compacta* section growing only about four to six inches in height are also highly desirable, being splendid for massing or beds, or for edgings, producing an effect that can probably be obtained by no other plant. All the sorts continue in bloom for a long season, and apart from their great usefulness for bedding are valuable for pot culture in the greenhouse, where they will give a beautiful display. Sow the seeds in February, March, or early in April, in pans or boxes of light rich soil; sow thinly, press down firmly, cover lightly, water, and place in a gentle heat. The young plants will be up in a few days, and soon as they can be fairly handled they should be pricked out about two inches apart in pans or boxes to strengthen, or potted singly into small pots, keep close for a few days, and when they are established give abundance of air, keeping close to the glass to induce a sturdy growth. May is soon enough for planting out, and a rather dry and sunny position is to be preferred. The dwarf kinds should be planted about eight inches or one foot apart; the others, which grow from nine inches to one foot in height, with a spreading habit, may be planted eighteen inches or two feet apart.

PHLOX DRUMMONDI GRANDIFLORA.

Phlox Drummondi nana compacta.

A BEAUTIFUL compact-growing class, many of the varieties only four or six inches high; admirable for pots, edgings, &c.

		per pkt.—s.	d.
406	Six choice varieties	2	6
407	Atropurpurea. Dark purple	0	6
408	Carminea. Bright carmine red	0	6
409	Rosea. Rose	0	6
410	Snowball. Pure white, very fine	1	0
411	Fireball. Brilliant scarlet	0	6
412	Victoria. Deep scarlet, splendid	0	6
413	Choicest mixed	1	0
414	„ „ smaller pkt.	0	6

Phlox Drummondi grandiflora.

THE *Grandiflora* varieties form a magnificent class; the plants are robust in habit, and the flowers, which are of various rich and beautiful colours, have in many of the varieties large conspicuous white eyes; the individual blooms are of fine substance and scarcely inferior in size to the perennial sorts, and are a decided improvement on the old varieties of *P. Drummondi*.

		per pkt.—s.	d.
415	An assortment of 12 splendid varieties	3	6
416	„ „ 8 „ „	2	6
417	Alba. Pure white	0	6
418	Atropurpurea. Dark purple	0	6
419	Carminea. Beautiful carmine, white eye	0	6
420	Coccinea. Brilliant scarlet	0	6
421	Coccinea striata. Beautiful scarlet-striped	0	6
422	Rosea. Delicate rose, white eye	0	6
423	Stellata atropurpurea. Purple, white eye	0	6
424	Violacea. Violet blue, white eye	0	6
425	Splendens. Fine vivid crimson, white eye	0	6
426	Stellata splendens. Brilliant crimson, with white eye, fine	1	0
427	Choicest mixed. In beautiful variety	1	0
428	„ „ smaller pkt.	0	6

Phlox Drummondi—Original Class.

VERY SHOWY AND FREE-FLOWERING.

		per pkt.—s.	d.
429	An assortment of 12 brilliant varieties	2	6
430	„ „ 6 „ „	1	6
431	Choicest mixed. In beautiful variety	0	6
432	„ „ smaller pkt.	0	3

Perennial Phloxes.

THE many beautiful varieties of this splendid class of hardy perennials are too well known to need any description of ours. The seed we offer has been carefully saved from our fine collection of choice named flowers, and may be expected to produce some really fine varieties.

		per pkt.—s.	d.
433	Tall varieties. Splendid mixed	1	0
434	Dwarf „ „ „	1	6

From Mr. J. BIRCH, Hythe.

Feb. 20th.
"The Asters and Phlox grown from your seed last year were the finest I ever saw, and were much admired by all who saw them."

Daniels' Choice Florists' Flower Seeds.

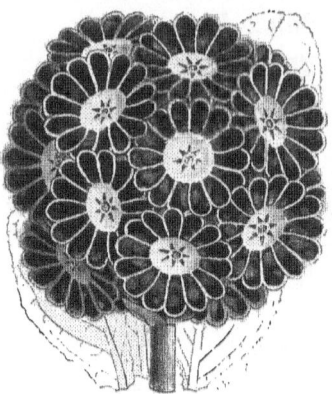

POLYANTHUS, GOLD-LACED.

From Mrs. RAYMOND SMITH, Cirencester,
May 20th.
"The Seeds I had from you last season turned out remarkably well.
The Gold-laced Polyanthus producing some grand flowers."

SWEET WILLIAM, DANIELS' PRIZE.

From EDWARD VAUGHAN, Esq. Carmarthen
March 31st.
"The Begonia Seed I had from you last year turned out most
satisfactorily, and produced some first-class double flowers."

Polyanthuses.

THE fine old hardy Gold-laced Polyanthus, which blooms about the same time as the Primrose, is a great favourite in most gardens, and too well known to need any description. The new varieties of *Giant* and *Magenta King* are very fine, and should be grown by all who are not already familiar with them.

per pkt.—s. d.

435	**Gold-laced.** Fine dark varieties, from a choice collection, beautifully laced	...	...	...	...	2 6
436	" "	...	...	smaller pkt.	1 6
437	**Cloth of Gold.** Fine yellow	...	...	...	1 6
438	**Hose-in-hose varieties.** Choice mixed	...	...	1 0
439	**Magenta King.** Very fine	...	...	...	1 6
440	**New Giant.** Crimson ⎫ Fine showy varieties for bedding				1 0
441	" " White ⎬ out, &c.				1 0
442	" " Yellow ⎭				1 0
443	**Choice mixed.** Good showy sorts	...	...	...	1 0
444	" "	...	...	smaller pkt.	0 6

Hardy Primroses.

A BEAUTIFUL free-flowering class of hardy plants, which has been highly improved of late years, invaluable for Spring gardening. The hybrid varieties vary in colour from the palest and most delicate sulphur-yellow, through all the soft shades of rose and purple to the most intense and brilliant crimson. In a mild season many of the varieties will commence blooming in the Autumn and continue through the Winter, but from the beginning of April to the middle of May they are generally in full bloom, and present a most lovely appearance. A partially shaded border, with a westerly aspect, will grow them to perfection in almost any moderately rich soil.

per pkt.—s. d.

445	**Large-flowered Hybrids.** A grand strain of beautiful high-coloured flowers, all of the true Primrose type, with the flowers large and brilliant; very fine					2 6
446	" "	...	...	smaller pkt.	1 6
447	**Very choice mixed.** From a good collection	...	...	1 0
448	**Crimson Beauty.** Rich crimson, splendid	...	...	2 6
449	**White Queen.** Pure white, beautiful	...	...	2 6
450	**Common Yellow**	...	...	...	0 6

Sweet William, Daniels' Prize.

WE have given great attention for several years past to our splendid strain of these, which we have much pleasure in offering. The sorts embrace a great variety of the choicest auricula-eyed, margined, selfs, &c., of the most brilliant types. The flowers are beautifully formed, of good substance, and are almost invariably awarded First Prize wherever exhibited.

per pkt.—s. d.

451	**DANIELS' PRIZE MIXED.** In beautiful variety	...	...	1 0
452	" "	...	...	smaller pkt.	0 6
453	**Dark crimson.** Splendid colour	...	...	0 4
454	**Double Pure White.** A fine variety	...	...	0 6

Violas—Bedding.

A PROFUSE-FLOWERING and invaluable class of hardy perennial bedding plants, continuing in bloom from early Spring till late in the Autumn months. Highly desirable for Spring gardening, and afford some charming effects in association with Spring-flowering Bulbs, &c. The following list includes the finest varieties in cultivation, and which we highly recommend.

per pkt.—s. d.

455	**An assortment of 6 splendid varieties**	...	...	3 6
456	**Admiration.** Splendid dark violet, yellow eye	...	...	1 0
457	**Cornuta alba.** White	...	...	...	0 6
458	**Blue Perfection.** Dark bluish purple	...	...	1 0
459	**Canary.** Large splendid light yellow flowers	...	...	1 6
460	**Sensation.** Very fine purple	...	...	...	1 0
461	**Magnificent.** Deep rich purple, large flowers, very fine	...	1 0
462	**Mauve Queen.** Light mauve, fine	...	...	0 6
463	**Golden Sovereign.** Rich golden yellow	...	...	1 0
464	**Snowflake.** Splendid pure white	...	...	1 0
465	**Choicest mixed**	...	...	...	1 0
466	" "	...	...	smaller pkt.	0 6

Daniels' Choice Florists' Flower Seeds.

ZINNIA ELEGANS FL. PL.

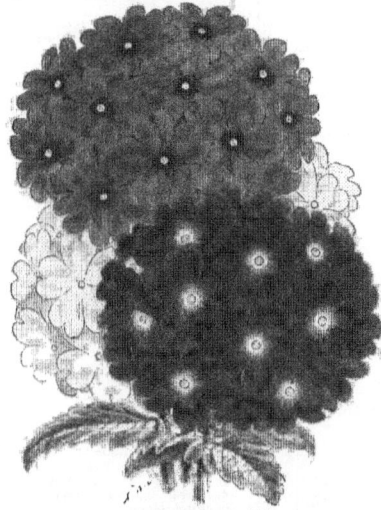

VERBENA HYBRIDA VARS.

Zinnia elegans fl. pl.

THERE is no class of annual flowers which has been so highly improved of late years as the double-flowered Zinnias, which may now be pronounced almost perfection. The flowers, which are large and perfectly double, range in colour from white to the most intense scarlet, orange, rose, salmon, purple, &c., and, considering their easy cultivation, should be grown freely in every garden.

		per pkt.—s.	d.
467	An assortment of 12 splendid varieties ...	2	6
468	„ 6 „ ...	1	6
	New Giant Double. A very fine new class of a robust habit of growth, and producing perfectly double flowers of an immense size, and of the most brilliant and beautiful colours; splendid for exhibition.		
469	„ An assortment of 8 beautiful varieties	2	6
470	„ Choicest mixed ...	1	0
471	Sulphur yellow. Finest double ...	0	4
472	Scarlet „ ...	0	4
473	Salmon Red „ ...	0	4
474	Purple „ ...	0	4
475	White „ ...	0	4
476	Golden Yellow „ ...	0	4
477	Rose „ ...	0	4
478	Choicest mixed „ ...	1	0
479	„ smaller pkt.	0	6
480	New dwarf, double. Splendid mixed ...	1	0
481	Darwini fl. pl. Beautifully imbricated double flowers	1	0
482	Haageana fl. pl. Distinct, small, double-flowered variety, orange, height one foot, trailing ...	0	6

Verbena hybrida.

Sow in February or March in pans or trays of light rich mould, and place in a gentle heat. As soon as the young plants have made three or four leaves pot them off singly into small pots, keep close till established, when they should be placed near the glass and have plenty of air, gradually harden off and plant out in May where intended to flower. Seedling Verbenas are almost invariably very vigorous in growth, and if raised from a good strain of seed will produce some charming flowers.

		per pkt.—s.	d.
483	Candidissima. Fine pure white ...	1	0
484	Dark blue, white eye. Very fine ...	1	0
485	Auriculæflora. Beautiful large-flowered varieties with conspicuous white eyes ...	1	0
486	Defiance. Scarlet, fine...	1	0
487	„ compacta. New. Rich scarlet, very dwarf	1	0
488	Carnation-striped. From a fine collection ...	1	0
489	Choicest mixed, in beautiful variety ...	1	0
490	„ „ „ „ smaller pkt.	0	6

Wallflowers.

THE double German varieties are exceedingly fine, throwing up noble spikes of handsome double flowers in April and May; they are, however, rather less hardy than the single-flowered sorts, and should have the benefit of a more sheltered position when planted out. The single varieties are highly desirable for Spring gardening, producing a great profusion of their finely-scented flowers, and in a mild season often bloom throughout the Winter.

		per pkt.—s.	d.
491	Double German, an assortment of 12 vars.	3	6
492	„ „ 6 „	2	0
493	„ „ blue. Very fine and double ...	0	6
494	„ „ dark brown. Extra ...	0	6
495	„ „ canary yellow. Beautiful...	0	6
496	„ „ very choice mixed ...	1	0
497	„ „ „ smaller pkt.	0	6
498	Single, Golden Tom Thumb. Golden yellow, dwf.	0	4
499	„ Harbinger. Rich dark brown, very curly	0	4
500	„ blood red. Deep colour, finely scented ...	0	3
501	„ Cloth of Gold. Splendid large yellow ...	0	6
502	„ fine mixed	0	3

DANIELS' GENERAL LIST OF FLOWER SEEDS.

For Cultural Instructions see page 93.

ABBREVIATIONS.

hA Hardy annual.
hhA Half-hardy annual.
tA Tender annual.
hB Hardy biennial.
hhB Half-hardy biennial.
tB Tender biennial.
hP Hardy perennial.
hhP Half-Hardy perennial.

From **Mr. HENRY ASHCROFT.**
Newburgh.

"I took the following Prizes with flowers grown from your Seeds—
First Prize for Asters at Newburgh
First, Second, and Third with Asters at Upholland
First Prize with African Marigolds at Upholland"

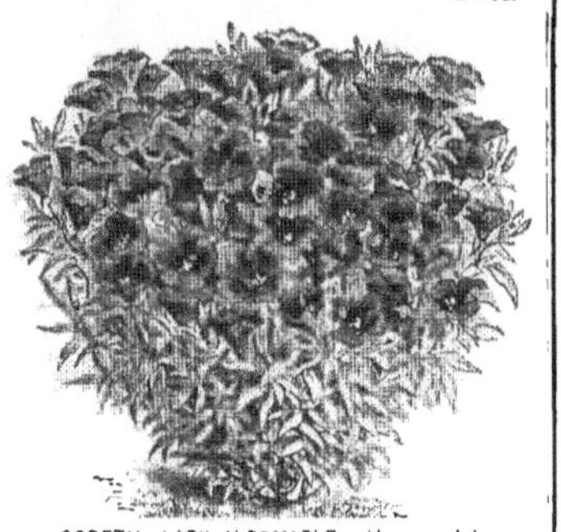

GODETIA—LADY ALBEMARLE. 6d. *per packet.*

ABBREVIATIONS.

tP Tender perennial.
spr Spreading or trailing.
cl Climbing.
gs Greenhouse shrub.
s Plants of a shrubby habit of growth.
st Stove plants.
Bb Having bulbous or tuberous roots.

From **Mr. CHARLES H. DANCER,**
Manitoba, Canada.

"At a Flower Show held here last year Mrs. Dancer took **six First Prizes** for flowers grown from your Seeds, and many of them were much admired. Nothing like the **Double Fringed Petunias** which had been grown in the open air, had ever been seen here before."

Those Perennials and Biennials marked with an asterisk (*) will bloom the first year from seed.

N.B.—In ordering, the numbers only will suffice, but as the numbers are altered every year, the date of Catalogue should also be given.

No.	Name.	Hard Dur.	Ht in feet.	Colour.	Months of Flowering	Per Pkt.	Observations.
						s. d.	
503	**Abronia umbellata**	hhA	spr.	pink	Jn to Sp	3	} Pretty Verbena-like annuals, excellent
504	„ **arenaria**	„	„	yellow	„	4	} for rockwork, &c.
505	**Abutilon, mixed hybrids**... ...	gs	6-8	various	My to An	1 6	Handsome greenhouse plants.
506	**Acacia lophantha**	hhP	3-5	yellow	„	4	Beautiful plant for pot culture
507	**Acanthus mollis**	hP	3	pink & white	Jn to Sp	6	Fine herbaceous plant.
	Acroclinium, *see page* 90.						
508	**Æthionema grandiflora**	„	1	rose	My & Ju	6	Beautiful hardy border plant.
509	**Ageratum, Imperial dwarf blue** ...	hhA	½	blue	Jn to Oc	4	} Valuable bedding plants of dwarf
510	„ „ „ **white** ...	„	„	white	„	4	} habit, exceedingly floriferous.
511	**Agrostemma coronaria atro-sanguinea**	hP	2	dark crimson	Jy to Sp	3	Fine showy perennial.
512	***Alonsoa linifolia**	hhB	1½	orange scarlet	Jy to Oc	6	} Excellent for mixed borders or as pot-
513	„ „ **gracilis** (new) ...	„	„	„	„	6	} plants, showy and pretty. A. myrti-
514 *	„ **myrtifolia**	„	„	scarlet	„	6	} folia is a fine new species, having
515 *	„ **Mutisi**	„	1	blush & scarlet	„	6	} large handsome flowers.
516	**Alstrœmeria, choice mixed** ...	hhB	2	various	Ju to Au	4	Fine new varieties.
517	**Alyssum maritimum**	hA	½	white	Ju to Oc	3	Useful for edgings, borders, &c.
518	„ **saxatile compactum** ...	hP	„	yellow	Ap & My	4	Fine for rockwork or borders.
519	**Amaranthus melancholicus ruber**	hhA	1-1½	blood red fol.	Jn to Sp	4	} A brilliant class of plants for decora-
520	„ **salicifolius**	„	„	scarlet	„	4	} tive purposes. A. salicifolius is very
521	„ **tricolor giganteus**	„	1½	var. col. leaf	„	6	} useful for conservatory decoration.
522	**Anagallis grandiflora coccinea** ...	„	½	scarlet	Jn to Oc	6	} Very pretty free-flowering annuals for
523	„ **Indica**	„	„	blue	„	3	} beds, rock-work, &c. A. grandiflora
524	„ **fine varieties, mixed** ...	„	„	various	„	4	} coccinea is very fine.
525	**Anchusa angustifolia**	hP	2	azure blue	„	6	} Beautiful Forget-me-not-like flowers, fine for bedding out or bouquets.
526	***Anemone coronaria, finest mixed**	„	1	various	Fe to An	3	Beautiful early flowering vars.
527 *	„ **fulgens**	„	„	brill. scarlet	Ap to Jn	6	Very showy.
	Antirrhinum, *see page* 66.						
528	**Aquilegia alpina superba** ...	„	1½	blue & white	My to Jy	6	
529	„ **Californica hybrida** ...	„	2	orange yellow	„	6	*Columbines.* This class of hardy peren-
530	„ **chrysantha**	„	2½	pale yellow	„	6	nials will thrive in almost any soil or
531	„ „ **grandiflora alba** (new)	„	„	white	„	1 0	position, and are admirably suited for
532	„ **cærulea**	„	„	sky blue	„	6	shrubbery borders, large rockeries,
533	„ „ **hybrida**	„	„	blue & yellow	„	1 0	or permanent beds where not often
534	„ **glandulosa vera**	„	1½	dk. blue & wh.	„	1 0	disturbed, and where they form
535	„ **Skinneri**	„	„	scarlet & yell.	„	6	beautiful objects. They vary in
536	„ **Stuarti**	„	2	blue & white	„	1 6	height from two to three feet. A.
537	„ **caryophylloides fl. pl.** ...	„	„	striped	„	6	glandulosa vera and cærulea hybrida
538	„ **mixed, single and double**	„	„	various	„	3	are especially worthy of notice.
539	„ **double, white**	„	„	white	„	3	
540	**Arabis alpina**	„	½	„	Mr to My	3	Early flowering rock or border plant.

Flower Seeds, General List (continued).

No.	Name.	Hard Dur.	Ht in feet.	Colour.	Months of Flowering	Per Pkt.	Observations.
						s. d.	
541	Asperula azurea setosa	hA	1	blue	My to An	3	Pretty sweet-scented annual.
	Asters, French and German, see pages 57, 59.						
542	Aster tenella	,,	½	mauve	Au & Sp	3	Dwarf annual *Michaelmas Daisy*.
543	Aubrietia Leichtlini	hP	,,	carmine rose	Mr to Ju	1 0	} Charming dwarf-growing plants of
544	,, græca	,,	,,	blue	,,	6	} spreading habit. First-class for
545	,, violacea	,,	,,	bright violet	,,	6	} rockwork or dry borders.
	Auricula, see page 66.						
	Balsam, see page 66.						
546	Bartonia aurea ...	hA	1½	golden yellow	Jy & Au	3	Showy hardy annual.
	Begonia, tuberous-rooted, see page 67.						
547	Beet, dwarf dark-leaved ...	hB	1	dk. pur. fol.	Ju to No	6	Fine variety for bedding.
548	,, Chilian	,,	2	variegated fol.	,,	6	} Brilliant and handsomely marked foliage. Splendid in Autumn.
549	Borecole, variegated ...	,,	,,	,,	Oc to Mr	6	Very handsomely variegated.
550	Brachycome iberidifolia ...	hhA	1	blue	Jy & Au	3	*Swan River Daisy.* Very pretty.
551	Browallia elata grandiflora ...	,,	1½	,,	Ju to Oc	6	} Beautiful plants for pots in the green-
552	,, Roezli	,,	,,	white & blue	,,	6	} house or conservatory.
553	Cacalia aurea	hA	1	orange	Jn to Au	3	} Useful hardy annuals, for bouquets,
554	,, coccinea	,,	,,	scarlet	,,	3	} &c.
555	Calandrinia speciosa ...	,,	spr.	bright purple	Ju & Jy	3	} Showy annuals for borders, rockwork,
556	,, alba ...	,,	,,	pure white	,,	3	} or any warm situation.
557	,, umbellata ...	hP	½	brill.mag.pur.	Ju to Au	6	Remarkably brilliant perennial.
558	Calceolaria, shrubby, mixed	hhP	1	various	My to Oc	1 6	Useful bedding-out varieties
	,, hybrida, see page 68.						
559	Calendula officinalis Meteor	hA	1½	orange & yel.	,,	3	} Double-flowered *Pot Marigolds,* in
560	,, Prince of Orange ...	,,	,,	orange	,,	3	} bloom till late in the Autumn.
561	Callirhoe pedata nana compacta...	hhA	1	crimson	Ju to Oc	6	Brilliant annual.
562	Calliopsis atrosanguinea ...	hA	2	dark brown	Jy to Sp	3	} Well-known brilliant and useful
563	,, Burridgii	,,	,,	yel. & brown	,,	3	} annuals, remaining in bloom for a
564	,, Drummondi ...	,,	1½	golden yellow	,,	3	} long time. Well adapted for grow-
565	,, tinctoria	,,	2	yel. & brown	,,	3	} ing in and near large towns, and
566	,, nana, dwarf vars. mixed ...	,,	,,	various	,,	6	} exceedingly useful for cutting.
567	Campanula medium, Dean's hybd.	hB	2½	,,	Ju to Au	1 0	} *Canterbury Bells.* These are a highly
568	,, ,, single blue	,,	,,	dark blue	,,	3	} interesting and desirable class of
569	,, ,, ,, white	,,	,,	pure white	,,	3	} handsome flowering plants for the
570	,, ,, ,, rose	,,	,,	rose	,,	4	} decoration of the garden. The large
571	,, ,, ,, mixed	,,	,,	various	,,	4	} bells of the pure white varieties are
572	,, ,, double mixed	,,	,,	,,	,,	3	} especially handsome, and should be
573	,, ,, calycanthema,blue	,,	,,	blue	,,	6	} freely grown for the contrast they
574	,, ,, ,, alba	,,	,,	white	,,	6	} afford with most other flowers. The
575	,, ,, ,, rosea	,,	,,	rose	,,	6	} double-flowered vars. are very fine.
576	,, Loreyi	hA	1	blue	,,	3	} C. pyramidalis and alba form very
577	,, pentagonia ...	,,	,,	purple	,,	3	} useful and handsome pot plants,
578	,, pyramidalis ...	hP	3	blue	,,	3	} whilst C. turbinata is a splendid
579	,, ,, alba	,,	,,	white	,,	3	} dwarf growing sort for the garden,
580	,, turbinata ...	,,	1	blue	,,	4	} rockeries, &c.
581	Candytuft, New carmine...	hA	,,	carmine	My to Au	6	} Useful and exceedingly showy annuals
582	,, creamy white	,,	,,	creamy white	,,	6	} for beds, rockwork, borders, &c.,
583	,, extra dark crimson	,,	,,	crim. purple	,,	6	} and afford a brilliant display of
584	,, Dobbie's New Spiral	,,	,,	pure white	,,	4	} colour for a long period. The new
585	,, purple ...	,,	,,	purple	,,	3	} carmine, creamy white, dark
586	,, white rocket ...	,,	,,	white	,,	3	} crimson, and Dobbie's New Spiral,
587	,, mixed	,,	,,	various	,,	3	} are very beautiful varieties, and should be grown in every garden.
588	,, New dwarf crimson	,,	½	crim. purple	,,	6	} A beautiful new class, of a dwarf
589	,, ,, mixed	,,	,,	various	,,	6	} habit of growth, exceedingly fine for edgings, rockwork, &c.
590	*Canna Indica coccinea ...	hhP	3	scarlet	Jy to Sp	6	} Handsome-foliaged plants, excellent
591	* ,, Nepalensis... ...	,,	3	yellow	,,	6	} for the sub-tropical garden or the
592	* ,, gigantea	,,	6	dark red	,,	6	} greenhouse. Soak the seeds in mod-
593	* ,, zebrina superba ...	,,	,,	scarlet	,,	6	} erately warm water for about 12
594	* ,, fine varieties, mixed ...	,,	3-6	various	,,	4	} hours before planting.
595	Cannabis giganteus ...	hhA	6-8	orn. fol.	Ju to Oc	4	*Giant Hemp.* For sub-tropical garden.
596	Capsicum, Prince of Wales ...	,,	1½	yel. fruit	,,	6	} Fine ornamental pot-plants, bearing
597	,, Tom Thumb ...	,,	,,	scarlet fruit	,,	6	} a profusion of handsome berries.
598	Carduus benedictus ...	hA	3	white	Jy to Sp	3	*Ornamental Thistle.*
	Carnation, see page 68.						
599	Castilleja indivisa... ...	hhA	½	brilliant crim.	,,	6	Very brilliant and beautiful.

Flower Seeds, General List *(continued).*

No.	Name.	Hard Dur.	Ht in feet.	Colour.	Months of Flowering	Per Pkt.	Observations.
						s. d.	
600	Centaurea candidissima (ragusina)	hhr	1	white foliage	Jy to Sp	1 0	Handsome silvery-foliaged plants for bedding out or the greenhouse.
601	„ Clementei ...	„	„	„	„	1 0	
602	„ cyanus minor, blue	hA	2	dark blue	„	3	*Cornflowers.* Showy hardy annuals.
603	„ „ mixed	„	„	various	„	3	Useful for bouquets.
604	„ depressa ...	„	1½	blue	Jy & Au	3	Very useful for bouquets.
605	„ „ rosea	„	„	rose	„	3	
606	Centranthus macrosiphon	„	1	red	Jy to Sp	3	Showy border annual.
607	Cerastium Biebersteini	hP	„	white	„	6	Useful white-foliaged bedding plants.
608	„ tomentosum	„	„	„	„	3	
609	Chamærops humilis	gs	6	orn. foliage	Fe to Ap	6	*Dwarf Fan Palm.* Very ornamental.
610	Chamæpeuce casabonae ...	bhu	1	lilac	Ju to Au	1 0	*Fishbone Thistle.* Curious.
611	Chelone barbata coccinea	hP	3	scarlet	Jy & Au	3	Pretty Pentstemon-like flowers.
612	Chrysanthemum Burridgeanum ...	hA	1½	crim. wh. yel.	Jy to Sp	3	
613	„ coronarium imbricat. fl. pl.	„	„	various	„	1 0	Showy annuals for mixed beds or borders. C. Burridgeanum and C.
614	„ „ sulphureum pl.	„	„	pale yellow	„	3	Eclipse are exceedingly handsome,
615	„ tricolor aurea (Cloth of Gold)	„	„	yellow	„	3	the latter producing the most beau-
616	„ segetum grandiflorum	„	„	gold yellow	„	3	tiful and richest colours; all the
617	„ inodorum plenissima, fl. pl.	hh	2	white	„	3	varieties are easy of cultivation.
618	„ atrococcineum	hA	1½	crimson	„	3	Exceedingly floriferous, and very
619	„ Dunnetti album fl. pl.	„	„	white	„	3	useful for cutting.
620	„ carinatum, Eclipse	„	„	various	„	6	
621	„ „ Golden Feather	„	„	crim. wh. yel.	„	3	
622	„ frutescens ...	hhr	2	white	Ap to Oc	6	*Marguerites,* or *Parisian Daisies.*
	Indicum, see page 67.						
623	Cineraria candidissima ...	„	1½	yellow	Ju to Au	6	Silvery-foliaged bedding plant.
	hybrida, see page 69.						
624	Cistus, Rock, finest mixed	„	1	various	„	3	*Rock Rose.* Very handsome.
625	Clarkia elegans, double white	hA	2	white	Jy to Sp	4	
626	„ „ Purple King	„	„	purple	„	4	An exceedingly useful class of hardy
627	„ „ Salmon Queen	„	„	salmon	„	4	annuals, admirably suited for sowing
628	„ integripetala, double rose	„	1	rosy pink	Ju to Oc	3	in patches, &c., in mixed borders.
629	„ „ alba, double white	„	„	pure white	„	3	and are very easy of cultivation.
630	„ „ limbata	„	„	pink & white	„	3	The integripetala varieties, and C.
631	„ „ Tom Thumb	„	1	rosy pink	„	3	pulchella marginata are very hand-
632	„ pulchella ...	„	„	„	„	3	some. The new varieties of elegans
633	„ „ alba	„	„	pure white	„	3	are also very fine and desirable.
634	„ „ marginata fl. pl.	„	„	pink & white	„	3	
635	„ mixed ...	„	„	various	„	3	
636	Clematis hybrida, choice mixed ...	hP	cl.		My to Oc	1 0	Valuable hardy climbers.
637	Clianthus Dampieri ...	gs	4	scarlet & blk.	Ap to Jy	1 0	*Parrot-beak plant.* Magnificent.
638	Clintonia pulchella	hhA	½	blue & white	Ju to Sp	6	Beautiful little plant for pots, borders, rockwork, &c.
639	Cobœa scandens ...	hhr	cl.	purple	My to Oc	6	Well-known useful climbers.
640	„ alba	„	„	white	„	1 0	
	Cockscombs, see page 69.						
	Coleus, see page 67.						
641	Collinsia bicolor ...	hA	1	lilac & white	My to Au	3	Much admired and useful annuals.
642	„ candidissima	„	„	white	„	3	C. verna is a charming variety,
643	„ multicolor ...	„	„	var. coloured	„	3	seeds of which must be sown in
644	„ verna	„	„	sky bl. & wh.	Ap & My	6	August as soon as ripe.
645	Collomia coccinea...	„	1½	scarlet	Jy to Oc	3	Useful for bees, pretty.
	Columbine (see Aquilegia).						
646	Commelina cœlestis...	hhP	„	sky blue	Ju to Au	3	An attractive plant with fine glossy foliage.
647	Convolvulus major, crimson	hhA	cl.	crimson	Jy to Oc	3	A fine class of hardy annual climbers
648	„ „ white	„	„	white	„	3	suitable for covering walls, trellis,
649	„ „ purple	„	„	purple	„	3	wire-fencing, arbours, &c.,&c. Very
650	„ „ rose	„	„	rose	„	3	pretty in association with Tropæo-
651	„ „ striped	„	„	various	„	3	lum canariense.
652	„ „ mixed	„	„	„	„	3	
653	„ minor, dark purple	hA	1	dark purple	„	3	The true dark purple variety, ex- ceedingly rich-coloured.
654	„ „ crimson violet	„	„	crim. violet	„	6	Splendid variety.
655	„ Mauritanicus ...	hhP	trl.	lavender	Jy to Sp	3	Useful variety for hanging-baskets, rockwork, &c.
656	Convallaria majalis ...	hP	1	white	Ap to Ju	6	*Lily of the Valley.*
657	Cowslip, common field ...	„	½	yellow	My & Ju	4	*Primula elatior.*
	„ American (see Dodecatheon meadia).						
658	Cuphea platycentra ...	hhP	1	scarlet	Jy to Oc	6	Useful bedding plant.
	Cyclamen, see page 69.						

Flower Seeds, General List *(continued).*

LARKSPUR. No. 745.   GODETIA. No. 701.   CANDYTUFT. No. 584.

No.	Name.	Hard Dur.	Ht in fect.	Colour.	Months of Flowering	Per Pkt.	Observations.
						s. d.	
659	Daisy, double red	hP	½	dark red	Ap to Jy	1 0	*Bellis perennis*—well known useful
660	„ „ white ...	„	„	white	„	1 0	plants for Spring gardening, edg-
661	„ „ mixed	„	„	various	„	1 0	ings, &c.
	Dahlia, *see page 70.*						
662	Datura atropurpurea plenissima...	hhA	„	dark purple	„	6	Splendid large-flowered varieties.
663	„ Huberiana fl. pl.	„	1	white	„	4	Very handsome for mixed borders.
	Delphinium, *see page 70.*						
	Dianthus, *see page 70.*						
664	Digitalis maculata superba ...	hP	3	sptd. vars.	Jy & Au	6	*Foxgloves.* A showy class of hardy
665	„ monstrosa alba ...	„	4	white	„	4	perennials admirably suited for
666	„ very choice mixed ...	„	3	various	„	3	shrubbery borders, &c. D. maculata superba is very fine.
667	Dodecathoon meadia	„	1	purple	Ap to Ju	1 0	*American Cowslip.* Valuable hardy perennial.
668	Eccremocarpus scaber ...	hhP	cl.	orange	Jy to Sp	6	Handsome climber of quick growth.
669	Echeveria secunda glauca ...	gP	¼	yellow .	Ju to Sp	1 6	Useful succulent bedding plant.
670	Echinops ritro	hP	3–4	azure blue	Ju to No	6	Singular and handsome border plant.
	*Edelweis, *see page 90.*						
	Egg Plant (*see Solanum*).						
671	Erinus alpinus	„	„	rosy purple	Ap to Ju	6	Beautiful little alpine plant.
672	*Erysimum Peroffskianum ...	hB	1¼	orange	Jy to Sp	3	Showy hardy annual.
673	Erythræa Muhlenbergia ...	hA	„	rose & white	„	6	Beautiful hardy annual.
674	Erythrina crista galli ...	gS	15	scarlet	My to Jy	6	*Coral Tree.* Greenhouse shrub.
675	Erythrolæna conspicua ...	hhu	4	or. carmine	Jy & Au	1 0	
676	*Eschscholtzia crocea fl. pl. ...	hB	1	orange	Jy to Sp	6	
677	* „ „ alba fl. pl. ...	„	„	white	„	6	Brilliant and exceedingly showy
678	* „ grandiflora carminea ...	„	„	carmine	„	6	plants. E. grandiflora rosea, Man-
679	* „ Mandarin	„	„	scarlet	„	4	darin, and the double-flowered
680	* „ Californica alba ...	„	„	white	„	3	varieties are very fine.
681	* „ crocea	„	„	orange	„	3	
682	Eucharidium Breweri ...	hA	„	rosy lilac	My to Au	1 0	Free-blooming, pretty annuals, some-
683	„ grandiflorum album ...	„	„	white	„	3	what resembling the Clarkias, but
684	„ „ roseum ...	„	„	rose	„	3	more compact in habit. E. Breweri is very fine.
685	Eutoca viscida	„	„	deep blue	My & Ju	3	Pretty annual with sky-blue flowers.
	Evening Primrose (*see Œnothera*).						
686	Flos Adonis	„	1½	scarlet	Jy & An	3	*Pheasant's-eye.* Showy annual.
	Foxglove (*see Digitalis*).						
	Fuchsia, *see page 67.*						

Flower Seeds, General List *(continued)*.

No.	Name.	Hard Dur.	Ht in feet.	Colour.	Months of Flowering	Per Pkt.	Observations.
						s. d.	
687	*Gaillardia hybrida grandiflora ...	hp	2	various	Jy to Oc	1 0	Saved from choice named flowers.
688	„ amblyodon	hha	„	deep red	Jy to Sp	3	Splendid plants for beds or borders.
689	* „ picta fistulosa	hhp	„	crim. yellow	„	3	Very showy.
690	„ „ Lorenziana... ...	hha	1	red and yellow	„	6	New and beautiful variety
691	Gentiana acaulis	hp	¼	dark blue	Ap to Jy	1 0	Beautiful early flowering border plant.
	Geranium, *see* Pelargonium *page* 72.						
692	Geum coccineum fl. pl.	„	2	scarlet	Ju to Oc	3	Double Ranunculus-like flowers.
693	Gilia achillæfolia alba	hA	1¼	white	Jy to Sp	3	Very pretty free-flowering annuals,
694	„ „ major	„	„	blue	„	3	suitable for patches on mixed beds
695	„ nivalis	„	„	white	„	3	or borders, or for rockwork.
696	„ tricolor	„	„	various	„	3	
697	Gladiolus gandavensis, mixed ...	hhp	3-4	„	Jy to Oc	1 0	Saved from choicest sorts.
698	Glaucium luteum	hA	2	yellow	Jy & Au	3	*Horned Poppy.* Curious.
	Gloxinia, *see page* 71.						
	Golden Feather (*see Pyrethrum aureum*).						
699	Godetia, Duke of Fife	„	1	satiny crim.	Jy to Sp	6	
700	„ Duchess of Fife	„	„	wh. & carmine	„	6	Magnificent class of free-flowering
701	„ Duchess of Albany ...	„	„	pure white	„	6	hardy annuals deserving of the
702	„ Lady Albemarle	„	„	crim. scarlet	„	6	most extensive culture. Duchess of
703	„ reptans insignis	„	„	white & crim.	„	3	Albany, Duke of Fife, Duchess of
704	„ The Bride	„	2	white & scarlet	„	3	Fife, Lady Albemarle, and General
705	„ General Gordon	„	1	deep crimson	„	6	Gordon, are especially worthy of
706	„ Bridesmaid	„	„	rose & white	„	6	notice, the flowers being of immense
707	„ Butterfly	„	„	wh. spt. crim.	„	6	size and charming appearance.
708	„ 6 choice varieties... ...	—	—	—	—	1 6	
709	Gourd, small ornamental vars. ...	hhA	cl.	yellow	Jy to Oc	6	Pretty climbers with ornamental fruit
710	Grammanthes gentianoides ...	„	½	scarlet	Ju to Oc	6	Excellent for hanging-baskets, pots, &c.
711	Grevillea robusta	gs	—	—	—	6	Beautiful greenhouse shrub.
712	Gypsophila elegans	hA	1½	pink	Jy to Sp	3	A fine annual from the Crimea.
713	Hawkweed, red	„	2	red	„	3	
714	„ white	„	1½	white	„	3	Useful and showy annuals.
715	„ yellow	„	„	yellow	„	3	
	Helianthus (*see Sunflower*).						
	Helichrysums (*see Everlasting Flowers*).						
716	Heliotrope, splendid mixed ...	hhp	1	greyish blue	My to Oc	6	Deliciously fragrant bedding plants.
717	Heracleum giganteum ...	„	6-8	„	Ju to Oc	3	*Giant Cow Parsnip.* Fine plant for shrubberies and waste places.
718	Hibiscus Africanus major	hA	2	lemon, dk. eye	Jy to Oc	3	Handsome annual.
	Hollyhock, *see page* 71.						
719	*Honesty, purple or lilac ...	hB	„	lilac	Ju & Jy	3	*Lunaria biennis* varieties. Fine for
720	* „ white	„	„	white	„	6	shrubbery borders, &c.
721	Honeysuckle, French, red	hp	„	red	„	3	Showy perennials, excellent for grow-
722	„ „ white ...	„	„	white	„	3	ing under trees, on mixed borders, &c.
723	Humulus Japonica	hhA	cl.	—	—	6	*Japanese Hop.* Rapid and useful climber for trellises, &c.
724	Iberis Gibraltarica ...	hp	¾	pink & white	Ap & My	4	Fine hardy perennials for rockwork
725	„ sempervirens ...	„	„	white	„	3	or borders.
726	Ice Plant	hhA	spr.	„	Jy & Au	3	Useful for garnishing.
727	Impatiens Sultani... ...	gp	1	magen. crim.	Ja to Dec	1 0	Splendid pot plant for the greenhouse.
728	Ionopsidium acaule ...	hA	½	violet	Ap to Oc	3	Charming little plant for rockwork.
729	Ipomœa coccinea ...	hhp	cl.	scarlet	Jy & Au	3	
730	„ hederacea superba ...	hhA	„	blue & white	Jy to Oc	4	Beautiful climbers for the greenhouse
731	„ Leari	gp	„	violet & white	Ju to Sp	6	verandahs, trellises, &c.
732	„ rubro-cærulea	„	„	blue and red	Au to Oc	6	
733	Ipomopsis elegans	hhp	5	scarlet	Au & Sp	3	Splendid for beds or borders.
734	Isotoma axilaris	„	1	blue	Jy to Sp	3	Handsome long-blooming plant.
735	Jacobæa, double, crimson ...	hhA	„	crimson	„	3	Useful varieties for bedding out, to
736	„ „ rose	„	„	rose	„	3	cut for bouquets, &c.
737	„ „ white	„	„	white	„	3	
738	Kalanchoe carnea	gp	2	pink	Ja to Mr	1 6	Charming greenhouse plant.
739	Kaulfussia amelloides	hA	½	light blue	Jy & Au	3	
740	„ „ rosea	„	„	rose	„	3	Pretty little Aster-like plants of dwarf
741	„ atroviolacea	„	„	dark purple	„	3	habit.
742	„ kermesina	„	„	crimson	„	6	
743	*Lantana, choice mixed	hhp	1	various	My to Oc	6	Choice bedding or pot plants.
744	Larkspur, dwarf rocket, double ...	hA	„	„	Jy & Au	3	
745	„ candelabra-formed ...	„	„	„	„	4	Fine double-flowered varieties of
746	„ Emperor, choice mxd. dbl.	„	1½	„	„	6	various beautiful colours.
747	„ Stock-flowered ...	„	„	rosy scarlet	„	1 0	
748	„ Tall branching ...	„	3	various	„	3	

From **Mr. G. H. B. LAWSON**, Shanklin.
Mar. 3rd.
"The **Primula** and **Cineraria** I had from you last year turned out very fine the flowers of the Primulas measuring over two inches across."

From **Mr. ISAAC WILDMAN**, Government House Gardens, Londonderry.
Oct. 1st.
"I never grew better plants, or raised such a choice variety of flowers, as I did this season from the **Calceolaria** seed sent me."

AURICULA, CHOICE ALPINE.

HARDY HYBRID PRIMROSE.

MIGNONETTE, VICTORIA GIANT.

NEW DWARF STRIPED PETUNIA.

LOBELIA ERINUS COMPACTA.

EUCHARIDIUM BREWERI.

CLINTONIA PULCHELLA.

SHIRLEY POPPIES. No. 891.

THIS beautiful strain of Hardy Annual Poppy is perfectly hardy, and flowers profusely the first season from seed. The flowers are large, exceedingly graceful and elegant; the colours are pure, soft, and varied, and range from blush-white, rose, delicate pink, and carmine through innumerable tints to bright sparkling crimson; the petals have a glossy satin-like wavy surface of exquisite softness, which makes the flowers literally ripple with colour under the slightest movement. Per packet 1s.; smaller packet 6d.

SCHIZANTHUS PAPILIONACEUS.

DANIELS' PRIZE BLOTCHED PANSY.

DANIELS' TEN-WEEK STOCK.

BRACHYCOME IBERIDIFOLIA.

CHRYSANTHEMUM, "ECLIPSE."

LOBELIA FULGENS VICTORIA.

PHACELIA CAMPANULARIA.

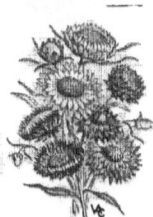

HELICHRYSUM, MIXED.

Flower Seeds, General List *(continued).*

No.	Name.	Hard Dur.	Ht in feet.	Colour.	Months of Flowering	Per Pkt.	Observations.
						s. d.	
749	**Leptosiphon aureus**	hA	½	golden yellow	Jy to Oc	3	Handsome showy annuals. L. densiflorus albus is one of the purest white flowers in cultivation. L. roseus and carmineus are lovely little compact-growing varieties of beautiful colours.
750	,, carmineus	,,	,,	carmine	,,	6	
751	,, densiflorus...	,,	1	lilac & white	,,	3	
752	,, ,, albus	,,	,,	pure white	,,	3	
753	,, roseus	,,	½	rose	,,	4	
754	,, French hybrids, mixed ...	,,	,,	various	,,	3	
755	**Leptosyne maritima**	,,	3	yellow	Jy to Sp	6	Very useful for cutting
756	**Lapageria rosea**	gP	cl.	rose	Ju to Oc	2 6	Beautiful stove or greenhouse climber
757	**Lavatera arborea variegata** ...	hhP	6-8	purple	Jy to Sp	1 0	Beautifully variegated foliage.
758	,, red	hA	3	red	Jy & Au	3	Showy hardy annuals.
759	,, white	,,	,,	white		3	
760	**Lavender, common garden** ...	hP	,,	lavender	,,	3	*Lavendula spica.* Well known.
761	**Layia elegans**	hA	1	yell. & white	,,	6	Pretty yellow flowers edged with white
	Lily of the Valley (*see Convallaria*).						
762	**Limnanthes Douglasi**	,,	½	white & yel.	My to Sp	3	Pretty dwarf annual.
763	**Linaria reticulata aurea purpurea**	,,	½	yel. & maroon	Jy to Sp	6	Pretty hardy annual.
764	**Linum grandiflorum rubrum** ...	hhA	1	crim. scarlet	Ju to Oc	3	Very brilliant and showy.
765	,, flavum	hP	,,	yellow	,,	4	Useful perennial for borders or pots.
766	**Lisianthus Russellianus**	gA		blue	Ju to Au	1 0	Beautiful greenhouse annual
	Lobelias, *see page* 74.						
767	**Lophospermum scandens**	hhP	cl.	blush	,,	4	Very useful climber.
768	**Love-lies-bleeding, red** ...	hA	2	crimson	Jy & Au	3	Showy border annuals.
769	,, ,, white ...	,,	,,	pale yellow	,,	3	
770	**Lupine, large blue** ...	,,	,,	blue	Jy to Sp	3	Suitable for mixed borders in front of shrubs, &c.
771	,, ,, yellow ...	,,	1½	yellow	,,	3	
772	,, ,, rose	,,	2	rose	,,	3	
773	,, ,, white	,,	,,	white	,,	3	
774	**Lupinus albo-coccineus**	,,	,,	scar. & white	Ju to Oc	3	These handsome and easily cultivated annuals certainly deserve their high popularity. L. subcarnosus is a strikingly handsome variety that continues in bloom for a long time. L. sulphureus superbus and albococcineus are beautiful.
775	,, ,, ,, nanus	,,	1	,,	,,	6	
776	,, Cruikshanki ...	,,	3-5	bl. wh. & yell.	,,	3	
777	,, hybridus superbus	,,	2	pur. ro. & wh.	,,	3	
778	,, subcarnosus ...	,,	1	dk. bl. & wh.	,,	3	
779	,, sulphureus superbus	,,	1½	sul. yellow	Ju to Sp	3	
780	,, nanus ...	,,	1	blue & white	,,	3	
781	,, ,, albus ...	,,	,,	white	,,	3	
782	,, polyphyllus ...	hP	4	blue	Ju to Au	3	Useful perennials for shrubbery borders, &c. L. polyphyllus tricolor is the finest.
783	,, ,, albus ...	,,	,,	white	,,	3	
784	,, ,, tricolor ...	,,	,,	various	,,	6	
785	**Lychnis Haageana**	,,	1	,,	Ju & Jy	3	Showy herbaceous perennials, with brilliant flowers.
786	,, fulgens	,,	,,	brill. scarlet	,,	3	
787	**Malva crispa**	hA	4	pink & white	,,	3	*Curled Mallow.* Useful for garnishing
788	,, moschata alba	hP	1	white	Jy to Sp	6	Fine showy hardy perennial.
789	**Malope grandiflora**	hA	3	crimson	,,	3	Brilliant and showy annuals of easy cultivation.
790	,, ,, alba	,,	,,	white	,,	3	
791	,, ,, rosea	,,	,,	rose	,,	3	
	Marigolds, *see page* 72.						
792	*Marvel of Peru. Choicest mixed	hhP	2-3	various	Ju to Au	3	Well-known useful perennials.
793	**Martynia fragrans**	hhA	2	str. crimson	,,	3	Large-flowered handsome annual.
794	**Mathiola bicornis**	,,	1	lilac	Ju to Sp	4	*Night-scented Stock.* Fragrant.
795	**Matricaria eximia crispa fl. pl.** ...	hP	2	white	Jy to Oc	6	*Double-flowered Feverfew.* Pretty.
796	**Maurandya Barclayana grandifl.**	hhA	cl.	blue	My to Sp	6	Fine and useful climbers.
797	,, ,, alba	,,	,,	white	,,	6	
798	**Mesembryanthemum tricolor** ...	,,	½	cr. wh. & pur.	Ju to Sp	3	Excellent for sunny rockwork, pretty Daisy-like flowers.
799	,, cordifolium variegatum ...	hhP	,,	rosy purple	,,	1 0	Useful for carpet bedding, &c.
	Mimulus, *see page* 74.						
800	**Mignonette, Miles' hybrid spiral**	hA	1½	pale buff	Jy to Sp	6	Superb varieties of comparatively recent introduction. Parson's white and Victoria Giant Red throw up noble spikes of deliciously fragrant bloom. The new "Machet" is also an exceedingly fine variety.
801	,, Parsons' white	,,	1	,,	,,	6	
802	,, dwarf compact	,,	½	reddish buff	,,	6	
803	,, Machet	,,	¾	pale buff	,,	6	
804	,, Golden Queen	,,	1	pale yellow	,,	6	
805	,, Victoria Giant Red ...	,,	2	red buff	,,	6	
806	,, common sweet-scented ...	,,	1	buff	,,	3	Very useful for ordinary purposes.
807	**Mina lobata**	hhA	12	orange scarlet	Jy to Oc	1 6	Splendid climber for trellises, &c.
808	**Musk Plant**	hP	½	yellow	Ju to Sp	4	*Mimulus moschatus.*
809	**Myosotis alpestris grandiflora** ...	,,	½	sky bl. yel. eye	,,	1 0	*Forget-me-nots.* Well-known beautiful little plants, invaluable for Spring gardening, &c. *M. disitiflora* is the best variety for Spring gardening. A partially shaded and rather moist position is most favourable.
810	,, azorica	,,	1	dark blue	,,	1 0	
811	,, ,, alba	,,	,,	white	,,	1 0	
812	,, disitiflora	,,	½	sky blue	Mr to Jn	1 0	
813	,, ,, alba	,,	,,	white	,,	1 0	
814	,, palustris (*the true Forget-me-not*)	,,	1	blue	Ju to Sp	6	

From **Mr. GEORGE MAGGS**, Bagstone, Falfield.
Feb. 2nd.
"The flowers I grew from your Seeds last year were very satisfactory; the **Zinnias** and **Rhodanthes** being especially fine."

From **Mr. D. SIMPSON**, Crook, Durham.
Jan. 25th.
"I obtained a packet of **Carnations** from you, and raised some splendid flowers, which I exhibited at three different Shows last year, taking First Prize each time."

Flower Seeds, General List *(continued)*.

No.	Name.	Hard Dur.	Ht in feet.	Colour.	Months of Flowering	Per Pkt.	Observations.
						s. d.	
815	**Nasturtium,** Tom Thumb, King ...	hA	½	rich scarlet	Jy to Sp	4	A brilliant and invaluable class of annuals very easy of cultivation. King of Tom Thumbs and Empress of India are the most brilliant of all. Among the others we may mention Golden King, cærulea rosea, and Ruby King as being particularly fine. Will thrive in almost any soil, but should have a sunny, rather dry situation, to bloom them to perfection.
816	„ „ Empress of India ...	„	„	deep scarlet	„	6	
817	„ „ dark crimson ...	„	„	dark crimson	„	3	
818	„ „ scarlet	„	„	scarlet	„	3	
819	„ „ Lady-bird	„	„	sptd, yel. & rd.	„	6	
820	„ „ cærulea rosea ...	„	„	bluish rose	„	3	
821	„ „ Golden King ...	„	„	golden yellow	„	6	
822	„ „ King Theodore	„	„	maroon	„	3	
823	„ „ Ruby King	„	„	purplish red	„	6	
824	„ „ Crystal Palace Gem	„	„	sulph. & mar.	„	3	
825	„ „ Pearl	„	„	cr. white	„	3	
826	„ „ yellow	„	„	yellow	„	3	
827	„ „ mixed	„	„	various	„	3	
	„ climbing (*see Tropæolum*).						
828	**Nemesia versicolor** ...	„	½	blue & white	Ju to Au	3	Useful for rockwork, pots, &c.
829	**Nerium Oleander**	gs	6	rose	Ju to Sp	6	Valuable greenhouse shrub.
830	**Nertera depressa**	hP	½	white	Ju to Au	1 0	Bears bright coral red berries.
831	**Nemophila atomaria atro-cærulea**	hA	spr.	deep blue	My to Sp	6	Extremely pretty early flowering annuals, useful for beds or borders, pots in the greenhouse, &c. N. insignis is fine for Spring gardening.
832	„ insignis	„	„	blue & white	„	3	
833	„ „ alba	„	„	white	„	3	
834	„ „ maculata grandiflr.	„	„	white & violet	„	3	
835	**Nicotiana affinis**	bhA	3	white	„	6	Fine for the sub-tropical garden. N. affinis has long white tubular flowers, deliciously scented.
836	„ macrophylla gigantea ...	„	6-8	pink	„	4	
837	„ Virginica	„	5-6	„	„	3	
838	**Nierembergia gracilis** ...	hhP	½	white & lilac	Ju to Sp	6	Useful for clumps, edgings, &c.
839	**Nigella damascena** ...	hA	1	pale blue	„	3	*Love-in-a-mist.* Curious.
840	**Nolana atriplicifolia** ...	„	spr.	blue & white	Jy to Sp	3	Pretty trailers, similar to Convolvulus minor.
841	„ „ alba ...	„	„	white	„	3	
842	**Nyctarine selaginoides** ...	hhA	„	white & pink	„	3	Excellent for rockeries, &c.
843	***Obeliscaria pulcherrima** ...	hP	2	crim. & yellow	Jy to Oc	3	Curious hardy perennial.
844	**Œnothera acaulis**	„	½	white	Ju to Au	6	A free-flowering class of plants useful for mixed beds, borders, &c. Œ. Lamarckiana is more suitable for shrubbery borders.
845	„ bistorta Veitchii ...	hA	1	yel. crim. spot	Jy to Sp	3	
846	„ Lamarckiana ...	hP	3	yellow	Ju to Au	3	
847	„ macrocarpa (Missouriensis)	„	spr.	„	Ju & Jy	4	
848	**Oxalis rosea**	hhA	¾	rose	Ap to Jy	6	Useful plants for rockwork, edgings, hanging-baskets, pots, &c.
849	„ „ alba	„	„	white	„	6	
850	„ Valdiviana...	hP	½	yellow	Ju to Oc	6	
851	„ tropæoloides	gBb	„	„	„	6	
852	**Oxyura chrysanthemoides** ...	hA	1	yel. & white	Ju to Au	3	Showy hardy annual.
853	**Pæony, Herbaceous, choicest dbl.**	hP	2	various	Ju & Jy	1 0	Showy herbaceous plants.
	Pansy, *see page* 73.						
854	**Papaver nudicaule** ...	hB	¾	yellow	Ju to Sp	6	*Iceland Poppies.* A beautiful and showy class, splendid for cut flowers.
855	„ „ alba ...	„	„	white	„	6	
856	„ „ miniatum ...	„	„	orange scarlet	„	1 0	
857	„ „ mixed ...	„	„	various	„	6	
858	„ Pavonium ...	hA	„	scar. & black	„	1 0	The Peacock Poppy, very fine.
859	„ umbrosum ...	„	1½	„	Jy to Sp	6	Fine new showy annual Poppies.
860	„ Danebrog ...	„	„	scar. & white	„	6	
861	„ Mikado ...	„	2	„	Ju to Sp	6	Very beautiful fringed variety.
862	„ orientale	bP	1½	rich scarlet	Jy to Sp	6	Grand variety for shrubbery borders.
863	**Passiflora cærulea** ...	„	cl.	blue	Ju to Oc	6	Valuable hardy climber for walls, &c.
	Pelargonium, *see page* 72.						
	Pentstemon, *see page* 72.						
864	**Perilla Nankinensis**	hhA	1½	dark purple	Ju to Au	3	Valuable dark-foliaged bedding plant.
865	**Pea, Sweet,** The Queen	hA	cl.	carmine strpd.	Ju to Oc	6	A beautiful and highly popular class of hardy annual climbers, deliciously fragrant, exceedingly useful for covering trellises, wire fencings, &c.; also invaluable for bouquets.
866	„ „ Butterfly	„	„	blue & white	„	6	
867	„ „ Invincible scarlet ...	„	„	scarlet	„	3	
868	„ „ Painted Lady ...	„	„	rose & white	„	3	
869	„ „ white	„	„	white	„	3	
870	„ „ black or purple ...	„	„	dark purple	„	3	
871	„ „ mixed, all colours ...	„	„	various	„	3	
872	„ „ Apple blossom (Eckford)	„	„	rose & white	„	1 0	Extremely beautiful new varieties, raised by Mr. Eckford, which are very superior to and distinct from the older sorts, the flowers being larger and the colours more brilliant. These are splendid for cut flowers, and where space is limited should certainly be grown in preference to the older varieties.
873	„ „ Boreatton „	„	„	crim. & rose	„	1 0	
874	„ „ Cardinal „	„	„	crim. scarlet	„	1 0	
875	„ „ Imperial Blue „	„	„	bright blue	„	1 0	
876	„ „ Indigo King „	„	„	maroon purple	„	1 0	
877	„ „ Isa Eckford „	„	„	delicate rose	„	1 0	
878	„ „ Orange Prince „	„	„	orange pink	„	1 0	
879	„ „ Splendour „	„	„	rose & crim.	„	1 0	
880	„ „ Eckford's **Superb** varieties, **mixed** ...	„	„	various	„	1 0	
881	„ „ „ „ smaller pkt.	„	„	„	„	6	

Flower Seeds, General List *(continued)*.

No.	Name.	Hard Dur.	Ht in feet.	Colour.	Months of Flowering	Per Pkt. s. d.	Observations.
882	**Pea, Sweet, a collection of 12 beautiful varieties,** including Mr. Eckford's new sorts, 7s. 6d.						
883	,, ,, **a collection of 6** ditto, 4s. 0d.						
884	**Pea, Everlasting, rose**	hp	cl.	rose	Ju to Sp	4	Fine hardy climbers of rapid growth.
885	,, ,, **white. Very fine...**	,,	,,	white	,,	1 0	
	Petunias, *see page* 76.						
886	**Phacelia campanularia**	hA	1	rich blue	Jy & Au	6	Superb new annual from California.
	Phloxes, *see page* 77.						
	Pink, *see page* 68.						
	Polyanthuses, *see page* 78.						
887	**Poppy, dbl. Pæony-flowrd. mixed**	,,	2-3	various	,,	3	Gorgeously coloured annuals, very effective for large mixed beds, shrubbery borders, &c. The new "Shirley" Poppies are especially worthy of mention, as the most beautiful and charming annuals that have been introduced of late years.
888	,, ,, **dwarf French** ...	,,	1½	,,	,,	3	
889	,, ,, **scarlet**	,,	2-3	scarlet	,,	3	
890	,, ,, **white**	,,	,,	white	,,	3	
891	,, **"The Shirley,"** *see page* 85.	,,	,,	various	,,	6	
892	,, **Carnation, finest double** ...	,,	2½	,,	,,	3	
893	,, **Ranunculus flowered, mxd.**	,,	,,	,,	,,	3	
894	**Portulaca grandiflora alba fl. pl.** ...	hhA	½	pure white	Ju to Sp	6	These constitute the most brilliant class of half-hardy annuals in cultivation. The plants are of a spreading habit of growth, only reach a height of from four to six inches, and are splendid for sunny rockwork, warm dry borders, pots in the greenhouse, &c. The seed has been carefully saved, and will produce a large percentage of fine double flowers, of strikingly handsome colours.
895	,, ,, **aurea fl. pl.** ...	,,	,,	golden yellow	,,	6	
896	,, ,, **rosea fl. pl.** ...	,,	,,	bright rose	,,	6	
897	,, ,, **splendens fl. pl.** ...	,,	,,	brill. crimson	,,	6	
898	,, ,, **Thellusoni fl. pl.** ...	,,	,,	crimson	,,	6	
899	,, ,, **choicest mixed dbl.**	,,	,,	various	,,	1 0	
900	,, ,, ,, smaller pkt.	,,	,,	,,	,,	6	
901	,, ,, **an assortment of 8 beautiful vars.,** one packet of each	,,	,,	,,	,,	1 6	
902	,, ,, **single-flowered, choicest mixed**	,,	,,	,,	,,	6	
903	**Potentilla, choice mixed, double...**	hp	2	,,	Ju to Au	6	Showy herbaceous perennials.
904	**Prince's Feather, giant**	hA	3	crimson	Jy & Au	3	Useful for large borders, &c.
	Primrose and Primulas, *see pages* 75, 78.						
905	**Pyrethrum parthenifol. aureum**	hp	½	wh., yel. fol.	Jy to Sp	4	*Golden Feather.* Valuable bedding plant
906	,, ,, **laciniatum** ...	,,	,,	,,	,,	6	A fine variety of compact growth.
907	,, ,, **selaginoides** ...	,,	,,	,,	,,	6	A fine acquisition.
908	,, **hybridum fl. pl., mixed** ...	,,	2	various	,,	1 0	New and highly improved class.
	Rhodanthe, *see page* 90.						
909	**Ricinus Borboniensis arboreus** ...	hhA	12	green fol.	,,	4	Stately plants with large handsome foliage, excellent for sub-tropical gardening. R. Borboniensis arboreus attains gigantic dimensions.
910	,, **major sanguineus**	,,	6-8	pale red fol.	,,	3	
911	,, **communis major**	,,	,,	green fol.	,,	3	
912	,, **Gibsoni**	,,	,,	red fol.	,,	6	
913	**Rocket, Sweet, purple**	hp	1½	purple	Ju to Au	3	Useful herbaceous perennials, very fragrant.
914	,, ,, **white**	,,	,,	white	,,	3	
915	**Rivinia humilis**	gp	2	,,	,,	6	Handsome plant for the greenhouse.
916	**Salpiglossis grandiflora, fine mixd.**	hhA	,,	various	Jy to Sp	6	Beautiful large-flowered annuals.
917	**Salvia splendens**	hhp	3	scarlet	Ju to Oc	6	Free-flowering handsome perennials for borders, &c. S. argentea has beautiful silvery foliage, quite covering the ground.
918	,, **patens**	,,	2	rich blue	,,	1 0	
919	,, **coccinea**	,,	,,	scarlet	Jy to Sp	4	
920	,, **argentea**	,,	½	silver fol.	,,	4	
921	**Sanvitalia procumbens fl. pl** ...	hA	spr.	yellow	Jy & Au	3	Useful hardy annual.
922	**Saponaria Calabrica**	,,	½	bright rose	Ju to Oc	3	Pretty and useful annuals for beds or borders. S. multiflora compacta and alba are charming new varieties of a fine dwarf habit of growth.
923	,, ,, **alba**	,,	,,	white	,,	3	
924	,, **multiflora compacta** ...	,,	¼	pink	,,	6	
925	,, ,, ,, **alba** ...	,,	,,	white	,,	6	
926	,, **ocymoides**	hp	spr.	pink	Jy & Au	3	Showy hardy perennial.
927	**Scabiosa atropurpurea major fl. pl.**	hB	3	various	Jy to Sp	3	Fine showy border plants. Excellent for cut flowers.
928	,, **candidissima fl. pl.** ...	,,	,,	white	,,	3	
929	**Schizanthus pinnatus**	hhA	1½	pk. wh. & blk.	Ju to Au	3	Elegant-growing half-hardy annuals excellent for mixed beds or borders or for pots in the greenhouse in Spring.
930	,, **papilionaceus**	,,	,,	crim.&yel.spt.	,,	6	
931	,, **retusus**	,,	2	crim. yellow	,,	3	
932	,, ,, **albus**	,,	,,	white	,,	3	
933	**Schizopetalon Walkeri**	,,	1	,,	My to Au	4	Beautifully fragrant annual.
934	**Scyphanthus elegans**	,,	6	yellow	Jy & Au	4	Useful half-hardy plant.
935	**Sedum azureum**	,,	¼	sky blue	,,	3	*Stone-crop.* Elegant little plant.
936	**Sensitive Plant**	tA	2	pale pink	Jy to Sp	6	*Mimosa pudica.* Ornamental for pots.
937	**Silene armeria rubra**	hA	1½	bright red	Ju to Sp	3	Bright profuse-flowering annuals. S. pendula and varieties are admirably suited for Spring gardening, and form a charming contrast with blue Nemophila, &c.
938	,, ,, **alba**	,,	,,	white	,,	3	
939	,, **pendula ruberrima** ...	,,	1	rosy carmine	My to Sp	3	
940	,, ,, **alba**	,,	,,	white	,,	3	
941	,, ,, **compacta**	,,	½	rosy carmine	,,	3	
942	,, ,, **new double** ...	,,	1	rosy pink	,,	4	

From **Mr. ALEXANDER LAURIE**, Cumbernauld, N.B.
"With the **Stocks** from your Seed I have taken three First Prizes already, and I mean to take two more. I grow the Giant Ten-week, and the Large-flowering; the latter can hardly be beaten."

"**Mrs. CAMPBELL** has been most successful for some years with the **Wallflower** Seed sent her, the double ones have always been magnificent, and quite the wonder of her friends, whom she always informs where to get the same."
Inverness, 3rd June.

Flower Seeds, General List (continued).

No.	Name.	Hard Dur.	1ft in feet.	Colour.	Months of Flowering	Per Pkt.	Observations.
						s. d.	
943	Solanum melongena purpurea	tA	1½	purple-fruited	Ju to Sp	4	Egg Plants. Excellent for garnishing purposes.
944	,, ,, alba	,,	,,	white-fruited	,,	4	
945	,, finest hybrids, mixed	hhP	,,	orn. fruit	Jy to No	6	Fine decorative plants for Winter.
946	,, hæmatocarpum	hhA	3	ornament. fol.	Jy & Au	6	Magnificent ornamental-foliaged plants for sub-tropical gardening.
947	,, Warscewiczii	,,	6	,,	,,	6	
948	Sphœnogyne speciosa aurea	hA	1	golden yellow	Jy to Sp	3	Showy hardy annual.
949	Spraguea umbellata	hhA	½	flesh	Jy to Oc	6	Fine for greenhouse or warm border.
	Statice (see Everlasting Flowers).						
950	Stellaria graminea aurea	,,	spr.	white	My to Oc	1 0	Golden Chickweed. Bright yellow foliage, useful for carpet bedding.
	Stocks, see pages 60 to 62.						
	Stock, Night-scented (see Mathiola)						
951	Streptocarpus, new hybrids	gP	½	various	Jy to Oc	1 0	Pretty pot plant
952	Sultan, Sweet, purple	hA	1	purple	Jy & Au	3	
953	,, ,, white	,,	,,	white	,,	3	Useful sweet-scented border annuals.
954	,, ,, yellow	,,	1½	yellow	,,	3	
955	Sunflower, large double	,,	5-6	rich orange	Jy to Oc	4	Fine decorative plants for the garden. The large double has immense double blooms of a rich orange yellow. Primrose Dame is a single-flowered variety with delicate prim-rose flowers, and is very distinct. The Miniature is a charming small-flowered single, useful for cutting.
956	,, ,, single	,,	,,	golden yellow	,,	3	
957	,, Miniature	,,	3-4	deep yellow	,,	6	
958	,, Primrose Dame	,,	5-6	delicate prmrs	,,	1 0	
959	,, Giant Yellow, single	,,	6-8	rich yellow	,,	3	
960	,, Dwarf, double	,,	3-4	deep yellow	,,	4	
	Sweet William, see page 78.						
961	Tacsonia insignis	gP	cl.	bril. crimson	Au to Oc	1 0	Superb greenhouse evergreen climbers, very brilliant.
962	,, Van Volxemi	,,	,,	dark crimson	,,	1 0	
963	Thunbergia, finest mixed	gA	,,	various	Ju to Sp	4	Beautiful little plants for pots, &c.
	Tobacco (see Nicotiana).						
964	Torenia Fournieri	,,	1	pur. & yellow	My to Oc	6	Pretty pot-plant for the greenhouse.
965	Tritoma uvaria grandiflora	hP	4	scar. & orange	Au to Oc	4	Handsome for large borders, &c.
966	Tropæolum canariense	hhA	cl.	yellow	Jy to Oc	4	Canary-creeper. Well known.
967	,, Lobbianum, brilliant	,,	,,	bril. scarlet	,,	4	Splendid and brilliant climbers or trailers for trellises, rockeries, large hanging-baskets, vases, &c. Should be grown in rather poor soil to induce the fullest development of bloom. The Lobbianum varieties are very handsome.
968	,, ,, Lucifer	,,	,,	intense scarlet	,,	6	
969	,, ,, Schultzi	,,	,,	rich scarlet	,,	4	
970	,, ,, Queen Victoria	,,	,,	striped	,,	6	
971	,, majus atrosanguineum	hA	,,	dark red	,,	3	
972	,, ,, Scheuermanni	,,	,,	yellow & red	,,	3	
973	,, ,, aurantiacum	,,	,,	orange	,,	3	
974	,, ,, mixed	,,	,,	various	,,	3	Common climbing Nasturtium.
975	Venus' Looking-glass, blue	,,	1	blue	Jy & Au	3	Useful hardy annuals for beds, borders, rockwork, &c.
976	,, ,, white	,,	,,	white	,,	3	
977	,, Navelwort	,,	,,	,,	,,	3	
978	Verbena, lemon-scented	gP	3-5	blush	Ju to Sp	1 0	Aloysia citriodora. Beautifully fragrant plant for greenhouse or window.
979	,, venosa, see page 79.	hP	spr.	purple	My to Sp	6	Valuable border-plant.
	,, hybrida, see page 79.						
980	*Veronica spicata	,,	1½	blue	Jy to Sp	3	Elegant herbaceous plant.
981	Violet, Sweet-scented, The Czar	,,	½	purple	Oc to Ap	6	Viola odorata. Well-known and popular favorites.
982	,, ,, white	,,	,,	white	,,	6	
983	,, ,, common	,,	,,	blue	,,	4	
984	Vinca rosea	gs	3-4	rose	Ju to Sp	6	Useful plants for the greenhouse.
985	,, ,, alba	,,	,,	white	,,	6	
	Violas, see page 78.						
986	Viscaria cardinalis	hA	1	bril. crimson	Au to Oc	3	Brilliant, profuse-flowering annuals, very easy of cultivation, and should be in every garden.
987	,, elegans picta	,,	,,	rose & crimson	,,	3	
988	,, oculata cœrulea	,,	1	blue	,,	4	
989	,, alba pura	,,	1	pure white	,,	4	
990	,, elegans striata	,,	,,	rose & crimson	,,	4	
991	Virginian Stock, red	,,	,,	red	My to Au	3	Early flowering annuals, useful for beds or borders; if neatly clipped will form a pretty and compact edging. The new Crimson King is very fine.
992	,, ,, white	,,	,,	white	,,	3	
993	,, ,, yellow	,,	,,	pale yellow	,,	3	
994	,, ,, Crimson King	,,	,,	crimson	,,	4	
995	,, ,, mixed	,,	,,	various	,,	3	
	Wallflowers, see page 79.						
996	Whitlavia grandiflora	hhA	1½	dark blue	Ju to Sp	3	Pretty border annual.
997	Wigandia caracasana	hhs	10	lilac	Jy to Sp	1 0	Splendid for sub-tropical garden.
998	Winter Cherry	hP	2	red fruit	—	3	Physalis alkakengi. Very useful for Winter decoration.
	Xeranthemum (see Everlasting Flowers).						
999	Zinnia linearis	hhA	1	yellow	Jy to Sp	6	Pretty Mexican species.
	Zinnia, see page 79.						

From Superintendent F. BULL, Tisbury.

May 12th.
"I have a beautiful show of Wallflowers and Pansies from the Seed you supplied me with; they are admired by all, there being none to equal them in this neighbourhood."

From Mr. JAMES FLETTON, Oundle.

"At Oundle Flower Show last year I took First Prize for Asters and First Prize for Stocks; they were much admired."

EVERLASTING FLOWERS FOR WINTER BOUQUETS

The popularity of Everlasting Flowers has been wonderfully on the increase during the past few years, and not without reason, for their culture is very easy and simple, and their flowers, if carefully gathered, dried, and preserved, will retain their beauty for years. Their bright and pleasing colours will be found of great service in the decoration of the Church or the home, in Winter, when other flowers are scarce. Many of the light varieties may be dyed of various brilliant colours; and, made up into bouquets with some of the Ornamental Grasses, are truly charming. Everlasting Flowers for preserving should be cut just as the blossoms are beginning to expand, or when they are not more than half open, and tied in bunches and hung up in a cool place to dry, with the flowers downwards. Small bunches are preferable for drying, as large bunches are apt to mould and spoil.

The Helichrysums are perhaps the most useful, and produce a great variety of brilliant and beautiful colours. *Rhodanthe maculata* and *Rhodanthe maculata alba* are two charming and elegant varieties of fine dwarf habit. *Rhodanthe maculata fl. pl.* is a fine new double-flowered variety of great merit. The Acrocliniums and Xeranthemums are also exceedingly useful, both for garden decoration or dried flowers.

GROUP OF HELICHRYSUMS

From **Mr. T. H. WAGSTAFF**, Duffield.

"I am pleased to state that the collection of **Zinnias** I had from you *turned out very satisfactorily. I gained First Prize* at our recent Show for them."

From **Mr. J. A. SHUFFREY**, Petersfield, Hants.

"I have the pleasure to inform you that I won the Bronze Medal of the Royal Horticultural Society at Petersfield Show with twelve **Zinnias** grown from the Seeds which I had from you. I am an amateur cultivating a garden without assistance."

From **Mr Z HODGSON**, New South Wales.

"I herewith enclose a P.O.O. for £1 for some of your **Flower seeds**, having seen, in one of my neighbour's gardens, the produce of some of your Seeds, and I should be pleased if I obtain like result."

From **Mr. H. REDDING**, Astwood Bank.

"I have the best bed of **Zinnias** from your Seed to be seen anywhere about here; I also obtained First Prize for them; also for **Stocks, Phlox Drummondi, and French Marigolds**, all produce from your Seed."

No.	Name.	Hard Dur.	Ht in feet.	Colour.	Months of Flowering	Per Pkt. s. d.	Observations.
1000	**Acroclinium roseum**	hhA	2	rose	Jy to Sp	3	Very useful and free flowering.
1001	" **roseum, double**	"	"	"	"	6	
1002	" **album**	"	"	white	"	3	
1003	***Ammobium alatum grandiflorum**	hP	"	"	My to Au	3	*Winged Sandflower.* Pretty.
1004	***Catananche bicolor**	"	"	white & blue	Jy to Oc	3	
1005	* " **cœrulea**	"	"	blue	"	3	
1006	**Gnaphalium fœtidum**	hA	1½	yellow	Jy to Sp	3	Useful *Everlastings.* G. leontopodium is a beautiful silvery white alpine variety of dwarf growth.
1007	" **leontopodium** (*Edelweis*) ...	hP	½	white	"	6	
1008	" **orientale fl. pl.**	"	1½	yellow	"	6	
1009	**Gomphrena globosa nana compac.**	tA	1	violet red	Ju to Sp	6	*Globe Amaranth.* Very pretty for the greenhouse during the Summer and Autumn.
1010	" " **alba**	"	"	white	"	6	
1011	" " **choice mixed** ...	"	2	various	"	6	
1012	**Helichrysum,** assortment of 12 beautiful vars. 2s. 6d.						A brilliant and splendid class of showy annuals that remain in bloom for a long period. Exceedingly useful to gather for vases, &c., for Winter decoration. The colours vary from dark crimson or purple to orange-scarlet and yellow, to pure white, and delicate rose, and are all very handsome (*see illustration*).
1013	" **scarlet**	hA	2½	scarlet	Jy to Oc	3	
1014	" **yellow**	"	"	yellow	"	3	
1015	" **purple**	"	"	purple	"	3	
1016	" **rose**	"	"	rose	"	3	
1017	" **white**	"	"	white	"	3	
1018	" **finest mixed**	"	"	various	"	3	
1019	" **minimum album**	"	1½	white	"	4	
1020	" " **luteum**	"	"	yellow	"	4	
1021	" " **roseum**	"	"	rose	"	4	
1022	" " **rubrum**... ...	"	"	dark red	"	4	
1023	" " **mixed**	"	"	various	"	6	
1024	**Helipterum anthemoides**... ...	hhA	1	yellow	"	3	Beautiful dwarf-growing varieties.
1025	" **corymbiflora**	"	"	white	"	3	
1026	" **Sandfordi**	"	"	yellow	"	3	
1027	**Rhodanthe atrosanguinea** ...	"	"	dark red	"	6	A charming group. R. maculata fl.pl. is a fine new variety, with handsome rose-coloured double flowers, whilst R. maculata alba is probably the most beautiful of all white everlastings.
1028	" **maculata**	"	"	rose & crim.	"	4	
1029	" " **alba**	"	"	silvery white	"	4	
1030	" " **fl. pl.**	"	"	rose	"	1 0	
1031	" " **mixed**	"	"	various	"	4	
1032	" **Manglesi fl. pl.**	"	"	rose	"	1 0	
1033	**Statice Bonduelli**	hA	1½	yellow	"	3	Very useful and showy varieties.
1034	" **spicata**	"	1	pink	"	6	
1035	" **candidissima**	"	1½	white	"	3	
1036	" **Suworowi**	"	2	rose	"	6	
1037	**Waitzia aurea grandiflora** ...	hhA	1	orange	"	6	Compact-growing, pretty annual.
1038	**Xeranthemum annuum superbissimum fl. pl.**	hA	"	purple	"	6	Very handsome and free-flowering everlastings. Excellent for garden decoration.
1039	" " " **album fl. pl.**	"	"	white	"	6	
1040	" **annuum purpureum** "	"	"	purple	"	3	
1041	" " **album** "	"	"	white	"	3	
1042	" " **roseum** "	"	"	rose	"	3	

Thirty-six varieties, one packet of each, post free, 6s. 6d.; 24 ditto, 5s.; 12 ditto, 2s. 6d.

Ornamental Grasses.

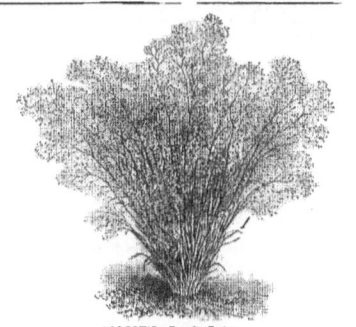
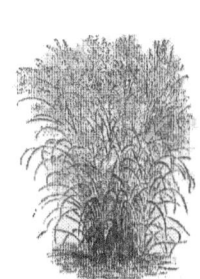

STIPA ELEGANTISSIMA.   AGROSTIS PULCHELLA.   PANICUM SULCATUM.

THE Ornamental Grasses form a very attractive and interesting class, their graceful and elegant forms and refreshing green colours giving a relief to the brilliancy of the more showy occupants of the flower garden. They can be gathered and dried in the same manner as Everlasting Flowers, and with the aid of dyes be made to assume many charming colours that will add greatly to their usefulness and attractiveness throughout the Winter season, and in combination with Everlasting Flowers, made up into Winter Bouquets, they form elegant and pleasing ornaments for the drawing-room. For this purpose the *Briza*, *Agrostis nebulosa*, *A. pulchella*, *A. minutiflora*, *Hordeum jubatum*, and *Lagurus ovatus*, are admirably suited. *Gynerium argenteum* is a grand variety, and undoubtedly the most noble of all the Ornamental Grasses for outside decoration, and as a single specimen on a lawn is unrivalled. It is perfectly hardy and will thrive in almost any soil or situation, but delights mostly in that which is near a lake, river, fountain, or any ornamental piece of water. *Isolepis tenella* forms a beautiful little pot plant for the greenhouse or window.

No.	Name.	Hard. Dur.	Ht in feet	Months of Flowering	Per Pkt.	Observations.
					s. d.	
1043	Agrostis nebulosa	ha	1½	Jy to Sp	3	
1044	„ pulchella	„	½	„	3	Graceful and extremely pretty varieties.
1045	„ minutiflora	„	1	„	6	
1046	„ purpurascens	„	„	„	3	
1047	Anthoxanthum gracile	„	„	„	3	Very fine.
1048	Arundo conspicua	hhp	6-8	Jy to Oc	6	Splendid for clumps.
1049	Avena sterilis	„	3	Jy & Au	3	*Animated Oats.* Curious.
1050	Briza gracilis (minima) ...	„	1	„	3	*The Maiden-hair Grasses.* A charming group. The new variety, geniculata is very fine
1051	„ maxima	„	„	„	3	
1052	„ geniculata	„	„	„	4	
1053	Bromus brizæformis ...	„	2	„	3	Fine ornamental species.
1054	„ patulus nanus ...	„	1	„	6	
1055	Coix lachryma	hha	„	„	3	*Job's Tears.*
1056	Chloris fimbriata	ha	„	„	3	Pretty variety.
1057	Erianthus ravennæ	hp	8	„	3	Handsome, similar to *Pampas Grass.*
1058	Eragrostis Abyssinica ...	hha	2	Au & Sp	4	*Love Grass.* Very graceful.
1059	„ elegans ...	ha	1½	„	3	
1060	„ maxima ...	„	„	„	6	
1061	Elymus caput Medusæ ...	hp	„	Jy & Au	3	Very fine varieties.
1062	„ giganteus ...	„	2½	„	4	
1063	Gynerium argenteum	„	8-10	Sp & Oc	6	*Pampas Grass of South America.* Handsome purplish plumes.
1064	Hordeum jubatum	ha	1	Jy to Sp	3	
1065	Isolepis tenella	hhp	½	Ju to Sp	6	Beautiful variety for pot culture.
1066	Lagurus ovatus	ha	1½	Jy & Au	3	*The Hare's-tail Grass.* Fine.
1067	Lamarckia aurea	„	1	„	3	Pretty dwarf variety.
1068	Maize, striped-leaved Japanese	hha	3-5	„	3	Fine ornamental plants for the sub-tropical garden, &c.
1069	„ Giant	„	6-8	„	3	
1070	Panicum sulcatum	hhp	1½	„	3	*Prairie Grass.* P. plicatum is a fine new variegated variety.
1071	„ virgatum	hp	3-5	Jy to Sp	6	
1072	„ plicatum fol. variegatis	hhp	1	„	1 0	
1073	Pennisetum longistylum ...	ha	2	Jy & Au	3	Very ornamental.
1074	Stipa elegantissima	hp	„	Jy to Oc	4	*Feather Grass.* Well-known and graceful varieties.
1075	„ pennata	„	„	„	3	
1076	Vulpia geniculata	ha	½	Jy & Au	4	Beautiful compact-growing varieties.

A collection of 25 varieties, 5s. 0d. | A collection of 12 varieties, 2s. 6d.

Showy Flower Seeds by Weight.

THE following showy, popular, and choice varieties, which are often required in larger quantities for sowing in beds, clumps, waste places, to rear for bedding out, &c., we can supply in quantities of not less than the half-ounce or half-pound of either sort, at the annexed low rates. *For descriptions see our General List of Flower Seeds.*

	per oz.—s.	d.
Amaranthus mel. ruber	1	6
Alyssum, Sweet per lb. 12s.	1	0
Antirrhinum, choice mixed	2	6
Aster, mixed German, double	5	0
,, **Pæony-flowered**,		
choice mixed	10	6
,, **dwarf Chrysan-**		
themum, choice mixed	10	6
,, **Victoria**, choice mixed	12	6
Aquilegia, choice mixed	1	6
Balsam, good mixed double	5	0
Bartonia aurea	1	0
Beet, dark-leaved, for		
bedding	1	0
*Borago per lb. 2s. 6d.	0	4
Briza maxima (Ornamental Grass)	1	0
Calandrinia speciosa per lb. 12s.	1	0
,, alba	1	0
Calliopsis tinctoria	1	0
,, **Drummondi**	1	0
Candytuft, extra dark		
crimson per lb. 12s.	1	0
,, white rocket ,, 10s.	0	9
,, purple ,, 10s.	0	9
,, mixed ,, 10s.	0	9
Canna, choice varieties, mixed	0	9
Canterbury Bells, blue	1	0
,, ,, choice mixed	1	6
Clarkia elegans, Salmon Queen	1	0
* ,, pulchella per lb. 7s. 6d.	0	8
* ,, alba ,, 7s. 6d.	0	8
* ,, integripetala fl. pl. alba	1	0
,, ,, rosea	1	0
Collinsia bicolor per lb. 10s.	0	9
,, alba	0	9
Convolvulus major, mixed	0	6
,, minor, dark purple	0	6
Chrysanthemum Burridgeanum	1	0
*Cyanus minor, mixed	0	6
Delphinium formosum	2	6
Dianthus Heddewigi, mixed	2	6
Digitalis (Foxglove), mixed	1	6
*Erysimum Peroffskianum per lb. 6s.	0	6
Eschscholtzia crocea per lb. 12s.	1	0
Flos adonis	1	0
*Gilia tricolor per lb. 4s.	0	6

	per oz.—s.	d.
*Gilia achillæfolia alba per lb. 4s.	0	6
Godetia, The Bride	1	0
,, reptans insignis	1	0
,, **Lady Albemarle**	1	6
,, Duchess of Albany	1	0
,, choicest mixed	1	0
Helichrysum, splendid		
mixed	2	0
Hibiscus Africanus	0	9
Kaulfussia amelloides	0	8
Larkspur, dwarf rocket per lb. 10s.	0	9
Leptosiphon densiflorus	0	9
,, ,, albus	0	9
*Limnanthes Douglasi per lb. 7s. 6d.	0	8
Linum, true scarlet		
per lb. 12s.	1	0
Lobelia speciosa	3	6
Love-lies-bleeding, red	0	8
Lupinus nanus per lb. 8s.	0	8
,, ,, albus	0	8
,, hybridus superbus	0	8
,, subcarnosus	1	0
Lupin, fine mixed per lb. 2s. 6d.	0	4
Maize, variegated Japanese	0	9
Malope grandiflora	0	9
,, ,, alba	0	9
Mathiola bicornis	2	0
*Mignonette, common		
per lb. 6s. 6d.	0	6
,, Victoria Giant	2	0
,, **dwarf compact**	1	0
,, **crimson giant**	1	0
Nasturtium, climbing, mixed	0	8
,, **Tom Thumb King**	1	0
,, ,, yellow	1	0
,, ,, rose	1	0
,, ,, mxd. per lb. 10s.	0	9
*Nemophila insignis per lb. 5s.	0	6
,, ,, alba ,, 5s.	0	6
,, maculata	0	9
*Œnothera bistorta Veitchi	1	0
Pea, Sweet, mixed per qt. 5s. 6d. ;		
per pint, 3s.	0	4
,, invincible scarlet	0	6
,, Painted Lady	0	6
,, white	0	6

	per oz.—s.	d.
Pea, Sweet, purple	0	6
Perilla Nankinensis	1	6
Petunia, good border varieties	4	0
*Phacelia campanularia	2	0
Phlox Drummondi, choice		
mixed	2	6
Pyrethrum, Golden Feather	2	6
Poppy, fine dbl., mxd. per lb. 10s.	0	9
Prince's Feather, giant	0	9
Ricinus Gibsoni	1	0
Saponaria Calabrica per lb. 10s.	0	9
,, ,, alba	1	0
Silene armeria rubra	1	0
,, ,, alba	1	0
,, pendula ruberrima	0	9
Schizanthus pinnatus	1	0
,, papilionaceus	1	0
Schizopetalon Walkeri per lb. 10s.	1	0
Sphœnogyne speciosa		
aurea	1	6
Stock, dwarf German ten-		
week, mixed (imported		
seed)	6	0
,, **large-flowered**		
dwarf ten-week, mixed		
(imported seed)	10	0
Sultan, Sweet, mixed	1	0
Sunflower, comu. single per lb. 5s.	0	6
,, fine double	1	0
Sweet William, fine mixed	1	6
Tropæolum Lobbianum, scarlet	1	6
,, **Lobbianum**, scarlet	1	6
Viscaria cardinalis	1	6
,, **elegans picta**	1	6
Venus' Looking-glass, blue	1	0
,, ,, white	1	0
Virginian Stock, red per lb. 10s.	0	9
,, ,, white ,, 10s.	0	9
,, **Crimson King**,		
splendid	1	0
Wallflower, single, mxd. per lb. 14s.	1	0
,, blood-red	1	0
Xeranthemum, double purple	1	6
,, ,, white	1	6
Zinnia, finest double	2	6

Those marked with an asterisk (*) are excellent for Bees.

Choice Flower Seeds in Mixture.

A BEAUTIFUL variety of pleasing colours for sowing freely in waste places in shrubberies, woodland walks, rockeries, covering large banks, &c., where they give a gay and cheerful appearance for a long period. Sow broadcast in March, April, or May, and give the seeds a slight covering after sowing, by drawing a rake over the ground. As most of the varieties contained in the mixture are perfectly hardy, a few sown in sheltered positions in August or September will stand through the Winter, and have a pleasing effect in early Spring.

Dwarf varieties, per lb. 5s. ; per oz. 6d.   Tall varieties, per lb. 5s. ; per oz. 6d.   *Not less than one ounce supplied.*

Flower Seeds in Penny Packets.

WE shall be pleased to supply seeds of all the most popular sorts of Flower Seeds in Penny Packets, our own selection, at the following rates Post Free.

100 packets in 100 choice varieties, 8s. ; 50 packets in 50 choice varieties, 4s. 2d. ; 25 packets in 25 choice varieties, 2s. 2d.

The Cottager's Packet of Choice Flower Seeds.

(Registered.)

Containing Twelve selected varieties, including Aster, Stock, Mignonette, Scarlet Linum, &c.
Post Free, 1s. 2d. ; two packets, 2s. 2d. ; twelve packets, 10s. 6d.

On the Rearing of Flowers from Seed.

Hardy Annuals.

THE many beautiful varieties of hardy annuals available for the Summer decoration of our gardens are worthy of a much more extensive growth, and a better cultural treatment than they usually receive, and, well-grown, will produce flowers of a size and brilliancy that will surprise many who are only accustomed to the weedy, starved representatives so often seen of this fine class. Although hardy annuals will thrive fairly in almost any soil or situation, some little preparation of the ground before sowing is necessary to grow them to perfection; and the first consideration is to reduce the surface to a fine and even tilth, carefully removing all large stones and clods, and if the soil be poor, working in a liberal quantity of well-decayed manure.

For a general display, perhaps the best time for sowing is about the middle of March, and for a later succession, April; but we have seen annuals sown in May, and even the early part of June, that have bloomed splendidly in the Autumn months. After sowing, the cultivation of hardy annuals is extremely simple, early and vigorous thinning out of the clumps or patches being nearly all that is necessary to ensure an abundance of fine plants, with a profusion of handsome flowers. Various methods are adopted in sowing; but perhaps the simplest and best plan for garden decoration is to sow in shallow furrows, in circles of from nine to twelve inches in diameter; or in rows or drills, their distance apart to be regulated according to the height of the plants when fully grown. When this is done in dry weather, an excellent plan is to fill the furrows with water and allow it to settle before sowing, carefully covering the seeds with the soil removed in the operation, and pressing down firmly with a trowel or flat piece of wood. Such large seeds as Nasturtiums, Lupins, and Sweet Peas may be covered to the depth of an inch; Convolvulus major and minor, not quite so deep; smaller seeds, such as Mignonette, &c., require but a slight covering. Hardy annuals may also be sown broadcast in mixture, in beds or patches, in waste places, shrubberies, &c., and have a very pleasing effect. For early spring decoration such fine varieties as Nemophila insignis and alba, Silene pendula, Limnanthes Douglasii, &c., may be sown in a sheltered position in August or early in September, and transferred as vacancies occur to where they are intended to bloom. Godetias also, in their many beautiful varieties, which are perfectly hardy, bloom much earlier and finer when sown in the Autumn and transplanted early in Spring.

Half-Hardy Annuals.

The great majority of half-hardy annuals require a long period of growth to develop the fine plants and blooms for which they are so much esteemed, and sowing should therefore commence as soon as convenient after the second week in February, and be continued to the end of March, or the middle of April. There are, however, some slight exceptions to this rule, as for instance, in the case of Zinnias and Marigolds, which should not be sown before the middle of March, and Ten-week Stocks, which may be sown as early as the middle of January, or early in February, and indeed treated thus will produce much finer blooms than those sown in March or April; whilst the finest Asters are produced from seeds sown the first and second weeks in April, and which should not, as a rule, be sown earlier. The beautiful Scarlet Flax (*Linum grandiflorum rubrum*) succeeds best treated as a hardy annual, and sown in April.

The most useful soil for raising plants from seeds, under glass, is composed of about equal parts of good rich loam, leaf-mould, and well-decayed manure from an old hot-bed, thoroughly incorporated with a sufficiency of coarse sand to render the whole fairly porous. In filling pots, pans, &c., with soil, it is of the first importance, after providing ample drainage, that the soil should be pressed down firmly before sowing the seeds, which will have the effect of providing a much more even moisture, and certainty of germination, than can be had by sowing on a loose and porous surface. Sow the seeds thinly, distributing as evenly as you can, and cover as lightly as possible with a sprink-

ling of fine soil, and after submitting them to a slight pressure from such as the bottom of a flower-pot, give them a careful watering and place in a gentle heat. When the young plants come up, place them as near as possible to the light, and give them on all favourable occasions a fair quantity of air, carefully avoiding, however, their exposure to the keen, drying east winds so often prevalent in Spring. When the plants have reached a size at which they can be handled, the choicer varieties should be carefully pricked out into pots, pans, boxes, &c., and placed in the greenhouse close to the glass, or in frames, &c., where on fine warm days they can have the full benefit of air and sun. This will enable them to make good sturdy plants with plenty of roots, that will transplant well, and produce an abundance of handsome flowers.

The best time for planting out depends very much on the season, and this operation should never be hurried if the weather be unfavourable, or proper attention cannot be given. Where heat is not available for the rearing of half-hardy annuals, they are easily raised by sowing in April, in pans or boxes placed under hand-lights, or in a cool frame close to the glass, the only difference being their blooming somewhat later. We have, indeed, seen a fine Autumn display of half-hardy annuals sown in May on the open border, and of Asters sown so late as the first week in June. We may add, that Lobelias for bedding out, cannot be sown too early in the year, some giving preference to those sown the preceding Autumn.

Hardy Perennials & Biennials.

With the exception of some few sorts, which require a somewhat different treatment, the greater part of these are best raised in the months of May, June, and July, in the manner recommended for hardy annuals, selecting, however, a somewhat cool and shady situation in preference to one exposed to much sun. Sow thinly, and when the plants are large enough, prick out on nursery beds to strengthen, and plant out early in Autumn, or in favourable weather in February and March, where they are intended to flower. Early sowing is decidedly the best, as it gives the plants a far better opportunity of becoming sufficiently strong to resist severe frost in Winter, and to bloom freely and finely in the coming Spring and Summer. This is especially the case in reference to double German Wallflowers and Brompton Stocks, which should not be sown later than the end of May. These being less hardy than most classed as such, should have the benefit of a more sheltered spot when finally planted out, which ought to be done if possible in July. Sweet Williams, unless sown early, will not all bloom the following year.

Greenhouse or Tender Annuals

The many fine varieties of such valuable plants as Balsams, Thunbergias, Amaranthuses, Celosias, Ipomœas, Cockscombs, &c., are richly deserving of cultivation wherever facilities exist for growing them. Their treatment in the young state closely resembles that of half-hardy annuals, a good light and rich soil with a liberal proportion of sharp sand being nearly all that is required to grow them to perfection. The chief difference in their culture, however, consists in their being sown somewhat earlier and on a stronger heat, and in pricking out the young plants as early as possible, singly into small pots; and as these fill with roots, shifting into larger, and so on, till they are transferred to the size in which it is intended to bloom them. The growth of the plants is very much assisted by occasionally watering with weak liquid manure; but this should be discontinued when the bloom is making its appearance, and tepid rain or soft water only should be used instead. Balsams, although classed as "tender," may be planted out in June, in sheltered positions in the open garden, and will make a fine display.

☞ Every packet of Flower Seed supplied by us bears all necessary cultural instructions printed on the envelope.

EXHIBITION GLADIOLUS.

Gladioli, Hybrids of Gandavensis.

We have much pleasure in drawing the attention of our customers to our fine list of Gladioli for the coming season, and also to the great reduction in price for many of the most splendid varieties, which are now placed within the reach of all.

We are large growers and importers of this charming flower, and for several years past have given particular attention to its successful cultivation. Our List has been carefully revised, and will be found to contain the most beautiful and distinct varieties. We send all Gladioli Free by Parcel Post at prices quoted.

Daniels' Special Collections of Gladioli—Carriage Free.

WE have much pleasure in recommending the following choice collections of named Gladioli, which will be found to contain a charming selection of the most beautiful and distinct varieties, specially selected for exhibition or decorative purposes.

A. 50 in 50 superb varieties as follows, price 36s.—
Africain, Amalthee, Andre Leroy, Argus, Baroness B. Coutts, Beatrix, Butterfly, Camille, Conqueror, Conquête, Diamant, Dr. Bailly, Eclair, Enchanteresse, Eugene Scribe, Figaro, Formosa, Ginevra, Grand Rouge, Harlequin, Horace Vernet, Jubilee, La Candour, Le Vesuve, Mdlle. Marie Mies, Maréchal Vaillant, Mary Stuart, Meyerbeer, Milton, Mons. Legouvé, Mount Etna, Murillo, Nereide, Neige et Fou, Ophir, Orpheus, Pactole, Phœbus, Phédro, Primatrice, Psyche, Rayon d'Or, Reine Blanche, Rossini, Rosa Bonheur, Schiller, Shakespeare, Sylvie, Therese de Vilmorin, Virginalis.

B. 25 in 25 superb varieties as follows, price 15s.—
Africain, Baroness B. Coutts, Beatrix, Camille, Conquête, Diamant, Eugene Scribe, Figaro, Ginevra, Grand Rouge, Horace Vernet, Le Vesuve, Meyerbeer, Mons. Legouvé, Murillo, Orpheus, Pactole, Phœbus, Phédro, Reine Blanche, Schiller, Shakespeare, Sylvie, Therese de Vilmorin, Virginalis.

C. 12 in 12 choice varieties as follows, price 8s. 6d.—
Africain, Baroness B. Coutts, Conquête, Grand Rouge, Horace Vernet, Le Vesuve, Murillo, Orpheus, Phédre, Reine Blanche, Shakespeare, Therese de Vilmorin.

D. 12 in 12 fine varieties as follows, price 5s.—
Conquête, Eugene Scribe, Figaro, Ginevra, Le Vesuve, Horace Vernet, Orpheus, Phédro, Reine Blanche, Sylvie, Schiller, Virginalis.

Gladioli in Mixtures from Finest Named and Seedling Sorts.

We can highly recommend our mixtures of these, which are very fine, and contain a great variety of superior flowers of many beautiful and varied colours.

	per 100	per doz.
Choicest mixed Seedlings, &c., from the finest sorts	20s. 0d.	3s. 0d.
White-ground varieties, extra fine mixed, from named sorts ...	,,	3s. 0d.
Rose and light red varieties, choice mixed, from named sorts ...	,,	3s. 0d.
Brilliant scarlet and dark varieties, choice mixed, from named sorts ...	,,	3s. 0d.
Yellow-ground varieties, very choice mixed, from named sorts ..	,,	3s. 6d.
Lilac and violet-ground varieties, fine mixed, from named sorts ...	,,	3s. 6d.
BRENCHLEYENSIS, well-known showy scarlet per 100, 10s. 6d.	,,	1s. 6d.
Snow White. Splendid new pure white each 6d.	,,	5s. 0d.

Gladioli—New and Select Varieties.

	each—s. d.
African. Slaty-brown on scarlet ground, streaked scarlet and white, conspicuous white blotch	0 7
Albatross. Very large spike, with large well-expanded pure white flowers. Superb variety	12 6
Amalthee. White, with large violet-red blotch	0 6
Andre Leroy. Fine deep red, white stripe	1 0
Argus. Dazzling fiery scarlet, centre pure white	0 6
Aurora de Feu. Flowers of a bright rose colour, passing to scarlet, with golden-yellow centre	3 0
Baroness Burdett-Coutts. Delicate lilac tinged with rose, flamed rosy-carmine; magnificent variety	1 8
Beatrix. Pure white ground, flushed carmine lilac	0 6
Blanc Frisé. Fine creamy white, large, well-expanded flowers, the edges of the petals fringed or crimped	6 6
Buffalo Bill. Large spike of cherry-red flowers with yellow blotch and centre stripe; very fine	3 6
Butterfly. Yellow ground, flaked with carmine	0 6
Camille. Magenta lilac, shaded darker lilac	1 6
Conqueror. Carmine flowers with pure white blotch	0 6
Conquete. Bright cherry-rose, with white blotch	0 6
Dismant. White, streaked with carmine; splendid	0 6
Doctor Bailly. Dazzling scarlet; carmine blotch	1 6
Doctor Hogg. Well shaped spike with open flowers to the extent of a foot in length, flowers tolerably large, well opened, banded and striped slatish purple	3 6
Doctor Masters. Well shaped compact spike of a superb colour; flowers large, bright rose, strongly flushed with dark purple; blotch amaranth	6 6
Eclair. Bright scarlet, with broad white bands	0 6
Enchanteresse. Very large flowers, of a satiny pale lilac-white, streaked violet-red on one or two sepals	1 9
Erigone. Magnificent flowers, streaked and banded carmine, on a white ground, with rich carmine blotch	2 6
Eugene Scribe. Tender rose, blazed with carmine	0 6
Fantome. Fine spike of enormously large flowers; pure white, slightly glazed and streaked at the edges with rosy lilac. Remarkable for the great size of the flowers	4 6
Figaro. Light orange red, large white blotch	0 6
Formosa. Large perfectly shaped spike; flowers of a very delicate satiny rose, thinly striped with carmine on the edges; blotch creamy white	1 0
Gerbe de Feu. Long well furnished spike of most brilliant and dazzling scarlet flowers, with a large creamy white blotch. A variety of grand effect	4 6
Ginevra. Beautiful cherry-rose, flushed with red, central line of petals pure white; splendid spike	0 6
Grand Rouge. Remarkably fine spike of large flowers of a bright scarlet colour, with small violet blotch. First Class Certificate R.H.S.	1 6
Grandeur a Merveille. Very handsome spike with immense well opened flowers of a satiny lilac white, very slightly speckled and streaked with rose	3 6

	each—s. d.
Harlequin. Salmon rose, flaked carmine on a yellow ground, well-shaped flowers	0 9
Horace Vernet. Bright purplish-red, with large pure white stain; a grand variety	0 7
Jubilee. Fine spike of large bright carmine flowers, splendid variety of a very bright and pleasing colour	1 0
La Candeur. White, lightly striped carmine-violet	1 0
Le Veuve. Intense scarlet, magnificent spike	0 9
Mademoiselle Marie Mios. Delicate rose, flamed with carmine, blotch rosy purple; magnificent	1 6
Marechal Vaillant. Brilliant scarlet, white stain	1 3
Mary Stuart. White, tinged with rose, and flamed with bright carmine-cherry; very beautiful	1 6
Meyerbeer. Brilliant scarlet, flamed with vermilion	0 6
Michel Ange. Crimson, white blotch	3 0
Milton. Cherry-rose, flamed with red; extra	0 6
Minos (Souchet). Long spike of salmony-rose, flowers profusely flushed and blotched cherry-red	3 0
Mons. Legouve. Bright red, with white lines	0 6
Mont Blanc. Immense pyramidal spike, with very large flowers, creamy white at first, soon changing to snowy white, small violet blotch	6 6
Mount Etna. Brilliant velvety scarlet, white bands	1 0
Mr. Patrick. Splendid spike, with very large and numerous very brilliant scarlet flowers, with violet blotch on a lilac ground; extra fine	6 6
Murillo. Fine cherry-rose on light ground, white stripe down the middle of each petal; beautiful	0 7
Nereide. Beautiful pearly rose colour, suffused with lilac, blotched bright violet; a very lovely colour	1 6
Neige et Feu. Cherry-red, ivory-white blotch	1 6
Ophir. Dark yellow, with purple stain; fine	0 6
Orpheus. Rose, blazed with carmine; magnificent	0 6
Pactole. Beautiful yellow, slightly tinged with rose	0 6
Phedre. Pure white, flamed with cherry-rose	0 6
Phœbus. Brilliant red, with large pure white stain	0 6
Pollux. Bright carmine, with brown-red on the edges, fine white blotch	1 6
Primatrice. Rose, tinged lilac, carmine blotch	0 6
Psyche. Satin rose, flamed with dark carmine	0 6
Rayon d'Or. Creamy yellow, flaked rosy purple	0 6
Reine Blanche. White, with dark carmine blotch	0 6
Rosa Bonheur. White, tinged lilac, dark blotch	1 0
Rossini. Dark amaranth red, with white lines	0 9
Schiller. Sulphur yellow, with large carmine blotch	0 6
Shakespeare. White, very slightly suffused with carmine-rose, large rosy blotch; magnificent	0 6
Sylvie. White, edged with delicate cherry-rose	0 6
Therese de Vilmorin. Very fine tall spike of splendid flowers, creamy white passing to pure white, with a few fine purplish rose stripes; superb	1 0
Virginalis. White, bordered and flamed carmine	0 6

NEW HARDY HYBRID GLADIOLI
With Large Stained or Blotched Flowers.

This fine new race of Hybrid Gladioli blooms somewhat earlier than those of the Gandavensis section, and are much more hardy, so hardy, in fact, that their bulbs do not need to be lifted in Winter. The flowers are very striking and handsome in appearance, all having conspicuous blotches on the lower petals, whilst the colours are very diversified and beautiful. These will be found splendid alike for garden decoration or for cut flowers.

	each—s. d.
Alsace. Pale sulphur, with blood red blotch	0 9
Admiral Courbet. Fiery scarlet, side petals blotched velvety red	0 9
Enfant de Nancy. Purplish scarlet, lower petals deep velvety crimson	0 8
E. V. Hallock (new). Sulphur-white, with large blood red blotch on yellow disc; large, well-formed	3 0
Incendie. Bright vermilion rose throat, lower petals purplish scarlet	0 6
Lafayette. Salmon-yellow, with large crimson blotches; very large flowers	0 6
Lemoinei. Creamy white tinted rose, crimson blotches; very free	0 6
Madame Lemoinier. Pure white, with maroon blotch, spike erect, and very early; very choice for cutting	1 0

	each—s. d.
Mount Etna. Velvety scarlet, with yellow blotch; very curly and effective	1 6
Sceptre d'Or. Beautiful chrome yellow, with large velvet black blotch	1 6
Venus de Milo. Pure white passing to rose, with maroon blotch, flowers large and perfect	3 0
Victor Hugo. Rosy yellow, vermilion blotch on yellow ground	1 0
Voltaire. Violet carmine, with maroon blotch on yellow ground; extra	1 0
W. E. Gumbleton. Rosy purple, striped carmine, velvet blotches on yellow disc	0 8
12 choice varieties, our selection from the above,	9s.
6 " " " "	5s.
Choice mixed, in beautiful variety, per 100, 24s.; per doz., 3s. 6d.	

Lilies (Lilium).

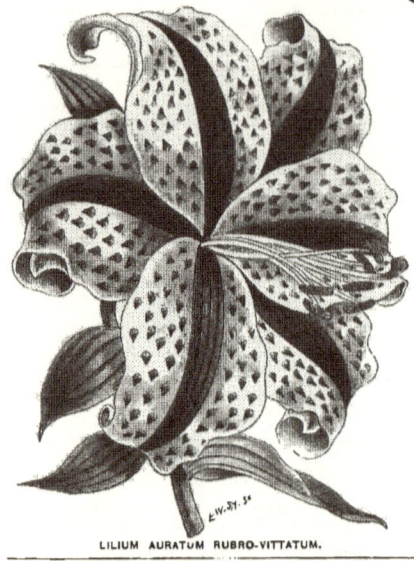

LILIUM AURATUM RUBRO-VITTATUM.

each—s. d.

AURATUM (Golden-rayed Lily of Japan). The beautiful large-flowered variety, white with yellow stripes and brownish-red spots; deliciously fragrant, extremely hardy, first-class for pot culture. One of the most useful and beautiful Lilies in cultivation. Having secured a large consignment of fine bulbs, of this superb variety, we are able to offer at the following low rates:—
No. 1. Good flowering bulbs
per doz. 6s.; 6 for 3s. 6d. 0 8
No. 2. Larger „ „ ... per doz. 10s. 1 0
No. 3. Extra fine „ „ English grown
per doz. 15s. 1 6
A few extraordinarily fine bulbs per doz. 24s. 2 6

AURATUM rubro-vittatum. Magnificent new variety, immense flowers, petals pure white, with a distinct broad band of deep crimson down the centre
2s. 6d. and 3 6
„ **virginale.** Very large flowers, white, with pale yellow bands; most beautiful variety ... 5 0
„ **platyphyllum.** Gigantic flowers of great substance, very broad petals, white, with yellow bands, slightly spotted; very fine ... 5 0
Batemani. Apricot yellow; a fine variety ... 0 9
Browni. Large creamy white trumpet-shaped flowers, outside of petals brownish purple colour 3s. 6d. to 5 0
Candidum. The old favourite White Lily per doz. 3s. 0 4
Chalcedonicum (Scarlet Turk's Cap). Splendid old variety, flowers medium sized, reflexed, and of a deep rich scarlet colour; finely effective per doz. 12s. 1 3
Colchicum (*Szovitzianum*). Pale yellow, spotted with black; finely scented per doz. 15s. 1 6
Croceum. Light orange, spotted black per doz. 5s. 0 6

each—s. d.

Davuricum fulgidum. Deep orange red flushed with yellow, very showy ... per doz. 7s. 6d. 0 9
Giganteum (the noble Himalayan Lily). White, with broad bands of crimson violet ... 3s. 6d., 5s., and 7 6
Humboldti. A fine species, growing about five feet high, with large golden-yellow flowers, spotted purple 2 6
Krameri. A beautiful variety, with flowers of similar form to those of Auratum, but of a beautiful pink colour; deliciously scented ... 2 6
Longiflorum. A fine early flowering, dwarf growing species, beautiful trumpet-shaped flowers, white, sweet-scented, and six to eight inches in length; should be in every garden ... per doz. 4s. 6d. 0 6
„ **Harrisii.** A fine new form, producing a great profusion of its beautiful pure white deliciously scented flowers. Will bloom three or four times in succession without the bulbs being rested. Splendid for pot culture in the greenhouse and for forcing :—
Good flowering roots ... per doz. 6s. 0 7
Extra strong roots ... per doz. 7s. 6d. 0 9
„ **Eximium.** First-rate for forcing in Winter and Spring. Long trumpet-shaped flowers; pure white ... ... per doz. 10s. 6d. 1 0
„ **Giganteum.** Immense pure white trumpets, splendid for pot culture ... per doz. 10s. 6d. 1 0
Martagon (Turk's Cap). Purple per doz. 7s. 6d. 0 9
„ **album.** Pure white-flowered forms of the preceding; extremely scarce ... 3s. 6d. and 5 0
„ **Dalmaticum.** A magnificent variety, with deep velvety crimson purple flowers 3s. 6d. and 5 0
Pardalinum. Bright scarlet shading to orange, spotted maroon; large flowers ... 1 6
Parryi. A new and beautiful Californian variety, with large rich golden yellow flowers ... 3 6
Philadelphicum. Vermilion scarlet, spotted black 1 6
Pomponium verum. An elegant species, with bright scarlet flowers ... per doz. 7s. 6d. 0 9
Pulchellum. Deep red, orange centre ... 1 6
Pyrenaicum (the Yellow Martagon). Deliciously scented flowers, yellow, spotted black per doz. 9s. 0 9
Speciosum (*Lancifolium*). A fine hardy class; excellent for pot culture; deliciously scented.
„ **album.** Pure white, beautiful per doz. 15s. 1 6
„ **Krœtzeri.** Pure white; the finest variety 1 6
„ **melpomene.** Rich dark crimson; splendid bulbs; a fine variety for pots 1 0
„ **punctatum.** White, rose-spotted ... 1 0
„ **rubrum.** White, spotted and shaded crimson 0 9
„ **roseum.** White, crimson-spotted ... 0 9
„ **multiflorum.** Fine variety ... 1 6
Superbum. A fine yellow Lily with purple spots. Flowers often produced 15 to 20 on a stem
per doz. 7s. 6d. 0 9
Tenuifolium. Dwarf, glittering scarlet; splendid variety ... ... per doz. 16s. 1 6
Testaceum (*Excelsum*). Nankeen-coloured flowers, delightfully fragrant; four feet high per doz. 10s. 6d. 1 0
Thunbergianum alternans. Rosy scarlet, tinged apricot ... ... per doz. 10s. 6d. 1 0
„ **atrosanguineum.** Scarlet, spotted black 0 9
„ **aurantiacum multiflorum.** Yellow ... 0 6
„ **fulgens.** Crimson, mottled with yellow
per doz. 7s. 6d. 0 9
Tigrinum splendens. The finest of the Tiger Lilies. Orange scarlet, black spots ... per doz. 5s. 0 6
„ **fl. pl.** Scarlet, spotted brown, very double ... 1 0
Wallichianum. Magnificent variety from the Himalaya Mountains, producing immense long trumpet pure white flowers on stems four feet high; a splendid variety for pot culture 3s. 6d. and 5 0
Washingtonianum. A grand Lily, growing four to five feet high, large white flowers, shaded lilac ... 3 6

We have many other species and varieties of choice Lilies in stock, which from want of space we are unable to enumerate.

Lilies in Collections—our own selection.

Carefully arranged Collections of Lilies, 6s., 9s., 12s., 18s., 24s., and 30s. per dozen.

Anemones and Ranunculi for Spring Planting.

DOUBLE-FLOWERED ANEMONES.

GIANT RANUNCULI.

Anemones in Mixture.

	per 100. s. d.	per doz. s. d.
Giant French, single. Very fine and floriferous, much superior to the common Dutch varieties	5 0	1 0
Choice Seedlings, double blue. Beautiful varieties, producing handsome double flowers, very superior to the ordinary mixtures	10 6	1 6
,, ,, ,, scarlet	7 6	1 0
,, ,, ,, all colours	6 6	1 0
,, ,, single, very fine and beautiful	4 6	0 8
Dutch, finest mixed, double, fine roots ... per 1000, 35s.	4 6	0 8
,, ,, single, fine roots ... per 1000, 21s.	2 6	0 6
Scarlet, finest double. Fine roots ...	6 6	1 0
,, ,, single. Strong roots ...	3 0	0 6
Pure White, single, "The Bride." Splendid ...	10 6	1 6

Superb Double-flowered Anemones.

PRODUCING large, handsome, double flowers of various beautiful colours; some of the varieties are strikingly brilliant and attractive. These are admirably suited for pot culture, and planted in patches of three or five form charming groups for the flower border.

Choicest mixed ...   . per 100, 6s.; per doz. 1s.

Superb New French—
Double Chrysanthemum-flowered.

A distinct and brilliant class.

Choice mixed ...   . per doz. 4s. 6d.

Anemone Fulgens.

BEAUTIFUL large-flowered varieties with dazzling vermillion scarlet blooms, which continue from February to May. Thrive best in a rich loamy soil.

Fulgens. Single scarlet, very fine ...   . per doz. 1s. 6d.
Fulgens fl. pl. A fine new double scarlet   ...   ...   ,, 1s. 6d.

Ranunculi.

THE Ranunculi are very free flowering and beautiful. They will succeed in almost any soil or position, and planted any time up to the middle of April will bloom abundantly during the Summer.

French Giant. Very fine   ...   ... per 100, 3s. 6d.; per doz. 8d.
Persian, choicest mixed. In beautiful variety
 per 1000, 35s.; per 100, 4s.; per doz. 8d.
Scotch, splendid mixed ...   ...   ,, 5s.; ,, 9d.
Turban, Daniels' Giant. A splendid and robust-growing class, very superior to the common Turban varieties; grows to the height of eighteen inches; each plant producing from forty to fifty splendid double flowers   ...

	per 100. s. d.	per doz. s. d.
	4 6	0 9
Scarlet. Admirably adapted for filling beds, ribbon borders, or massing	2 6	0 4
Mixed. All colours ... ... per 1000, 25s.	3 0	0 6

Hyacinthus (Galtonia) Candicans.
(THE CAPE HYACINTH.)

THIS splendid hardy bulbous-rooted plant grows from three to four feet high. It blooms in Autumn, and throws up large loose spikes of white bell-shaped flowers. Planted in groups of three, five, or more, it is very handsome and effective amongst roses or shrubs. It blooms about the same time as the well-known scarlet Gladiolus Brenchleyensis, and grown together, the two plants when in bloom are very effective.

Hyacinthus candicans. Fine strong flowering bulbs
 Per 100, 10s. 6d.; per doz. 1s. 6d.

Tuberous-rooted Begonias.

DOUBLE BEGONIA.

From T. H. ROBERTS, Esq., Redhill.

Nov. 16th.

"All the Myrobella I had from you last year has done well."

We have much pleasure in offering roots of our grand strain of Tuberous-rooted hybrid Begonias, which have been grown and selected at our Nurseries during the past season, and which for form, size and substance of flower, and beauty and variety of colouring will be found second to none in the country. The individual blooms of many of the single-flowered varieties are of immense size—often measuring four to five inches across—of splendid form and substance, and the colours range from the most intense dark crimson through all the shades of scarlet, salmon, cerise, and yellow to the purest white, the plants being of a fine dwarf sturdy habit of growth. They will be found splendid for pot culture and for bedding out; much superior to Geraniums, as they continue in full bloom through the wettest season and late into the autumn, when Geraniums have but a poor appearance. The double-flowered also include some magnificent flowers, in an equal variety of colouring to the single. These, although not so showy and useful for bedding out as the single-flowered, are superb for pot culture in the greenhouse.

SINGLE-FLOWERED.

			per doz. s. d.	each. s. d.
Crimson and Scarlet	...	...	7 6	0 9
Rose and Carmine	...	...	7 6	0 9
Pink and Salmon	...	...	7 6	0 9
Primrose and Citron	...	Strong Flowering Tubers	7 6	0 9
Pure white	...		7 6	0 9
Extra choice mixed. Selected flowers	...		9 0	—
Choice mixed. In beautiful variety	...		6 0	—
Mixed showy sorts	...	per 100, 30s.	4 6	—

DOUBLE-FLOWERED.

			per doz. s. d.	each. s. d.
Extra choice. Very fine selected flowers		Strong	18 .0	—
Choice selected flowers. Very good		Flowering	12 0	—
Mixed. In beautiful variety	...	Tubers	9 0	—

Tuberoses.

TUBEROSE—AMERICAN PEARL.

From Dr. ROBERTS, Crouch End.

Nov. 14th.

"The Roses I had from you have done exceedingly well. I shall require some more soon."

These deliciously fragrant and exceedingly useful flowers are much more easily grown than is generally supposed, and will well repay the little trouble that is necessary to have them in perfection. For early forcing, pot singly into five or six-inch pots, as early in the season as the bulbs can be obtained, and plunge in a good moist heat, withholding water till the foliage makes its appearance, when water may be given abundantly till the flower-buds are formed, when they may be removed to the greenhouse or conservatory and less water given. For Autumn blooming, pot singly into five or six-inch pots in March or April, using a light rich compost, and plunge the pots about six inches above their rims in cocoa-nut fibre, coal ashes, or any light material, under the stage of a greenhouse or in a cool pit or frame; when the foliage of these makes its appearance they should be removed and plunged under a south wall, removing them to the greenhouse or indoors as the flower-buds are formed. Dry roots may also be planted in sheltered places in the open ground, from the middle of April to the latter part of May, and will produce beautiful flowers in Autumn if taken up, potted, and kept in a close warm house or pit for a few days when coming into flower, and will furnish a supply of valuable bloom in the greenhouse almost up to Christmas.

		per doz. s. d.	each. s. d.
Double American "Pearl." Fine new dwarf variety from the United States; deliciously fragrant, with large double flowers, pure white .... per 100, 17s. 6d.		2 6	0 3
" African grown. Very fine roots " 21s.		3 0	0 4

Miscellaneous Bulbous-rooted Plants, &c.

Bravoa Geminiflora (The Twin Flower). A beautiful little Summer and Autumn blooming, hardy bulbous-rooted plant, bearing erect spikes of rich scarlet cerise coral-like tubular flowers; very pretty
per doz. 5s.; each 6d.

Colchicum speciosum. Beautiful large-flowered hardy plant from Asia Minor, producing noble, Crocus-like, bright rosy purple flowers in Autumn and having handsome foliage in Spring. Will thrive in any soil where undisturbed; splendid for clumps on border per doz. 8s.; each 9d.

Schizostylis coccinea. A remarkably handsome, perfectly hardy, evergreen bulbous plant, with beautiful crimson-scarlet flowers per doz. 2s. 6d.; each 3d.

Sternbergia lutea (syn. Amaryllis lutea). A splendid hardy Autumn-flowering bulb, with yellow Crocus-like flowers per doz. 3s.; each 4d.

Tigridia—Canariensis } (Tiger Flowers)   per doz. 3s.; each 4d.
Pavonia   per doz. 2s. 6d.; each 4d.

Grandiflora alba. Creamy white, spotted with red, and having a violet centre; a fine novelty, very beautiful; quite hardy per doz. 4s.; each 6d.

PALM- PHŒNIX RECLINATA.

BEGONIA—REX VARIETY.

DAPHNE INDICA ALBA.

Greenhouse & Stove Plants

Allamanda Hendersoni. Beautiful stove plant
each 2s. 6d. and 3s. 6d.

Aralia Sieboldi variegata. Beautiful plant
each 3s. 6d. and 5s.

Araucaria excelsa (_Norfolk Island Pine._) A fine plant for
the conservatory each 3s. 6d. and 5s.

Aspidistra lurida variegata. A very beautiful and
distinct plant, with handsomely variegated foliage each 3s. 6d. and 5s.

Azalea Indica. We offer a choice collection, including the
finest varieties, all in good healthy flowering plants, varying in height
from about ten inches to sixteen inches from the pots. Our own
selection, per doz. 24s., 30s., 40s., 50s., and 60s., according to size and
variety; each 2s., 2s. 6d., 3s. 6d., 5s., and 7s. 6d.

Azalea Mollis. Fine healthy plants well set with flower-buds
each 1s. 6d., 2s. 6d., and 3s. 6d.; per doz. 18s. to 30s.

Begonias, Rex varieties (_see illustration_). Well-known
beautiful foliaged plants, for the greenhouse or conservatory
each 1s. 6d. and 2s. 6d.

Caladiums. The most beautiful varieties each 2s. 6d. and 3s. 6d.

Camellia Japonica. Our collection of these includes all the
finest of the English and continental varieties, and our plants are
amongst the healthiest and best budded we have ever seen. The
height of plants from the pots varies from about a foot to eighteen
inches. Our own selection, per doz. 30s., 40s., 50s., and 60s.;
each 2s. 6d., 3s. 6d., 5s., and 7s. 6d.

Clerodendron Balfouri. Useful climber each 2s. 6d.

Cobæa scandens variegata. Useful climber for the
greenhouse each 1s. 6d. and 2s. 6d.

Coprosma Baueriana variegata. Beautiful green-
house plant, with handsomely variegated foliage each 1s. 6d. and 2s. 6d.

Crassula jasminioides. Pure white flowers, similar in
form to those of Jasmine or Bouvardia; capital greenhouse plant,
good for cutting each 6d.; per doz. 5s.

Daphne Indica alba. Pure white, deliciously scented
variety each 2s. 6d., 3s. 6d., and 5s.

Daphne Indica rubra. Very sweet each 2s. 6d. and 3s. 6d.

Eucharis Amazonica. The most useful variety
each 2s. 6d., 3s. 6d., and 5s.

Eurya latifolia variegata. Very useful plant for the
greenhouse each 2s. 6d.

Ficus elastica (_India-rubber Plant_) each 1s. 6d. and 2s. 6d.

Gloxinia hybrida grandiflora. Fine flowering bulbs
in beautiful variety. Our selection, per doz. 9s., 12s. and 18s.

Greenhouse Ferns. A fine selection
per doz. 6s., 9s., 12s., and 18s.

Lapageria rosea. Well known beautiful greenhouse climber
each 2s. 6d., 3s. 6d., and 5s.

Lapageria alba. Lovely pure white wax-like flowers
each 7s. 6d. and 10s. 6d.

Palms. A nice assortment of choice plants, suitable for the dinner
table each 3s. 6d. and 5s.

Passiflora princeps. Lovely stove climber, with large
scarlet flowers each 2s. 6d. and 3s. 6d.

Primula obconica. Pretty evergreen species, bearing
numerous umbels of pale lilac flowers; makes an excellent pot plant
for the greenhouse or cool pit, and is in bloom throughout the Winter
each 6d., 1s., and 1s. 6d.

Stephanotis floribunda. Well known beautiful climber
each 2s. 6d. and 3s. 6d.

Swainsonia galegifolia alba. Lovely clusters of
pure white pea-like flowers; very free bloomer each 2s. 6d.

Tacsonia van Volxemi. Brilliant climber for the greenhouse each 1s. 6d. and 2s. 6d.

Greenhouse Plants in choice variety, our selection,
per doz. 18s., 24s., 30s., and 40s.

Hybrid Perpetual Roses.

MARCHIONESS OF LORNE.

This magnificent and beautiful class of Roses is better than any other adapted for garden and pot culture, and for exhibition. They continue in flower from the early part of June to the end of October, and are by far the most desirable for general cultivation. Our stock of these comprises many thousands of the newest and choicest varieties in standards and dwarfs, and the past season having been very favourable to their growth, the plants we offer will be found unusually well grown and vigorous, and may be expected to produce a fine display of bloom next season.

Hints on Cultivation.—Generally speaking the Rose will thrive in any good garden soil, but as it has a decided preference for that which inclines to the clayey or loamy, it is advisable in planting, where the soil is not of a suitable nature, to make for each plant a hole of about eighteen inches diameter, removing a sufficient quantity of soil to admit of about a bushel of good rough loam with the addition of a fair quantity of well-decayed stable manure incorporated, in which to place the roots. If planting be done in dry weather in Autumn or in Spring, the roots of the plants should be well watered before filling in with soil, and at all times the standards should be firmly staked and tied to prevent their disturbance by the wind. To ensure a vigorous growth, Roses should be cut back the first season from planting to two or three eyes or buds on each shoot. The best time to do this is about March, but a longer succession of bloom may be had by pruning some at intervals from the new year to the beginning of April. November is perhaps the best month for planting, but it may be done with perfect safety any time from October to March.

Hybrid Perpetual Roses in Collections.

These collections are carefully made up to ensure a fine variety, and customers ordering may depend on their giving the most unqualified satisfaction. In all cases good healthy plants will be sent, and in the best variety of colour, &c., that can be included in the number given, but in all instances the selection must be left to ourselves.

CARRIAGE FREE. IMPORTANT NOTICE.

To meet the requirements of many of our numerous customers, we send all these collections Carriage Free to any part of the British Isles at prices quoted, and we make no charge for packing.

	Stds. & Half-Stds.	Dwarfs.
12 in 12 of the most select vars.	£1 4 0	£0 10 6
12 in 12 good and popular vars.	0 18 0	0 7 6
25 in 25 of the most select vars.	2 0 0	1 0 0
25 in 25 good and popular vars.	1 15 0	0 14 0
50 in 50 of the most select vars.	3 15 0	1 10 0
50 in 50 good and popular vars.	3 5 0	1 7 6
100 in 50 of the most select vars.	7 0 0	3 0 0
100 in 50 good and popular vars.	6 10 0	2 10 0

Miscellaneous Roses.

MOSS ROSES—Dwarfs only—

Common Moss. Rosy blush, mossed well up the bud per doz. 10s. 6d.; each 1s.
White Moss. Pure white, beautifully mossed per doz. 10s. 6d.; each 1s.

PROVENCE OR CABBAGE ROSES—

Old Provence. Rose colour, very fragrant ... each 9d.
White Provence. White, beautiful bud ... each 9d.

CRIMSON CHINA. Dark crimson, dwarf and pretty; an old favourite ... per doz. 10s. 6d., each 1s.

AUSTRIAN COPPER. Distinct and beautiful, golden terra-cotta colour, flowers single ... per doz. 10s. 6d., each 1s.
PERSIAN YELLOW. Deep golden yellow, full, double flowers, beautiful ... ... 10s. 6d., each 1s.
RUGOSA. Beautiful single-flowered Japanese species, fine glossy foliage, and bright purplish crimson flowers ... each 1s. 6d.
RUGOSA ALBA; A white-flowered variety of the above, beautiful in bud ... ... each 1s.

Roses—Tea-scented and Noisette.

This beautiful class is distinguished by the peculiar and delightful fragrance of the flowers, and the many charming tints and shades of yellow, rose and salmon colour not to be found amongst the hybrid perpetuals. The individual blooms are of exquisite form, and invaluable for button-holes or bouquets. They are especially suited for pot culture in the conservatory, and planted outside on slightly raised beds in a sheltered position, and given a slight protection in Winter, they will furnish some beautiful flowers throughout the Summer and Autumn.

Our own selection, in choice variety, plants mostly established in pots, per doz. 15s., 18s., and 21s.

	Dwarfs—s. d.			Dwarfs—s. d.
Anna Olivier. Flesh-coloured rose	1 6		**Perle des Jardins.** Straw colour	1 6
Belle Lyonnaise. Deep canary yellow	1 6		**Primrose Dame.** Primrose yellow, apricot centre;	
Bouquet d'Or (Noisette). Deep yellow, coppery			fine form; very free flowering	2 6
centre	1 6		**Princess of Wales.** Rosy yellow, centre deeper	1 6
Catherine Mermet. Flesh-coloured rose	1 6		**Reve d'Or** (Noisette). Deep yellow	1 6
Celine Forestier (Noisette). Pale yellow	1 6		**Safrano.** Bright apricot; beautiful	
Comtesse de Nadaillac. Bright rose, with yellow	1 6		**Souvenir d'Elise Vardon.** White, centre pale	
Comtesse Riza du Parc. Salmon rose, shaded			yellow	1 6
with copper	1 6		**Souvenir d'un Ami.** Salmon and rose	1 6
Devoniensis. White, tinted yellow, beautiful	1 6		**Souvenir de S. A. Prince.** The finest White	
Duchess of Edinburgh. Deep glowing crimson	1 6		Tea Rose offered in late years; it has all the good	
Etoile de Lyon. Fine saffron yellow, large	1 6		qualities of *Souvenir d'un Ami*, with flowers of	
Francisca Kruger. Copper yellow, shaded peach,			the purest white. Three First Class Certificates,	
large and full	1 6		and now well-known from its frequent exhibition	
Gloire de Dijon. Buff, with orange centre. A well-			at various Rose Shows as a good exhibition Rose	
known old favourite 1s. 6d., 2s. 6d., 3s. 6d., 5s., and	7 6		2s. 6d. and	3 6
Homere. Rose, centre salmon	1 6		**Sunset.** Rich tawny saffron colour 1s. 6d. and	2 6
Innocente Pirola. Pure white, slightly rosy	1 6		**The Bride.** A pure white sport from *Catherine*	
Isabella Sprunt. Sulphur yellow	1 6		*Mermet*; most valuable for cutting purposes	2 6
Jean Ducher. Salmon yellow, shaded with rose	1 6		**THE PURITAN** (Hybrid Tea). This fine white	
Lady Castlereagh (new). Soft rosy yellow	2 6		Rose is exceedingly valuable for forcing. The buds	
Lady Mary Fitzwilliam. Delicate flesh colour	1 6		when opening are slightly yellow, changing to pure	
Madame Bravy. Creamy white	1 6		white as they expand, whilst they have the most	
Marechal Niel (Noisette). Beautiful golden yellow.			delicious perfume	2 6
Well known 1s. 6d., 2s. 6d., 3s. 6d., and	7 6		**THE METEOR** (Hybrid Tea). Rich velvety crimson,	
Marie Guillot. White, slightly tinted with yellow	1 6		without the slightest tint of purple; a constant and	
Madame Falcot. Apricot yellow, very distinct	1 6		free bloomer, very vigorous in growth and with no	
Madame Lambard. Bright red, a fine variety	1 6		tendency to mildew. A capital Rose for Winter	
Madame Margottin. Deep yellow, centre rosy	1 6		blooming under glass, and first-class for the Summer	
Madame de Watteville. Salmony white, edged			season out of doors	2 6
with bright rose and pink; beautiful and distinct	1 6		**Vicomtesse de Cazes.** Yellow, centre deeper	1 6
Marie van Houtte. Lemon yellow edged with			**Vicomtesse Folkestone.** Creamy pink	1 6
lively rose, medium size, good form, beautiful	2 6		**W. F. Bennett.** Crimson, large and double	2 6
Mrs. James Wilson (new). Deep lemon yellow,			**William Allen Richardson** (Noisette). Fine	
margined rose, very fine	3 0		deep orange yellow, very showy and distinct; a	
Niphetos. Pale lemon, changing to white 1s. 6d. and	2 6		gem for buttonholes and bouquets	
Perle de Lyon. Deep yellow; splendid	1 6		1s. 6d., 2s. 6d., 3s. 6d., and	5 0

Climbing Roses, Hardy and others.

The following list of Climbing Roses includes the most useful and beautiful varieties in cultivation. For pillars, walls, or arches in exposed positions the fine old varieties of Ayrshire, Evergreen, Banksia, Boursault, Cheshunt Hybrid, Gloire de Dijon, and Aimee Vibert are the most desirable; whilst for greenhouse work the beautiful Marechal Niel, Climbing Niphetos, and Climbing Devoniensis are the best.

	s. d.			s. d.
Aimee Vibert (Noisette). Small pure white flowers			**Evergreen, Donna Maria.** Pure white	1 0
in large clusters; very hardy	1 0		" **Felicite Perpetuelle.** Creamy white	1 0
Ayrshire, Dundee Rambler. White, edged pink	1 0		" **Leopoldine d'Orleans.** White, tipped	
" **Queen of the Belgians.** Pure white	1 0		red	1 0
Banksia alba, or white. Pure white	1 6		" **Myrianthes.** Blush, edged rose	1 0
" **lutea,** or yellow. Fine yellow	1 6		" **Rampant.** Pure white	1 0
Boursault (Rosa alpina), Amadis, or crimson	1 0		**Gloire de Dijon** (T). Buff, with orange centre,	
Cheshunt Hybrid. Bright cherry carmine, large			well known, superb variety 1s. 6d., 2s. 6d., and	3 6
open flowers; a very hardy and strong grower	1 0		**Marechal Niel** (Noisette). Beautiful golden yellow	
Climbing Devoniensis (T). Magnificent strong-			of the most lovely form and delicious fragrance;	
growing variety, flowers creamy white with blush			well known, superb variety	
centre; deliciously scented 1s. 6d., 2s. 6d., 3s. 6d., and	5 0		1s. 6d., 2s. 6d., 3s. 6d., and	5 0
Climbing Niphetos. A fine new, rapid growing,			*****Waltham Climber, No. 1.**) Light crimson	2 0
climbing tea-scented variety; shoots running to			*****Waltham Climber, No. 3.**) Dark crimson	2 0
twenty feet in one season, flowering on lateral			**William Allen Richardson** (Noisette). Fine	
shoots from their main stems continuously; blooms			deep orange yellow, very showy and distinct; a	
of a purer white than those of the old variety, not			gem for buttonholes and bouquets	
showing the pink tinge, and even more delicately			1s. 6d., 2s. 6d., 3s. 6d., and	5 0
scented. First Class Certificate R. H. S.				
2s. 6d., 3s. 6d., and	5 0		* Seedlings from the well-known Gloire de Dijon.	

Miscellaneous Fruit Trees, &c.

APPLE, P ASGOOD'S NONSUCH.

The large and steadily increasing demand for all kinds of choice Fruit Trees, &c., furnishes a sure indication that good English-grown fruit is, year by year, becoming more appreciated, and it is clearly shown by the splendid samples being brought to our markets and sold at highly remunerative prices, that by planting only really choice varieties, and with good cultivation, Apples, Pears, and other fruits can be grown in this country of a size, flavour, and quality altogether surpassing those of foreign production.

Wherever space in the garden will admit, fruit of some kind should be grown, as apart from its great usefulness in point of domestic economy, its great value as a health agent cannot be fairly over-estimated where it is freely used in the household.

For small gardens such compact-growing fruits as dwarf or pyramid Apples and Pears, Gooseberries, Currants, Raspberries, and Strawberries are the most useful, and where there is a good south wall a Vine or Peach should be planted, whilst a wall with a westerly aspect will do well for Cherries or Pears, and a north wall is well suited for Currants. In planting in the garden be careful to plant at such a distance apart that the plants get the full benefit of light and air, the result of over-crowding being but too often barrenness or inferior quality.

In very dry weather young fruit-bearing trees of Apples, Pears, Plums, &c., are much benefited by a liberal supply of water, which promotes a healthy growth and prevents cracking of the fruit. Dwarf or pyramid trees are also rendered more fruitful by being partially lifted every other year and having the roots slightly pruned.

The various stocks of choice Fruit Trees we offer include all the best varieties of their respective kinds in cultivation. The plants will be found well grown, strong, and healthy, with abundant fibrous roots, and in the best possible state for removal.

The prices quoted per dozen for Apples, Pears, Gooseberries, Currants, &c., are for our own selection of kinds, and are governed principally by the size and strength of the plants supplied. When the selection is left to us, customers may rely on only the best sorts being sent.

APPLES.

Dwarfs or Bushes in fine variety per doz. 10s. 6d.; each 1s.
Dwarf Trained ... ... each 3s. 6d.
Pyramids, our own selection of varieties
     per doz 21s. to 54s.; each 2s. to 5s.
Standards, our own selection of choice varieties
     per doz. 18s., 21s., 24s.; each 1s. 6d. to 2s. 6d.

EARLY AND SECOND EARLY APPLES.

D denotes dessert, K kitchen.

Devonshire Quarrenden (D.), Duchess of Oldenburg (K.), Eckinville Seedling (K.), Irish Peach (D.), Juneating (D.), Keswick Codlin (K.), Kerry Pippin (D.), King of the Pippins (D.), Lord Suffield (K.) Stirling Castle (K.), Worcester Pearmain (K.D.).

MEDIUM EARLY APPLES.

Adams' Pearmain (D.), Aromatic Russet (D.), Bess Pool (D.K.), Blenheim Orange (D.K.), Cellini (D.K.), Cox's Orange Pippin (D.), Cox's Pomona (K.), Doctor Harvey (K.), Gloria Mundi (K.), Kentish Fillbasket (K.), Lane's Prince Albert (K.), Lord Grosvenor (K.), Mère de Menage (K.), New Hawthornden (K.), Peasgood's Nonsuch (K.), Ribston Pippin (D.), The Queen (K.), Yorkshire Greening (K.).

LATE APPLES.

Alfriston (K.), Annie Elizabeth (K.), Beauty of Kent (K.), Court of Wick (D.), Court Pendu Plat (D.), Dumelow's Seedling (K.), Golden Pippin (D.), Golden Russet (D.), Keddleston Pippin (D.), Lady Henniker (K.), Lord Burghley (D.), Normanton Wonder (K.) (*Dumelow's Seedling*), Old Nonpareil (D), Reinette du Canada (D.K.), Scarlet Nonpareil (D.), Sturmer Pippin (D.), Warner's King (K.).

And many others.

NEW APPLE—Beauty of Bath.

This fine new early Dessert Apple, on account of its earliness, extremely handsome appearance, good flavour, and free cropping qualities, will eventually, both for market purposes and private use, take the leading place among first early Apples.

The "Beauty of Bath" is fit for use at the end of July and early part of August. It immediately follows the Juneating, and is earlier than the Irish Peach, from which it is quite distinct The fruit is of medium size, round and flattened, the ground colour a yellowish green, beautifully striped and spotted with crimson toward the sun; the flesh is firm and pale yellow, and it has a brisk, sub-acid flavour far superior to that of other early apples. It is a certain and free cropper. Our stock trees have not failed once during the last six years, and it will on this account be a valuable market variety.

Strong Maiden Trees, each 1s. 6d. and 2s. 6d.

Miscellaneous Fruit Trees, &c. (continued).

PEAR, PITMASTON DUCHESSE.

PEARS.

Dwarfs or Bushes in fine variety
per doz. 10s. 6d ; each 1s.
Dwarf Trained ... ... per doz. 37s. 6d. ; each 3s. 6d.
Pyramids ... per doz. 21s. to 5¼s. ; each 2s. to 5s
Standards per doz. 18s., 21s., & 24s. ; each 1s. 6d. to 2s. 6d.
" **Trained** ... ... each 5s.

PITMASTON DUCHESSE (see illustration).

A superb and most valuable variety. The fruit are very large and handsome, and of first-rate quality. The tree is hardy and an excellent bearer. In season from October to December.

Dwarfs or Bushes ... ... each 1s. 6d.
Pyramids ... each 2s. 6d., 3s. 6d., and 5s.
Standards ... ... each 2s.
Dwarf Trained ... ... each 3s. 6d. to 5s.

EARLY AND SECOND EARLY PEARS.

Beurré d'Amanlis, Beurré Giffard, Beurré Superfin, Citron des Carmes, Doyenne d'Eté, Durondeau, Gratioli of Jersey, Jargonelle, Souvenir du Congrès, Williams' Bon Chrétien, Williams' Victoria.

MID-SEASON PEARS.

Althorp Crassanne, Beurré Clairgeau, Beurré d'Aremberg, Beurré de Capiaumont, Beurré Diel, British Queen, Brockworth Park, Conseiller de la Cour, Chaumontel, Doyenné du Comice, Duchesse d'Angoulême, Fondante d'Automne, Gansel's Bergamot, Hessle, Louise Bonne of Jersey, Marie Louise, Marie Louise d'Uccle, Napoleon, Passe Colmar, Triomphe de Jodoigne, Van Mons Leon le Clerc.

LATE PEARS.

Bergamot d'Esperen, Beurré Rance, Easter Beurré, Josephine de Malines, Knight's Monarch, Ne Plus Mouris, Winter Nelis.

STEWING PEARS.

Catilluc ; Uvedale's St. Germain.

And others.

Grape Vines.

Our stock of these is a very fine one; the canes have been grown from eyes without bottom-heat, and are remarkably well ripened, short-jointed, and the buds are thoroughly matured and plump.

The fruiting canes we offer are strong and stout, from eight to ten feet in length ; and if cultivated in pots will bear from eight to twelve bunches each next season.

H denotes those varieties that require to be grown in a heated vinery.
C denotes those suitable for growing in a cool vinery.

Strong planting canes, in pots ... ... each 5s.
Fruiting canes, in pots, very fine ... each 7s. 6d. to 10s. 6d.

Alnwick Seedling (H.)	Muscat of Alexandria (H.)
Black Alicante (H.)	Muscat Hamburgh (H.C.)
Foster's Seedling (C.)	Mrs. Pearson (H.C.)
Gros Colmar (H.)	Madrosfield Crt. Muscat
Gros Maroc (H.)	(H.C.)
Hamburgh, Black (C.)	Sweetwater, Buckland (C.)
Lady Downes' Seedling	West's St. Peter's (H.)
(H.)	White Syrian (H.)

Apricots—
Breda, Hemskirke, Kaisha, Large Early, Moor Park, Royal, Shipley's or Blenheim, &c., &c.
Dwarf Trained, very fine ... ... each 5s. to 7s. 6d.
Standard Trained ... each 7s. 6d. to 10s. 6d.

Nectarines—
Albert Victoria, Downton, Elruge, Early Newington, Hardwick Seedling, Lord Napier, Pineapple, Pitmaston Orange, Rivers' Orange, Roman, Victoria, Violette Hative, &c.
Dwarf Trained ... ... each 5s. to 7s. 6d.
Standard Trained ... each 10s. 6d. to 21s.

Peaches—
Alexandra, Barrington, Condor, Dr. Hogg, Early Beatrice, Early Rivers, Grosse Mignonne, Noblesse, Royal George, Stirling Castle, &c.
Dwarf Trained, very fine ... ... each 5s. to 7s. 6d.
Standard Trained, fine ... each 10s. 6d. to 21s.

Plums—
Angelina, Belgian Purple, Burdett, Coe's Golden Drop, Early Prolific, Golden Gage, Greengage, Huling's Superb, Jefferson's, Kirke's, Magnum Bonum, Mitchelson's, Orleans, Pond's Seedling, Prince Englebert, Prince of Wales, The Czar, Transparent Gage, Victoria, Washington, &c.
Dwarf Maidens ... ... per doz. 10s. 6d. ; each 1s.
" **Trained** ... per doz. 37s. 6d. ; each 3s. 6d.
Pyramids ... ... per doz. 21s. ; each 2s.
Standards ... ... per doz. 21s. ; each 2s.
" **Trained** ... ... each 5s.

Miscellaneous Fruit Trees, &c. (*continued*).

GOOSEBERRY, WHINHAM'S INDUSTRY.

Cherries—
Archduke, Bigarreau, Downton, Elton, May Duke, Morello, Ohio Beauty, &c., &c.

Dwarf Trained per doz. 40s. to 54s.; each 3s. 6d. to 5s.
Standards ... ... per doz. 21s.; each 2s.
" Trained ... per doz. 54s.; each 5s.
Pyramids ... ... per doz. 21s. to 54s.; each 2s. to 5s.

Chestnuts, Spanish—
Standards ... per doz. 10s. 6d. to 21s.; each 1s. to 2s.
Banks' Prolific | Common

American Fruiting Blackberry—
Wilson Junr. This magnificent Blackberry is undoubtedly one of the largest, finest, and most prolific in cultivation, producing very large, glossy black fruit, of delicious flavour, in immense quantity each 9d.; per doz. 7s. 6d.

Figs—
Strong Plants, in pots ... ... each 2s. 6d.
Fruiting Plants, in pots ... each 3s. 6d. to 7s. 6d.

From **MRS. FURSDON**, Cadbury.
Nov. 4th.
"Mrs. Fursdon writes to Messrs. Daniels to say she received the **Apple Trees** safe, and was especially pleased with them."

From **CHAS. STUHLMAN, Esq.**, Battersea.
July 16th.
"The Dwarf-trained Fruit Trees are very healthy. The **Morello Cherry** bearing a good amount of fruit, this, the first year after planting."

From **Mr. ROBERT DIXON**, Shiplake.
Dec. 16th.
"I enclose cheque for your account. I am very pleased with the **Fruit Trees** you sent me."

Gooseberries.
A good collection of the best Lancashire Prize and other varieties.

Strong Bushes in good variety per 100, 21s.; per doz. 3s.
Lancashire Prize. Splendid large-fruited sorts
Our selection, per doz. 4s. 6d. and 6s.

WHINHAM'S "INDUSTRY" A superb new variety, bearing a wonderful profusion of large handsome fruit, which are of a dull red colour when ripe. This is one of the best and most prolific gooseberries in cultivation, and has proved itself invaluable for culinary and market purposes.
Strong bushes, per 100, 40s.; per doz. 6s.; each 8d.

British Crown | Overall
Broom Girl | Pilot
Companion | Pitmaston Greengage
Crown Bob | Red Champagne
Drill | Red Warrington
Duck-wing | Rifleman
Governess | Roaring Lion
Gunner | Rough Red
Ironmonger | Slaughterman
Lancashire Lad | Snowdrop
Leader | Thumper
Lion's Provider | Whitesmith
London | Yellow Champagne
And others.

Currants.
Strong bushes ... per 100, 21s. to 35s.; per doz. 3s. to 6s.

BLACK CHAMPION. A very fine and remarkable variety, bearing large bunches of handsome, globular, richly-flavoured fruit, the individual berries, when well grown, being equal in size to medium-sized grapes. It is a vigorous grower, wonderfully prolific, and retains its splendid colour and freshness for a much longer time than other varieties; undoubtedly the best of all the black currants. Was awarded a First Class Certificate by the Royal Horticultural Society, and pronounced by the Committee to be the finest Black Currant ever seen at South Kensington.
Strong young bushes, per doz. 4s. 6d.; each 6d.

BLACK— | RED—
Common | Cherry
Lee's Prolific | La Fertile
Naples | New Giant
Ogden's | Raby Castle. Fine
WHITE— | Red Dutch
Dutch | &c., &c.
Transparent White

Raspberries.
Per 100, 12s. to 20s.; per doz. 2s. to 3s.

Fastolf | Red Antwerp
Fillbasket | White Antwerp

Baumforth's Seedling. A fine new variety; fruit very large, of the most beautiful crimson colour; an abundant bearer of good habit. Per 100, 25s.; per doz. 4s.

Nuts and Filberts.
We have a very fine stock of these in good strong bushes, comprising such fine varieties as Cosford, Kentish Cob, Filbert, white, red, purple-leaved and frizzled, Norwich Prolific, &c.

Dwarf Bushes in good variety
per 100, 45s. to 60s.; per doz., 6s. and 9s.

Strawberry Plants—Select List.

Strawberries when well-grown are wonderfully prolific, and constitute one of the most profitable crops, really good fruit always meeting with a ready sale at high prices. These delicious and wholesome fruit should be grown freely in every garden where there is room for them. As will be seen, our collection of choice Strawberries, a select list of which we offer below, contains all the finest varieties in cultivation.

New Strawberries.

"Latest of All" (LAXTON).

A GRAND new seedling from *British Queen* crossed with *Helena Glaede*. The fruit is very large, exceeding in size that of either parent, and is certainly the finest flavored and largest late Strawberry yet introduced. The flesh is firm and white, the flavour vinous, yet luscious and quite equal to that of *British Queen*, which it most nearly approaches in appearance, but ripening from ten days to a fortnight after it ... ... per 100, 20s.; per doz. 3s. 6d.

A. F. Barron (Laxton). A cross between *Sir J. Paxton* and *Sir Charles Napier*. Very fine. First Class Certificate, Royal Horticultural Society per 100, 7s. 6d.; per doz. 1s. 6d.

Commander (Laxton). A cross between *British Queen* and *President*, and said to be even superior in flavour to *British Queen*. One of the most distinct and splendid Strawberries yet raised ... ... per 100, 7s. 6d.; per doz. 1s. 6d.

Laxton's Noble. Large and handsome fruit. Early and very prolific. Will be universally grown
per 100, 5s.; per doz. 9d.

NEW STRAWBERRY—LAXTON'S "NOBLE."

	per 100—s.	d.		per 100—s.	d.		per 100—s.	d.
Alpha	5	0	James Veitch ...	5	0	Prince Arthur ...	3	6
Aromatic ...	5	0	Keen's Seedling	3	6	Royalty ...	5	0
Auguste Nicaise	5	0	King of the Earlies	5	0	Sir Charles Napier	3	6
British Queen ...	5	0	Kitley's Goliath	3	6	Sir Harry ...	3	6
Dr. Hogg ...	5	0	Lucas ...	5	0	Sir Joseph Paxton	5	0
Duke of Edinburgh	5	0	Marguerite ...	3	6	The Captain ...	5	0
Elton (*syn. Elton Pine*)	5	0	Premier ...	3	6	Vicomtesse H. de Thury	3	0
Filbert Pine ...	5	0	President ...	5	0	Waterloo per doz. 1s.	7	6
Frogmore Late Pine	5	0						

1000 in 10 choice varieties ... 35s. 0d.   **100 in 10 choice varieties** ... 5s. 6d.

Asparagus.

AN abundance of fine Asparagus may be grown with less than half the expense usually incurred in making costly "beds," and will succeed admirably on most soils when planted in lines or clumps on the Kitchen Garden borders, or amongst dwarf-growing Fruits where the space will admit, a liberal cultivation being all that is required to ensure the best results. We consider March and April the best months for planting in the open ground. The strong roots we offer will be found very fine for forcing.

Connover's Colossal. Two and three years old
per 100, 5s. and 7s. 6d.
True Giant. Two and three years old ... per 100, 3s. 6d. and 5s.

Sweet and Pot Herbs.

WE have a fine collection of these, including the following useful sorts:—

			per doz.—s.	d.
Balm	...	...	4	0
Chamomile	...	...	4	0
Chives	...	each 6d.	5	0
Horehound	...	...	4	0
Hyssop	...	...	4	0
Lavender	...	each 6d.	5	0
Mint, Lamb	...	...	4	6
,, Pepper	...	...	4	0
Marjoram, Pot	...	...	4	0
Pennyroyal	...	each 6d.	5	0
Rosemary	...	each 8d.	6	0
Rue	...	...	4	0
Savory, Winter	...	each 6d.	5	0
Sorrel, Giant French	...	each 6d.	5	0
Tarragon	...	each 6d.	5	0
Thyme, Lemon	...	each 6d.	5	0
,, Common	...	...	4	0
Wormwood	...	...	4	0

The most useful varieties assorted, our selection, per doz. 4s.; per 100, 25s.

Sea Kale.

Strong planting roots
per doz. 1s.; per 100, 7s. 6d.
Good strong roots, for forcing
per doz. 1s. 6d.; per 100, 10s. 6d.
Extra strong roots, for forcing; very fine
per doz. 2s.; per 100, 15s.

Rhubarb.

Strong plants of the following, each 9d.; per doz. 7s. 6d.

Johnson's St. Martin's
Scarlet Defiance
Royal Albert
Myatt's Victoria

Paragon (Kershaw). The most wonderfully prolific kind known; as much as £240 has been made off a single acre for market purposes
each 1s.; per doz. 10s. 6d.

The Queen (new). Very early, the stalk a beautiful red quite through, each 1s.; per doz. 10s. 6d.

CARNATIONS.

1 GERMANIA.
2 BIZARRE CARNATION.
3 MRS. REYNOLDS HOLE.

Carnations & Picotees

Our collection of these is very fine, and includes all the choicest of the yellows, scarlets, flakes, bizarres, and fancy varieties. Our Grounds are peculiarly well suited to their cultivation, and in consequence of the past favourable Season, we are enabled to offer unusually strong, well-rooted, and healthy plants from pots at the following cheap rates.

NEW AND VERY CHOICE SORTS.

Alice Ayres. Pure pearly white, the centre petals delicately marked with carmine, most beautiful form, very full   each 1s.

Amber. An amber-coloured self, medium size, very distinct and pleasing, extra fine; has been awarded three First Class Certificates   each 1s. 6d.

Amy Herbert (1891). A fine deep-bodied rose self, showing bright cerise by artificial light; an enormous flower   each 2s.

Cara Roma (new). A beautiful rich glowing maroon with a soft blending of mulberry, a large flower of fine substance   each 1s. 6d.

Comte de Chambord. A new variety, possessing very considerable attractions, large flesh-white flowers   each 1s. 6d.

Countess of Paris. Delicate flesh colour, fine bold flower   each 2s. 6d.

Duke of Fife (new). Clear soft salmon-scarlet, one of the largest and finest ever introduced   each 3s.

Germania. Pure soft yellow self, with broad flat smooth petals, of extra large and fine form, long intact pod, a first-rate grower, and altogether the best yellow self known. F.C.C., R.H.S.   each 1s. 6d.

Gloire de Nancy. Large pure white clove-scented   each 8d.

La Neige (Perpetual, new). Splendid new pure white, of dwarf robust habit; first class for pot culture   each 3s.

Leander (1891). Intense deep yellow self, a fine heavy shell-like petal, especially useful in wet seasons, as it withstands the heavy rains better than most of its class   each 3s.

Miss Joliffe (Perpetual). Pale pink, dwarf habit, very fine flowering, splendid for Winter blooming   each 1s.

Montague (1891). Rich deep scarlet, a very large flower of splendid form and substance; said to be the finest scarlet variety ever offered to the public   each 3s. 6d.

Mrs. Frank Watts. The finest White Border Carnation in cultivation. The flowers are very large and full, smooth edge, of a beautiful pure white, very fragrant, and do not burst   each 1s. 6d.

Mrs. Reynolds Hole. Quite a new and altogether novel shade of colour amongst Carnations, somewhat difficult to describe—salmon-apricot is the nearest blending of colour to liken it to; possessing a vigorous constitution, producing a great quantity of both foliage and flowers, and has been awarded several First Class Certificates   each 1s. 6d.

Mrs. F. Gifford (1891). A pure flaky white, petals very slightly fringed, good form and immense size; rich clove-scented   each 2s.

Raby Castle. Clear soft salmon-pink, neatly fringed; very pleasing   each 1s.

Redbraes (Picotee). White ground, edged with purple; fine   each 1s.

Sir Charles Wilson (Perpetual). Scarlet, shaded with carmine, very large flowers   each 2s. 6d.

Souvenir de la Malmaison. Well known grand old variety with delicate pink flowers   each 1s. 6d.

The Coroner. Rich scarlet, early and free   each 1s. 6d.

CARNATIONS & PICOTEES IN COLLECTIONS.

50 in 50 choice named sorts...	...	...	40s.
25 in 25 extra choice sorts ...	...	...	21s.
25 in 25 standard varieties ...	...	...	17s. 6d.
12 in 12 extra choice sorts	...	...	12s.
12 in 12 good sorts ...	...	...	9s.
12 in 12 popular varieties	...	...	6s.

PERPETUAL or TREE CARNATIONS IN POTS—
A good collection of choice sorts, per doz. 18s., 21s., 24s., and 30s.

YELLOW AND YELLOW-GROUND CARNATIONS AND PICOTEES—
Including all the leading varieties, our selection   per doz. 18s.

SELECTED BORDER CARNATIONS (Seedlings)—
All good double flowers, and in fine variety   per doz. 4s. 6d.

Crimson Clove. The fine old spice-scented variety per doz. 5s.; each 6d.

Blush Clove. Lovely soft blush colour; finely scented per doz. 6s.; each 8d.

Striped Clove (Coquette). White spotted and striped with crimson each 1s.

White Clove. Pure white, deliciously scented per doz. 5s.; each 6d.

Select Hardy Florists' Flowers.

Garden Pinks.

Her Majesty (new). We have much pleasure in drawing attention to this charming novelty, which is far away the finest and best White Garden Pink in cultivation. The plants are of sturdy compact growth, the flowers are very large, resembling those of a Carnation, pure white, and of the most delicious fragrance. Splendid as a cut flower, and a first-class variety for forcing. Has been awarded Nine First Class Certificates   per doz. 15s.; each 1s. 6d.

Mrs. J. M. Welsh. This is a very charming new variety, outvieing considerably that now well-known and universally appreciated white variety, *Mrs. Sinkins.* In habit it closely resembles the variety mentioned, and produces quite as freely large entire pure white flowers, lacking the green centre and the tendency to burst which is sometimes exhibited in the case of *Mrs. Sinkins*
   per doz. 7s. 6d.; each 9d.

Mrs. Sinkins. The largest pure white grown, dwarf free habit, very hardy   per doz. 5s.; each 6d.

Old double white fringed   per doz. 2s. 6d.

Early Blush. Blush pink, large double fringed flowers
   per doz. 4s. 6d.; each 6d.

Choice named varieties. Including the most beautiful laced sorts, our selection   per doz. 4s. and 6s.

Perennial Gaillardias.

(Gaillardia hybrida grandiflora.)

SPLENDID hardy perennials. The very large and beautiful flowers are almost unique in their charming blendings of the many rich shades of brown, maroon, and golden yellow, and being of good substance are first-class to cut for indoor decoration, as the blooms will last a week in water. The plants, which are of a bushy habit of growth, attain about 2½ feet in height, will thrive in any soil, and produce a profusion of their lovely flowers from June to October.

	each—s.	d.
Admiration. Vermilion, edged with golden yellow ...	2	6
Addison. Crimson, edged with gold	1	0
A-la-Mode. Very large red, shaded yellow	2	0
Banquo. Orange, red centre, fine	1	0
Bellini. Crimson, yellow edge; fine	2	0
Diana. Deep crimson with golden edge	1	0
Grandiflora. Rich crimson, edged yellow	1	0
Lutea. Very fine yellow	0	9
Maximus. Blood crimson, edged golden yellow ...	1	6
Perfection. Brilliant scarlet, edged with yellow ...	1	0
Splendida. Very rich crimson, margined orange yellow	1	0
Splendidissima plena. Double crimson, gold edge	2	6
Superbum. Deep crimson, with broad yellow edge ...	1	0
Vivian Grey. Yellow, a grand flower ...	2	6

Choice named varieties, our selection
   per doz. 12s. and 18s.

Choice mixed seedlings, will produce some beautiful flowers   per doz. 4s. 6d.; 6 for 2s. 6d.

Delphiniums.

SINGLE AND DOUBLE-FLOWERED.

THESE fine hardy plants are deserving a place in every garden; they continue in bloom for a long time in Summer, many of the varieties producing spikes of bloom one foot to two feet in length, and of the most intense and delicate colours.

Belladonna (Single). Very pale blue, a lovely shade of colour, splendid for cutting. Plant of dwarf habit each 9d.

Choice named sorts, our selection   per doz. 6s. and 9s.

Perennial Phloxes.

MAGNIFICENT hardy plants, in bloom from July to November. The flowers, which are produced in grand spikes, are of the most beautiful form, and the colours range from the most intense crimson and scarlet to the purest white, and white with delicately coloured eyes. Will succeed well planted out in Spring and grown as Chrysanthemums. We have a fine collection of these, upwards of 100 varieties, including the most charming flowers in cultivation.

Early-flowering—Angus, Clipper, Forerunner, Hercules, Mrs. Miller, John Forbes, King of Purples, Mrs. Walker, &c.

Late-flowering—Annabel, Aurora, Chas. Pearson, Decius, Gloire de Poiteau, Jessie Laird, Mrs. Laing, Miss Balfour, Roi des Blancs, Roi des Roses, Telephone, The Mc Newman, W. Kilgour, and many others.

Strong Plants established in pots, our own selection, in beautiful variety to name
   per doz. 4s. 6d., 6s., and 9s.; per 100, 30s. and 40s.

Potentillas.

DOUBLE AND SINGLE-FLOWERED.

VERY free-flowering and useful hardy perennials, growing about two feet high. The flowers are of a rich velvety texture, and vary in colour from crimson and maroon to orange and golden yellow.

12 in 6 choice varieties, our selection 9s.; 6 for 5s.

Double-flowered Pyrethrums.

THESE fine plants produce a great variety of beautiful flowers in all the shades of crimson, carmine, rose, to pure white. The individual blooms are as double and finished as those of good Asters which they resemble, and are extremely useful for cutting.

Strong established Plants in choice named variety. Our selection   per doz. 6s. and 9s.

Single-flowered, in brilliant variety to name   per doz. 6s.

Herbaceous Pæonies, Double-flowered.

WELL-KNOWN, magnificent, hardy, herbaceous plants for the shrubbery border, &c.; will thrive in almost any soil or situation, but to be grown well should be planted in an open position and not disturbed for several years. We have a splendid named collection of these, including the newest and best sorts, the flowers ranging in colour from pure white to the deepest crimson and purple. Cut when just expanding, the blooms will last a long time in water.

Choice named varieties. Our own selection ... ... per doz. 12s., 15s., 18s., 21s., and 24s.
Fine varieties, mixed, without names ... ... per doz. 9s.

Miscellaneous Bedding Plants, &c.

READY FOR SENDING OUT DURING MAY AND JUNE.

The prices quoted are for fine strong plants from single pots. All orders for these will be executed in the same rotation as received.

Not less than 50 supplied at the rate per 100, or 6 at the rate per dozen.

LOBELIA, KING OF THE BLUES.

	per doz.—s.	d.
Ageratum. Dwarf. Blue ... per 100, 17s. 6d.	2	6
Alternanthera amœna. Bright red foliage		
per 100, 17s. 6d.	2	6
„ **aurea nana.** Clear golden yellow foliage	3	0
Alyssum (*Koniga*). Silver-variegated per 100, 17s. 6d.	2	6
Arabis lucida variegata. Dwarf, yellow variegated foliage; capital edging plant	4	0
Begonia Saundersi. A capital free flowering variety, growing twelve to eighteen inches high, with bright coral red flowers	5	0
Begonia, tuberous-rooted, *see page 98.*		
Calceolaria. Golden Gem ... per 100, 21s.	3	0
Cannas. In variety, fine for centres of beds ...	6	0
Centaurea candidissima. Beautiful silvery foliage, dwarf ... ... per 100, 21s.	3	0
Coleus. Verschaffelti splendens. Fine and effective variety for bedding per 100, 25s.	4	0
Dahlias, *see page 120, 121.*		
Daisies, *see page 109.*		
Diplacus Californicus. Similar in habit to Pentstemon, flowers orange buff	4	0
Echeveria secunda glauca ... per 100, 21s.	3	0

	per doz.—s.	d.
Fuchsias. In beautiful variety, including best sorts 4s. and	6	0
Funkia lanceolata marginata. Handsome variegated foliage, a good edging plant	5	0
Gazania splendens. Beautiful golden yellow flowers, dwarf ... ... per 100, 21s.	3	0
Geraniums, Bedding.		
Crimson Henry Jacoby. Splendid dark per 100, 30s.	4	0
Crystal Palace Gem. Beautiful „ 24s.	3	6
Golden Brilliantissima. Splendid dwarf ...	4	0
Pink, Master Christine „ per 100, 24s.	3	6
Salmon, Mrs. G. Smith ... „ 24s.	3	6
Scarlet, Vesuvius. Splendid bedder „ 21s.	3	0
Verona. Golden foliage, pink flowers	6	0
White, Virgo Marie ... per 100, 24s.	3	6
Golden Tricolor. Lady Cullum „ 30s.	4	0
„ Sophie Dumaresque „ 30s.	4	0
„ In line variety to name ... each 9d.	8	0
Silver Tricolor. Lass o' Gowrie, Mrs. John Clutton, Mrs. Laing ... ... each 6d.	5	0
Silver-leaved. Avalanche. Pure white flowers ...	6	0
„ Charming Bride	6	0
„ Flower of Spring per 100, 24s.	3	6
„ Happy Thought „ 30s.	4	0
„ May Queen	6	0
„ Mrs. Mappin. White flowers ...	6	0
„ Prince Silverwings per 100, 24s.	3	6
Bronze-leaved. Black Douglas „ 30s.	4	0
„ Marechal McMahon „ 30s.	4	0
Geraniums, Ivy-leaved. Splendid for baskets, stumps, vases, or for bedding out; abundant bloomers, and much superior to Zonals in a wet season. Choice named double flowered varieties „ ... ... 4s. 6d. and	6	0
Geraniums, Zonal. Single-flowered. New and choice sorts ... ... 9s. and	12	0
Single-flowered. Choice named sorts 4s. 6d. and	6	0
Double-flowered. New varieties, very fine ...	10	6
„ Choice named sorts ... 6s. and	9	0
Heliotrope. White Lady. Fine for bouquets ...	4	0
Mixed sorts ... ... per 100, 21s.	3	0
Lobelia. Blue Stone ... per 100, 17s. 6d.	2	6
King of the Blues (*see illustration*). Dark blue, with conspicuous white eye, very pretty per 100, 18s. 6d.	3	0
Pumila grandiflora ... „ 17s. 6d.	2	6
White Perfection ... „ 17s. 6d.	2	6
Cardinalis Victoria. Splendid scarlet ...	6	0
Marguerites or Parisian Daisies. Yellow or white ... ... per 100, 24s.	3	0
Mesembryanthemum cordifolium variegatum. Splendid bedding plant	2	6
Myosotis, *see page 100.*		
Pansies and Violas, *see page 100.*		
Pentstemons. In beautiful variety ... 4s. and	6	0
Petunias. Fine mixed Seedlings per 100, 17s. 6d.	2	6
Pyrethrum. Golden Feather ... „ 7s. 6d.	1	0
Salvias. Scarlet, Blue, White. Beautiful showy plants	3	0
Verbenas. Scarlet ... per 100, 21s.	3	0
Pink, purple, and white ... each „ 21s.	3	0
In twelve beautiful varieties to name „ 30s.	4	6

Miscellaneous Spring-flowering Plants

PANSY—MR. BENNETT.

Alpine Auriculas. The Alpine Auriculas in their many beautiful varieties are eminently suited alike for Spring flowering, in pots in the greenhouse, or the open border. The flowers from our improved strain are exceedingly brilliant and varied in colour.

Choice Named sorts per doz. 12s., 18s., and 24s.

Selected Seedlings. Strong plants, from our very fine strain per doz., 4s. 6d.
,, ,, Smaller plants ,, 2s. 6d.

Double Daisies. Well known beautiful and brilliant little plants for edgings of beds or borders, which continue in bloom throughout the months of April and May; the dark crimson and pure white are very handsome.

Large crimson ... per 100, 16s.; per doz. 2s. 6d.
Large white ... ,, 16s.; ,, 2s. 6d.
Large pink ... ,, 12s.; ,, 2s. 0d.

Hepaticas. These are amongst the most charming Spring-blooming plants we possess, and should certainly be found in every garden. The beautiful variety *H. angulosa* forms lovely compact masses of tender blue flowers, that form a delightful contrast with most other plants. The varieties of *H. triloba* are also very beautiful, and desirable alike for clumps on the permanent border or as edgings thereto.

	each—s.	d.
Angulosa. Sky blue; beautiful per doz. 7s. 6d.	0	9
Triloba alba. Single, white	0	9
,, **cærulea.** Single, blue ...	0	6
,, ,, **fl. pl.** Double blue ...	1	6
,, **rubra.** Single, red	0	9
,, ,, **fl. pl.** Double, red ...	1	0

Myosotis dissitiflora (Forget-me-not). Exceedingly valuable Spring-flowering plant, producing a great profusion of bright sky blue flowers; a fine bedding variety, the best of all Forget-me-nots per doz. 3s. 6d.; each 4d.

Bedding Pansies and Violas. The Pansies and Violas are amongst the very best of our Spring and Summer flowering bedders. They are wonderfully free-flowering and pretty, and will thrive in almost any soil, but should not be planted in a hot dry position. A spot where they are shaded from strong sunshine for some part of the day, a north or west border suits them admirably, and a fair supply of weak liquid manure in dry weather will keep them in splendid flower.

Ardwell Gem. Sulphur yellow, dwarf habit. A profuse bloomer per doz. 4s. 6d.; each 6d.

Blue King. Magnificent variety, producing an abundance of large deep ultramarine blue flowers, which continue from early Spring till late in Autumn; should be in every garden per 100, 16s.; per doz. 3s.; each 4d.

Cliveden Purple. Fine large flowers of a rich bright purple colour, a constant bloomer per 100, 16s.; per doz. 2s. 6d.; each 3d.

Cloth of Gold. Beautiful bright yellow with dark centre, very effective for Spring gardening per 100, 16s.; per doz. 3s.; each 4d.

Duchess of Sutherland. Mauve and white each 6d.

Favorite. Bronze purple per doz. 4s.; each 6d.

Golden Gem. Deep golden yellow, a free grower and first rate bedder per doz. 3s.; each 4d.

Holyrood. Deep indigo-blue, with dark blotch, one of the finest per doz. 6s.; each 9d.

Jeffrey's White. Pure white, dwarf per doz., 6s.; each 8d.

Lottie. Mauve, dense bloomer ,, 4s.; ,, 6d.
Max Kohl. Dark purplish maroon ,, 4s.; ,, 6d.
Mont Blanc. White, very free ,, 4s.; ,, 6d.
Mr. Bennett. Large, beautiful, pure white flowers, with a lovely blue blotch in centre per doz. 4s. 6d.; each 6d.
Souvenir. Rich lavender ,, 4s. 6d.; ,, 6d.

Our own selection, per 100, 21s.; per doz. 4s.

Show and Fancy. A splendid collection of choice named sorts, our own selection per doz. 6s. and 9s.

Erica. Herbacea (carnea). A procumbent little shrubby evergreen plant; flowers deep flesh-coloured with black anthers, produced in wreath-like spikes, from middle of January to end of March per doz. 7s. 6d.; each 9d.

Carnea alba. A pure white-flowered variety of the preceding, very fine per doz. 10s. 6d.; each 1s.

Primroses and Polyanthuses. A beautiful and indispensable class of brilliant Spring-flowering plants, blooming at the same time as Narcissi and many other bulbs; many of the single-flowered varieties are exceedingly handsome.

Double White ... ... per doz.; each 6d.
,, **Lilac** ... ... ,, 5s.; ,, 6d.
,, **Yellow** ... ... ,, 5s.; ,, 6d.
,, **Purplish-crimson** ,, 10s.; ,, 1s.

Single "Harbinger." A superb large-flowered, early blooming variety, with lovely white flowers with an orange centre per doz. 10s. 6d.; each 1s.
,, **mixed hybrids.** Very fine and brilliant per 100, 17s. 6d.; per doz. 2s. 6d.

Polyanthus, Gold-laced. Fine seedlings, all good flowers per doz. 3s. 6d.

Primrose "Pompadour." The true old dark crimson, double-flowered variety, splendid per doz. 18s.; each 1s. 6d.

Oxlip, Prince of Orange. Large trusses of rich orange-coloured flowers, very fine each 1s.

Wallflowers. Old Double yellow. A fine plant for Spring decoration ... 3 for 2s.; each 9d.
Old Double dark red or purple. Very useful and fine old sort 3 for 2s.; each 9d.

Clematises.

These magnificent hardy climbers are highly popular amongst amateur growers, and considering their great beauty, freedom of blooming, and the facility with which they may be trained on any kind of wall, trellis, verandah, or pillar, and in almost any aspect, it is surprising that Clematises are not found in abundance in every garden. The plants we offer are established in pots, and can be removed at any time of the year. The sorts blooming after June are the best for bedding purposes; they flower on the young wood, and therefore require before growth commences in Spring, to be cut down to within six or twelve inches of the ground, as likewise do all the late-flowering kinds; and early sorts, flowering from May to July on the old wood, should be pruned similarly to Roses. When the selection of sorts is left to ourselves, customers may rely on our sending a really good variety.

CLEMATIS—JACKMANII SUPERBA.

	Months of Flowering.	each. s. d.
Albert Victor. Deep lavender	My Jy	1 6
Ascotiensis. Azure blue, large	Jy Sp	1 6
Beauty of Surrey. Greyish blue	Jy	2 6
Beauty of Worcester. Large and handsome, producing double and single flowers on same plant, lovely bluish violet, pure white stamens	Ju Oc	2 6
Belle of Woking. Silvery grey, double	Ju	1 6
Blue Gem. Pale cærulean blue	Jy Oc	2 6
Countess of Lovelace. Bluish lilac, double	Ju Jy	2 6
Duke of Edinburgh. Rich violet purple	My Jy	1 6
Duchess of Edinburgh. Double white	Ju Jy	2 6
Duchess of Teck. Pure white, mauve bar	Jy Oc	1 6
Earl of Beaconsfield. Rich royal purple	Jy Oc	2 6
Enchantress. White, flushed with rose	Ju Jy	1 6
Fair Rosamond. Blush white	My Ju	1 6
Flammula. Sweet-scented. White	Jy Oc	1 0
Fortunei. Creamy white, rosette form, sweet-scented	Ju Jy	1 6
Gipsy Queen. Dark velvety purple	Jy Oc	1 6
Henryi. Beautiful large creamy white, most hardy variety	Jy Oc	2 6
Jackmanii alba. Fine white, very distinct	Jy Oc	2 6
Jackmanii. Intense violet purple	Jy Oc	1 6
Jackmanii superba. A very fine variety somewhat similar to "Jackmanii," but later than that variety, and the colour more intense, the flowers frequently with five and sometimes six petals	Jy Oc	2 6
Jeanne d'Arc. Greyish white	Ju Oc	2 6
La France. Deep violet, purple dark anthers, large and robust	Jy Oc	1 6
Lady Bovill. Greyish blue, cupped	Jy Oc	2 6
Lady Caroline Neville. French white	Jy Oc	2 6
Lanuginosa.. Pale lavender	Jy Oc	2 6
Lanuginosa candida. Tinted greyish white	Ju Oc	2 6
Louis van Houtte. Bluish purple	Ju Oc	2 6
Lucie Lemoine. Double, white	Ju Jy	2 6
Madame van Houtte. White, mauve tint	Jy Oc	2 6
Miss Bateman. White, red anthers	My Jy	1 6
Mrs. Baron Veillard. Distinct light lilac rose; a new and handsome variety of the Jackmanii type, flowering from July to October; very free bloomer, vigorous grower	Jy Oc	3 6
Mrs. S. C. Baker. French white	My Ju	1 6
Mrs. Hope. Satiny mauve	Ju Au	2 6
Mrs. Geo. Jackman. Satiny white, beautiful	Ju Oc	2 0
Star of India. Reddish plum	Jy Oc	1 6
Symeana. Delicate lavender blue, deeper bars	Jy Oc	1 6
Venus Victrix. A fine double-flowered variety, delicate lavender blue, beautiful form	Jy Oc	2 6
William Kennett. Deep lavender	Ju Oc	2 6

	Months of Flowering.	each. s. d.
Othello. Dark velvety purple	Ju Oc	2 6
Princess of Wales. Deep bluish mauve	Jy Oc	2 6
Purpurea elegans. Deep violet purple	Jy Oc	2 6
Robert Hanbury. Bluish lilac	Jy Oc	2 6
Sir Garnet Wolseley. Slaty blue	My Jy	1 6

Choice named varieties from the above list, our own selection, per doz. 18s., 24s., and 30s.

Clematis indivisa lobata.

WE offer fine plants of this beautiful evergreen greenhouse species. The foliage is of a dark olive green and of great substance; the flowers are of the purest white, very fragrant, and produced in wonderful profusion. Highly recommended as a greenhouse climber. The flowers are very neat and exceedingly useful for cutting.   Fine strong plants, each 2s. 6d.

Hardy Climbing and other Plants

SUITABLE FOR TRAINING ON WALLS, &c.

These are mostly grown in pots, and can be supplied and planted at any time of the year with perfect safety.

	each—s. d.
Ampelopsis (*Virginian Creepers*). Well-known beautiful climbers, the leaves changing to a deep crimson scarlet colour in the Autumn.	
Veitchi. Small-leaved, very beautiful variety	1s. & 1 6
Hederacea. Common Virginian Creeper	... 1 0
Sempervirens. Evergreen	... 1 6
Hoggi. Large-leaved, fine variety ...	... 1 6
Aristolochia sipho. Deciduous ...	... 1 6
Azara microphylla. Beautiful plant for walls	... 1 6
Berberidopsis corralina. Evergreen, crimson flowers	1s. 6d. &
Bignonia radicans (*Trumpet Flower*) ...	... 1 6
Buddlea globosa. Orange globoso flowers ...	... 1 6
Ceanothus. Gloire de Versailles. Large panicles of sky blue flowers, fine ...	... 2 0
Azureus. Pale blue	... 2 0
Divaricatus. Very pale blue	... 1 6
Chimonanthus fragrans. Very sweet-scented	... 2 0
Cotoneaster microphylla ⎱ Very handsome with berries	1 0
Simmondsi ⎰ in Autumn	1 0
Escallonia macrantha. Evergreen, with bright rosy crimson flowers, very pretty ... 1s. 6d. &	2 6
Ivies (*Hedera*)—	
Cavendishi. Silver-margined	... 1 6
Clouded Gold. Fine	... 1 6
Irish. Strong-growing, very useful per doz. 10s. 6d.	1 0
Madeiriensis variegata. Fine robust-growing variety, beautiful silver-edged foliage 1s. 6d. &	2 6

	each—s. d.
Ivies (*Hedera*)—	
Palmata. Handsome variety	... 1 0
Ragneriana (*The Giant Ivy*). Very large, beautiful foliage, quite distinct ...	... 1 6
Tricolor. Very pretty	... 1 6
Jasminum (*Jasmine*)—	
Nudiflorum. Yellow, blooms in December	... 1 0
Officinale. White, very sweet-scented ... 9d. &	1 0
Kerria Japonica fl. pl. Double yellow flowers ...	1 6
Lonicera (*Honeysuckle*)—	
Aurea reticulata. Golden-veined foliage ...	... 1 6
Flexuosa. Evergreen	... 1 6
Halli. Pure white, evergreen, fine ...	... 1 0
Early White ⎱ Well-known deliciously-scented	1 0
Late Red Dutch ⎰ varieties	1 0
Scarlet Trumpet ⎰	1 6
Magnolia grandiflora. Exmouth variety, very fine ... ... 2s. 0d. to	10 6
Passiflora caerulea. Common blue Passion-flower ...	1 0
"Constance Elliott." A seedling from P. caerulea, flowers pure white; sweet-scented	1 6
Periploca graeca. Rapid climber	1 0
Pyracantha Laelandi. Red-berried and splendidly effective plant in Autumn and Winter 1s. 6d. &	2 6
Pyrus Japonica. Valuable early Spring-flowering plant, rich scarlet, exceedingly handsome 1s. 6d. &	2 6
Wistaria sinensis. Large clusters of lilac mauve coloured flowers ... ... 1s. 6d. &	2 6
alba	... 2 6

Choice Hardy Climbers, our own selection, 10s. 6d. and 15s. per doz.

Flowering & Ornamental Foliaged Deciduous Trees & Shrubs.

SOME fine effects may be produced in the garden or the shrubbery border by the judicious planting of the following ornamental trees and shrubs. Such graceful plants as Weeping Willows and Mop-headed Acacia are well suited for planting amongst dwarf-growing shrubs, and will also form nice specimens on the lawn, whilst a back ground or line of such choice subjects as Double Scarlet Thorn, Acer negundo variegata, Prunus Pissardi, Laburnums, Purple Beech, planted alternately, produce the most exquisitely beautiful effects when in full bloom and leaf in May and June.

Acer negundo variegata. Beautiful silver-edged leaves. Dwarfs and dwarf-standards, each 1s. to 1s. 6d; half-standards, standards, and pyramids, each 1s. 6d. to 2s. 6d.

Ailanthus glandulosa. Per doz. 8s., 10s., and 12s.

Arbutus unedo. Strawberry-tree, each 1s. 6d.

Ash, Weeping. Fine standards, each 3s. 6d. to 7s. 6d.

Aucuba Japonica (*mas. et fœm.*). Each 1s. to 3s. 6d.

Beech, Copper. Each 1s. 6d. to 6s.

"   Fern-leaved. Each 2s. to 3s. 6d.

"   Purple. Each 1s. 6d. to 6s.

Berberis Darwini. Elegant evergreen shrub, bearing yellow flowers, followed by orange-coloured berries, each 1s. to 3s. 6d.

Berberis, Purple-leaved. Handsome, each 1s.

Bird Cherry (*Cerasus padus*). Each 1s.

Catalpa Kæmpferii. Each 2s. 6d.

"   syringifolia. Each 1s. and 1s. 6d.

Cherry, Double-blossomed. Standards, each 2s. and 2s. 6d.

Chestnut, Horse. Per doz. 4s. and 9s.; each 6d., 1s., 2s. 6d., and 3s. 6d.

"   " Scarlet. Standards, each 2s. 6d. and 3s. 6d.

Elder, New Golden. Each 1s.; per doz. 9s.; per 100, 50s.

"   Scarlet-berried. Each 1s.

Holly, Gold-variegated ⎱ Beautiful varieties, each 2s. 6d.

"   Silver Queen ⎰ to 10s. 6d.

Japanese Maples. Beautiful varieties, quite hardy, each 3s. 6d. and 5s.

Laburnum, English or Common. Each 1s. and 1s. 6d.

Liquidambar styraciflua. Each 1s.

Lilac, Marie Legraye. A grand variety bearing immense clusters of pure white deliciously-scented flowers, dwarfs, each 1s. 6d.

"   Charles X. Numerous clusters of deep purple flowers, very fine variety; dwarfs, each 1s. and 1s. 6d.

"   Common. Each 1s. and 1s. 6d.

Lime, Red-twigged. Each 1s. to 3s. 6d.; per doz. 10s. 6d. to 30s.; extra large 5s.

Mountain Ash. Common, each 6d. to 1s. 6d.

Oak, Scarlet. Each 1s. to 2s. 6d.

"   Turkey. Variegated, standards, nice heads, each 2s. 6d. and 5s.

Philadelphus (*Syringa* or *Mock Orange*). Each 1s. and 1s. 6d.

Poplar, Golden-leaved. Each 1s. to 2s. 6d.

Prunus Pissardi. A new Japanese Plum, with dark crimson-purple foliage, very beautiful in Autumn; dwarfs, each 1s.; standards, each 2s.

Rhus cotinus (*Smmach*). Slender panicles of flowers in Summer forming hairy tufts; curious, each 1s. 6d.

Ribes sanguinea. Red-flowered American Currant, each 1s. and 1s. 6d.

Robinia inermis (*Mop-headed Acacia*). Standards, each 2s. 6d., 3s. 6d., and 5s.

"   hispida (*Rose Acacia*). Standards, each 2s. 6d. & 3s. 6d.

Spiræa arisefolia. Large panicles of white flowers, very fine, each 1s. and 1s. 6d.

Sumach, Stag's Horn. Each 9d. to 1s. 6d.

Thorn, Double Scarlet (Paul's). Splendid dwarfs, each 1s.; fine pyramids and standards, each 1s. 6d. to 2s. 6d.

Willows, Weeping. Fine standards, each 2s. 6d. and 3s. 6d.

Hardy Perennial Flowering Plants.

We have a fine collection of these popular, interesting, and beautiful plants, which are daily coming more and more into favour with the Gardening Public. All the varieties are perennial, extremely hardy, and many of them produce flowers of the most exquisite beauty, which are very valuable for cutting, whilst the dwarfer growing sorts are admirably suited for rockeries, or edgings. No special soil or position is necessary, as with but very few exceptions, they will thrive almost anywhere, and with a moderate collection, a charming variety and succession of bloom may be had throughout the Spring and Summer. The plants we offer are all grown in pots, and may be removed at any time or season.

CHRYSANTHEMUM MAXIMUM.

Adonis vernalis. This is a beautiful, early, Spring-blooming plant, with clear golden yellow flowers, known as the "God of Love." The individual blooms are very large comparative to the size of the many-times divided foliage, its general height being six inches. It will thrive in any kind of soil and most situations, and is perfectly hardy
             per doz. 4s. 6d. ; each 6d.

Anemone—Japonica alba. One of the very best Autumn-blooming plants we have. Blooms produced in great profusion, and of a beautiful pure white
             per doz. 5s. ; each 6d.
   ,,   ,,   **rosea.** Similar to preceding, but flowers of a beautiful rose colour   per doz. 7s. 6d. ; each 9d.

Anthemis tinctoria pallida. An exceedingly beautiful Marguerite, with pale sulphury yellow flowers. The blooms are very useful for cutting, and last a long time in water. Grows 2½ feet to 3 feet high ...   per doz. 5s. ; each 6d.

Aubrietia Leichtlini. A beautiful dwarf-growing plant, with numerous bright purplish crimson flowers; a gem for dry rockeries, &c. ...   ...   per doz. 10s. 6d. ; each 1s.

Asters (*Michaelmas Daisies*).
   ,,   **Dumosus.** Flowers bright purple, 2½ feet high, flowers in September   ...   ...   each 9d.
   ,,   **Formosissimus.** A distinct and beautiful species, flowers rosy purple; height four feet   each 9d.
   ,,   **Novæ Angliæ.** Large bluish-purple flowers; blooms in October   ...   each 9d.

Anthericum. Beautiful hardy border plants, bearing elegant spikes of pure white flowers in Spring; height about eighteen inches. These are exceedingly useful for cut flowers and should be found in every garden.
   ,,   **Liliago** (St. Bernard's Lily) per doz. 5s. ; each 6d.
   ,,   **Liliastrum** (St. Bruno's Lily)
             per doz. 7s. 6d. ; each 9d.
   ,,   ,,   **major.** Very fine; pure white; splendid for bouquets ...   per doz. 10s. 6d. ; each 1s.

Auriculas, Alpine (*see page* 109).

Calliopsis lanceolata. The best of the family, and one of the most showy hardy perennials in cultivation. The flowers are large, of a bright golden yellow colour, and produced in the greatest profusion per doz. 7s. 6d. ; each 9d.

Campanula isophylla. Beautiful dwarf trailing species, bearing large lilac blue salver-shaped flowers; a gem for pots   ...   ...   per doz. 5s. ; each 6d.
   ,,   ,,   **alba.** A white form of the preceding
             per doz. 5s. ; each 6d.
   ,,   **persicifolia alba grandiflora.** A fine upright growing variety, with large pure white flowers each 1s.
   ,,   **persicifolia alba grandiflora pl.** Produces spikes two feet high, of pure white double flowers, useful for cutting   ...   ...   each 9d.
   ,,   **pyramidalis** (*The Chimney Campanula*). Long spikes of blue, salver-like flowers; excellent for single specimens in herbaceous border or for pots   each 6d.
   ,,   ,,   **alba.** A white flowering form of the preceding; makes a fine pot plant ...   each 9d.
   ,,   **turbinata pallida.** A beautiful dwarf compact-growing variety, producing a profusion of beautiful silvery lilac-coloured bells that continue for a long time   strong clumps, per doz. 10s. 6d. ; each 1s.

Chrysanthemum latifolium. A very showy Marguerite, its bold pure white flowers, with yellow centre, are two to three inches across; splendid for cutting, and invaluable for Autumn decoration ...   each 9d.
   ,,   **leucanthemum semi-duplex.** A fine novelty, with large pure white semi-double flowers
             per doz. 10s. 6d. ; each 1s.
   ,,   **maximum** (*see illustration*) (true). A beautiful free-growing plant, only two feet high, and covered with a profusion of large pure white Marguerite-like flowers, that continue for a long period; splendid for cutting
             per doz. 10s. 6d. ; each 1s.
   ,,   **uliginosum.** A very strong-growing Autumn-flowering species, with pure white Marguerite flowers
             each 9d.

Cheiranthus alpinus. A dwarf neat-growing species; flowers lemon-yellow, borne in great profusion in Spring; very effective, and ought to be in every garden
             per doz. 3s. ; each 4d.

Cypripedium spectabile. The most splendid of this interesting family, growing about two feet high, and producing numerous large delicate rose and white flowers; hardy ...   .   per doz. 24s. ; each 2s. 6d.

Delphiniums (*see page* 107).

Hardy Perennial Flowering Plants (*continued*).

Dielytra spectabilis. A beautiful and indispensable plant, with lovely bending sprays of deep rose-coloured flowers and handsomely divided foliage. First-class for shady borders, pots in the greenhouse, &c. It is perfectly hardy and forces well strong plants, per doz. 6s.; each 8d.

  ,,   **spectabilis alba.** A beautiful variety of the preceding, having pure white flowers; fine for pots each 1s. 6d.

Dodecatheon Jeffreyanum. A beautiful perennial, a native of the Rocky Mountains, producing large umbels of Cyclamen-like blossoms, rose-coloured, with a yellow ring at the orifice of the reflexed corolla each 2s. 6d.

  ,,   **meadia** (American Cowslip). From the rich woodlands of North America; an elegant Spring-flowering plant worthy of more extended cultivation; flowers purple, inclining to colour of the peach-blossom, in a loose umbel, each blossom drooping elegantly per doz. 5s.; each 6d.

Doronicum austriacum. Bright golden yellow flowers in Spring; very showy ... per doz. 7s. 6d.; each 9d.

  ,,   **Harpur Crewe** (*plantagineum excelsum*). A magnificent variety, growing three to four feet high, bearing bold golden yellow flowers three to four inches across. First-class for cutting, and an almost perpetual bloomer per doz. 10s. 6d.; each 1s.

Echinops ritro. A fine perennial, growing three to four feet high, bearing numerous globular heads of blue flowers each 9d.

Erigeron aurantiacus. A fine new variety, growing about nine inches high and bearing bright orange-coloured flowers as large as a crown piece. A very free bloomer per doz. 7s. 6d.; each 9d.

Erigeron (Stenactis) speciosa superba. Beautiful border perennial, growing about three feet high, covered for a long time with beautiful large bright purple flowers with yellow centre; very fine per doz. 7s. 6d.; each 9d.

Funkia, or Plantain Lily. Fine hardy border plants, the flowers of *F. subcordata grandiflora* almost equalling those of the Eucharis. The leaves are large, heart-shaped, and are finely effective for clumps on mixed borders, as edgings to large beds of sub-tropical plants, etc.

  ,,   **lanceolata.** Dwarf-growing; lilac purple flowers per doz. 5s.; each 6d.

  ,,   ,,   **marginata.** A form of the preceding, with beautifully variegated leaves per doz. 5s.; each 6d.

  ,,   **sieboldi.** Glaucous foliage and pink Lily-like flowers; very beautiful ... ... each 9d.

  ,,   **subcordata grandiflora.** A beautiful variety with bright green foliage per doz. 5s.; each 6d.

Gaillardias (*see page* 107).

Galega officinalis alba. Produces a profusion of white Pea-shaped flowers; useful for cutting ... each 6d.

Gentiana acaulis. Intense blue, very fine per doz. 7s. 6d.; each 9d.

  ,,   **verna.** One of the most brilliant of all Alpine flowers; one to three inches high, forming dense tufts of intense blue flowers per doz. 7s. 6d.; each 9d.

Geum coccineum plenum. Height about two feet, bearing a profusion of double, bright scarlet flowers; first-rate for cutting ... ... per doz. 8s.; each 9d.

Harpalium rigidum. Rich golden yellow flowers with a black disc, resembling a small Sunflower per doz. 5s.; each 6d.

Helenium pumilum. Beautiful Autumn-blooming plant, eighteen inches high, bearing a profusion of bright yellow flowers ... ... per doz. 7s. 6d.; 3 for 2s.; each 9d.

  ,,   **autumnale.** Bright yellow flowers; fine for Autumn display ... ... each 9d.

Helianthus multiflorus plenus (*Perennial Sunflower*). Height three to four feet, beautiful golden yellow double flowers in Autumn per doz. 8s.; each 9d.

  ,,   **Soleil d'Or.** A fine variety, with deep orange yellow double flowers ... ... each 1s.

Helianthus (Harpalium) lœtiflorus. Similar in growth and foliage to *Harpalium rigidum*, but with semi-double flowers, and coming into bloom later each 9d.

Helleborus (Christmas Rose). *H. niger* and *H. niger maximus* are undoubtedly the finest hardy Winter-flowering plants in cultivation, producing beautiful white flowers through the Winter; useful for potting for greenhouse decoration, and are worthy of extensive cultivation when grown outside. The flowers are much improved in their purity of whiteness and size, if hand-lights or bell-glasses are placed over them just prior to and during the blooming season.

  ,,   **Niger** (*Christmas Rose*) Fine pure white, abundant bloomer ... per doz. 10s. 6d.; each 1s.

  ,,   ,,   **maximus.** A fine variety, large pure white flowers, splendid; should be in every garden per doz. 24s.; each 2s. 6d.

  ,,   **atrorubens.** Flowers purplish red, very numerous in clusters; blooms in Mid-Winter per doz. 15s.; each 1s. 6d.

Hemerocallis. Kwanso fl. pl. variegata. One of the most beautiful hardy variegated plants in cultivation; is also admirably suited as a decorative plant for the greenhouse or conservatory per doz. 7s. 6d.; each 9d.

  ,,   **flava.** A beautiful hardy border plant, producing in June and July large umbels of beautiful Lily-like flowers, of a bright yellow colour, and finely scented per doz. 4s. 6d.; each 6d.

  ,,   **fulva.** Bronzy orange, shading to crimson per doz. 3s. 6d.; each 4d.

  ,,   **disticha fl. pl.** Large, double, bronzy yellow flowers; very fine ... ... each 1s.

Hepaticas. These are amongst the most charming Spring-blooming plants we possess, and should certainly be found in every garden.

  ,,   **Angulosa.** Sky blue; beautiful per doz. 7s. 6d.; each 9d.

  ,,   **triloba alba.** Single, white ... each 0s. 9d.

  ,,   ,,   **cærulea.** Single, blue ... ,, 0s. 9d.

  ,,   ,,   **fl. pl.** Double, blue ,, 1s. 6d.

  ,,   ,,   **rubra.** Single, red ... ,, 0s. 9d.

  ,,   ,,   **fl. pl.** Double, red ,, 1s. 0d.

Heuchera sanguinea. It forms a neat compact tuft of deep cordate leaves, of a light green colour and slightly hairy. The flower stems are slender and much branched, from twelve to eighteen inches in height, covered with bright crimson tubular flowers lasting in bloom the whole of the Summer ... ... per doz. 10s.; each 1s.

Inula glandulosa. A fine hardy plant, growing about two feet high, and bearing large, single, Helianthus-like yellow flowers ... ... each 1s.

Lathyrus latifolius albus (*The White Everlasting Pea*). Beautiful clusters of pure white flowers; exceedingly useful hardy climber ... ... per doz. 10s. 6d.; each 1s.

Lychnis dioica rubra fl. pl. A plant of great beauty, exceedingly useful for cutting; large double crimson flowers; a first-class border plant ... each 9d.

  ,,   **viscaria splendens plena.** A distinct and splendid variety, growing about eighteen inches high and bearing a profusion of large, double, brilliant rose-coloured flowers per doz. 7s. 6d.; each 9d.

Matricaria inodora grandiflora pl. Flowers pure white; useful for cutting ... ... each 6d.

Œnothera acaulis vera. A beautiful dwarf-growing species, with large white flowers; very distinct per doz. 7s. 6d.; each 9d.

  ,,   **macrocarpa.** A fine hardy perennial, forming a trailing mass of foliage covered with large soft yellow flowers ... ... each 6d.

  ,,   **Youngi.** Height two feet, with deep golden yellow flowers; a first-class hardy plant per doz. 7s. 6d.; each 9d.

Papaver nudicaule (*Iceland Poppies*). Most useful and beautiful hardy flowers. They are very graceful in habit of growth, having attractive bright green foliage formed in tufts, the flowers rising on slender stems about one foot high, and are charming as cut flowers.

  ,,   **nudicaule.** Bright pale yellow per doz. 5s.; each 6d.

Hardy Perennial Flowering Plants (*continued*).

SENECIO PULCHER.

Papaver nudicaule alba. Pure white per doz. 5s.; each 6d.

"   **miniatum.** Brilliant orange-scarlet per doz. 5s.; each 6d.

* "   **bracteata** (true). A charming species, with immense deep blood-crimson flowers ... each 1s.

* "   **Royal Scarlet.** The flowers are unequalled for size and brilliancy, measuring when fully expanded twelve inches in diameter, and are of a glowing scarlet colour ... ... each 1s. 6d.

* *Large-flowered Perennial Poppies, very showy and splendid flowers, first-class for mixed or shrubbery borders.*

Pæonies, Herbaceous (*see page* 107).

Phloxes, Perennial (*see page* 107).

Physalis alkekengi (*Winter Cherry*). Bears numerous bright berries, which are most attractive in late Autumn ... ... each 6d.

Phlox subulata. (Dwarf Spring-flowering Phloxes). Beautiful, compact-growing varieties, forming dense cushions of lovely flowers, that continue for a long time; splendid for rockeries, edgings, or massing.

"   "   **frondosa.** Dense evergreen foliage, lovely pink flowers, dark centre per doz. 4s.; each 6d.

"   "   **verna.** A very beautiful trailing species; flowers large, deep rose colour   per doz. 4s.; each 6d.

Polemonium Richardsoni. Beautiful hardy perennial, blooming in June, height eighteen inches, flowers sky blue with golden yellow anthers; very pretty   each 9d.

"   **Himalaicum.** Vigorous habit of growth, with large branching spikes of azure blue flowers, 1 inch to 1½ inch across; very handsome ... ... each 1s.

Potentillas (*see page* 107).

Pyrethrums (*see page* 107).

Primroses and Polyanthuses. A beautiful and indispensable class of brilliant Spring-flowering plants, blooming at the same time as Narcissi and many other bulbs; many of the single-flowered varieties are exceedingly handsome.

Double White ...	...	per doz. 6s.;	each 8d.
" **Lilac** ...	...	" 6s.;	" 8d.
" **Yellow**	...	" 6s.;	" 8d.
" **Purplish-crimson**	" 10s.;	" 1s.

Single "Harbinger." A superb large-flowered, early blooming variety, with lovely white flowers with an orange centre. Strong plants in pots per doz. 10s.; each 1s.

"   **mixed hybrids.** Very fine and brilliant per 100, 17s. 6d.; per doz. 2s. 6d.

Polyanthus, Gold-laced. Fine seedlings, all good flowers ... ... per 100, 21s.; per doz. 3s. 6d.

Rudbeckia Newmanni. A splendid hardy free-flowering plant, height about two feet; flowers golden yellow with black centres ... ... per doz. 5s.; each 6d.

Scabiosa caucasica. Large, handsome, pale lilac blue flowers, four to six inches across, fine for cutting, one of the best perennials grown; good flowering plants ... each 1s.

Senecio pulcher (*see illustration*). A very fine hardy perennial, flowers large, purplish crimson with yellow centre, three feet high; a fine Autumn bloomer ... each 9d.

"   **doronicum.** Large golden-yellow flowers on stems twelve inches in height; a first-class plant; fine for cutting ... ... each 6d.

Spiræa aruncus. A handsome, stately-looking, border plant, from three to five feet high, with magnificent plumes of creamy white flowers ... ... each 1s.

"   **astilboides.** A beautiful Japanese species, about two feet high, producing dense plumes of feathery white flowers; easily grown in pots or borders each 2s. 6d.

"   **filipendula fl. pl.** Numerous corymbs of double white flowers and pretty fern-like foliage, very hardy and desirable ... ... each 9d.

"   **palmata** (*Crimson Meadow Sweet*). A very fine border plant, flowers rich crimson. Is well described by its popular name ... ... each 9d.

Trillium grandiflorum (*Large-flowered White Wood Lily*). A very pleasing plant for moist shady nooks, flowers snowy-white on stems about one foot high ... each 9d.

Tritoma nobilis. The grandest of the group, immense spikes of orange red flowers, on stems six to seven feet long. In bloom from August to December per doz. 10s. 6d.; each 1s.

"   **uvaria grandiflora.** Crimson and orange flowers, very fine spikes of bloom   per doz. 10s. 6d.; each 1s.

Trollius Europæus. Beautiful Spring-flowering plant, with large, globular, lemon-coloured and delicately scented flowers ... ... per doz. 7s. 6d.; each 9d.

Herbaceous and Alpine Plants in Collections.

WE have a fine collection of these which from want of space we are unable to catalogue. The following collections, which are offered at a very cheap rate, include the most beautiful and useful sorts for border and rockery decoration, and if our customers when ordering will kindly say for which purpose they are required, they may rely on having the very best selection that can be given for the prices quoted.

Carefully selected collections of the most useful and interesting kinds, our own selection.

100 in 50 choice varieties	...	... 25s. 0d.	25 in 25 choice varieties	... 7s. 6d.
50 in 50 " "	...	... 14s. 0d.	12 in 12 " "	... 4s. 6d.

PLANTS AND ROOTED CUTTINGS OF CHOICE FLORISTS' FLOWERS.

PACKAGE AND CARRIAGE FREE AT PRICES QUOTED.

• For new varieties see List of Novelties on coloured paper.*

We have much pleasure in offering Plants and Rooted Cuttings from our splendid collections of Choice Florists' Flowers, to which we have added many varieties of great merit during the past season. We would particularly draw the attention of our patrons to our superb collections of Dahlias, Chrysanthemums, Fuchsias, and Zonal Pelargoniums, which include all the newest and most select varieties in cultivation.

Abutilons.

Beautiful free-flowering plants for pots in the greenhouse, continuing in bloom throughout the Winter. Planted out in May will bloom finely in the garden till killed by the frost; very useful for cut flowers.

	each—s. d.
Aurea globosa. Orange red, fine	0 9
Baron Rothschild. Large, beautiful, sulphury-yellow flowers; very distinct and handsome ...	1 6
Boule de Niege. Pure white, very vigorous ...	0 6
Cyrus. Orange pink, beautiful	1 0
Esperance. Rosy pink, large flowers	1 0
Grand Duke. Indian red, very fine ...	0 9
M. Jules Marty. Clear orange yellow flowers; beautiful ...	1 0
Orange Perfection. Brilliant orange red ...	1 0
Osiris. Beautiful pink, very large	1 0
Queen of the Yellows. Pale yellow, beautiful...	1 0
Sanglant. Deep rich scarlet, a splendid and remarkable colour hitherto unknown in Abutilons	2 0
Thompsoni fl. pl. Flowers double, orange veined with crimson, the foliage beautifully variegated	0 9
White Queen. Large, beautifully formed flowers of the purest white	1 0

Beautiful varieties, our own selection to name
per doz. 4s. 6d and 6s.; 6 for 2s. 6d. and 3s. 6d. —

GROUP OF SINGLE BOUVARDIAS.

Bouvardias.

each—s. d.

The most beautiful and charming of all flowers to cut for bouquets, button-holes, or table decoration; the colours range from the purest white through the delicate shades of pink and rose to the most intense and brilliant scarlet and crimson. They are easy of cultivation, and grown in the same way as Winter-flowering Pelargoniums will bloom to perfection.

	each—s. d.
Alfred Neuner. Pure white, double	0 9
Angustifolia. Brilliant scarlet, dwarf	0 9
Elegans. Scarlet, splendid	0 9
Hogarth fl. pl. Double, scarlet, very fine ...	0 9
Jasminoides. Beautiful, pure white ...	0 6
Longiflora flammea. Deep pink	0 6
Queen of Roses. Bright rose	0 6
Priory Beauty. Delicate pink	0 9
President Cleveland. A fine sturdy-growing free-flowering variety, bearing lovely trusses of deep crimson-scarlet flowers; splendid	1 0
President Garfield. Delicate rose	0 9
Sang Lorraine. New double, beautiful vermilion-scarlet	1 0
The Bride. Beautiful pure white, compact ...	0 9

Choice varieties, our own selection to name
per doz. 4s.; 6 for 2s. 6d. —

Coleus.

each—s. d.

Well-known, easily cultivated plants of remarkable beauty, should be grown freely in every greenhouse.

	each—s. d.
Ada Sentance. Green, carmine and purple centre...	0 6
Beauty of Cambridge. Large, beautiful foliage, crimson splashed with green and gold, all the leaves having a bright gold edge; very handsome	1 0
Cloth of Gold. Clear golden yellow, shaded green...	0 6
Conqueror. Leaves cream-coloured at the base, crimson in the centre, surrounded with black, and have a distinct bright green edge ...	0 9
Countess of Dudley. Large bright green leaves, veins and centre creamy white	0 6
Edith Sentance. Beautiful variety ...	0 6
Ellen Terry. Green, veined yellow, crimson centre	0 9
Henry Irving. Crimson maroon, edged with gold ...	0 9
J. L. Toole. Green, veined and splashed with gold and crimson; fine	0 6
Magenta Queen. Very fine and brilliant ...	0 6
Lady Birkbeck. Medium sized leaves, cream coloured centre and veins, interspersed with delicate green and splashed with crimson; beautiful ...	0 9
Lord Beresford. Crimson, edged with black ...	0 6
Lord Rosebery. Leaf black, edged with carmine ...	0 9
Sir E. Birkbeck. Crimson centre, edged black, extreme edge bright green with crimson veins ...	0 9
Sir Peter Eade. Centre of leaf bright carmine surrounded with black, clear green edge; superb ...	0 9
Pride of the Market. Crimson, green, lake, and cream-coloured; very distinct	0 6
Princess Irene. The centres cream-coloured, splashed with crimson, the edges delicate green ...	0 9
Vesuvius (King). Very large, round, pointed leaves, golden green at the base, the upper parts a rich bright crimson, finely edged with golden yellow ...	0 9

Choice named varieties, our own selection; rooted cuttings
per doz. 3s. 6d.; 6 for 2s. —

Chrysanthemums.

GRAND VARIETIES OF RECENT INTRODUCTION.

The following superb varieties after careful trial have proved to be flowers of exceptional merit, most of them have received high awards at our late shows, and will be in great demand for next season's exhibitions.

Will be supplied in April, all in strong young plants from single pots, Carriage Free at prices quoted.

LOUIS BOEHMER.

The Pink Ostrich Plume Chrysanthemum, "LOUIS BOEHMER."

This superb new variety was exhibited for the first time in England at the Royal Aquarium, Westminster, in November 1890, when it made a very favourable impression amongst Chrysanthemum growers. The flower is of good size, and similar in form to *Mrs. Alpheus Hardy*, and like that variety, has the beautiful yet strange-looking silky hairs or glands on the reverse of the petals; its colour, however, is a charming silvery lilac pink, the petals being of good substance, whilst the plant is of a good sturdy habit of growth. This is a splendid novelty. Each 1s. 6d.

BEAUTY OF CASTLEWOOD (Japanese). A fine bold flower of the most perfect form, petals very broad and incurved, closely covering the centre; the outside of petals a clear bright orange, the inner surface bright velvety crimson. A first-class exhibition variety. Each 1s. 6d.

CENTENARY (Japanese). A sport from *Lady Lawrence*, with the same broad petals and splendid form; colour, a beautiful primrose yellow; a grand flower. Each 1s. 6d.

DELAWARE (Anemone). Very large double flowers, white guard petals with pale yellow centre; the finest Anemone-flowered variety yet sent out. Each 2s. 6d.

E. G. HILL (Japanese). Immense blooms of brightest golden yellow, full and very double, lower petals sometimes shaded carmine; an elegant variety of strong habit. First Class Certificate and Medal. Each 2s.

FLORENCE DAVIS (Japanese). Large beautiful flowers with long drooping petals, greenish white, passing to pure white. Splendid habit, and first-class for exhibition. Each 2s. 6d.

GLOIRE DU ROCHER (Japanese). Bright orange amber, flushed crimson. A splendid flower, said by many of the best judges to be the flower of the season. Each 2s.

HARRY E. WIDENER (Japanese). Bright lemon yellow without shading; flowers large on stiff stout stems, incurving and forming a large rounded surface, splendid. Winner of the Blanc Prize, Philadelphia Exhibition. Each 2s.

JOHN DYER (Japanese). Good strong grower, broad petals of extra substance, perfectly double; colour, chrome yellow, striped the entire length of the petals with fine red lines. A fine show flower. Each 1s. 6d.

LILIAN B. BIRD (Japanese). A remarkable variety introduced from Japan. The flower is large, the petals long, thin, and tubular, with a tendency to incurve; colour, a delicate pale salmon pink; very striking and beautiful. Each 1s. 6d.

MDLLE. MARIE HOSTE (Japanese). Very large double flower, with broad stout petals; colour, pale rose, a very beautiful flower. First Class Certificate. Each 2s.

MR. A. H. NEVE (Japanese). Very large flower, broad flat drooping petals; colour, a beautiful silvery blush. Two First Class Certificates. Each 1s.

MRS. LIBBIE ALLEN (Incurved Japanese). Large well-formed flowers; colour, a beautiful pure yellow. A fine show flower. Each 2s. 6d.

MRS. E. W. CLARKE (Japanese). Deep amaranth purple, reflex, silvery rose. Flowers very large, petals broad and incurving; a very fine variety. F.C.C. Each 1s.

MISS ANNA HARTSHORNE (Incurved Japanese). Blush pink, changing to pearly white. A superb double flower of immense size. One of the very finest productions of late years. Two First Class Certificates. Each 2s.

ROBERT CANNELL (Incurved). Quite a new colour in this section, being an exceedingly bright chestnut-red; the reverse of the petals a deep golden-yellow, a beautiful combination, and one of the most effective in the whole of the section. First Class Certificate, National Chrysanthemum Society. Each 1s. 6d.

VIOLET ROSE (Incurved Japanese). A grand double flower of perfect form, very free in colour; a beautiful combination of violet and rose. First-class for exhibition. Each 1s. 6d.

VIVIAND MOREL (Japanese). This is undoubtedly the finest new Japanese variety of the past season. The flower is of immense size, with long gracefully drooping petals; colour, a pale rosy pink shading to white; magnificent exhibition variety. Two First Class Certificates. Each 2s.

W. H. LINCOLN (Japanese). Immense full double flowers, slightly incurved; colour, a beautiful golden yellow like *Jardin des Plants*. Silver Medal, Boston; First Class Certificate. Each 2s.

Twelve superb varieties, our selection from the above ... ... 15s. 0d.

Six " " " " ... ... 8s. 6d.

Chrysanthemums—General Collection.

JAPANESE—New and Select Varieties.

The following 6d. each, except those priced; strong plants in pots in May, 9s. per doz.

Ada Spaulding (Incurved Japanese). The flowers are large and of splendid form and substance. The lower half of the flower is of a deep rich pink colour, shaded purple rose, the upper half of a beautiful pearly white. Each 1s.

Avalanche (Japanese). One of the grandest white Chrysanthemums; the flowers are of immense size without being coarse, the colour is pure, and the plant of good habit. Each 9d.

Etoile de Lyon (Japanese) Deep lilac, shaded silvery grey; enormous flowers, sometimes ten to twelve inches across; capital exhibition flower.

Eynsford White (Japanese) Beautiful pure white flowers as large as those of *Avalanche*, but much broader petals; splendid exhibition flower. Each 1s.

George Daniels (Japanese). Large flowers; silver white, reverse purple-rose, splendid. F.C.C.

L. Canning (Japanese). A grand new pure white of splendid size; plant of short-jointed, sturdy habit, said to be an improvement on *Avalanche*.

M. E. A. Carriero (Japanese). A magnificent flower, white, the reverse of the petals a delicate blush rose; a fine exhibition variety. Each 1s.

Mr. H. Cannell (Japanese). Yellow; a fine showy flower; first-class for exhibition.

Mrs. Irving Clarke (Japanese) (Volunteer). Delicate rose pink, high centre, first-rate in form and size; a fine novelty. Each 1s.

Mrs. Alpheus Hardy (Japanese). (*The White Ostrich Plume Chrysanthemum.*) Flowers large, beautiful pure white, the backs of the petals covered with silky hairs, most lovely variety, but difficult to flower.

Mrs. Andrew Carnegie (Japanese). Deep bright crimson; a fine flower, and plant of good habit.

Mrs. James Carter (*syn. Thistle*). A small flowered Japanese variety, with very fine thread-like petals, opening a pale yellow, and changing to pure white; a charming variety for cut flowers. Each 9d.

Mrs. F. A. Spaulding (Japanese). Bright nankeen yellow, long broad incurving petals, reverse of petals salmon rose; a grand exhibition flower. Has won silver cup, medal, and several certificates. Each 1s. 6d.

Stanstead White (Japanese). Purest white flowers, semi-incurved, very long petals, immense size; a magnificent variety for exhibition. Each 1s.

Sunflower (Japanese). Clear golden yellow, by far the best yellow Chrysanthemum in cultivation; has received two or three First Class Certificates. Each 9d.

Sunset (Japanese). An immense flower of gorgeous and remarkable appearance. It is semi-double, the petals very long, broad, and drooping, colour a rich orange yellow, marbled with brown, red, and crimson; a grandly effective variety. Each 1s.

W. W Coles (Japanese). Bright red, long broad flat petals, the brightest and clearest of this colour yet introduced; a first-rate novelty; splendid.

JAPANESE—Older Varieties.

Rooted cuttings, our own selection, 2s. 6d. and 3s. 6d. per doz., customers' selection, 4d. each; strong plants in pots in May, 6s. and 9s. per doz.

Anna Delaux, Belle Paule, Boule d'Or, Brise du Matin, Criterion, Comte de Germiny, Don Quixote, Edwin Molyneux, Edouard Audignier, Gloire de Toulouse, Golden Dragon, Grandiflora, Japonais, Jeanne Delaux (*syn. F. A. Davis*), J. A. Laing, La Charmeuse, Lady Selborne, L'Africain (*syn. George Gordon*), L'Or de France, L'Or du Rhin, Madame Baco, Madame John Laing, Madame Payne, Madame de Sevin, Madame C. Audiguero, Madame Feral, Mdllo. la Croix, Mdlle. Paul Dutour, Mrs. Falconer Jameson, Mrs. C. W. Wheeler, M. Bernard, M. Freeman, M. Romaine, M. Thibaut, Pelican, Rosea superba, Safranum, Sarah Owen, Source d'Or, Souvenir du Japon, Thunberg, Triomphe du Nord, Val d'Andorre.

EARLY-FLOWERING JAPANESE.

Splendid varieties, blooming three to five weeks earlier than other sorts; very useful for cutting.

Bouquet Estival, Dame Blanche, E. G. Henderson & Son, Ete Fleuri, G. Wermig (*syn. Golden Madame Desgrange*), J. H. Laing, La Reine, Mandariu, Madame Desgrange, Mrs. Hawkins, Roi des Precoces, W. C. Boyce, William Holmes.

INCURVED—New and Select Sorts.

John Lambert (Incurved). A sport from *Lord Alcester*. The flowers are of a beautiful light buff, shaded with rose; it has all the grand qualities of the parent, and will take rank as one of the finest incurved varieties in cultivation. Each 1s.

Mrs. S. Coleman (Incurved). Bright golden bronze, shaded rose, a sport from *Princess of Wales*; a fine variety, has received six Certificates. Each 9d.

Miss M. A. Haggas (Incurved). A sport from *Mrs. Heale*, colour a beautiful light golden yellow, with all the splendid qualities of the parent. Has received three First Class Certificates. Each 9d.

Miss Violet Tomlin (Incurved). Beautiful bright purple violet, a sport from *Princess of Wales*. A fine variety, especially valuable on account of its colour. Has been awarded three First Class Certificates. Each 1s.

INCURVED—Older Varieties.

Rooted cuttings, our own selection, 2s. 6d., 3s. 6d., and 6s per doz.; customers' selection, 4d. each; strong plants in May, 6s. and 9s. per doz.

Alfred Salter, Antonelli, Aurea multiflora, Barbara, Baron Beust, Beauty of Stoke, Beverley, Bronze Jardin des Plantes, Cherub, Empress of India, Eve, Faust, General Bainbridge, George Glenny, Golden Empress of India, Golden Queen of England (*syn. Emily Dale*), Guernsey Nugget, Hero of Stoke Newington, Isabella Bott, Jardin des Plantes, Jeanne d'Arc (*syn. Mad. M. Tezier*), John Salter, Lady Hardinge, Lady Slade, Lady Talfourd, Lord Derby, Lord Wolseley, Mabel Ward, Miss Mary Morgan (*syn. Pink Perfection*), Mr. Gladstone, Mrs. Dixon, Mrs. George Rundle, Mrs. Norman Davis, Mrs. Heale, Mrs. Haliburton, Mrs. J. Crossfield, Mr. Bunn, Prince Alfred, Princess of Wales, Princess Imperial (*syn. Lord Alcester*), Princess of Teck (*syn. Christmas Number*), Princess Beatrice, Refulgence, Venus, White Globe, White Venus.

Chrysanthemums.

REFLEXED VARIETIES—Select List.

Boule de Niege. Pure white, very fine.
Cullingfordi. Beautiful crimson scarlet.
Chevalier Domage. Deep yellow, fine.
Christine. Peach colour, very good.
Cloth of Gold. Bright golden yellow, splendid.
Dr. Sharpe. Magenta, very fine.

Golden Christine. Very showy.
King of Crimsons. Deep bright crimson.
Mrs. Hope. Pale rose, shaded lilac.
Mrs. Forsyth (*White Christine*). White, pale lemon centre.
Perle des Beautes. Crimson.

Our own selection, per doz. 3s. 6d.; each 6d.

LARGE ANEMONE-FLOWERED.

Mrs. Judge Benedict (new). Flower of good size, a light blush on opening changing to pure white, guard petals very broad, high lemon centre; a charming flower   Each 1s.

Gluck. Deep yellow self, fine.
J. Thorpe, Jun. Bright yellow, very fine.
Lady Margaret. Very large, pure white, splendid flower.
Madame Robert Owen. Pure white, a very fine and distinct variety.
M. Charles Lebocqz. Citron yellow, tinted carmine, large flower.
Prince of Anemones. Lilac blush, fine.
Sœur Dorothee Souille. Pale lilac, centre white. 6d. each.

POMPONES AND HYBRIDS.

Our own selection, per doz. 2s. 6d., 3s. 6d., and 4s. 6d., customers' selection, 4d. each.

William Westlake (new). Rich golden yellow, suffused with a reddish tint, fine shaped flowers.   Each 1s. 6d.

Amy, Argentine, Aurora Borealis, Bijou d'Horticulture, Bouquet Fleuri, Creme, Diamant, Eliza Dordan, Exposition de Chalon, Flambeau Toulousain, James Forsyth, La Favorite, La Purete, Lilacee, L'Orangere, Maid of Kent, Marabout, Maroon Model, Mdlle. Marthe, Mdlle. Marthe Golden, Mrs. Cullingford, New York, Osiris, Pacquerette, Perle des Beautes, Poudre d'Or, Progne, Reine d'Or, Rubra perfecta, Sœur Melanie, Soiree d'etc, St. Thais.

POMPONE—Anemone-flowered.

Astarte. Amber shaded gold, 6d.
Antonius. Bright yellow, beautiful, 6d.
Eugene Lanjaulet. Yellow, orange disc, 6d.

Madame Sentir. Pure white, charming, 6d.
Madame Montels. White, with golden yellow centre, 6d.
Magenta King. Magenta guard petals, yellow disc; fine, 6d.

Single-flowered Chrysanthemums.

This beautiful class is becoming very popular. The flowers resemble the Marguerites in form, but vary in colour from crimson, pure yellow and rose, to the purest white; all the flowers have yellow centres, which give them the most charming appearance. These should be grown abundantly wherever cut flowers are in demand.

	each—s. d.
Admiral T. Symonds. Golden yellow, a large handsome flower, three to four inches across. If disbudded resembles a Sunflower	0 9
Coachman. Beautiful pure white; late	0 6
Ethel Smith (new). Rosy crimson, distinct and beautiful, a charming flower for cutting	1 6
Exquisite. Pure white, shaded delicate pink; a lovely flower	0 6
Jane. Pure snow white, most beautiful variety	0 6
Miss Ellen Terry. Rosy pink, very pretty	0 6
Miss Cannell. White, first-rate for cutting	0 6
Souvenir de Londres. Crimson red, very fine. F.C.C.	0 9
Yellow Jane. Deep yellow, twisted petals; handsome	0 6

Our selection, 3s. 6d. per doz.

Marguerites or Parisian Daisies (Chrysanthemums).

Beautiful free-flowering half-hardy plants, in bloom almost throughout the year. Exceedingly useful for cut flowers, especially during the Winter months. Planted out in May they form beautiful objects in the garden, and will continue in bloom till killed by the frost, or the plants may be lifted in Autumn, repotted and transferred to the greenhouse, where they will continue in beautiful bloom throughout the Winter.

Cloth of Gold. A very free-flowering and beautiful variety, with large, bright, golden-yellow flowers of good substance. Almost a perpetual bloomer. Highly recommended.   3 for 2s.; each 9d.

Etoile d'Or Improved. Pale yellow, free-branching habit, and a great bloomer; splendid for cut flowers 3 for 1s. 6d.; each 8d.

Frutescens. Numerous pure white flowers with glaucous green foliage   4 for 1s.; each 4d.

   ,,   "Bedding Gem." A beautiful dwarf-growing variety, only about a foot high, a sport from the *Old Marguerite*. The foliage is of a rich soft yellow, resembling the *Golden Feather*, and the plant being of compact symmetrical growth, it will prove of great value for window boxes or bedding out.   Per doz. 9s.; each 1s.

Crassula jasminioides.

   each—s. d.

Beautiful pot plant for the cool greenhouse, growing about nine inches high, and bearing heads of pure white Jasmine o r Bouvardia-like flowers per doz. 5s.   0 6

Campanula isophylla.

   each—s. d.

Beautiful dwarf trailing species, bearing large lilac blue salver-shaped flowers; a gem for pots 3 for 1s. 3d.   0 6
Alba. A white form of the preceding   3 for 1s. 3d.   0 6

Plants and Rooted Cuttings of Choice Florists' Flowers *(continued)*.

FUCHSIA—COUNTESS OF ABERDEEN.

Fuchsias.

Our list of these has been carefully revised, and includes only really good
sorts that can be highly recommended. These beautiful flowers are not
only admirably suited for pot culture indoors, but if planted out in
May they will form beautiful objects in the garden, and bloom profusely throughout the Summer and Autumn.

New and very choice sorts, our selection   per doz. 6s. ; 6 for 3s. 6d.
Twelve choice named varieties, our own selection   ... 3s. 6d. and 4s. 6d.
Six   „   „   „   ... 2s. 0d. and 2s. 6d.

New and Select Varieties—

Those marked (*) are double-flowered.   each—s. d.

*MRS. E. G. HILL. This magnificent Fuchsia will be
found one of the most splendid ever sent out. The plants
are short-jointed and sturdy in growth, with beautiful dark
green foliage. The flowers are of an immense size, the tube
and sepals being of a deep rich scarlet colour, the corolla a
beautiful creamy white, veined with pink ; grand variety .. 1 0
Countess of Aberdeen. A beautiful dwarf-growing, free-
flowering variety. Both the sepals and corolla being white,
it is quite unique and totally distinct from any other Fuchsia,
whilst its elegantly formed flowers and neat habit will make
it a general favourite 1 0
Beauty of Clyffe Hall. Tube and sepals blush white, corolla
rich bright carmine pink ; beautiful 0 6
Beauty of Lavington. White tube and sepals, rosy carmine
corolla ; very fine 0 9
*Compacta superba. Beautiful dwarf compact habit of growth;
tube and sepals light crimson, corolla violet blue ... 0 9
*Colonel Domine. A magnificent variety, with large splendidly
formed perfectly double flowers ; sepals a bright rich scarlet,
corolla a beautiful creamy white veined with pink ; superb 0 9
Loveliness (Lye). Creamy tube and pale blush sepals,
very long and stout, pale violet pink corolla   ... 1 0
*M. Berraud Massard. Tube and sepals light scarlet,
well reflexed ; the corolla very double, lilac-coloured,
scarlet at base of petals. Splendidly-formed flowers 1 0
Madame Millot Robinet. Immense flowers; tube
and sepals waxy white ; corolla rosy crimson   ... 1 0
*Madame Jules Chretien. Large well-shaped
flowers, tube and sepals crimson, corolla beautiful
white, veined red 0 6
Madame Rozain. A truly grand variety, bearing
immense flowers of the most elegant form ; the tube
and sepals a deep rich scarlet crimson colour, the
corolla a charming creamy white ; most beautiful,
and distinct from all others 0 9
*Magnificent. A grand variety, bearing immense
double flowers of splendid form and fine effect.
The sepals, which are well reflexed, are of a bright
rich crimson colour, the corolla a deep violet blue ... 1 6
*Morope. Fine double flowers, rich crimson scarlet,
with dark purple corolla 1 0
*Miss Lucy Finnis. Corolla pure white, tube and
sepals coral red ; very large, splendid form   ... 0 6
Miss Lizzie Vidler. Red, lilac corolla ; fine   ... 0 6
*Molesworth. A fine compact-growing variety,
bearing an abundance of very large, well-shaped
flowers ; the tube and sepals are of a bright deep
carmine-crimson colour ; the sepals are well reflexed,
and display the unusually large and full double
white corolla to great advantage 0 9
*President Gunther. Beautifully formed flowers ;
corolla double, of a bright reddish purple colour,
sepals light crimson 0 6
*Raphael. Immense double flowers, tube and sepals
crimson, corolla violet splashed with red 0 9
Rose of Denmark. White, pink corolla ; beautiful 0 6
Star of Wilts. White, rosy crimson corolla ; splendid 0 6
Sunray. Foliage handsomely variegated 0 6
Walter Long (Lye). Bright pale coral-red tube and
sepals, clear violet corolla 1 0

each—s. d.

Diadom (Lye). Delicate blush tube and sepals, pale
magenta corolla, broadly edged with brilliant carmine 0 9
*Edelweiss. Scarlet, white corolla ; very fine   ... 0 6
Earl of Beaconsfield. A splendid hybrid variety,
flowers over three inches long, carmine, with deep
carmine corolla 0 6
Emily Bright. White tube and sepals, corolla bright
carmine 0 6
Ernest Renan. Large, beautiful flowers, tube and
sepals waxy white, well reflexed ; corolla rosy crimson 1 0
*Esmeralda. Light crimson tube and sepals, corolla
lilac blue, heavily splashed with red ; very distinct and
beautiful 1 0
Final. Tall and graceful growing variety, with large,
finely reflexed flowers ; tube and sepals crimson ;
corolla rich violet 0 9
*Frau Emma Topfer. A remarkable dwarf-growing
variety, with extraordinarily large, peculiar-looking
flowers, tube and sepals bright rosy coral, corolla rosy
blush 0 9
General Gordon. Very large well-formed flowers ;
corolla a bright purple, tube and sepals scarlet   ... 0 6
Gem of Lavington (Lye). White tube and sepals,
very delicately tinted with the palest pink, very
stout carmine corolla, flushed with soft violet   ... 1 0
General Garfield. Rich crimson, carmine corolla .. 0 6
Jason. Deep crimson tube and sepals, corolla dark
purple ; fine and distinct 0 6
Jupiter. Large, beautiful double flowers ; sepals well
reflexed, brilliant scarlet ; corolla, a deep plum violet 1 6
*Joseph Rosaine. Scarlet, purple corolla ; very fine 0 6
Lye's Excelsior. Creamy tube and sepals, tinted
with emerald, stout and well reflexed ; rich deep rosy
magenta corolla flushed with carmine 0 9
Lye's Favorite. White, deep rose corolla ; splendid 0 6
*La France. Large handsome double flowers of beautiful
form ; the sepals a bright rich scarlet, the corolla a
bright light violet 0 9
Lady Doreen Long. White tube and sepals ; deep
pink corolla 1 0
*Le Cygne. Crimson tube and sepals, corolla white ... 0 9
Lord Wolseley. Splendid large flowers, brilliant
scarlet, with bright purple corolla, striped with red 0 9

From **Miss O'KEIFFE,** Gowran, Kilkenny.

May 1st.
"The Fuchsias, particularly 'Esmeralda,' sent last year were the admiration
of all."

Plants and Rooted Cuttings of Choice Florists' Flowers (*continued*).

Dahlias—Show and Fancy.

Our collection of Show and Fancy Dahlias includes all the newest and choicest varieties in commerce, and is one of the most complete and finest in the kingdom. We annually raise many thousands of these beautiful flowers, for which we have a very large and increasing demand. Customers wishing to secure special varieties should therefore kindly send us their orders as soon as convenient. Our prices for Dahlias as quoted are for strong plants from single pots, ready in May, carefully packed and sent free by parcel post. Should our customers however prefer to have them sent in pots the charge will be 6d. per doz. extra; when sent in this way we enclose extra plants in part compensation, but do not pay carriage.

PRICES OF SHOW AND FANCY DAHLIAS.

		s.	d.			s.	d.
New and very choice sorts ...	... per doz.	9	0	Good exhibition varieties ...	... per doz.	6	0
,, ,, ,, ...	... 6 for	5	0	,, ,, ,, ...	... 6 for	3	6

Our own selection of popular and beautiful varieties, per 100, 31s. 6d.; per doz. 4s. 6d.; 6 for 2s. 6d.

New and Select Varieties.

S denotes Show, F Fancy.   *Those not priced 6d. each.*

Alice Emily (S.). Delicate buff yellow, a brighter and purer yellow at the edge of each petal, and toward the centre of the flower, petals beautifully formed, splendid outline, very constant. This variety was awarded a First Class Certificate last year at every place it was shown, including Crystal Palace, Aquarium, Trowbridge, and Royal Horticultural, 1s.

Buffalo Bill (F.). Buff, striped with vermilion, large, and very constant, 1s.

Buttercup (S.). Yellow tinged with red, very fine.

Colonist (S.). Chocolate and fawn, very distinct.

Comte de la Saux (F.). Deep lilac, striped with dark crimson, very fine, dwarf habit, 1s.

Condor (S.). Buff shaded orange.

Crimson Globe (S.). Crimson, a large deep flower, well up in the centre, good form, very constant and free. First Class Certificates at Royal Horticultural, Aquarium, and Trowbridge, 1s.

Crown Prince (S.). Yellow shaded buff, a fine flower.

Dewdrop (S.). Dark primrose.

Diadem (S.). Deep crimson, fine and constant.

Dorothy (F.). Fawn coloured, flaked with maroon.

Duchess of Albany (F.). Pale orange, striped with crimson.

Duke of Connaught (S.). Dark crimson, large.

Duke of Fife (S.). Fine rich cardinal, large, with great depth of petal. First Class Certificates at Aquarium and Crystal Palace, 1s.

Edmund Boston (F.). Orange, striped crimson.

Ethel Britton (S.). Blush white, edged purple.

Falcon (S.). Light fawn.

Flag of Truce (S.). White, faintly flaked lilac.

Gaiety (F.). Yellow, striped red, and tipped white; very striking, 9d.

General Gordon (F.). Yellow, striped scarlet; very fine.

Goldfinder (S.). Yellow, tipped with red.

Gloire de Lyon (S.). Pure white, immense flowers.

Glow-worm (S.). Orange scarlet, high centre; a good show flower, 9d.

Grand National (S.). Yellow, very fine.

Harry Keith (S.). Rosy purple, very fine and constant.

Hartie King (F.). Orange, striped crimson and scarlet.

Henry Bond (S.). Bright rosy lilac, superb.

Henry Eckford (F.). Yellow, striped scarlet.

Illuminator (S.). Dark red, shaded orange; large.

James Cocker (S.). Purple, large and good.

James Vick (S.). Purplish maroon.

John Hickling (S.). Clear bright yellow, of grand form and constant, excelling by far all other yellows. First Class Certificates at Royal Horticultural and Aquarium, 1s.

Joseph B. Service (S.). Rich yellow, very fine.

Joseph Green (S.). Clear bright crimson.

Jessie Mackintosh (F.). Red, tipped with white.

King of Purples (S.). Purple, very fine.

Lottie Eckford (F.). White, beautifully striped with purple.

Majestic (S.). White ground, edged and shaded with purple, large, and in every way a fine flower. First Class Certificate at Crystal Palace, 1s.

Maggie Soul (S.). Blush white, edged purple.

Major Barttelot (F.). Orange, heavily striped maroon; large, 9d.

Matthew Campbell (F.). Buff or apricot, beautifully striped with crimson, 9d.

Maud Fellowes (S.). French white, tinted and shaded with purple; a grand show flower, 1s.

Miss Browning (F.). Yellow, tipped with white.

Miss Fox (S.). Blush ground, heavily edged with lake; a splendid variety. First Class Certificate at Trowbridge, 1s.

Mrs. Gladstone (S.). Delicate blush, with white centre; a most charming flower.

Miss Henshaw (S.). Pure white, large.

Mrs. J. Grieve (S.). Yellow, large and fine form.

Mrs. Langtry (S.). Cream colour, edged with crimson; splendid.

Mrs. N. Halls (F.). Bright scarlet, tipped with white.

Mrs. Stancombe (S.). Canary yellow, tipped with fawn.

Muriel (S.). Clear yellow, a splendid flower.

Nellie Cramond (S.). Purple, shaded cerise, distinct.

Pioneer (S.). Dark velvety maroon, almost black; distinct.

Polly Sheffield (F.). Lilac striped and speckled with crimson, 9d.

Plutarch (F.). Buff, striped and splashed with crimson.

Primrose Dame (S.). Primrose yellow, large.

Purple Prince (S.). Rich purple, large and constant.

Reliance (S.). Fawn colour, very prettily shaded with pink, fine form. First Class Certificate at Royal Horticultural, 1s.

Rev. J. B. M. Camm (F.). Yellow, flaked with red.

Richard Dean (S.). Deep purple, splendid form.

Salamander (F.). Yellow, striped with red.

Shirley Hibberd (S.). Dark shaded crimson.

Sir J. Bennett (S.). Yellow, scarlet edge, splendid.

Sunrise (S.). Bright magenta, distinct and beautiful, 9d.

Sunset (F.). Yellow, flaked and striped with scarlet; a most telling flower, 1s.

T. W. Girdlestone (F.). Lilac, heavily flaked and splashed with deep maroon, a grand fancy flower, 1s.

Volunteer (S.). Bright cardinal red, a fine useful flower, with every good property, 1s.

Walter H. Williams (S.). Bright scarlet, splendid.

And many others.

CACTUS-FLOWERED DAHLIAS.

(See Coloured Plate.)

The Cactus-flowered Dahlias with their many brilliant and charming tints and shades of colouring, form a magnificent class either for garden decoration or for exhibition, and certainly no class of flowers has risen so highly in the public estimation of late years as these. The flowers last a long time in water when cut, and apart from their great value as exhibition flowers, they are exceedingly useful to cut for indoor decoration. We have made some splendid additions to our list, and as will be seen below, our collection of Cactus-flowered and Decorative Dahlias includes all the finest varieties.

GRAND NEW VARIETIES.

Strong Plants ready in May.

	each—s. d.		each—s. d.
BEAUTY OF ARUNDEL (*see coloured plate*). Most superb variety. A sport from *Juarezi*, which it resembles in form and in every particular except colour, which is a brilliant glowing crimson, the tips of the petals shaded bright rosy purple. First Class Certificate R.H.S.	2 6	**DUKE OF CLARENCE.** Large handsome flowers of true Cactus form, colour deep rich maroon crimson with fiery scarlet shading towards the top of petals, dwarf in habit and wonderfully free-flowering. A grand exhibition variety. Awarded two First Class Certificates	2 6
BLACK PRINCE (*see coloured plate*). A remarkable and splendid variety, undoubtedly the finest and best dark Cactus Dahlia yet raised. The flowers are large, finely formed, and of a rich purplish-black colour. First Class Certificate N.D.S.	1 6	**HARRY FREEMAN** (*see coloured plate*). Finest pure white Cactus Dahlia yet sent out. A great improvement on *Henry Patrick* in having the flowers of more Cactus-like formation. Very free-flowering and of great value for cutting. First Class Certificate	1 0
CANNELL'S FAVORITE (*see coloured plate*). A very beautiful variety, quite distinct in colour, which is of a most attractive and fashionable tint, being a charming yellow bronze or old gold. A very fine flower. First Class Certificate	2 6	**MARCHIONESS OF BUTE.** A very pleasing variety, a great improvement on the variety *Charming Bride*. The colour is a pure white, the petals being tipped with bright delicate rose	1 0
ROBERT MAHER (*see coloured plate*) Bright clear yellow, a very free bloomer of good habit. The finest yellow Cactus Dahlia yet sent out. First Class Certificate	1 0	**MRS. J. DOUGLAS** (*see coloured plate*). A true Cactus Dahlia of a most peculiar and charming shade of colour, which is perhaps best described as a bright pinkish salmon. A fine flower and free bloomer. First Class Certificate	1 6

Twelve new and very choice varieties, including the sorts shown on Coloured Plate 12s. 6d.
Six new varieties as on Coloured Plate ... ... 8s. 6d.

Cactus-flowered and Decorative Dahlias.

OLDER VARIETIES—GENERAL LIST.

Strong Plants ready in May.

The Decorative Varieties are intermediate between the Cactus and Show and Fancy.

	each—s. d.		each—s. d.
Amphion. Chrome-yellow flushed with cerise, long pointed petals, very fine and distinct	1 0	**Lady E. Dyke.** Yellow, medium size; very free	0 9
Annie Harvey (*Semi-cactus*). Deep maroon crimson	0 6	**Lady Kerrison.** Yellow, edged with crimson	0 9
Asia. Delicate rosy peach blossom, very beautiful	0 9	**Lady Marsham.** Deep salmon; splendid flower	0 9
Beauty of Brentwood. Similar in form to *Juarezi*, of a distinct bright purple shade; very showy. First Class Certificate (Grand National)	1 0	**Mikado.** Orange buff, very fine and distinct	0 9
		Miss Barry (new). Bright rich purple; large and splendid flower	1 0
Centennial (new). Magenta crimson with side margins of deep maroon, very distinct	1 0	**Mr. G. Reid** (Decorative). White, tipped with rosy lilac a beautiful variety of good size and substance	1 0
Cochineal (*Semi-cactus*). Rich deep crimson	0 6	**Mrs. Hawkins.** Soft primrose yellow, shaded delicate fawn on the outer petals; a charming flower	0 8
Charming Bride. White, tipped with rosy pink, fine	0 9	**Panthea.** Reddish salmon, with long graceful petals of the *Juarezi* type: a superb flower	0 9
Constance (*The White Cactus Dahlia*). Pure white	0 8	**Prince Albert Victor.** Deep rich scarlet	0 9
Empress of India. Large, splendidly formed flowers; colour, deep crimson and maroon shaded with black	0 9	**Professor Baldwin.** Brilliant scarlet; splendid	0 9
		Picta formosissima (*Meteor*) Orange yellow edged with scarlet	0 6
Fascination (Decorative). Lovely bright lilac-rose, each petal being conspicuously marked with a pure white stripe; charming variety	0 9	**Sir Trevor Lawrence.** Bright cherry scarlet, shaded purple, fine	0 9
Germania Nova (Decorative). A distinct and beautiful variety; colour, a soft mauve-rose; the tips of the petals beautifully laciniated	0 9	**William Darville.** Bright magenta purple, with pointed, recurved petals; very distinct	0 9
General Gordon. Bright scarlet, good form	0 6	**William Pearce.** Bright golden yellow	0 6
Henry Patrick. Beautiful pure white; splendid	0 9	**William Rayner.** Beautiful bright salmon buff	0 9
Honoria. Pale amber, long pointed petals	0 9	**W. T. Abery** (Decorative). A most beautiful semi-double-flowered variety; colour, a pale lemon-yellow almost white, each petal being distinctly edged with brilliant scarlet. Plants only about 2½ feet high 3 for 2s.	0 8
Juarezi (*The True Cactus Dahlia*). Brilliant scarlet, large Cactus-like flowers, very showy and effective	0 8	
King of Cactus. Light crimson red; immense flowers, very showy	0 6	**Zulu.** Deep maroon purple, almost black; splendid	0 9

New and very choice varieties, our selection ... ... per doz. 4s.; 6 for 5s.
Choice selected sorts, our selection ... ... per doz. 6s.; 6 for 3s. 6d.
Showy and popular varieties, our selection ... ... per doz. 4s. 6d.; 6 for 2s. 6d.

New Cactus Flowered Dahlias 2

3

Single-flowered Dahlias.

THE Single-flowered Dahlias are charming as cut flowers, and splendidly effective when well staged for exhibition. They commence blooming about the end of July, and are resplendent with a profusion of their lovely flowers till killed by the frost in Autumn. The small or medium sized flowers are the most useful, either for exhibition or decorative purposes, as it is found they retain their beauty for a much longer period when cut than the larger blooms. We have made some fine additions to our list of these, which contains the choicest varieties in commerce.

New and very choice varieties, our selection ...	... per doz. 9s., or 6 for 5s.
Very good sorts, our selection	... per doz. 6s., or 6 for 3s. 6d.
Good showy and popular varieties, our selection	per doz. 4s. 6d., or 6 for 2s. 6d.

NEW AND SELECT VARIETIES.

Cleopatra. Deep velvety crimson, very rich and of good substance; flowers medium sized and nicely recurved ... ... — 1 0

Claudia. Medium-sized flowers; reddish salmon, beautifully tipped with delicate mauve, and having a dark crimson ring round the disc; strikingly beautiful ... ... — 1 6

Duchess of Albany. An exceptionally distinct variety of quite novel colours, soft mauve, edged with pale buff brown, beautifully recurved, dwarf and free. Two First Class Certificates, R.H.S. and National Dahlia Society ... ... — 1 0

Duchess of Fife. Beautiful amber, with side edgings of reddish orange. First Class Certificate, National Chrysanthemum Society ... — 1 0

Duchess of Westminster. Pure white, splendid — 0 8

Eclipse. Beautiful rosy mauve and salmon, with a broad crimson ring round the disc; very charming and distinct. Has been awarded several First Class Certificates ... ... — 1 0

Formosa. Brilliant rich scarlet, rather small, beautifully formed flowers; first-rate for exhibition — 0 6

Guleilma. Pure white, with broad margins of golden buff; medium-sized flowers of good shape; very distinct. First Class Certificate, National Dahlia Society ... ... — 1 6

James Scobie. Yellow, beautifully striped and flaked with scarlet; one of the finest exhibition flowers. First Class Certificate R.H.S. ... — 0 9

John Downie. Rich scarlet, splendid form; a fine exhibition flower ... ... — 0 9

Miss Glasscock. Medium-sized flowers, slightly recurved; colour a soft clear lavender, margined with pale mauve; a beautiful and delicate-looking variety ... ... — 1 6

Miss Henshaw. Pale primrose, edged with white, beautiful form ... ... — 0 9

Miss Jefferies. A most charming variety and one of the grandest exhibition flowers. It has a peculiar combination of colour, rendering it very effective. The colour is a lovely blending of mauve and magenta, with a conspicuous red ring at the base of the petals ... ... — 0 9

Miss Ramsbottom. Flowers of a lovely pink colour, shaded cerise, quite new and distinct, medium size and perfect in form. First Class Certificates, National Dahlia Society and National Chrysanthemum Society ... ... — 0 9

Miss Roberts. Bright clear yellow, beautifully formed flowers ... ... — 0 9

Miss Louisa Pryor. Deep velvety crimson, with golden yellow disc, a splendid flower ... — 0 9

Mr. Riley. Deep carmine-crimson, with golden disc, splendid form ... ... — 0 9

Mrs. Barker. Pale buff, shaded red, and sometimes edged with gold; fine ... ... — 0 9

Mrs. Charles Daniels. Sulphury white, edged with crimson; a very distinct and showy variety — 0 9

Mrs. J. Coninck. Pure white, shaded with pale mauve, very beautiful form and colour ... — 0 9

Northern Star. Bright red, margined with deep golden yellow; small, well-formed flowers on stiff, wiry stems; very showy and distinct. Has been awarded three First Class Certificates ... — 1 0

Paragon. Deep maroon, edged with crimson ... — 0 6

W. C. Harvey. A striking novelty, and one that must become a favourite. It is a bold, handsome flower, with petals of great substance and slightly reflexed, and of a rich yellow, shaded with orange, having a distinct red ring at the base. First Class Certificate, National Dahlia Society ... — 0 9

White Queen, Improved. Pure white, good form — 0 6

And others.

(For the New "Marguerite" Dahlia *see* page 56.)

New Tom Thumb Single Dahlias.

A QUITE new and distinct race of Dahlias raised by Mr. T. W. Girdlestone, Secretary to the National Dahlia Society, and remarkable for their dwarf habit, compact growth, and consequent suitability for bedding purposes. The plants are of a close compact habit of growth, and do not generally exceed twelve inches in height, whilst the brilliantly coloured flowers are produced in great profusion. The number of varieties is at present very limited, but we may soon expect a great variety of beautiful flowers in this class. Will be found splendidly effective for edging of large beds or shrubbery borders, or for filling small beds, &c.

Bo-Peep. Height of plant, exclusive of flower stems, 15 inches, to top of bloom 22 inches, flower 3¼ inches across, very free blooming maroon self, dark ring round disc, petals rather pointed ... — 1 6

Bootles. Height of plant, exclusive of flower stems, 12 inches, to top of bloom 16 inches, flower 3 inches across; colour rich velvety red ... ... — 1 0

Lilliput. Height of plant, exclusive of flower stems, 10 inches, to top of bloom 14 inches, flower 2¾ inches across; colour light scarlet, lined orange, petals somewhat pointed ... ... — 1 6

Maud. Height of plant, exclusive of flower stems, 18 inches, to top of bloom 22 inches, flower 2¾ inches across; colour extremely rich velvety dark scarlet (almost deeper than scarlet), very striking, perfectly formed flower ... ... — 1 6

Miniature. Height of plant, exclusive of flower stems, 11 inches, to top of bloom 15 inches, flower 3¼ inches across; clear bright yellow ... ... — 1 0

Midget. Height of plant, exclusive of flower stems, 10 inches, to top of bloom 14 inches, flower 2¼ inches across, flower curried perfectly erect; colour pure bright scarlet; bright green glossy foliage ... — 1 0

Mignon. Height of plant, exclusive of flower stems, 9 inches, to top of bloom 12 inches, flower 2¼ inches across; colour bright clear pink, white ring round disc, very distinct and pleasing. Might be described as a dwarf *Marian Hood* ... ... — 1 6

Pearl. Height of plant, exclusive of flower stems, 11 inches, to top of bloom 15 inches, flower 3¼ inches across, very handsome and well-formed flower; colour deep mauve self, most distinct and effective ... — 1 0

Tom Tit. Height of plant, exclusive of flower stems, 12 inches, to top of bloom 18 inches, flower 3 inches across; colour clear orange scarlet with very distinct and telling light yellow eye round disc; elegant toothed foliage ... ... — 1 0

Plants and Rooted Cuttings of Choice Florists' Flowers (*continued*).

NEW POMPONE DAHLIAS.

Pompone or Bouquet Dahlias.

A brilliant and charming class, of a neat compact habit of growth, with beautifully formed, perfectly double, miniature flowers, which are produced in profusion throughout the Summer and Autumn. The colours vary from deep crimson and brilliant scarlet to the softest primrose, pure white, &c., three colours being sometimes blended in the same flower. Invaluable for cutting.

NEW VARIETIES.

Crimson Beauty. This is the best Crimson Pompone ever raised, very dwarf in habit of growth, and remarkably free flowering. The blooms are of medium size, perfect in form, and of the richest crimson colour   each 2s. 6d.
Eden. Deep shaded crimson; a small, compact, well-formed flower. 4 ft.   ...   .   each 9d.
Eurydice. Blush, tipped with purple; very pleasing; flowers profusely. 4 ft.   ...   ...   each 9d.
Fairy Tales. Delicate primrose; fine shape; free and distinct. 3 ft.   ...   .   each 9d.
Little Ethel. White, often tipped with purple; very pretty and free. 3 ft.   ...   ...   each 9d.
Mittie Wood. Primrose, edged with bronze; a very profuse bloomer. 3 ft.   ...   ...   each 9d.
Red Indian. Deep coral red; charming. 3 ft.   each 9d.
Salmon Queen. A distinct and beautiful variety, with numerous medium-sized, well-formed blooms of a light salmon colour, deepening towards the tips of the petals to a rich reddish salmon   ...   each 2s. 6d.
Whisper. Clear yellow, edged with gold; very attractive; extra fine. 2½ ft.   ...   .   each 9d.

GENERAL LIST.

Strong Plants ready in May.

New and extra choice sorts   per doz. 6s.; 6 for 3s. 6d.
Our own selection   ...   ...   „ 3s. 6d. and 4s. 6d.
    „   „   ...   .   6 for 2s. and 2s. 6d.

Brilliant, Burning Coal, Catherine, Chameleon, Comte von Sternberg, Dandy, Darkness, Don Juan, Dora, Eccentric, E. F. Junker, Fair Helen, Fashion, Favorite, Gazelle, Grace, Gem, Golden Gem, Hector, Iolanthe, Iscult, Janet, Lady Blanche, Lady Jane, Leila, Little Arthur, Little Duchess, Little Prince, Mignon, Prince of Liliputians, Profusion, Pure Love, Rosalie, Royalty, Sensation, Thomas Moore, Titania, Virginal, White Aster, White Button, William Carlisle.

PELARGONIUMS—Show, Fancy and Regal.

WE have a very choice collection of these beautiful and highly popular flowers, which we offer in fine healthy plants, well set with flower-buds, at prices as below. Our collection includes such fine varieties as Beauty of Oxton, Bush Hill Beauty, Captain Raikes, Dorothy, Duchess of Albany, Duchess of Edinburgh, Duchess of Teck, Emperor of Russia, Gold Mine, Kingston Beauty, Masterpiece, Pink Perfection, Prince Arthur, Prince of Novelties, Prince of Wales, Princess of Wales, Queen Victoria, Triomphe de St. Maude, Volonte National Alba, Rob Roy Improved, and many other new and beautiful sorts.

New and select vars., fine plants   per doz. 21s. and 24s.
Very fine sorts, good plants   ...   „ 15s. „ 18s.
Very fine sorts, smaller plants   ...   „ 9s. „ 12s.

Gold and Silver Tricolor Geraniums.

Lady Cullum, Sophie Dumaresque, Lass o'Gowrie, Mrs. Laing, Mrs. John Clutton, and other beautiful varieties   ... per doz. 5s.; each 6d.

Sweet-scented Geranium.

Lady Plymouth. Handsomely divided silver-variegated foliage, deliciously scented   .. 3 for 2s.; each 9d.

SHOW AND REGAL PELARGONIUMS.

Single-flowered Zonal Pelargoniums.

NEW SINGLE ZONAL PELARGONIUMS.

Zonal Pelargoniums.

We have a grand collection of these superb flowers, including all the finest of recent introduction. A great improvement has been made in these of late years, and the flowers and trusses of some of the varieties attain an immense size. The individual blooms of many of the specimens grown at our Nurseries during the past season measured upwards of seven inches in circumference being at the same time of the most perfect form, and of the most exquisite colours.

New Zonal Pelargoniums (Pearson's 1890, &c.)

	each—s.	d.
Agnes. White, very pure; a large and splendid flower	1	6
Duchess of Portland. Bright rosy pink, colour beautifully clear and distinct; flowers of good form	1	0
Ethel Lewis. Rose pink, white blotch on upper petals; the largest and most perfect flower in this class	1	0
Katherine Moreton. Salmon, light edge; very large in both pip and truss, and perfectly formed; habit very good; a beautiful variety	1	0
Launcelot. Salmon scarlet, very fine pip and truss	1	0
Phœnna. Scarlet, shaded magenta, white eye; will make a grand decorative or exhibition plant	1	0
Phryne. Cerise, shaded plum colour; the flowers, though not perfect in outline, are produced in grand trusses, making it a most effective variety	1	0
Sappho. Salmon rose. This though not so large as some of our seedlings, is a desirable acquisition from its novel colour; it promises also to be a good bedder	1	0
Sir Percivale. White; flowers large and well shaped, perfectly pure in colour; a fine winter bloomer	1	6
T. Hayes. Dark crimson; fine pip and truss; a very telling kind in the way of *A. Albrecht* and *J. Gibbons*, but much richer and darker in colour	1	6
Souvenir De Mirando (Lemoine). Lower petals rosy carmine, fading to white at the base; upper petals white, tipped carmine; a most striking novelty	1	0

Single Zonal Pelargoniums.

New and select varieties, very choice ... per doz. 9s.
Twelve in 12 superb varieties, our selection
                      4s. 6d. and 6s.
Six in 6 superb varieties, our selection 2s. 6d. and 3s. 6d.

Select Varieties.

	each—s.	d.
Ajax. Brilliant vermilion, immense flowers	0	9
Alcides. Rich deep scarlet, white eye	0	9
Alex. Albrecht. Rich dark scarlet	0	9
Aline. Pure white, splendid flower	0	9
Amy Amphlett. Purest white; blooms well shaped and freely produced; plant of good habit	1	0
Cato. Bright orange scarlet, very large	0	9
Celia. Magenta rose, beautiful and distinct	0	9
Chas. Mason. Brilliant vermilion, perfect shape	0	9
Clara Palethorpe. Blush white, suffused with pale pink, very delicate and pretty, dwarf habit	0	9
Dr. Orton. Deep crimson, splendid	0	6
Eccentric. Salmon, shaded with orange	0	9
Edith Little. Delicate rose, very charming	0	9
Ellen Clarke. Bright orange salmon	1	0
Falstaff. Rich shade of plum colour, shading to scarlet at the edge of the petals, very showy	1	0
Flamboyant. Brilliant scarlet; flowers very large and of fine form; plant dwarf, and good habit	1	0
G. Dore. Pretty novelty in the mottled salmon class; the shades are difficult to describe, being a mixture of salmon, pink, and orange	1	0
Guinevere. Creamy white; splendid truss and pip	1	0
Herminius. Scarlet, shaded magenta, fine	0	9
International. White, very large and fine form	0	9
James Douglas. Rich dark crimson, superb	0	9
Jno. Lorraine Baldwin. Scarlet, white eye	0	9
Lady Chesterfield. Salmon, suffused with orange	0	9
Lady Francis Russell. Clear rose pink	0	9
Lord Chesterfield. Crimson magenta, magnificent	0	9
Lord Tredegar. Scarlet, suffused with plum	0	9
Lucy Mason. Mottled salmon, large and distinct	0	9
Mary Caswell. Delicate pink, beautiful form	0	9
Mary Clarke. Salmon, shaded with pink and red	1	0
Mercedes. Salmon, tinted orange	0	9
M. Myriel. Crimson scarlet, white eye	0	9
Mrs. David Saunders. Pale lilac pink	0	9
Mrs. Gordon. Rich crimson, white eye	0	9
Mrs. H. F. Barker. Dark rose	0	9
Mrs. Holford. Salmon, large and splendid	0	9
Mrs. Johnson. Rosy lilac, beautiful	0	9
Mrs. Lord. Deep crimson, beautiful form	0	9
Mrs. Norman. Salmon. One of the finest things ever sent out	1	0
Mrs. Norris. Scarlet, with white eye	0	9
Mrs. Robertson. Bright deep pink, white eye	0	9
Mrs. Wilders. Bright scarlet, white eye	0	9
Norissa. Orange cerise, beautiful	0	9
Norah. Delicate rosy salmon	0	9
Omphale. Beautiful salmon pink, very large	0	9
Opal. A beautiful shaded salmon, in the style of *Sissie*, but more pink. This is a great advance in size and shape on anything before offered in this class	1	0
Orestes. Carmine rose, beautiful	0	9
Perdita. Salmon, shading off to white at the edge	1	0
Plutarch. Bright orange scarlet, with white eye	0	9
Queen of the Belgians. Pure white ... 2 for 2s.	0	9
Rev. R. D. Harries. Salmon scarlet, soft shade	0	9
Rev. Dr. Morris. Rich vermilion scarlet	1	0
Rhodope. Bright orange, flushed with pink	0	9
Rhada. Rose colour. Chiefly valuable from being one of the best Winter blooming sorts we have ever raised	1	0
Rosy Morn. Delicate rosy pink; flower not large, but an entirely new and distinct colour	1	0
Ruby. Scarlet crimson, with white eye, fine	0	9
Stella Massey. Blush pink; a most delicately beautiful flower, very perfect in form. Good habit	1	0
Tristrain. Crimson scarlet, with white eye, very fine	0	9
W. Bealby. Rosy scarlet, very good habit	0	9

Plants and Rooted Cuttings of Choice Florists' Flowers (*continued*).

DOUBLE-FLOWERED IVY-LEAVED PELARGONIUM.

Double-flowered Ivy-leaved Pelargoniums.

No class of plants has been so highly improved within the past few years as these, and few persons can form any idea of the splendour and beauty of many of the newer sorts. The flowers of some are as double and well-formed as the most perfect Rose or Camellia, and the colours range from pure white to the most intensely brilliant magenta, crimson, scarlet, delicate rose, lilac, mauve, &c. Magnificent for pots or hanging-baskets in the greenhouse or conservatory, or for garden decoration, whilst as cut-flowers they are charmingly beautiful.

Now and select varieties per doz. 6s.; 6 for 3s. 6d.
Choice varieties, our selection
per doz. 3s. 6d.; 6 for 2s.

	each—s.	d.
Andro Theuriet. Bright rich amaranth	0	9
Abundance. Deep rosy lilac, fine	0	6
Alice Crousse. Violet purple, tinged crimson	0	9
Bernardo Marone. Deep rosy pink	0	9
Cardinal Lavigerie. Very fine and brilliant semi-double flowers; colour, a beautiful bright fresh scarlet	1	6
Congo. Lilac rose, with lighter edges	0	6
Cuvier. Beautiful rich violet purple, very fine	0	9
Daniels Bros. Charming violet carmine colour	0	9
De Quatrefages. Large, beautiful, well-opened flowers; colour, a deep bright rosy purple; very fine	1	0
Edmund About. Brilliant cerise; very double	0	9
Francisque Sarcy. Rosy crimson, splendid	0	9
Futuro Famo. Brilliant amaranth purple	0	9
Galilee. Bright rosy pink; large, beautifully formed	0	9
General Briere de Lisle. Scarlet, splendid	0	9
General de Negrier. Scarlet carmine	0	9

Double-flowered Ivy-leaved Pelargoniums (*continued*).

	each—s.	d.
Girofloe (new). A very fine, compact, sturdy-growing variety, producing large trusses of fine, splendidly formed double flowers; colour, a rich bright purplish crimson; will prove an exceptionally fine variety for pot culture	2	0
Jeanne d'Arc. White, suffused with lavender	0	6
Le Printemps. Beautiful salmon rose	0	9
Louis Thibaut. Light crimson scarlet, very fine	0	6
Madame Crousse. Delicate rose, large flowers	0	6
Madame Sylvain May. Cerise pink	0	9
Madame Thibaut. Brilliant crimson cerise	0	9
M. de Lesseps. Crimson scarlet, very fine flowers	0	9
Mdlle. Marie Fabre. Splendid carmine cerise	0	9
Mdlle. Laura Daix. Charming rosy crimson	0	9
Merveille. Rich magenta crimson, magnificent	1	0
Mignonne. Delicate bright rose, splendid form	0	6
Murillo. Large, deep crimson flowers	0	9
Robert Owen. Large, deep rosy carmine	0	9
Rosacina. Brilliant carmine scarlet colour	0	9
Soleil Couchant. Bright rosy mauve	0	9
Souvenir de Charles Turner. Splendid variety, large, well-formed flowers; beautiful deep rose	0	9

Double-flowered Zonal Pelargoniums

Splendid double and massive flowers of the most charming and brilliant colours; in many of the varieties the flowers are beautifully formed, whilst they are all much more durable than those of the single-flowered varieties.

Now and select varieties ... per doz. 9s.; 6 for 5s.
Choice varieties, our selection
per doz. 4s. 6d. and 6s.; 6 for 2s. 6d. and 3s. 6d.

Select Varieties.

	each—s.	d.
Attraction. Light lilac pink, beautiful	0	9
Baronne de Villeneuve. Beautiful carmine-rose	1	0
Californian Gold. Brilliant orange-scarlet, double flowers, large and beautiful	1	0
Carolus Duran. Dark crimson, splendid	0	9
Charles Daniels. Brilliant magenta crimson	1	0
Ernest Bach (new). Flowers very large, semi-double; upper petals brilliant scarlet, lower petals a beautiful cerise. A very fine and brilliantly effective variety	2	0
Graf Herbert von Bismarck. Brilliant scarlet	0	9
Grand Chancellor Faidherbe. Deep rich scarlet	0	9
Le Cid. Deep rich scarlet; splendid flowers and truss	1	0
Le Cygne. Pure white, splendidly formed flowers	0	9
M. Alois Frey. Delicate salmon rose	1	0
Madame J. Causse (new). Salmon, with rosy orange centre; magnificent truss of splendid double flowers; extra	2	0
Madame Gilbert. Lovely bright fresh rose	0	9
Marquise de l'Aigle. Brilliant carmine pink	1	0
M. Adrien Corret. Cerise, tinged with vermilion	0	9
M. Prudent-Besson. Bright purple, shaded violet	0	9
Meteor. Brilliant orange scarlet	0	9
Ministre Constans. Deep mottled salmon	0	9
Mr. W. Bealby. Light crimson-cerise, splendid	0	9
Penelope (new). Dark amaranth crimson, flamed with scarlet; flowers very full and double, and borne in superb trusses; very fine and distinct	2	0
Perle Blanche. Magnificent variety, producing pure white flowers, perfectly double and of the most splendid form	1	0
Secretaire Daurel. Deep carmine-cerise, splendid	0	9
Sir Trevor Lawrence (new). Beautifully formed, full double flowers; colour, a bright deep rose; a fine trusser, and a splendidly effective variety	2	0
Soleil Levant. Cerise-pink, splendidly formed	0	9
Surpasse Edouard Barker. Vermilion rose	0	9
Triomphe de France. Salmon-red, the edges of a beautiful creamy white; splendid	0	9
Vesuvius. Intense vermilion scarlet	0	9

Plants and Rooted Cuttings of Choice Florists' Flowers (*continued*).

TROPÆOLUM "COMET."

Tropæolum "Comet."

An extremely beautiful, free-flowering, and graceful-growing variety; splendid for pots or hanging-baskets in the greenhouse or conservatory. The blooms, which are elegantly formed, are of the most intense deep brilliant scarlet colour, and form an admirable contrast with the rich glaucous green foliage of the plants. It blooms profusely throughout the Summer and Autumn months, and with a moderate warmth will bloom freely throughout the Winter and Spring

each 6d.; 3 for 1s. 3d.; per doz. 4s. 6d.

Impatiens Sultani.

(THE SULTAN'S BALSAM.)

each—s. d.

This is without doubt one of the most brilliant and beautiful plants of recent introduction. Its flowers, which are single, are of a beautiful bright magenta rose colour, and are produced in the greatest profusion throughout the year, forming a splendid plant alike for the greenhouse, conservatory, or the dinner-table. It is a fine perennial, easily cultivated, and should be in every greenhouse ... 3 for 1s. 3d. 0 6

Francoa ramosa.

(THE BRIDAL WREATH PLANT.)

Beautiful half-hardy plant, throwing up long sprays of pure white flowers 0 6

Heliotropes.

each—s. d.

Very useful for pots in the greenhouse, deliciously scented.

Beautiful varieties to name. 6 for 2s. 3d.; per doz. 4s. —

Queen of Violets. Dark violet with white eye, very free-flowering and of good habit per doz. 3s. 6d. 0 4

White Lady. Fine variety for bedding, and potted may be had in bloom in the greenhouse throughout the Winter; deliciously scented per doz. 3s. 6d. 0 4

Petunias.

NEW DOUBLE-FLOWERED FRINGED.

A superb new class, producing large brilliantly coloured blooms embracing all the most beautiful shades of colour, the edges of the petals being beautifully fringed.

New Fringed, Double. A superb new class, having all the blooms beautifully fringed.

Our own selection to name per doz. 6s.; 6 for 3s. 6d. —

Single-flowered Fringed. Very large, beautifully fringed flowers per doz. 4s. 6d.; 6 for 2s. 6d. —

DOUBLE-FLOWERED PETUNIAS
(Original Class).

A highly improved and beautiful class for pot culture.

Crimson King. Fine variety ... 3 for 1s. 3d. 0 6

Alba maxima. Superb pure white ... 3 for 2s. 0 9

Fine varieties, our selection

per doz. 4s. 6d.; 6 for 2s. 6d. —

Pentstemons.

Beautiful showy plants, with graceful spikes of brilliant and delicately coloured flowers, resembling the Foxglove somewhat in form of flower and habit of growth; height about two feet. Splendid for garden decoration and for cut flowers.

Choice named sorts, our selection

per doz. 3s. 6d.; 6 for 2s. —

Streptosolen (Browallia) Jamesoni

each—s. d.

A beautiful cool-greenhouse plant, growing to the height of three to five feet, bearing at the extremity of its branches dense panicles of thirty to forty flowers; in colour a pale orange at first, but changing to a bright cinnamon. It is a free and vigorous grower, and makes nice compact specimens if stopped from time to time. Strong young plants ... ... 3 for 2s. 0 9

Lantanas.

In beautiful variety 6 for 1s. 6d.; per doz. 2s. 6d. —

Mimulus.

Daniels' Large-flowered Hybrids. Splendid sorts in beautiful variety per doz. 2s. 6d.; 6 for 1s. 6d. —

Musk.

Harrison's Giant. Splendid variety of a robust habit of growth, fine for pots ... per doz. 2s. 6d. 0 4

New Double-flowered. Beautiful double yellow flowers quite as large as those of the old single form, but bearing no seed.

Strong young plants in April; 3 for 2s. 0 9

Swainsonia galegifolia alba.

Beautiful plant for the greenhouse, with clusters of pure white pea-like flowers ... ... 3 for 2s. 0 9

LILY OF THE VALLEY.

Lily of the Valley.

For early forcing single crowns of these should be planted about twelve in a five-inch pot, with the buds well above the surface. Cover the crowns with a little moss or an inverted flower pot for about ten days, and place them in a good heat of say 85 or 90 degrees; water frequently with tepid water, and if judiciously looked after they will bloom in four or five weeks from the time of potting. Good single crowns are much the best for the purpose. Clumps or single shoots can be supplied up to the end of April.

Fine strong clumps of the best variety for forcing.
per doz. 10s. 6d.; each 1s.
Selected Single Shoots, German. Produce splendid heads of bloom, much superior to the Dutch   per 100, 7s. 6d.; per doz. 1s.

Spiræa Japonica.

Perhaps the most elegant and useful of all plants for early forcing. Lovely and chaste spikes of elegant white inflorescence, and is singularly adapted for pot display, table or hand bouquets, &c., and by judicious forcing may be had in abundance at Easter. It will last well in almost any situation when in bloom. It is besides perfectly hardy, and can be grown on the open border.

Strong clumps for forcing   per doz. 6s.; each 8d.

Spiræa Astilboides.

This fine new variety is one of the most handsome of hardy herbaceous perennials, and has been certificated both by the Royal Horticultural and the Royal Botanic Societies on account of its great merit. The stems grow from two to three feet high, and are terminated by compound feathery branches of elegant white flowers, which are produced in the greatest profusion. A charming and effective plant for pot culture.

Strong plants ... ...   per doz. 15s.; each 1s. 6d.

Violets—Sweet-scented.

THESE deliciously-scented and ever welcome favourites, so extremely useful as cut flowers for bouquets, button-holes, &c., may, with a little management, be had in abundant bloom throughout the Winter and Spring months—a time when they are especially valuable. The stock plants should be divided in April or early in May and planted out in rich soil in a partially shaded position, the doubles in rows one foot apart and nine inches apart in the rows, the singles one foot apart each way. As growth commences, the young shoots or runners should be removed and the plants should be watered in the evening in dry weather, whilst if extra fine plants are required, they should have a mulching of well-decayed manure from an old mushroom bed or cucumber frame. Towards the end of September the plants may be lifted and planted into specially prepared frames placed in a south aspect, and partially filled with stable litter, leaves, &c., with about six or eight inches of soil on the top. The plants should be placed sufficiently close together to fairly fill the space without crowding, and should be as near the glass as the foliage will admit. When planted, give a thorough watering and keep close for a few days, after which admit air freely at every opportunity through the Winter. The glass may be entirely removed in sunny weather when there is no frost, and in all mild weather plenty of ventilation should be given. *Marie Louise, Count Brazza's,* and *Neapolitan* are the best of the doubles to be grown in this way, and when treated as recommended above will produce some grand flowers.

Double-flowered vars.

	each—s.	d.
Belle de Chatenay White. New double; pure white, tipped with bluish purple; very double per doz. 6s.	0	9
Belle de Chatenay Blue (new). A fine dark-blue-flowered variety of the above; very fine and double	0	9
Count Brazza's Neapolitan White (*syn.* Swanley White). Magnificent variety; large, double, pure white flowers, deliciously scented; the finest of all double white Violets; splendid for bouquets. per doz. 7s. 6d.	0	9
De Parme. Deliciously fragrant flowers of a delicate pale lavender purple, in great profusion per doz. 6s.	0	9
Duchess of Edinburgh. Blue, fine per doz. 5s.	0	6
Mademoiselle Bertha Barron (new). Flowers a beautiful indigo blue, deliciously scented per doz. 10s. 6d.	1	0

	each—s.	d.
Marie Louise. A fine variety, large double flowers, rich lavender blue, with white centres per doz. 5s.	0	6
Neapolitan. Lavender blue, flowers very large and double, profuse bloomer ... per doz. 3s. 6d.	0	4
Queen of Violets. Flowers large, double, white, slightly tinted with violet rose; finely scented ...	0	6

Single-flowered vars.

	each—s.	d.
Odoratissima. Similar to *Victoria Regina* ...	0	8
Rawson's White. A very free-flowering and beautiful variety, producing immense quantities of deliciously fragrant pure white flowers per doz. 10s. 6d.	1	0
The Czar. An almost constant bloomer per doz. 3s.	0	4
Victoria Regina. Large, fragrant, fine-shaped flowers, on strong flower-stems per doz. 3s. 6d.	0	4
Wellsiana. Very large, deep rich purple, superior to *Victoria Regina* ... per doz. 7s. 6d.	0	9

Choice Hardy Coniferous Plants.

	each—s. d.	s. d.
Abies canadensis (*Hemlock Spruce*). Very graceful	1 0	to 1 6
„ Douglasii. Very ornamental ...	1 6	„ 2 6
„ glauca. Beautiful glaucous-green foliage	3 6	„ 10 6
„ Engelmanni. Fine variety ...	3 6	„ 10 6
Araucaria imbricata (*Chilian Pine*) ...	5 0	„ 10 6
Cedrus Atlantica. Very hardy ...	2 6	„ 5 0
„ deodara. One of the most graceful and useful	1 6	„ 10 6
Cryptomeria elegans. Very hardy and useful	1 6	„ 7 6
„ Japonica. Very ornamental ...	2 6	„ 5 0
Cupressus—		
Lawsoniana. Very useful	1 6	„ 5 0
„ alba spica. Very handsome ...	2 6	„ 10 6
„ argentea. Very distinct ...	3 6	„ 10 6
„ erecta viridis. Beautiful up-right-growing variety, dark green foliage	1 6	„ 5 0
„ lutea. Beautiful golden foliage	3 6	„ 10 6
„ pyramidalis alba. spica. Very handsome and distinct ...	3 6	„ 10 6
Juniperus Chinensis aurea (*Golden Juniper*)	3 6	„ 21 0
„ Virginiana (*Red Cedar*) ...	1 0	„ 3 6
Picea lasiocarpa. Fine for single specimen	5 0	„ 10 6

	each—s. d.	s. d.
Picea Nordmanniana. Very handsome	2 6	to 10 6
„ pinsapo. Handsome and distinct	2 6	„ 10 6
Pinus cembra. Beautiful variety ...	2 6	„ 5 0
Retinospora plumosa. Very ornamental	1 6	„ 5 0
„ argentea } Extremely handsome ...	1 6	„ 5 0
„ aurea }	1 6	„ 5 0
„ squarrosa. Fine glaucous foliage	2 6	„ 5 0
Taxus baccata (*Common Yew*). Fine young plants	1 0	„ 5 0
„ elegantissima. Beautifully varie-gated	2 6	„ 10 6
„ fastigiata (*Irish Yew*). Very distinct, upright-growing ...	1 6	„ 10 6
„ aurea variegata. Golden-variegated	3 6	„ 10 6
Thuja Lobbi. Very hardy and ornamental	1 0	„ 5 0
„ occidentalis (*American Arbor-vitæ*)	1 0	„ 3 6
„ „ Vervæneana. Beautiful golden variety	1 6	„ 5 0
Thujopsis borealis. Fine dark green foliage	1 6	„ 5 0
„ dolabrata. Very handsome ...	2 6	„ 7 6
„ „ variegata. Beautiful silvery foliage	3 6	„ 7 6
Wellingtonia gigantea. Nice young plants	2 6	„ 7 6

Hardy Evergreen Shrubs & Coniferous Plants.

We have a fine collection of these in sturdy healthy young plants, all of which were transplanted during the past season, and are in splendid condition for removal.

Our own selection of sorts, { in good variety } ... ... height 1 to 1½ ft., per doz. 9s. ; per 50, 30s. ; per 100, 55s.
 „ 1½ to 2 ft., „ 12s. ; „ 40s. ; „ 75s.
 „ 2 to 3 ft., „ 18s. ; „ 65s. ; „ 110s.

RHODODENDRONS—Garden Hybrids.

The cultivation of these beautiful hardy evergreen flowering shrubs has been greatly on the increase since the discovery that peat soil is not absolutely necessary for their successful growth. Sandy peat free from stagnant moisture probably suits them best, but they will do well in sandy loam or even clayey loam, if free from calcareous matter, whilst we have seen many beautiful specimens growing in ordinary light garden soil. The colours of the flowers range from the richest and most intense crimson to the most delicate shades of rose and pure white, the masses of beautiful bloom having a charming appearance with the rich dark green foliage.

Choice named varieties. Our own selection, according to size each 2s. 6d., 3s. 6d., and 5s. ; per doz. 24s., 30s., and 40s.
 „ „ „ Standards and half-standards each 7s. 6d. to 21s.
Unnamed Hybrids. Good kinds, producing a beautiful variety per doz. 12s., 18s., 24s., and 30s.

Iris Germanica.

These beautiful hardy plants are very easy of cultivation, and will thrive and bloom freely in almost any soil or position, and always leave a fresh and pleasing appearance. We have a fine collection of these, including upwards of fifty of the most distinct and beautiful sorts. The best time for planting these, and the *Kæmpferi* varieties, is in March or April.

Choice named varieties, our selection per doz. 6s. and 9s.
Very choice mixed per doz. 3s. 6d. ; per 100, 24s.

Iris Kæmpferi.

These form a splendid group of extremely beautiful and distinct varieties, the flowers of some of which attain an immense size, and the colours vary from crimson, blue, purple, rose, to the purest white. A rich, moist, loamy soil with partial shade is the most favourable, and they must have abundance of water during the summer months, to grow them well.

Choice named varieties per doz. 18s., 24s., and 30s.
Choice mixed seedlings .. per doz. 6s. and 9s.

Choice Bouquets and Cut Flowers.

We grow many thousands of Plants specially for our supply of **Choice Cut Flowers**, which we furnish in season from the following superb assortment:—

Abutilons, in variety	Chrysanthemums, Pure White,	Lily of the Valley
Arum Lilies	&c.	Narcissi, of sorts
Azaleas, Pure White and	Deutzia gracilis	Orange Blossom
others	Heaths, of sorts	Orchids, in variety
Begonias, Greenhouse and	Heliotropes, Sweet-scented	Primulas, Double White
Stove varieties	Hyacinths, White Roman and	Roses, Tea-scented and others
Bouvardias, the most beau-	others	Spiræa japonica
tiful sorts	Lapagerias, Rose, White	Stephanotis floribunda
Camellias, in variety	Lilacs, Pure White (forced)	Violets, Sweet-scented
Cyclamens, of sorts	Lilies, Pure White	

And many other Choice Greenhouse and Stove Flowers.

MEMORIAL WREATHS AND CROSSES. Made up with choicest pure white natural flowers and Maidenhair Fern, arranged in the most beautiful style, and guaranteed to give the highest satisfaction

each 7s. 6d., 10s. 6d., 12s. 6d., 15s., 21s., 31s. 6d., and 42s.

BRIDES' BOUQUETS. Exquisitely made up with choicest pure white flowers only   each 7s. 6d., 10s. 6d., 15s., and 21s.
BRIDESMAIDS' BOUQUETS. Made up with pure white and delicately tinted flowers, or to order

each 5s., 7s. 6d. and 10s. 6d.

BUTTON-HOLE BOUQUETS. White or coloured flowers   each 1s., and 1s. 6d.; per doz. 10s. 6d. and 15s.
LADIES' DRESS BOUQUETS OR SPRAYS. Beautifully made up to order   each 2s., 6d., 5s., and 7s. 6d.
LOOSE CUT FLOWERS AND FERN. For table and other decorations supplied in liberal quantity in boxes.

each 2s. 6d., 3s. 6d., 5s., 7s. 6d., 10s. 6d., 15s., 21s., 31s. 6d., and 42s.

By our careful and perfect system of packing, the Wreaths, Bouquets, &c., we supply, will stand a journey of fully two days if necessary, and then reach their destination in beautifully fresh condition.

All orders are despatched promptly on receipt, if required, but customers residing at a distance should give, if possible, at least two days' clear notice before the flowers are required.

From W. S. LONG, Esq., Windsor.	From Mr. H. M. WILKIN, Aldreth.	From Mr. J. HALL, Silverstone.
April 7th. "The Bride's Bouquet and Bridesmaids' Flowers supplied to Saxlingham gave every satisfaction."	Oct. 21st. "I have much pleasure in thanking you for the Wreaths you sent yesterday, and in stating that they have been admired by every one who has seen them."	Nov. 4th. "The Wreaths came to hand in splendid condition, and we were very pleased with them."

Index.

NORWICH: FLETCHER AND SON, HORTICULTURAL PRINTERS AND LITHOGRAPHERS.

EXPORT DEPARTMENT.

UR rapidly increasing Export and Colonial Trade is at once evidence of the general satisfaction given by the good results of our Seeds, and a gratifying return for the care and attention we give to our Foreign Department. Our experience in packing seeds for export, the care we exercise in the selection of stocks, and our improved method of packing, almost invariably give the highest satisfaction. We have numerous customers in India, Australia, New Zealand, China, Africa, Canada, United States, &c., to whom we shall at all times be pleased to refer new customers with respect to the superior quality of our Seeds.

The increased facilities for forwarding parcels of Garden Seeds direct to the purchaser by means of the "Foreign and Colonial Parcel Post," is annually placing us in more immediate communication with a large and important circle of our Foreign and Colonial Friends. Whilst our clients and ourselves now reap the advantages of a low and uniform cost of transit, we can at the same time be assured of regularity and certainty of delivery.

FLOWER SEEDS POST FREE.—All Orders for Flower Seeds in packets, over 10s. in value will be forwarded Post Free to any part of the World.

KITCHEN GARDEN SEEDS POST FREE.—All Orders for Kitchen Garden Seeds (excepting Peas and Beans) in packets, to value of 20s. and upwards, will be sent free to any part having Parcel Post communication with Great Britain.

Remittances must accompany all Orders from Clients not having ledger accounts.

Goods delivered, Carriage Paid, at Ship's side at any British Seaport.

In larger export orders our trade is rapidly increasing, and whilst thanking our esteemed correspondents for their confidence, we respectfully solicit their kind recommendations, and shall have much pleasure in forwarding Catalogues in all instances when requested.

Our shipping arrangements receive careful attention, best means are adopted in all cases to secure the most expeditious transit at the lowest